To Mum and Dad. For always believing.

BOTH WAYS

Visit us at www.boldstrokesbooks.com

BOTH WAYS

by
Ileandra Young

2018

BOTH WAYS

ISBN 13: 978-1-63555-298-0

THIS TRADE PAPERBACK ORIGINAL IS PUBLISHED BY
BOLD STROKES BOOKS, INC.
P.O. BOX 249
VALLEY FALLS, NY 12185

FIRST EDITION: NOVEMBER 2018

CREDITS
EDITOR: RUTH STERNGLANTZ
PRODUCTION DESIGN: STACIA SEAMAN
COVER DESIGN BY JEANING HENNING

CHAPTER ONE

Keep still, will you? I only want to do this once." Pippa locates a suitable vein and jabs her needle into my upper arm.

I hiss behind my teeth and fight the urge to clench my fist. "You enjoy that way too much."

She depresses the plunger on the syringe, forcing fifteen fluid ounces of thin green fluid into me. "Just doing my duty. Can't fault me for that."

Her smile is smug and knowing. Like usual.

A chill prickles at the site of the needle. It spreads up my arm, a thread of ice that spirals out across my shoulder and chest. No matter how many times I go through this, it still freaks me out.

Pippa removes the needle and dumps the syringe into a bright yellow bucket at her side, the one with the word *biohazard* written on the side in huge black letters.

I roll down my sleeve and pedal my arm.

"What are you doing?"

"I'm done, right? I need to get out of here."

She lifts another syringe, this filled with purple fluid dotted with silver specks. "Not before your shot for turbo coagulate and dialysis."

"Already?"

"Six months. Just like always."

I sigh. This one hurts more than the lupine immunity shot. "We can't skip it?"

The level look she gives me offers all the answer I need.

"Fine, but hit the other arm, okay? Last time I couldn't lift my gun for three days."

Pippa smirks and helps herself to the sleeve on my left side. This time, she takes her time finding the right spot, running her fingertip over and over the crook of my elbow until she locates the vein she wants. "Steady," she mutters.

I close my eyes.

The needle goes in.

At first there's nothing, just slight pressure as the plunger goes down. Then the burn begins, chasing away the cold like a river of fire. It floods my arm within seconds, then my chest, and fast across the rest of my body. Sweat breaks out on my forehead. The examination room spins.

"Lie back, Dani. Come on, or you'll pass out."

"I'm fine."

"Lie back. I'm not kidding."

I obey, reclining on the soft, padded cushions while my fingers prickle with pins and needles.

To the left, Pippa disposes of the second syringe and grabs a clipboard from the cupboard. She scribbles a line of notes and ticks a couple of boxes, her features creased in concentration.

Posters on the far wall blur in and out. I focus on making them clear, skimming the heading across the top: *Clear Blood Foundation: Supernatural Information Sheet #41*. Sheets one to forty are nowhere in sight, but sixty-five peels from its position on the back of the assessment room door. I narrow my eyes at it and pick out details on the toxicity of faerie blood.

"In small quantities, faerie blood is comparatively harmless unless ingested. If at any point you suspect contamination by faerie blood—"

"What are you talking about?"

"The poster. Fae."

Pippa grins and hands me a small square of cheese and a plastic cup of milk. "Nice try. You know those things off by heart. I'm not letting you go for at least another ten minutes."

Busted.

"Come on, I need to get back to work."

"This *is* work. Enjoy lying down for a second. It won't kill you."

"It's boring."

She massages the back of her neck, then perches on the only other chair in the room, a narrow, high-backed thing against the far wall. "Then talk to me. I've not seen you for ages."

I roll the cheese between my fingers. Sip the milk. Full fat. Yuk. "I'm good. It's crazy at work, but it keeps us all with something to do."

"Same here. Jimmy's disappeared, so we're covering his workload."

"Who?"

"Tech guy, the one with the patches on his cheek. A couple are on holiday so we're short anyway, but he's dropped off the grid."

"Sick?"

"Probably. Or high." She gestures for me to keep drinking. "He does it all the time. No doubt he'll show up on Monday wondering why we're so upset."

"Fire him."

"Not my job. Anyway he's too good, leading some amazing chemical advances. Too bad for him if he misses the cool stuff."

Another glug of the milk. I cringe. Far too creamy and rich for me. "Did you go for that job yet?"

"The researcher one?" Pippa rubs her stomach. "No, I—I'm not sure it's a great idea right now."

"You'd be great at it. No one has a mind like you."

She smiles. "And you? What about that team leader role?"

I shove the cheese into my mouth, chew and swallow in one. "No thanks. I have a hard enough time managing my own problems—why on earth would I want to be responsible for someone else's?"

"Because you're capable."

"You sound like Mum."

Shrug. "It's true. And before I forget..." She pulls a fat leather watch from her pocket and overhands it my way.

I catch it and slip the straps around my right wrist. It's huge: a big round face and Roman numerals in place of numbers. Heavy too, but only now do I feel dressed and complete. "Thanks."

"How do you feel now?"

Still shaky, but I've no intention of telling her that. Instead I smile, swing my legs off the side of the bed, and put the remains of the milk on the table. "Bloody brilliant. Can I get back to HQ now?"

"Two more minutes. It's my neck on the line if you fall over when you leave. What are you doing later?"

"Probably sleeping. I had the late shift last night and another one tomorrow."

"So you couldn't come to dinner with me?"

"Of course I could. When?"

She smiles. "Eightish? That Italian place on West Side."

Can't help but shudder at that. "West Side? You sure?"

"I've got something to tell you. Thought it would be nice to do it over a quiet dinner."

Her eyes are bright and lively, lit with a mischievous light I remember well from when we were younger. "I guess we could—"

Loud rapping at the window cuts me off. Pippa jumps, one hand pressed her chest. I pull a knife from the sheath on my right ankle.

"Danika Karson?" calls a gravelly voice. "Danika Karson?"

I put the knife away. "Chill, Pip, it's just Norman."

She exhales hard and fast. "Can't it use the door like everyone else?"

"Would you, if you had wings?"

Outside the window is a scaly, cat-sized creature with tiny gossamer wings. Spider-like, it clings to the brickwork and gazes through the glass with black beady eyes. "Danika Karson?"

"Yeah, yeah, I heard you."

As soon as the window opens, it's inside, skittering along the wall and along the table with a flick of its barbed tail. It flops to the floor, then across the tiles, across my boot, and up the leg of my jeans. Tiny claws scratch my skin through the denim as it works up my body and onto my shoulder.

"Danika Karson?"

"It's me, idiot, you know it's me. Just give me the message."

The chittarik flicks out a long forked tongue, lapping at my cheek. Only then does the inflection change. "Danika Karson." It lifts its chin, exposing a flapping pocket of skin lined with tiny scales. A small, narrow tube nestles inside.

"Thanks."

"Danika Karson," it says once more. Brief pressure on my shoulder, then the chittarik is airborne, fluttering awkwardly back to the window. It wobbles on the sill for two precarious seconds before throwing itself out into the air beyond.

Pippa gasps. "We're on the fifth floor."

"He'll be fine." Already I'm opening the tube and scanning the contents. The paper inside is blue. Damn.

What the hell have I done now?

"I know that look. What's going on?" Pippa arrives at my shoulder, straining to see the note.

"There's a car waiting for me outside."

Her eyebrows lift. "What did you do this time?"

Wish I could tell her. Instead, I tuck the message and the tube in my pocket and snatch up my kit. Jacket too. "I'd better find out."

"Take it easy. No heavy lifting, complex machinery, or—"

"I know, Pip, this isn't my first medical. Speak later." I'm gone before she can reply.

❖

Out on the street, my ride waits on the pavement edge, a black limo with smoky windows and a private number plate. Slouched against the bonnet, smoking, is a short, sallow-skinned figure with warty features and a long, crooked nose. He grunts on seeing me and tosses the remains of his cigarette in the gutter.

"Agent Karson?"

I show him my ID.

"Good. Get in."

"Where are we going?"

He glares, hot, yellow stare intense and searching. "I'm not allowed to tell you that."

I'd argue, but there's little point. Goblins are stubborn to the point of lunacy, and there's no reason to believe this one will be any different.

He wears plain blue, no emblems, crests, or weapons. Not a SPEAR driver, then.

He waddles round to the passenger door and pops it open, sweeping a bow so low and extravagant I can't decide if he's making fun of me. Probably.

Inside, the seats are plush and leather. A tiny fridge holds three bottles of water; beside that's a button to raise and lower the privacy partition. A glance at the dim windows tells me the glass is reinforced as well as smoked.

What the hell is this?

A door slams. The limo rocks. A moment later we're on the move, pulling away from the pavement in a smooth U-turn.

I sit back, fasten my seat belt, and drop my jacket into the footwell. "To the races, Jeeves."

A grunt from up front. Then, with a whispering hiss, the partition slides up.

Well *someone* is certainly lacking a sense of humour.

Outside, Angbec fizzes with bright, excited energy. I press my nose to the glass, enjoying the sight of it from a position of comfort and ease. Not often do I visit this end of the city without chasing someone, or needing medical assistance.

Restaurants, shops, bars, and clubs, all clustered together in an untidy mishmash. *Edane* establishments stand side by side with human ones, normal and accepted. This area, affluent and expensive, is beautiful and perhaps the most metropolitan part of the city. In amongst the humans walk other creatures, from goblins to fae. They mingle easily, a sight that continues to fascinate even after so many years.

I spot a bus shelter under repair, broken glass pulled away by two men in high-vis jackets. The poster beneath is pitted and torn, but just visible on the flapping paper is a bright, sunny face and six words picked out in foot tall lettering: *New Law, New Order, New Mayor.* In smaller letters beneath that, a quick call to action: *This year, vote for unity, vote for change.*

A snort catches in my throat. Unlikely that this new candidate can be any worse than our current mayor; most parties have the same stance on *edanes.*

The limo turns right, into the financial district.

No shops now, but large imposing buildings, often with security posted outside.

Five minutes later we stop outside a Victorian era building with columns, flags, and two security trolls posted outside. They wear blue vests and blank, vapid expressions.

"City Hall?" My chest tightens.

Really, what the hell have I done?

❖

The goblin opens my door and I exit the car with my hands thrust into my pockets.

Like other buildings in this district, City Hall's exterior is decorated in posters and pennants of blue. From a banner above the entrance, a stern-faced man with frown lines and a crew cut stares down on all those who dare enter. *Vote Mikkleson* demands the signage beneath.

No thanks. At least the other guy knows how to smile.

I hurry up the steps and pull on the doors, wary of the trolls to either side. Either they know to expect me or they're off duty, because neither moves as I slip through. Inside, the foyer is a high-ceilinged, echoing space, with elegant decor and gleaming marble. The Angbec city crest glitters on the floor, picked out in mosaic tiles of red, green, yellow, and blue.

I walk to the reception desk, straight into a woman who promptly drops every folder, poster, and badge she holds.

The whole lot fans across the floor, a whispering rush that does nothing to mask her grunt of frustration.

"Bugger, I'm sorry." I scrabble to retrieve the sheets and folders, bundling them up into my hands. A couple get crushed, but not before I see smaller versions of the poster outside the building—*Vote Mikkleson*—and the familiar colours of the Clear Blood Foundation logo.

The woman grabs the packet of badges and a couple of the folders and huffs a curl of hair out of her eyes. "No trouble, neither of us was paying attention."

I freeze, one hand flopped pointlessly on one of the folders.

She's blond. Full, bow-shaped lips teased with the faintest lick of pink lipstick. Her dress suit is grey, just like her eyes, and fitted close to a figure that is obviously willowy and slender. Her shoes match too.

Wow.

"Uh, hi?"

She grins. Even her smile is perfect, white and dazzling. "Good afternoon."

"Yeah. Um. Hi."

She holds out her hand and, for a truly crazy moment, I wonder if she expects me to kiss her fingers. Just in time I realize she wants her papers and posters. Or a handshake.

"I'm Amelia Smythe, nice to meet you."

I shake the proffered hand, then hand over the slightly crushed papers. "Danika Karson."

Her eyebrows give the faintest twitch. "*Agent* Danika Karson?" Her gaze skims my face, then my shoulders, lingering on the gun tucked beneath my left arm. The stare is hot and intense, the grey of her eyes deep and all encompassing. They must be contact lenses, right?

"Yeah, I guess."

Again she reaches for my hand. This time her grip lingers, cool fingers tightly gripping mine. "Then it's truly an honour to meet you. I'm a great…follower of your work."

My brain is goo. The most I can manage is a timid, "Huh?"

"With SPEAR? Youngest woman to join the regiment since their foundation, yet the operative with the highest capture rate ever known. Exceeded only by your exceptional kill rate." Her breathing hitches on the words *kill rate*.

My heart fights to escape my chest. "Just doing my job."

"Indeed. And you enjoy your job?"

For the first time during this encounter, my words are firm and confident. "No, I love it. I'm making a difference. Protecting people."

She squeezes my hand one last time. Some of the intensity leaks from her eyes. "Good. One should enjoy their profession and yours is...important. Again, good to meet you. Have an enjoyable day." She settles her belongings more firmly in hand and strides away.

I watch her go, confused by the little shudder that ripples down my back. There's something familiar about her, but a woman that beautiful isn't one I'm likely to forget easily.

"Everything okay, Agent?"

I yelp, leaping round to face the source of the voice. That goblin, my chauffeur, wearing a smug grin.

"I'm fine. What do you want?"

"You forgot this." He holds out my jacket.

I snatch it away and hurry towards reception.

❖

Behind the desk, as wide as my bed is long, a woman pauses her phone conversation long enough to smile and point to a screen on the right.

She nods as I sign in. "Take this guest ID and wear it at all times. Go to the security desk where they'll frisk you before heading upstairs."

"I got a summons through my chittarik, any idea what it's about?"

She taps a few buttons on her keyboard, then studies her own screen. "Nothing here, I'm afraid. They'll tell you more upstairs."

The unease swells, but there's not much I can do.

At the security checkpoint, another security guard, this one human, waits with a metal detector in his hand and a Taser on his hip. He waves to a shallow tray on the edge of a conveyor belt that runs into a scanning machine.

"Place all your belongings in the tray and raise your arms."

"That'll take a while—are you sure?"

"Rules. Get on with it."

I bite my tongue over the snarky response and begin the laborious process of pulling off all my gear. Purse, ID wallet, gun, silver darts, a pack of chewing gum, and three red Biros with the ends chewed off. Next my utility belt which holds two throwing knives, three holy water phials, a pack of UV glow sticks, three clips of SPEAR issue bullets (wood, lead, and silver), a coil of silver chain, a daisy pressed between two sheets of greaseproof paper, and a single pebble of smooth, red-flecked obsidian. Oh, and all the other knives secreted across my body.

The guard heaves a sigh.

"I did warn you."

He shoves my tray through the scanner, then waves the wand of his metal detector back and forth across my body. It bleeps going over my watch. "Off."

"It's just a watch."

"Take it off and put it in the tray."

I wrap my hand around it. "I take this thing off once a day and that's when I go to bed. Beyond that and you're shit out of luck."

His free hand drifts towards the Taser. "I won't say it again, miss."

"It's *Agent*, and you can get bent, tubby gut."

His lips draw back, showing blunt, nicotine-stained teeth.

I lean my weight onto the balls of my feet.

Bring it on, arsehole.

"Let her in, Bobby." This voice comes from beyond the checkpoint, from a man standing at the bottom of the stairs. He studies me, small dark eyes bright with interest.

Oh hell.

The security guard lowers his hand. "But, sir—"

"I called her here, and I'm already behind schedule. Let her in."

The guard steps back, sweeping a hand across his body to gesture the way through. I treat him to the sweetest smile I can manage before gliding through the checkpoint. It trills and lights up with red warning lights, which stop as the guard slaps a button on the side.

"Cheers, chief."

Closer to the man on the stairs, I give him a quick once-over. Tailored suit. Crew cut. Shiny shoes. The scent of cigar smoke on his breath.

"Good to meet you, Agent Karson." He extends a hand.

I take it and immediately bite back a gasp at his savage grip on my fingers. "Yeah, and who are you?"

He frowns and steps to the right, revealing another of those garish posters, *Vote Mikkleson* in big, angry letters, and I take a closer look at the stern face above it.

Oh. Shit.

CHAPTER TWO

Sebastian D. Mikkleson. Ex-Marine, weapons specialist, and current mayor of Angbec.

He sits behind an overlarge desk in an overlarge chair, sipping from an overlarge mug of overstrong coffee. Thick, bushy eyebrows hang low over his deeply set eyes, grey to match the finely shaped beard and tash across his powerful jaw. I'd say his campaign poster has had a little of the airbrush treatment.

The room matches the desk, obnoxiously big, but spartan. Panelled walls and deep green carpets, like the study or drawing room of some period drama. Another door besides the one I used stands on the left, slightly ajar. A soft voice comes from beyond it.

Mikkleson sets the coffee down and retrieves a cigar from an ashtray on the corner of the desk. A long stream of blue-grey smoke billows from his mouth. "You're prettier than I expected."

"And you're older."

The eyebrows dip lower. "Miss Karson—"

"Agent."

He grunts. "*Agent* Karson, thank you for coming to see me at such short notice."

"Didn't get much choice, did I?"

"You're agitated, Miss—Agent Karson. Apologies. I'll admit that summons wasn't the most diplomatic way to get your attention, but it worked, and once I explain, I'm sure you'll understand why I did it."

I sit back, arms folded. I feel naked without the gun beneath my arm, but at least I have my watch. Oh, and the four-inch stiletto blade hidden in my ponytail. In your face, tubby gut.

"I need you to find someone."

I wait.

He stares.

"I'm not a...people finder, Mr. Mikkleson—"

"*Mayor* Mikkleson."

Touché.

"Why haven't you been to the police?"

He rolls the cigar between his fingers then relights it, watching the nub of ash on the end grow. "This is a sensitive matter. So close to election day, I can't afford to have this matter made public, as it no doubt would be if the police became involved."

"So hire a private detective."

"I am."

"I'm a SPEAR agent. We don't hunt missing persons."

"I know exactly what you do, Agent Karson, and that's why I want you. You're the best SPEAR has and your record highlights you as the best possible candidate."

"Oh yeah? And what parts of my record are we talking about?"

He continues to stare. I glare right back.

This guy may be ex-military, but I'm pretty sure he's never stared down a vampire caught up in blood mania, or a werewolf in moon fever. If he's waiting for me to break, we'll be here a while.

"I'm willing to pay," he says at last, "a significant sum for your time, trouble, and, of course, your vow to secrecy."

I stand. "Sorry, Mr. Mayor, but no. I'm not available for private hire." I walk to the door.

"They have my son, Agent."

Damn. I was so, so close.

❖

I turn away from the door with a sigh. "Who has your son, Mr. Mayor?"

"I'm not sure."

Still near the door, I wait. And wait some more.

This time he looks away, fiddling with the end of his cigar, which is no longer smoking. "I haven't heard from him for a week and a half. Usually he checks in, at least for money, but there's been nothing. I went to his house and it looks normal, no signs of a struggle or forced entry."

He shows me a photo from his inside pocket. It shows a lanky lad with scruffy hair and goth style clothing. He wears dark, miserable make-up and blows smoke rings at the camera.

"I found this in the sitting room." Mikkleson pulls a plastic evidence bag from a drawer in his desk.

I take it, watching his face, wary of the creases around the corners of his eyes.

He's scared.

The bag contains a narrow plastic tube, the length of my index finger. A large hole at one end shows traces of fine green dust.

My breathing hitches. "Shit."

"I'm glad you understand. I also found this." Another bag, this one holding large flakes of a thick black substance that crumbles as I tighten my grip.

"Fuck." The single exclamation flees my lips before I can catch it. "At his house?"

Mikkleson nods, no longer able to meet my gaze.

I return to my seat and kick both heels up onto his flawless, polished desk. "Start from the top."

He glances at my boots, then my face. A sigh. "A few weeks ago the police raided a Faerie Dust cookhouse outside the Veranna estate. My manifesto includes a crackdown on supernatural crime and—"

"I don't need the pitch. Just tell me what's going on."

His lips tighten beneath the moustache. "Agent—"

"I'm tempted to leave right now and let the civvie bashers know our mayor's son is a drug addict. You've got sixty seconds to convince me not to."

His eyes widen. "The raid went well. We arrested twelve people, and half that number won't see the outside world for five years."

"So?"

"So, that was the largest cookhouse in the city. There are others, but none of them produce with the speed and quality that one did. Someone high up the chain is losing a lot of cash."

I drop the bags on the table.

Faerie Dust. A highly addictive substance made from the bones of grass gnomes and a bunch of other chemicals I can't pronounce. The mix results in a fine dust that the user snorts for a wild, soaring high. And, if they're unlucky, paranoia, mania, and violent fits. And death.

"Revenge, then?"

"Maybe. I'm an important man and this…cripples me." Mikkleson grits his teeth. "And there are other signs of vampire involvement, beyond the residue I found at the house."

Ah. Now it makes sense. But I want to hear him say it.

"I don't suppose you've reported this to SPEAR?"

"Nobody knows. Surely you understand the delicate nature of this situation. I'm on the verge of winning the city for my third term. I can't afford a scandal right now."

"And you're trusting me, because…?"

He leans back. "Come now. Agent Danika Karson, youngest female agent since the regiment's foundation, highest vampire kill rate in the city."

"In the country, actually. Last I checked."

He chuckles. "I'm willing to pay you significant sums of money if you can find my son and keep it quiet."

I bite my lip. This still feels wrong. Off, somehow. "But I'm not for hire."

The drawer rumbles again; this time as he pulls out a pen and a pad of sticky notes. He scribbles on the top sheet, rips it free, then slaps it on the table. "Are you sure?"

A glance at the numbers on that tiny slip of pink paper and my mouth drops open.

"That's right. Half now, and the other half on completion. I'll throw in a bonus too, if you deal with the ones that took him."

It's an insane amount of money. Even for a man like this.

He smiles now, slow and smug. "Not bad is it? Perfect for that little project of yours."

I sit straight. "Excuse me?"

"Don't worry, I won't tell anyone. But that house won't stay on the market forever. If you truly want to buy it, you'll need to act fast before someone else scoops it up. Cipla is popular these days, given the new renovation project."

I grip the edge of the desk, my knuckles tight and pale. "How do you know about that?"

"It's my job to know."

"The hell it is." My voice leaps in volume. "And when you say *deal with them*, what exactly are we talking about?"

"I'm talking about the SPEAR agent with the highest vampire kill rate in the country, doing what she does best."

I force my fingers to relax. "This has to be a trick. Did Quinn put you up to this?"

"I assure you, no trick."

"You're asking me to break the law."

"I'm asking you to take on a job doing something we both know you enjoy."

"Vampires have rights."

He grunts. "They shouldn't."

Can't argue with that. But my gut won't let it lie. "And if I take this case, what then?"

Mikkleson leans across the desk, his cigar forgotten. "You find my son with the utmost speed, tell no one of your actions, and enjoy a significant payment when you're done." One hand twitches the pen back and forth across his fingers, in nervous spirals.

"No. Sorry, but I can't."

"I'll double the fee."

I stumble, halfway from my seat. It takes every scrap of willpower to keep moving towards the door. "No."

"Agent." He hurries from behind his desk. Footsteps pound the carpet. "Please, I've no one else." An instant later he grabs my shoulder and spins me round. "You've got to—"

My fist flies at his face.

Ex-Marine weapons specialist Sebastian Mikkleson is pretty fast. But he's not a SPEAR.

Though he ducks my fist, he drops straight into my knee, which I've already hiked upward. It slams into his chin, cracking his teeth together.

Mikkleson cries out, dropping at my feet.

The door flies open.

I turn again, whipping the stiletto from my hair, holding it in a reverse grip, feet spread wide.

A troll lumbers through the door, knocking its head on the frame. It looks at Mikkleson, then me, before roaring. It lurches at me, an attack I dodge easily with lighter, quicker feet. I end up on the desk, ready to jump again.

"Stand down." Mikkleson spits a glob of red-tinged saliva at the floor. "Cobble, I said *stand down*."

The troll blinks stupidly, pointing at me, then the stiletto blade.

"I'm fine. Go away. Now."

I tense, prepared to spring.

The troll offers me one last confused glance before plodding out. Once more it knocks its head and a fine rain of dry soil cascades down its shoulders. The door slams.

I breathe again.

Mikkleson stands, thumbing blood from a cut on his lip. "You're the best agent SPEAR has. If you don't help me, my son is going to die."

"How old is he?"

"Fifteen."

I sigh. Jump off the table. As I return to the door, I tuck the stiletto back into my hair. "When you transfer that money, just send twenty per cent or my accountant will go nuts. Divide the other thirty between my mum and sister."

Confusion wells in Mikkleson's eyes, followed swiftly by relief. "Thank you. Thank you, Agent Karson."

"Don't thank me yet." I drag the door open. "I need to find him first."

❖

I use the cab ride back to HQ to ponder Sebastian Mikkleson. While I can see why he'd prefer to keep the matter under wraps, I'm surprised he'd turn to SPEAR. No, I'm surprised he'd turn to *me*. My personal stance on vampires aside, my skill as an agent isn't the only part of my reputation to travel ahead of me.

Unlike City Hall, SPEAR headquarters is a vast modern monstrosity, built just after the inauguration of the Supernatural Creatures Act in 2027. Three floors high and five deep, the building houses training, office, and living spaces for the city's population of SPEAR agents. It also has laboratories, holding cells, and interview rooms designed for all manner of supernatural guests.

The staff entrance is a small, nondescript door to the side of the building, almost invisible in the face of the revolving glass ones presented to the public. I enter my code, allow the retinal scanner to verify me, then walk through, into the darkness. The door swishes shut on hydraulic hinges.

Silence.

Blue light flickers from a sensor in the ceiling, scanning up, down, left, right. A fine mist of cool fluid hits my left cheek, followed by a jet of something warmer on the right.

Blue fades to green.

"Authorized," chirps a mechanical voice. "Karson, Danika. Agent 2024011904A05."

Darkness lifts as the hidden door ahead of me slides open from bottom to top.

Beyond the security measures, the staff side of HQ resembles a mash-up between a sci-fi novel and a vintage American police station. Open plan, with a sea of desks arranged haphazardly at the far end. The rest of the space is wide open, currently empty except for one man with a mop and bucket, scrubbing absently at a liquid red stain on the floor. My gaze travels up to the other two floors, exposed by a gap in the centre that extends right the way to the top floor's ceiling. Men and woman walk back and forth, some with stacks of papers, others with weapons, all with the same steely focus in their eyes.

In the centre, hanging from the ceiling, is a replica of the SPEAR insignia: a pair of crossed swords above a single arrow, both surrounded by flares of light, picked out with gold inlay. Our motto is carved beneath it, some pretentious rubbish in Latin that I've never bothered to translate. I know roughly what it means anyway, since it describes what I do every day: protect and serve, learn and understand, hunt and exterminate.

On the right, behind a Plexiglas wall, a batch of new recruits work through training exercises with our hand-to-hand coach. One trips and lands on his face before a woman who enthusiastically punches the air. A second later, she falls and slams into the Plexiglas nose first.

Behind them both, our training coordinator grins and flexes his huge, bat-like wings. His lips move and though the room is soundproofed I know what he's saying. *Again, little meatsicles. Again.*

Bloody gargoyles.

I cross the open area, gaze pinned on my desk.

Metal slides sharply over something soft. Soft breathing. Light footsteps.

I dart left, flinging myself down and to my knees on the wooden floor. I turn as I slide, facing the direction I've come in time to see the man bearing down on me, axe in hand. He yells, a wordless bellow of exertion, as he brings the weapon round towards my head.

I lean flat on my back, blinking as the air swishes past my face.

Then I'm kicking out, flipping back onto my feet, then down again, sweeping with my left leg.

The axe flies from his grip as he hits the floor, skidding off the wooden surface to the carpet that marks the start of the desks.

My fingers close on the stiletto, and then I'm on him, point pressed to his throat, my knees weighing down on his forearms. "Too slow, Noel."

He struggles for brief seconds before relaxing beneath me. He mutters something in Spanish, then adds, "I thought I had you that time. You were miles away, sí?"

"And you breathe loud enough for six men. Better luck next time." I hop off his body and tuck the blade back into my hair. When I offer my hand, he grips it tight and bounds to his feet.

"Where you been, chica? The boss wants you."

My lips twist. "I got a summons."

Noel's eyes widen. "Guau, what have you done now?"

"Um…" I weave through the maze of desks towards my own. "Nothing, just some admin cock-up at City Hall."

My gut curls into uncomfortable knots.

"You okay, Dee-Dee?"

I clear my throat. "Fine."

"Fancy a training session later? I got new moves to show you." He kicks and jabs at the air, light, quick motions on the balls of his feet. "I get you this time, sí?"

"Maybe another time."

"Oh, come, come." He smiles, an expression so light and sunny I almost want to give in. "We make bets on it."

"Not today."

My desk, when I reach it, is covered with small brown pellets. Some are furry, others are moist, all of them stink like the waste bins of a butcher's shop. "Damn it, Norman. I told you to use the tray."

The chittarik peeps out from under my desk, small, pointed face looking rueful. Kinda. "Danika Karson?"

"Yeah, yeah, come here, you daft thing."

Clicking and chittering, he crawls up my jeans like before and settles on my shoulder. The hard, curved beak nuzzles my ear, then gently nips my lobe. An apology, I hope.

Noel chuckles. "You could use the post staff, like normal person."

"And miss the love and affection of my little baby?" I pet Norman on the back of the head and he purrs softly. Or I think he does. The sound is a gurgling cross between a growl and a whimper, but that usually means he's happy. "Anyway, it pisses off Quinn something rotten. A few shit pellets on my desk is a small price to pay."

A soft, staged cough. "Speaking of…"

I spin around in time to catch Quinn sneaking up on me.

Norman gives a little hiss, and I put my hand on his back, pressing him onto my shoulder. Just in case. "Quinn."

"Karson." Her thin lips draw back in an ugly sneer. "Where have you been?"

Knowing better than to wing it, I pull the message tube and blue slip of paper from my pocket.

"What have you done now?"

Noel snickers.

I grit my teeth. "Clerical cock-up."

"Good. Then I need you to look into a couple of missing persons cases."

"What?"

"Angbec police are swamped with calls from The Bowl. They want a SPEAR to check it out."

"We aren't missing persons—"

"You are. For now."

My face flushes with heat. Norman growls against my cheek. I shift my grip to the base of his tail.

"If it has to be an Alpha, at least put a G3 on it. I have other cases. *Edane* cases."

Quinn's smile is as broad as it is fake. "Taken care of. Thought you'd be pleased since you enjoy working alone so much. Without the backup of a team or the authorization of a G7."

Bitch.

"I don't enjoy—"

"That'll be all, Karson. Report back to me at the end of the week." She nods at Noel and stalks off.

Norman lunges off my shoulder. Only a quick dive stops him chasing down Quinn. I hug him to my chest, whispering softly, crooning nonsense while he twitches and struggles.

"I know, baby, I know. She's a hateful witch. Don't worry, I'll take you to shit on her desk later, okay?"

Noel slaps my shoulder. "I'll be in the sparring room. Join me if you want to blow off steam, sí?" He makes a beeline to his own desk.

❖

I sit and scoop dried and fresh droppings into the tray stashed beneath my desk. That done, I skim through the various message tubes dotted across my workstation. Test results, lab reports, case summaries. Nothing I can't deal with later.

While Norman sits on my head and helpfully tangles his talons in my locs, I kick my legs on the desk, pull out my mobile, and dial.

"Hey, Dani, this isn't a great time." Pippa's words are clipped and hushed, nothing like her usual chirpy self.

"Quinn just reassigned all my cases and dumped me on civvie basher babysitting duty. How she got as far as Grade Seven is beyond me, the woman is a total bitch. I could strangle her—"

"So head a team instead of avoiding your own—take the team leader role."

I snap my mouth shut. She has a point.

"Is that Danika?" A second voice thrums through the phone line.

My fingers tighten on the mobile.

"No, it's—" The rest of Pippa's lie goes unheard as a scuffle ensues on the other end.

That new voice: "Danika? Danika, baby, is that you?"

I slump in my chair. "Hey, Mum."

"When are you coming to see me? It's been so long."

"I'm sorry, I—"

"What have I done that you won't return my calls?"

Six blind dates in three weeks? Each one an unmitigated disaster. From allergic reactions to the prawn salad, right up to escape through a toilet window, I'd say that's reason enough to avoid talking with my mother. And date number seven.

"I've been busy. Work is crazy and—"

"Take a holiday. All that fighting and hunting and chasing, you deserve some R and R. How are your menses this month?"

My fingers tighten on the phone. Norman stops tugging on my hair and slithers down my cheek to peer into my eyes.

Yeah, he gets it.

I lift him away from my face and dump his tiny body on the desk. "You know our protection shots muck up our cycles. Ask Pippa, she'll tell you. Anyway, I'm fine."

Mum harrumphs like an angry horse. "Shouldn't be allowed. How are agents supposed to plan for families if the drugs you take destroy your inner body balance?"

Deep breath in. Then out. I'm not having this conversation again. Not now. "Mum, can you pass the phone back? I'm trying to arrange dinner."

Delighted squeal. "Oh, perfect. I was thinking it's time we sat down together. Tonight? How's eight thirty?"

"Actually, Pip and I were—"

"Make sure you change before coming out. No T-shirts or trainers. What about a skirt? Or a dress? That red one with the ruffled hem?"

I heave, just enough to bring a bitter taste to my mouth. "I don't do dresses."

"I thought you liked red?"

"I do, but—"

"Good. Wear that and the earrings I got you for Christmas."

I cover my eyes with my arm, silently cursing my big mouth.

"Sure, Mum. Whatever you say."

"Great. Now, we're going now. The pair of us will see you later. Phillipa has some exciting news she can't wait to share, right, darling?"

Mumbles of assent from the background.

"Of course you do. See you later, Danika. Eight thirty, don't be late." Gone.

Norman stares at me, black eyes wide and unblinking.

At the far end of the office, another rookie slams face first into the Plexiglas divide.

Yeah. Suddenly the thought of some one-on-one sparring seems a wonderful idea.

❖

Sweat streams down my jaw and chest. Stiffness in my right shoulder and leg highlight where Noel clipped me with a couple of lucky shots.

He stands in front of me now, the practice sword resting on his shoulder, body at an angle. His hair is mussed up and one cheek darkens with a fresh bruise. He walks favouring his left leg and a tiny trickle of blood runs from a gash on his forehead. I've never seen him look so happy.

"See?" he cries. "I told you, sí, I told you. One day, I beat you. Today is that day."

Swap my own sword from my left hand to my right. "Not a chance, González." My hips creak in complaint, but that doesn't stop me assuming the next defence stance.

To the right of us, Link lowers his wings across his shoulders and folds his bulky arms. Eight feet tall, with thick skin the colour of a holly blue butterfly, he grins, flashing fangs. "He has you, Karson. You're tired."

"And you're ugly," I snap.

He chuckles. "Careful, little meatsicle, careful. You're good but I can still crush you."

"Never managed it yet, buddy."

"You may be faster, but I'm bigger, stronger—"

"Shut up and let me concentrate."

We've pulled in a sizeable crowd, fighting as we have for the last half hour. Many of my colleagues stand with their faces pressed to the Plexiglas, and more than a handful of them are passing around money.

Can't help but wonder who they're betting on.

In the middle of them, Quinn glares at us, her face a glorious picture of rage.

Noel spies me looking. "You know, you could stop baiting her."

"And she could stop being a stuffy old cow."

"Perhaps, instead, you do as she says? Just now and then?"

"She's incompetent. I know it, you know it, everyone does."

I flick the sword out and dart in, cutting high with a sharp feint before swinging low. The wooden blades clack together, a sound like twigs snapping.

"So do a favour for all of us, and take the G7 team leader role."

"You know I trust your judgement, but what the hell makes you think that would suit me?"

A shrug. "You are strong, clever, and talented. People resent you, sí, but they respect you too. You'd make a good leader."

"But then I'd have to put up with the likes of you day in, day out. Pass, thanks."

He takes the offensive, driving me back across the training floor with a flurry of jabs and slashes. I block them all, teeth gritted, eyes narrowed, focused wholly on the blade in my hand. Feels good to be physical like this.

His blade slices the air above my shoulder, a hair's breadth from my cheek.

"Ah, close, sí? You yield?"

"Screw you."

"Oh, Dee-Dee"—he pauses long enough to press his free hand to his chest—"I have asked again and again. Do you now, finally, admit your desire?"

"Do you have boobs?"

"No, no, I did away with those when I began training with the weights. Now, I am all muscle." A flex of his biceps to demonstrate.

"Then our deal hasn't changed. The day you beat me fair and square is the day I let you take me out. I'll even wear a pretty dress."

A sharp whistle through his teeth. "Now that I would like to see."

He stops, just for a moment, probably imagining exactly that. I seize the chance and flick out with my blade. The point slams into his chest, an obvious heart shot.

"Yes!" I toss the blade down and rub more sweat off my face. "Better luck next time."

Noel grunts and drops his blade beside mine. "Ah, one day, Dee-Dee. Not this day and perhaps that's best. I have much to do tonight."

"Watching porn in your underwear doesn't count as much to do."

Again that hand to the chest, and a stream of Spanish. "You wound me, Dee-Dee. So cruel, so cruel."

"Shut up, you love it."

"Sí, that I do." He winks and joins me in the corner of the sparring space where towels hang alongside a shelf stacked with bottles of water. He opens one and gulps heavily, Adam's apple bobbing. The empty bottle clatters into the bin beneath. "A gargoyle nests in a warehouse on Sith Street. Tonight, I take my team to catch it."

Link appears behind us, curious and wary. "Wild?"

A nod. "Any help you can offer would be much appreciated, amigo."

I leave them discussing the upcoming capture. Fascinating as it would be to see a wild gargoyle, right now, with the adrenaline rapidly leaking away, the only thought left in mind is that of a nap before dinner. Ugh. Dinner.

As I open the door, the excited chatter from the crowd becomes audible. Money changes hands and several agents pause to thank me or pat me on the back.

Glad to know I'm good for something.

Quinn snags my arm as I aim for the changing rooms. It takes every scrap of willpower I possess to refrain from punching her in the nose.

"Your form is sloppy and your footwork horrendous. Fight like that out there and you won't last a minute."

I pull the sweetest smile I can muster. "I'm always open to coaching. Should we go back in? We can go hand-to-hand."

She jerks free and scrambles back three awkward steps. "You think I have time to waste, coaching the likes of you? Speak to Link if you want extra training." Without meeting my gaze, she hurries away.

Bitch.

I stick two fingers in my mouth and whistle a sharp high-low-high trio of notes. "Norman?"

Bobbing like a balloon, Norman flies towards me above the heads of my fellow agents. He settles on my shoulder once more, nuzzling my cheek with his beak as I head for the showers.

CHAPTER THREE

I arrive early at the Italian place. Good thing too, because the heels I've worn to match this horrendous dress are near impossible to walk in. I totter through the tables, following the waiter who moves with the graceful, seamless glide of a supernatural.

Trust Pippa to pick an *edane*-owned venue.

The waiter leads me to a circular table positioned in the centre. When he pulls out a chair, I hang back, gripping my flimsy cotton shrug around my shoulders.

"No. Put us near the wall, close to the toilets or kitchens."

He stares.

My skin crawls.

His eyes are purple. Only the iris, but that's enough to tell me this vampire is at least two hundred years old.

What the hell is he doing waiting tables?

He leads me to a corner, illuminated by wall lights and a trio of candles in brass candelabra. Two of the chairs are positioned with their backs to the rest of the tables, but the third is against the wall offering a clear view to the left and right. Perfect.

"Ah," he nods, "SPEAR?"

There's no way he can know about the knife strapped to the outside of my left thigh, or the stiletto tucked into my updo, but that prickling discomfort in my skin intensifies. I force myself to think of my sister, to remember that this venue was her choice. It's the only way to stop myself leaving.

"This establishment is fully licensed and registered with the Clear Blood Foundation. If you're looking for—"

"It's my night off, Fangs. Just bring me the menu and a jug of water, okay?"

His lips tighten. "Very good, ma'am. May I hang up your outer garment?"

"Hell, no."

He leaves, and I exhale, shifting my legs to reassure myself of the knife hidden beneath the dress. I miss my gun, but it's better than nothing.

My water arrives with three glasses, each one ringing with a handful of ice cubes shaped like roses. More ice sculptures float in the jug that joins them, a mix of hearts and teardrops.

"Anything else, ma'am?"

"No."

His lips quirk at one corner. "Then here is the menu." He lays it in front of me and leaves.

Two minutes later, in a flurry of coat, scarf, and handbag, my mother crash-lands at the table. "Sorry I'm late, baby, I had errands. Seems Phillipa isn't feeling well."

My stomach knots. "Is she okay?"

Mum waves her hand. "Fine, just tired and nauseous, it's perfectly normal. We thought it best she stay home tonight and catch up with you tomorrow." She dumps her things on the now spare chair and grabs my menu.

I slump. "So she's not coming at all?"

"Nope. Just us." Mum beams over the top of the menu.

I sip my water and mentally scramble to find the upside of a meal with only my mother for company.

❖

The waiter is back again, his purple gaze hard and intense. He looks pointedly at the empty chair. "Your reservation was for three?"

Mum cuts in with a wave. "Yes, we're one short and—oh, what beautiful eyes you have."

"Thank you, ma'am. One of the more flattering changes my kind experiences upon changing."

Delight fills Mum's features. "You're a vampire. My baby is a SPEAR agent, you know. One of the best in the country."

I fight the urge to sink beneath the table. What could possibly convince her that my job is a suitable topic of conversation?

"I'm sure she's very talented and dedicated to her role."

"Too dedicated. It would be nice if she took a break sometimes."

"I can imagine." He clears his throat. "Would you care for a drink? Or further time to peruse the menu?"

Another flighty hand wave. "No, no, I'm ready." She skims the menu once more, then reels off her order. In Italian.

Guess that means her language class is going well.

The waiter beams and replies in kind, words which flow with the ease of a native speaker. He and Mum chat a moment longer before giggling. Like hyenas.

"Ma'am?" He faces me, eyebrows arched.

Git. I might not speak Italian, but I'll bet he doesn't speak Goblin or the Cold Blood Tongue.

"Um…" I grab the menu, flip it the right way up, and scan the list. Why the hell isn't it in English?

"She'll have the lasagne, please." Mum leans across me. "A side of salad as well. No dressing or parmesan."

No. Hell, no.

"Actually"—I lift a finger and point to the centre of the menu—"I prefer the look of this."

Mum strains to see the page.

Vampire waiter studies the choice, chuckles, and scribbles on his notepad. "Anything else, ma'am?"

Another pointless skim of the page. "This one."

More scribbling. "Very good, ma'am." He bows, clicks his heels, then walks off, smirking.

Mum watches me. I can feel her gaze like an itchy blanket across my shoulders. "Danika, baby, are you okay?"

"Fine. Just tired. Work is heavy this week."

"Tell me all about it."

I bite my lip. I could tell her about Quinn and my reassignment, but I could also gargle oven cleaner and rip off my fingernails.

"Phillipa told me you got a summons this morning. Are you in trouble again?"

"Why does everyone assume that?" I roll my eyes and pull off the shrug.

"Danika"—Mum bolts upright in her seat—"what happened?"

Too late I remember why I'd worn the pointless garment. "Nothing, I—"

"But those are new. On your arms and your chest. When did you get injured? Why didn't you tell me?"

I trace the new scars and remember the various injuries. A bite on my shoulder, claw slashes across my arm. A small round dot that, at the time, gushed stinking clots of blood and pus while the spriggan that stabbed me made a slick getaway. That one was close: two full months of recovery and desk work while the poison left my system.

"I'm fine, Mum."

She glares. "This job is too dangerous for a young woman like you. You've your whole life ahead of you. Why are you risking it fighting ghoulish monsters?"

The tablecloth receives the full weight of my stare. "I like my job."

"Don't pout. You know I'm proud of you."

I sigh and lean my chin on my hand. "Yes and I—"

"Elbows off the table, baby."

"Yes, Mum."

"Now, do you ever consider that your job is somehow off-putting?"

"Excuse me?"

She leans in, as if her words are a terrible secret. "All that hunting, shooting and killing, it's more of a man's job, wouldn't you say?"

"A quarter of my team are female. What does that have to do with anything?"

"It's intimidating. And you're a forceful personality. Perhaps that's why so many past relationships have been so brief?"

Well, that might be one of the reasons…

"Mum—"

"It's not a bad thing," she rushes on, as if sensing my rage. "Nobody wants you to be a doormat, but you could try being more feminine. Look how pretty you are with your hair up like that, and no weapons. Never thought I'd see the day."

Another twitch in my seat reminds me of the knife strapped to my thigh. "Well, like I said before, if men are intimidated by me, maybe they aren't right for me."

"Don't be silly. How else are you going to raise a family?"

Food arrives. One thing to be said for *edane* establishments, their service is super-speedy.

Good thing.

The waiter lays a steaming plate in front of my mother. Looks incredible—long twists of pale pasta smothered in sweet-smelling red sauce. With it, a wicker bowl of garlic bread dripping with butter and herbs. That one he handles with a single gloved hand.

My mouth waters. I search for my plate.

The insufferable smirk returns. "And for you, ma'am." He lays a plate in front of me.

Mum frowns. "When did you start eating mushrooms?"

"Um…" I force a smile. "Just thought I'd see what all the fuss is about."

"And this is also yours." The waiter places a small white bowl beside the plate.

Pasta shaped like trucks, cars, and planes, not a lick of sauce. The fork he sets beside it is bright green plastic, blunt enough to double as a spoon.

He loiters, hands clasped at hip height, shoulders bucking.

"This can't be what she ordered—"

"I assure you it is, ma'am. And if you recall, your daughter was quite firm in her order." He bows from the waist and spins on his heel. "Ladies, please enjoy your meal."

I stare at my selection of food.

Maybe after this I could stop for a burger.

Mum digs into her pasta, slurping juicy strands into her mouth. She gives an appreciative coo, then ploughs on. "You won't be this young and fit forever. What happens if your next injury cripples you? Or worse?"

"I can take care of myself."

"I don't want to lose you. Not you too."

Shame bubbles in my gut. I hide a cough beneath a slurp of water and end up spluttering icy droplets down my front. The face of my watch catches a flicker of light from the candles. So out of place while wearing this dress, but I don't care, and now, more than ever, I'm pleased to be seen wearing it.

"I know, Mum."

"He'd be proud too. You've done so much more than we ever believed possible."

That's a compliment. It has to be.

I smile and nibble the end of a pasta truck. Bland. Overcooked. Hours old.

"I miss him too, Mum."

She plays with gold ring on a chain around her neck, a larger version of the one on her left hand. "You're an amazing woman with so much to give. I don't want you to miss all the wonderful things a family can bring you. Love is for everyone."

"Even me?"

"Of course, don't be silly—" Her mobile rings. She fishes it from the depths of her bag while I silently curse myself.

I can stare down vampires, fight hand-to-hand with gargoyles, but I can't set matters straight with my mother? How long is she going to deny the truth? More important, how long am I going to let her?

Mum grins into the phone. "You made it? Wonderful. Yes, come in, we're at the back. We'd be thrilled to see you."

My heart gives a gleeful skip. Pip made it after all. Maybe she can take the edge off this emotionally barbed conversation.

The chair squeals as Mum shoves it back, standing so she can see above the tables. A moment later she's bobbing up and down and waving like a middle-aged football fan. "Over here...hello...can you see me?"

Several heads turn in our direction.

I cover my face with my hands.

She waves again, then scurries away from the table. "There you are. We've already eaten, but you can join us for dessert."

A chair screeches.

I look up, ready to thank my sister with the biggest hug I can manage.

Oh.

"Who the hell is this?"

❖

The man at my side is tall, with puppy-dog eyes and a toothpaste ad smile. Beneath the shirt sleeves and waistcoat is a body he plainly likes to show off; only an idiot would allow their tailor to stitch silk that tight by accident. His face is vaguely familiar, the look in his eyes more so. In fact, I know it well.

Not again.

"Mum—"

"This is Jackson Cobb. Jackson, this is my eldest daughter, Danika."

He holds out his hand. "Please, call me Jack, and it's nice to finally meet you. I've heard so much about you."

"What?"

His smile bumps up several watts. "It's so often, *Danika this, Danika that*, you sound superhuman. Great to see you're real after all."

I glance at Mum. She beams and shifts her chair left, leaving us closer together.

Oh no.

When the waiter returns, he bobs a short, polite bow at Jack and offers a set of dessert menus.

Again Mum says something in Italian. Jack uses English, though he makes valiant attempts at the complex pronunciations.

"And you, ma'am?"

"Bok ta'akt meir hal." I glare at the tablecloth. "Synq wen."

Long drawn-out pause.

The waiter clears his throat. "Arri tuk meckla shurri nah. Po'eck rar aye?"

Though nobody moves, the tension in the air is palpable. I ease my gaze up, meeting the gaze of our waiter who studies me through eyes taking on a bright silver sheen.

So he *does* know the Cold Blood Tongue. Shit.

I lift my hands, palm out, careful to keep each movement slow, smooth, and most of all non-threatening. "I'm going to rephrase that."

"Perhaps you should." His voice is low and bass, almost a growl.

I think about the knife on my thigh. The stiletto in my hair. Both might as well be on the moon.

I clear my throat. "Do you have any ice cream?"

"Vanilla. Strawberry. Chocolate. Mint."

I wince. "Then strawberry. Please."

"Of course." The waiter stomps away, carrying the dessert menus with him.

I exhale. Hadn't realized I'd been holding that breath.

Insensitive to mood, or unconcerned by it, Mum beams and lays a hand on Jack's shoulder. "I need to go. I promised Phillipa some painkillers on the way back. But I'm sure you'll take good care of Danika."

"Of course. And please allow me to collect the bill."

Mum nods and throws a wholly unsubtle look of approval my way. "That's very kind of you, Jack, thank you. Danika, be nice to him, won't you?"

No. She can't do this, she—She's already gone.

How did this happen? Is Mum so slick and cunning that she can now get me on a date without my realizing it?

Jack swivels in his chair. "Wow, she's a whirlwind. Quite the character, isn't she?"

"Mum? Yeah, she's something."

"Thinks highly of you."

"Mm-hmm."

He drums his fingertips against the tablecloth. "I always thought SPEAR agents were grizzled old guys with itchy trigger fingers and a beard full of breadcrumbs."

"What?"

He's watching me, gaze flicking back and forth across my face and down the neckline of my dress. "That's my experience. Supernatural crime fighters are generally old, jaded, and grey or young, cocky, and stupid."

"Have you been hanging around my office?"

He laughs. "Is that an invitation?"

"Only if you like mindless, poorly dressed women with nervous trigger fingers and hair extensions full of fake tan."

More laughter.

Maybe this won't be so bad.

❖

I'm surprised at how easy it is to talk to Jack. We discuss cars, TV, and music before dessert arrives, this time with a different waiter. Probably for the best.

Jack has a cheesecake, white, thick, and creamy, smothered in orange coulis. My ice cream is stacked three scoops high in a glass bowl, decorated with sliced strawberries and sparkly red dust.

I shove a spoonful into my mouth and fight to survive the onset of brain freeze.

"Teresa isn't the only one to brag about a SPEAR in the family." Jack cuts a tiny piece of the cheesecake with the side of his fork. "Pippa loves telling us about her big sister, the vampire slayer."

Juice slides down my chin. "How do you know Pip?"

"She works in my office."

"You're a researcher?"

He chuckles. "Once upon a time. Not so much now that I'm running for mayor. It's all so different now since the Interspecies Relations Act. The mayor actually has responsibilities."

I stare. My mouthful of ice cream becomes an uncomfortable ooze at the back of my throat. Finally, I recognize his face. "Wait, you're Jackson? Jackson *Cobé*?"

A boyish shrug. "I didn't have the heart to correct your mother—she was so excited to introduce us."

I drop my spoon. It spins off the bowl and hits the floor.

This is how I imagine kids feel when they meet Santa.

"Jackson Cobé of the Clear Blood Foundation? Host of the Supernatural Registry?"

Jack turns his head aside, a bashful gesture that smacks of careful practice, probably in front of a mirror. "It's not that big a deal."

"Oh, shut up." I hurry on, ignoring his wide, surprised eyes. "The Life Blood Serum is the single most important tool SPEAR has. We wouldn't be able to do our job if vampires were snacking on us every night. You're a hero."

"And you're very kind, but I'm afraid your colleagues might disagree."

I retrieve the spoon and stab it into the ice cream. "My colleagues are idiots. Vampires might be vicious killing machines, but the rest can be integrated. *Edanes* have so much to offer us, and that registry of yours is one way to let them."

"*Edanes?*"

"Extra mundanes."

"Catchy. I like it. You should be on my PR team."

"No, I shouldn't, people hate me. Anyway, SPEAR has thrown everything behind that git Mikkleson. I doubt I'd be much use singing from the wrong side of the hymn sheet."

Jack leans across the table, reaching for my hands. This close, I can see the tail end of a thin, trailing scar peeping out from beneath his watch. Faint streaks run down his jaw and throat.

Is this man wearing make-up?

He swirls his index finger over the back of my wrist. "I doubt very much that it's possible for anybody to hate you, Danika."

"Tell that to Quinn."

"Who?"

"My supervisor."

He smiles and grips my hand. "This Quinn is a fool."

True, but now isn't the time to go into that. In fact, now seems like the time to bolt.

"I need to go."

"But—"

I'm already up, snagging my shrug and flinging it around my shoulders. Two long strides and I remember the heels.

Baby steps, then.

Somehow I make it to my car without breaking my neck. The car park is empty but for a handful of vehicles at the far end, so I kick off the shoes and stand barefoot on the Tarmac, fumbling for my keys.

Jack catches up as I swing my door open, catching the edge with one hand.

"What's the hurry, baby doll? I thought we were having a nice chat."

"Long day."

"Busy saving the world?"

"Something like that." I tug on the door. "I need my beauty sleep."

He pulls the door wider and steps into the gap. His fingers trace a circle on my bicep, over the claw slash scars. Though he pauses to look, his smile never droops. "Beauty sleep is something you most definitely don't need." One arm curves around my waist, the other hand drifting up to my chin. He's strong and broader than he looks.

So distracted by this latest discovery, I'm slow to realize what he's doing. By the time I catch up, his hand is on my jaw, his lips on my mouth, tongue jabbing for entry against my teeth.

I punch him.

Jack drops like a rock, bumping his forehead against the door on the way down.

Bad. Bad Danika. Don't beat up civilians.

The rush of adrenaline gives way to cool irritation. I'm never going to forgive Mum for this. Not this time.

A quick step over Jack puts me in the driver's seat where I slam the door shut and dump my heels on the passenger seat.

The engine starts with a roar.

"Danika? Wait, Danika?"

No chance. I'm gone before he can stand.

CHAPTER FOUR

I'm half a mile away before the rage fades. Before my mind clears and I can see and understand what I've done.

"Damn." I slam my hands against the steering wheel. It hurts, but not as much as it might receiving my P45 tomorrow morning.

Cursing, I turn and speed back to the car park. Maybe I only stunned him?

The area is quiet when I arrive, just Jack under a street lamp, hugging some short, dark-haired woman. At his side, a sleek silver Jaguar stands with its door open.

My stomach turns.

Creep. That didn't take long.

Wait...

I slam my foot down, grinding through the gears as my wheels spin and screech.

Closer now, Jack's screams are loud and shrill, his frantic cries mingling with the snarls of the figure clawing at his throat.

I stab the button which lowers my windows and hurl one of my shoes through the widening gap.

It thunks off the head of the shorter figure, not hard, but enough to gain attention.

Wild silver eyes and long fangs glistening with streamers of drool.

Vampire.

I turn the car, toss the other shoe, then screech across the car park. Turn.

The creature releases Jack and follows, legs pumping with supernatural speed.

Again I floor the accelerator, hunched low over the wheel.

I hit the vampire travelling at a powerful fifty miles an hour. The impact throws me against the seat belt, dents my bonnet, and catapults the snarling figure twenty feet across the Tarmac. It rolls twice, then lies still.

"Jack!" Out of the car and running. There's blood on his face. His hands. "Are you okay?"

He blinks at me. "She...out of nowhere...talking, then teeth—she bit—"

"Look at me, Jack, look at my face. Hey!" At last I have his attention. I use the opportunity to scan assess his injuries. "It's just a graze, she didn't go deep. Get in your car and lock yourself in."

"She—vampire—they don't—"

I slap him. "Get in the damn car."

"But Life Blood—they're not supposed to—"

"For goodness' sake." With his heavy arm drawn across my shoulders, I hold his body close and guide him back to the Jaguar. His steps drag but at least he's moving.

At the car I shove him inside and slam the door.

"Don't move. I'm going to—"

A heavy impact numbs my entire right side. A moment later I realize I'm on the ground several feet away from Jack's car.

The vampire fights to get inside the Jaguar. The glass must be reinforced like my limo earlier, because repeated punches and kicks barely scratch it, though that won't last long.

I scramble up and wave my arms. "Hey, you." It pauses. "Yes, you, fang face, over here."

The next punch cracks the glass.

Jack yells.

Small chips of stone and grit catch between my toes, but that's still better than wearing heels. My sprint takes me back to the car and provides momentum for a flying roundhouse kick.

Jarring shudders race up and down my leg. Did I break my foot?

The vampire lands to the side, nursing its jaw.

Jack's car roars to life, squealing away with the rear fishtailing. Moments later, rear lights wink and vanish as it peels out of the car park.

Jackson Cobé...my hero.

Again the vampire stands, this time focused on me.

It snarls.

I yank the knife off my thigh holster.

We collide hard, and air flies out of me in a gushing whoosh. I stab at the eyes, but the vampire is fast and willow slender. She slithers out of my grip and slips behind me before I fully understand she's moved at all. I drop into a roll and spring up three feet away.

Fluttering fragments of red fabric litter the ground behind me.

"Watch it, this is the only dress I own."

More snarling and flexing fingers.

The next charge I'm ready for, ducking beneath groping hands and slashing with the knife. Blood rains across my face and shoulders, then the weapon skitters out of my hand and across the Tarmac. My hand throbs. The shoulder of my dress lists on the right, exposing half my bra.

"Damn you."

I turn. Dart back to the car.

Thunk.

She slams into my back and I thrust my hands out. It saves my face and nose, but both wrists creak as I twist on my belly.

Kick, kick, and kick again. The grip on my left ankle slips away, along with several strips of skin. Blood streams down my leg.

She snarls, the silver in her eyes intensifying.

Up again. Run. Faster. Faster.

I reach the car as the vampire catches me a third time, clawing for my face.

Jump kick.

Her head snaps back.

Elbow strike.

Down.

I leave her writhing and pop the boot. Inside, no SPEAR kit, but I do have rope, a hazard triangle, a spare tyre with the wheel missing, and my wheel nut wrench.

My fingers scrape the latter as she drags me down.

The tyre tips over the side and hits us both, surprising the vampire enough to give me precious half seconds.

I grab the wrench and swing it down, a two-handed grip.

Crunch.

The large end cracks off the back of her skull.

She slumps into stillness.

"Ugh, finally!"

❖

More of my dress tears as I wriggle out from beneath her. Throbbing in my hand and shoulder tells me I'll be aching in the morning. Blood on my leg is already clotting, courtesy of fast-acting coagulate drugs. The horrific slashes may not even scar. Yay.

A lone figure hurries across the car park, a quick *edane* stride.

I reach for the stiletto, then change my mind as I recognize the uniform of the restaurant waitstaff.

"Running to my rescue? I didn't know you cared."

The waiter from earlier slides to a stop beside me and the unconscious specimen on the floor. The silver leaks from his eyes, leaving behind the stunning purple.

Shame. That shade used to be my favourite colour.

"What happened?" He stares. "Is she—"

"Not yet. But I caught her attacking a human." A shrug. "She's done."

"But—"

"Law is law, Mr. Fangtastic. I'm taking her in."

He stiffens, fingers flexing.

I wait.

"Fine. Go ahead, Agent. Do your duty." He stalks away.

I heave a sigh and study the creature at my feet. Female, young, dark haired, petite.

Oh, well.

Without my SPEAR kit I've nothing to restrain her. A rummage through my car reveals nothing of use except the rope, which I use to hog-tie her wrists and ankles. For good measure, I force the tyre down over her head and shoulders, further trapping her arms.

It won't hold if she wakes, but perhaps I can reach HQ.

She twitches. Her eyelids flutter.

HQ is three miles from here, the Clear Blood Foundation a mere two. But I won't reach either location in a civilian car before she wakes fully, which leaves me with one option.

Great. Because this night needs to get a little bit worse.

❖

There are groans coming from the boot of my car. The occasional whimper.

My radio is broken so there's not much I can do to block it out. After a few minutes, the sounds stop.

On the outer edges of West Side, a small independent bookshop carries more than local authors and guidebooks. In the basement, a minor SPEAR safe house provides shelter, bed rest, and the occasional handful of mean weaponry.

I leave the car running as I knock on the door, rapping out a two-one-two-three pattern with my knuckles.

It opens after a few seconds, revealing a thin sliver of brown, warty face.

"No, no, no, not you." The door swings closed.

I jam my foot into the gap. "Let me in, Shakka—"

"No, damn it. They don't pay me enough to deal with you more than once a week."

"You get paid plenty, open up. I've got a wild fanger and I need to stash her until sunup."

Still he leans on the door. "Take her to HQ."

"Too far. Open the door."

Silence.

"Fine." I brace my weight and shove.

A cry, then the pressure lifts and the heavy wood swings wide. On the other side, Shakka rubs the end of his crooked, misshapen nose with a hand already missing one finger. "You're a bully, Karson, a sick, twisted bully."

It takes a moment to remember what he's talking about. "I thought you liked cow livers."

"Raw, you stupid human, not flambéed to a black, crunchy crust. You cost me my lunch."

"And you cost me my favourite flamethrower. I'd say we're square. Any holding rooms free?"

The little goblin tugs hard on the remains of his right ear, all mangled and torn. "Sure they're free, but we aren't equipped for vampires right now."

"We'll be fine."

"No, we won't. This is what I'm talking about. What have you got against following rules?"

With a grunt I return to the car.

The vampire is as I left her, tied hand and foot, wedged into my spare tyre. I heave her out with effort and drag her towards Shakka by the last dangling three feet of rope.

"Look at her. You think I can make it all the way to HQ in my knackered old banger?"

He looks at the vampire. Then me. Clothes, face, bare feet. "Gave you a walloping, did she?"

"Not as bad as I gave her."

He rubs his nose, focused on the deep indentation filled with thick, knotty scar tissue. "I do this, you owe me lunch. And not those awful dried livers either—I'm talking fresh. Twelve hours, max."

My stomach turns. "What about immediately frozen?"

"I said *fresh*, Human. Take it or leave it."

Again the vampire stirs. This time her eyes flicker enough to catch a glimpse of the silver shimmering beneath.

"Fine, fine, let me in. And get a cell ready."

"Of course. And remember, Human, you owe me." Shakka grins and hobbles into the building, gleefully dry-washing his thin, knobbly hands.

I follow, fighting hard not to think about what owing him means.

❖

By the time we reach the steel doors at the bottom of the basement, vampire in tow, the creature is lucid and starting to strain.

"Hurry up, Shakka."

Muttering, he leans in and punches a code into the number panel on the right hand side. A mechanical voice requests ID, and he pushes up on tiptoe to peer into the hole above it. A red line scans his eye, left, right, up, down.

The door hisses open. The scent of bleach wafts through.

Beyond the steel door, the holding facility stretches far beyond the boundaries of the shop above it. A wide, brightly lit space extends 650 feet, lined on either side by cells of various heights and sizes. All are fronted with bars as thick as my wrist, and a small keypad which activates the opening mechanism.

Down the centre, a recess in the floor houses weapons. Swords, knives, daggers, guns, and—my favourite—the huge, troll-made battleaxe, all accessed via key code.

I drag my struggling bundle through the first open door on the left.

The tyre groans and splits in three places.

Time to go.

I reach the other side and slam the door, as the ropes fray and snap. Seconds later, shreds of rubber fly through the air as the vampire frees herself with powerful flexes of her arms and wrists. She dives at me, checked only by the bars that hold fast against her charge. Then fizzing, cracking, and popping fill the air, and her eyes open wide as two thousand volts pump through her body.

Why do they always pull on the bars?

Shakka, hanging back near the main door, chuckles and picks something from between his teeth with a long, pointed fingernail. "They always do that."

The current breaks and she jerks away, retreating to the back of the cell with her knees drawn up to her chest.

"Are we done, Karson? Can I get some sleep now?"

I yawn, abruptly aware of how long I've been awake myself. Bed sounds marvellous. "Sure. I'll ring it in upstairs, then get out of your hair."

"Danika?"

I spin around, searching for the source of that voice. Not Shakka, he couldn't sound so soft and timid if he tried.

The vampire is standing again, close to the bars but far enough back that she can avoid the shock. The silver has faded from her eyes leaving behind a rich, golden brown the colour of ripe acorns. "Danika?"

"How do you know my name?"

She hesitates.

I point to the ceiling of her cell. "Those dots up there are linked to our sprinkler system. Guess what kind of water we keep in it."

She shudders. "He said *Karson* and I recognized the name. I didn't know it was you."

"Hi, Danika Karson, grade five, SPEAR. Who are you?"

She looks away.

"Fine. Enjoy your stay at Château SPEAR and, if I don't see you before then, enjoy your execution."

"Execution?" Her voice is the faintest of whispers. "I—but—you—"

"You attacked a civilian. Angbec's newest candidate for mayor. I doubt they'll bother with a trial."

Her lips wobble. "Mayor? I didn't know. I was only—I thought it was okay—"

My steps falter a short distance from the cell. "You thought it was *okay*?" I'm back at the bars, so close I can hear the hum of electricity coursing through the metal. "You thought it was okay to leap on an unsuspecting human and treat him like some walking Snack Pack?"

"No—"

"So maybe you don't care about the law? Or all the systems we've put in place to help you leeches?"

She flinches. "I don't know what you're talking about. I always obey the law, it's important, I—"

"Vampires in Angbec get their food from the Foundation. Remember? The Supernatural Registry? Donations? This ringing any bells?"

Her eyes widen. "I don't understand."

Behind me, picking something soft and yellow from the depths of his nostril, Shakka gives a low chuckle. "I don't think she's lying, Agent."

"Bull. She's a vampire. Of course she knows this stuff."

He grumbles but falls silent, leaving me to consider the vampire in the cell.

I can get a good look at her now, delicate pixie features and small, slender hands. Everything about her is dainty and cute. Except for the mouthful of fangs.

Vampires, growing more sly and cunning every day.

"You broke the law. Not only that but I caught you doing it. Then you attacked me. As soon as the sun rocks up, HQ will pick you up and that's it. Hope it was worth it."

My stomach warms with a strong sense of right and justice. Vampires, blood thieving scum we have no choice but to live with. But when one acts up like this, nothing gives me more pleasure than dealing with it.

I'm halfway to the door before she speaks again.

"There's a bounty on you, Agent Karson."

I raise my eyebrows. "Excuse me?"

"Among vampires. Anyone who finds you and kills you will be rewarded."

"Oh, really? By who?"

"The queen of our nest."

I snort. "This isn't the States, fang face. Vampires in Angbec don't nest. That's illegal too."

She swings a hand at the bars, jerking back at the last moment. "Why won't you listen? I—I want to help."

"You're a vampire." Again I make for the door. My fingers are on the handle this time.

"I'm not the only one hunting. We all do it. I thought that was the right way—we were all told…Just look it up. Check with the police. They'll tell you."

"Will you shut up—"

"Humans are going missing, right? More than usual? It's my nest, my family. We've been taking them from Misona because the public are less likely to care about vanishing homeless people."

I miss a step. Think back to Quinn and her irritating reassignment to The Bowl. Or, as it's officially named, Misona.

"Why should I believe you?"

"You can check, can't you? SPEAR must have links with the local police force."

I fiddle with a loc falling loose from my mangled updo. "If this is all some sick joke—"

"It's not. Please. I didn't know. I don't want to be bad."

"If this doesn't check out, I'll cut your head off myself, understand?"

She nods, timid and drawn in. "It's the truth."

"We'll see, fang face." I slip through the door and let it slam behind me.

❖

Back upstairs, Shakka sits in the cubby outside the steel door. Thin slicks of pink drool slide down his chin as he munches through bite-sized pieces of something small, brown, and squishy.

"How did it go?" He slurps a gobbet of the gooey stuff off his fingers.

"Fine. Where's the hotline?"

He points to a landline unit against the wall.

I enter my ID and wait for the line to connect.

"SPEAR switchboard," says the mechanical female voice. "Please state the agent or extension you require."

"Quinn, Francine. Agent A20191125A06."

"Please wait."

The line chirps, then rings. And rings.

I hang up.

"What the hell, Karson?"

"Quinn already hates me. I can't call in the middle of the night with conspiracy theories about vampires snatching humans off the street. She'd have me suspended."

Another slurp and Shakka is done eating. He sighs, burps, and slaps his stomach. "What now?"

I dial again.

"Angbec Police Force, this is Officer Tina Marks."

I press the phone tighter to my ear. "This is SPEAR agent Danika Karson, A20240119A05. I need to check a couple of details on a case I'm working."

Shuffling papers. A slurp of some fluid, probably coffee, if I know the civvie bashers.

"Don't you guys ever clock off?"

"Apparently not."

"What do you need?"

"An outline of all open missing persons cases."

Tina splutters into her coffee. "All of them? How long do you think I have?"

"That many?"

"Why do you think we asked you guys for help? Three of our team are off, and now all these people just vanish from The Bowl. We're good, but we aren't trained to deal with the people living down there, especially when short-staffed."

My chest tightens. "Ballpark figure?"

"This week?" She sighs. "Five. Last week, seven. And there's three outstanding from last month."

"Anything else you can tell me?"

"Not unless you come in. I shouldn't be sharing this on the phone as it is."

"Don't worry about it. Thanks." Disconnect and put the handset back on the cradle.

"What happened? Hey! Karson?"

I pause on the stairs back to street level. "It's not enough. I need to check it myself."

"I thought you were off tonight."

Shrug. "So did I."

CHAPTER FIVE

The drive to Misona takes half an hour, even so late at night. Outside my windows, Angbec transitions from beautiful, modern city to filthy, broken-down hovel in the space of half a mile. Deeper into the district, brightly lit shops and bars give way to boarded-up doorways and shattered windows. Figures wrapped in blankets curl beneath any available overhang and cars lining the pavement are rusted, dented, or burnt-out.

I slow the car, studying the slouched figures walking the otherwise abandoned streets. It's dark too, any moon- and starlight blocked by the height of the buildings in this area. And the street lamps certainly don't work.

The road branches left, angled towards a small play area between two blocks of flats. The swings and slide are mangled and broken, but the climbing structure offers some shelter. Beneath it, three figures huddle together, passing a bottle wrapped in carrier bags.

I stop the car and lean through my window. "Wendy, is that you?"

One of the figures bolts upright and dashes away from the climbing frame, stooped and round-shouldered but faster than most humans. Straight up to my door then crouching to peer through the opening. "My name is Wensleydale." A puff of whisky-scented breath gusts across my face.

"I need your help."

He glares and the meagre light from my overhead illuminates the golden glow in his eyes. "You've got a lot of nerve—"

"But not a lot of time. Anything weird been happening down here? People disappearing, increased fanger activity?"

"Not on my watch. This territory belongs to my pack and—"

"That's why I'm here. You're alpha, right? Shouldn't you know everything going on?"

Wendy cocks his head, scratching the tangled nest of wiry grey-black facial hair masking the lower half of his face. "I forgot how ballsy you are, girl. Yes, something weird is happening, but not with us—the humans. Someone or some*thing* is picking them off. Can't figure out who."

I tighten my grip on the steering wheel. "I really hoped you wouldn't say that."

A shrug. "Told the coppers, but they don't much care for a bunch of homeless wasters and druggies. Nearly blamed us, as if we have any use for a handful of piss-weak humans. No offence."

"None taken, you filthy mongrel."

"Meat sack."

"Puppy."

"Bitch."

"You wish."

He laughs and looks me over. "What's up? And who have you been fighting this time? Not another handsy date?"

"Fanger."

"Thought I smelled rot."

"Can't say much now, but you've confirmed enough that I need to keep checking."

"You don't sound happy about that."

"It's my night off."

Wendy peers deeper into my eyes. "You should take it easy. You humans are so soft and breakable, training can only get you so far."

"I didn't know you cared."

He snorts and walks back to the climbing frame. "The pack and I will do some sniffing around. Come back tomorrow."

❖

Halfway back to the bookshop, my mobile trills from the glove compartment. I pull over and press it to my ear. "Hello—"

"Danika, thank God—where are you?"

"Pip?"

"Mum said you were attacked by vampires."

"How the hell did she know?"

"Jackson called Mum to ask if you were okay, but of course she didn't know anything about it." Pippa's voice is shrill and panicked, fast and breathless. "He told her what happened and she rang me and I rang you but no one was answering and we've all been worried sick—"

"Steady, sis, calm down." I make soothing gestures with my hands, even though she can't see them. "I'm fine. Yes, there was a vampire, yes, I had to fight, but I dealt with it. Like always."

Long pause. And...a sob?

"Pip?"

"I was scared, Dani. I'm always scared for you, but you wouldn't answer your phone..."

My throat seizes up. "I'm sorry. I've been out on recon. My phone was in the car—"

"I want to see you."

"Now?"

Sniffle. "Later, then. Please come see me."

"Of course." I switch the phone to my other ear to check my watch. "Breakfast, okay?"

More sniffs. A honk like a goose and the rustle of tissues. "I love you, Danika."

"Me too, Pip. Sorry to scare you."

"It's fine. And don't worry about Mum, I'll ring her. You get back to work or sleep, or whatever it is you're doing."

"See you soon."

As I hang up and drive off again, I can't help but wonder if I've lied to my sister.

❖

Back at the bookshop, my vampire sits on the floor against the rear wall, knees hugged to her chest, eyes closed. Her lips move, but I've no idea what she's saying, not until she stiffens and turns my way.

"Hello, Agent."

I plant my hands on my hips. "Start talking."

"You verified what I told you?"

"Humans vanishing from The Bowl. Lots of them. Even the werewolves have noticed, and they don't care about anybody not covered in fur. So talk. How long have you been snatching humans? How many of you? Where are you based? Why aren't you using Foundation blood stores?"

She shudders and opens her eyes. "I—you're not—"

"Okay. Start slow, what's your name?"

"Rayne."

"And you've been a fanger for…?"

"A month."

My jaw drops. That's young for the levels of strength she showed earlier. "Who created you?"

"I—I—"

I pause to stop the alarm beeping on my watch. If sunrise is that close, I need to be quick. "What's your FID?"

Blank stare.

"The number they gave you when you registered."

"I don't have—we never—I mean, we don't—"

"You're not registered?" I grit my teeth. "Every new vampire is required, by law, to register with Clear Blood within three days of changing. They give you a number, log you to the system, and then, three times a week you visit them to get your blood."

Her eyes widen. "They give it to you?"

"What do you think the Life Blood Serum is for?"

Another bemused look.

I tangle my hands in my locs. "Clear Blood uses it to extend the shelf life of all donations. Any samples deemed unsuitable for human medical procedures are then offered to vampires. You know, so they don't run around snatching people off the street. Your maker must have told you this."

"We don't talk much."

"Great." A tic pulses below my left eye.

I've never liked vampires, not since Dad, but I hold a high level of disgust for the ones who change humans then disappear without teaching or explaining. It's as close to child neglect as an *edane* can get.

"You keep saying *we*."

Rayne hangs her head. "I didn't know. Back home we had nothing like this, vampires would just—" She sniffs. "But here, my family, they need food. We need to eat. So we bring a human each. Only bad ones, only cruel people. I didn't know about the blood stores—"

"How many of you?"

"Please—"

"How many?"

"Twenty? Fifty? We're not allowed to gather together so we're based all over the city. There could as many as one hundred."

My chest and stomach fill with cold. "And none of you are registered?"

She shakes her head.

I sit on the floor. It's that or fall.

"Are you all right, Agent?"

"Do I look all right?" Deep breath. "How long has this been going on?"

Rayne offers an apologetic shrug. "I arrived a week ago."

"Have others been travelling into Angbec?"

"Lots. For the past fortnight."

No wonder the missing persons figures have increased so sharply.

My legs wobble as I stand. "Tell me everything. Every single detail about what you leeches have been doing."

She stares. The tiniest rim of silver leaks into her eyes before she blinks it away. "Please, please, believe me. I didn't know. I would never have done these things if I knew there was another way."

"Prove it. Tell me who your creator is."

"I told you, she's our queen. She runs everything, gives the orders, decides who feeds and when. She's old, powerful, and—"

"Name."

"It's Vi—" Rayne's eyes roll back in her head. A thick, shuddering gasp rushes from her lips. She slumps sideways like a sack of rocks and hits the ground on her face.

"No!" I reach for the bars, just in time remembering the voltage running through them.

Ten more seconds.

A soft gong vibrates through the captivity space. The humming from the bars peaks, then dies.

Sunrise.

I'm into the cage in an instant, grabbing Rayne by the shoulders and shaking her. For the good it will do.

She's dead for the day.

What the hell do I do now?

❖

I'm still kneeling in the cell when Shakka returns. Rayne lies in front of me, boneless and limp, her eyes still freakishly open. I close them with the tips of my fingers.

He stops outside the cell. "Did you get anything?"

"She's not registered. And neither are the others she hangs out with."

"How many?"

"A lot."

Shakka's eyes widen. He rubs his mouth and mutters something obscene in Goblin. Though I can't follow it all, I know he understands. "What now?"

"Wait until sundown, I guess. She can tell me then."

"How? She'll be ooze well before then."

It takes me several seconds to catch up. "No. No, they can't. She's my only lead."

"She attacked a civilian."

"But all those unregistered vampires. I have to find out more."

Shakka wags a finger at me. "Whatever you're thinking, don't."

Am I so predictable?

I dart out of the cell and to the end of the holding area where a storage cupboard hides behind a false wall.

I drag it open and start riffling through, tossing aside sheets, pillows, overalls, and cleaning sponges. Right near the back, stacked neatly, is a pile of thick black body bags.

"Karson, no."

I carry one to the cell, unzipping the heavy steel teeth as I go.

"You can't. What about logging the capture? Hello? Are you hearing me? Log the damn capture, or else it's my neck on the line. Karson—"

"Shut up."

"You're risking disciplinary for a fanger. What's the matter with you?"

A couple of hours ago I would have asked the same thing, but this is bigger than me. Hauling one wild vampire off the street may be a good night's work, but if there's more?

"Don't you get it? These fangers could be anywhere, anyone. Without a FID, we've no way to capture, monitor, or even track one of these things."

"Don't care," he snaps. "Log her in, or I'll do it."

"One night, Shakka. That's all I need." I lay the bag on the ground and open it fully. "She attacked Jackson Cobé. If I let them take her, she's dead and my lead is gone."

"You humans don't pay me enough." He spits on the floor. "So you stick her in the bag, what then?"

"I'll figure it out."

"You're insane."

I grab Rayne by the shoulders and begin to roll her.

By the time I have Rayne in the bag, my arms and forehead are sheathed in a thin coat of cool sweat. The remains of my dress hang in further tatters. I'm sure Shakka is getting an eyeful, but I take comfort from the fact that I'm probably not his type.

"Hey, Shakka, why is the door open? Everything okay?" This voice, familiar as it is unwelcome, reaches us from the area beyond the steel door.

The goblin and I share a startled glance.

I crouch over the bag, jamming Rayne's arms and legs inside. "Stall them."

"How?"

"Think of something."

Grumbling, Shakka waddles up the steps.

I keep stuffing the bag.

Sweat drips off the end of my chin, onto Rayne's face. The salty droplets gather in the corners of her eyes, then spill over like tears. Her mouth is slightly open, pale tongue visible through the gap.

I lean closer.

Such smooth skin. Pale too, not vampire pale, but certainly paler than my Caribbean roots make me. A curl of dark hair fans across her forehead.

Can't remember ever being so close to a vampire I didn't intend to kill. There's an unsettling intimacy in seeing her like this, a powerful supernatural creature suddenly fragile and vulnerable.

I could kill her. Right now. I could take one of the stakes from the weapons store—hell, a pencil would do—and shove it through her chest until the ooze starts to flow. It would be so easy. No doubt she deserves it too.

Loud shouts float down the stairs. Growls. Something thudding and crashing, roaring.

Later. When I have the information I need.

Hiding places are sparse down here, but there is that storage cupboard. With one end of the body bag up on my shoulders, I drag the rest at an awkward half shuffle. The mess from my earlier search is still there, and I pull more junk down to make a pile on top of Rayne. Then I snatch a pair of overalls and hike the remains of the dress over my head.

The steel door slams open.

Through it stumble three SPEAR agents in full tactical gear, including Tasers, chains, and assault rifles. One carries a telescopic control pole and heaves hard on the end to tighten the noose.

A huge winged beast bursts through the door, purple skin, scales, and barbed tail. Six feathered darts protrude from its chest and stomach, one wedged between small, solid breasts.

"Okay now, steady. Take it through, you're covered."

Noel follows after the gargoyle, his rifle aimed and steady. He moves on quick, light feet, his grip never wavering. Until he spots me. "Dee-Dee?"

The gargoyle flicks out with its tail, the thick spikes clipping the rifle to send it spinning away across the holding area. The other three operatives move in, the one with the pole heaving up, then down. The beast crashes to the floor, snarling and spitting, wings beating up a whirlwind.

Cursing, Noel dives after his rifle. He catches it on the ascent and swings the weapon round to aim and fire in one smooth motion.

The tranquillizer hits the narrow strip of skin between jaw and shoulder, shuddering while the creature begins to slow. It roars again, this sound more frustrated than angry. A moment later, it slumps across the ground, breathing low and shallow.

"Use the cell at the back." Noel slings the rifle over his shoulder and dabs at the spots of blood on the back of his hand. "The big one. Make sure she has space. She'll be pissed when she wakes, sí?"

His teammates wrestle the gargoyle through the holding area, coordinating with a fascinating assortment of masculine grunts.

I pull the overalls on over my underwear.

"Dee-Dee, you changed your mind, sí? A fine treat for me after a long night's work."

"I just wanted to see the garg."

He arches an eyebrow. "Naked?"

"Why are you complaining? I thought you'd enjoy the view."

A grin. "Always, always, my dear. And what a view it is. The sight of your shapely beauty makes my passion swell."

"Passion? That's what you call it?" My cheeks are hot, and my heart pounding, but at least his eyes are on me rather than the pile of crap at my feet. I finish buttoning the shapeless garment and search the lower shelves for boots.

Noel leans against the wall beside me, his feet frighteningly close to the head end of Rayne's body bag. "So you see the creature now, what do you think? A fine specimen, sí?"

The other three operatives hurry out of the cell, the last one scooping his control pole to free the noose.

"You'd know best, I guess. Did you catch the pups too?"

He stares. "Pups?"

I bite my lip. "She's nursing. Couldn't you tell?"

"No one said anything about pups."

"Why do you think she put up such a fight? You put seven tranqs in her and she's still eyeing you like she's wondering what you taste like."

"Mierda," he mutters. "Men, we go. There are more. Babies. We must find them."

His agents share startled glances.

I sit to pull on a suitable pair of boots. "If it's any consolation, there won't be more than two. Gargoyles don't tend to have litters bigger than that."

Noel's face is a queer shade of green. He dashes up the stairs still yelling at the rest of his team, who follow sharing confused looks.

Moments later, the screech of spinning tyres tells me I'm in the clear.

Yay.

❖

Shakka limps down the stairs a short while later, leafing through a thick stack of papers.

"You call that stalling them?"

He glares. "And how do I stall an eight foot mother screeching for her babes? Anyway, you survived, didn't you?"

"Barely." I restack the shelves, uncovering Rayne's body bag which hasn't moved at all. "I need to get out of here before they get back. You helping?"

The papers flutter as he waves them in my face. "I've got paperwork to do."

"You should be thanking me. If I'd logged the vamp, that pile would be twice as thick."

He gives a low, menacing growl.

I keep my mouth shut and begin dragging the body bag towards the doors.

Now I need to figure out if my car's boot is light tight.

CHAPTER SIX

Traffic is sparse on the drive back. Mercifully. A handful of close calls remind me how little sleep I've had, but somehow I make it home.

I sit behind the wheel with the engine idling, watching the sky melt from rosy pinks into the paler blue of a crisp morning. Beautiful... if not for the vampire stuffed into the boot of my car.

"Danika, there you are. I was so worried." The voice, coupled with frantic tapping on my window, near sends me through the roof.

"Jack?" I squint through the glass.

He opens the door and crouches in the gap. "I got all the way home hating myself. I can't believe I abandoned you out there, alone and helpless. Forgive me?"

"I'm hardly helpless—"

"Did you get backup? Were there more agents after I left?"

I grip the steering wheel to keep my fingers off his throat. "I'm more than capable of handling a single vampire."

The wonderment in his eyes makes me grit my teeth.

"But she was so strong. I've never seen a vampire so wild before—"

"Why are you here?"

He leaps to his feet and opens the door wider. "I know you spoke to Pippa, but Terri said she couldn't rest until someone had seen you in person."

When the hell did Jack and my mother get on cutesy nickname terms?

"I'm fine and—"

"Good." Jack grins. Since I last saw him, he's changed his outfit, still tailored, still tight, but now pseudo-casual with hints of Eton boating club. Fresh make-up too, especially along the bottom of his jaw.

"What about the vampire?" he whispers.

Can't help but glance over my shoulder. "I took care of it."

Nerves force me from the car and onto the pavement. Jack immediately grabs my hands. "You were amazing out there."

"We're trained for this sort of thing."

"So all SPEAR agents are like you?"

Can't help but snort at that. Quinn would have a nervous breakdown.

Jack chuckles with me, a rich, full-bodied laugh that doesn't quite distract from the bemusement in his eyes.

"Are you just getting home? You must be exhausted."

"It's been a long night."

"I'll walk you up."

"I don't think that's a great idea—"

"It's the least I can do, then I'll reassure Terri that I've seen you safe and sound." He grasps my arm, finger swirling on the end of my elbow.

Again I glance at the back end of the car. It's light tight, right? It has to be.

Guess I'll find out later.

I have the time to lock the doors before Jack's grip tightens, towing me towards the door of my apartment block.

❖

Now I remember why people never visit my flat.

The door opens to a sea of my own slobbery: clothes, DVDs, and plates laden with crumbs strewn across the front hall and living area.

Jack lingers in the doorway, a hand over his mouth, unsuccessfully hiding his distaste.

"I don't usually have guests." Six different bras, three odd socks, and a blouse make a mismatched heap in my arms as I zoom around the room. I toss the lot into the kitchen, silently promising I'll clean up later.

"It's fine—"

"Oh yeah? Mum would have a fit if she knew you'd seen this."

"I won't tell if you don't." He smiles again, eyes bright with the double entendre.

A thong and an off-white pair of granny pants slide from my grip. After a moment of thought, I leave them on the sofa, put my hands on my hips, and offer my best attempt at a coy smile. "Secrets? Whatever would my mother say?"

He leans as if to sit, changes his mind, then perches on the arm of the sofa. "What she doesn't know won't hurt her." His eyebrows lift suggestively. "Though I'm sure she wouldn't mind if I—"

"Danika Kar? Son-son? Karson, Karson, Karson, Kaaaaaaaa!" In a flurry of wings and shedding scales, Norman bursts from my bedroom. He loops my head, tight, frantic circles, before diving, screeching, at my face.

I catch the flustered creature before it can reach my eyes. "Hey. Hey, baby, it's okay. I'm okay."

"Dan-dan kaaar," he wails, nuzzling my cheek with his sharp, pointy beak.

Jack scrambles back so fast, his hip slams the back of my sofa. "Is that a chittarik?"

I bump the little creature up to my shoulder. "His name is Norman."

"Norman? Like a pet?"

A shrug. "I rescued him from the river six months ago. He'd fallen in and soaked his wings, no way he was getting out. I tried to put him back in the nest, but the other chicks wouldn't let him stay. I thought they were going to peck his eyes out."

"Chicks and the mother reject anything that doesn't smell right."

I nod and shift Norman to the other shoulder to stop him gnawing my hair. "He bonded with me while I was trying to figure out what to do. After that, I couldn't let him go."

"Bonded?"

"He started calling my name every three seconds and following me all over the place. Couldn't even take a shower unless he was there."

"It imprinted on you." Jack inches forward, one hand outstretched. "I didn't know chittarik did that. In fact, I've rarely seen one up close outside the carrier unit. Incredible." He gets within two feet of me before Norman dives off my shoulder, claws extended, tiny fangs gnashing.

With a yelp, Jack throws himself back. His feet catch in the arms of a bra I missed, and he tumbles over onto his back.

I snatch the furious creature out of the air and jam him, squirming and squawking, under my arm. "Yeah, and he doesn't like men much. Especially around me. I wouldn't get much closer if I were you."

"Karson," yells Norman, as if to prove the point. "K-kar son-kar!" Jack scrambles to his feet. "But chittarik are pests."

"Tell me something I don't know."

"They're a Class B *edane* mini beast—you can't keep it here."

I hold Norman at eye height and pull some silly faces. "No, no, baby. Don't listen to the mean, mean man. Of course you can stay with me." He hisses softly and brushes his tail against my cheek.

"*Mean man?*" Jack clears his throat. Then, the smile is back, all teeth, twinkling eyes, and perfume ad perfection. "Clearly you have this in hand. I...I need to go. Someone needs to tell Terri you're in one piece."

"Thanks." Another saccharine smile, still making kissy faces at Norman.

At the door, he pauses to shake the bra off his heel. "By the way, that chittarik is female. It's subtle, but the barbs on the end of the tail are shorter on the males." He shrugs. "Thought you should know."

The door clicks shut.

I exhale. "You—I kiss Norman's beak—"are an angel, you know that? I was running out of ways to gross him out."

The chittarik cocks its head to study me through one beady eye. "Danika Karson?"

"So, you're a girl, who knew?" Suddenly I'm laughing, roaring, hugging the scaly body tight to my chest. "A girl who doesn't like men. No wonder we get on so well. Guess you need a new name."

"Danika Karson."

"No, that's taken. What about Normina? Or Gertrude? Or Prudence? Norma?"

"Dan. Son, kar-kar, Danika."

I put him—no, her—back on my shoulder. "Good. Pleased to meet you, Norma, I'm—"

"Danika Karson?"

"Yeah, okay, smart-arse."

❖

I give up on trying to keep Norma inside. Each time I head to the door, she makes such a fuss that I worry about the neighbours. In the end, I head down to street level with her riding on my head, clawing and fussing with my locs.

Most other residents are out for the day, since they work more traditional jobs than mine, but I know one or two are either old and retired or too bum lazy to work. Whichever they are, I need to avoid them while dragging that hefty body bag into the service lift.

Outside, a fat ginger cat peers down at me from the stone wall fronting the block. It hisses as I walk by, arching its back and laying both stubby ears flat to its head.

Norma growls right back, a protective snarl that sends the moody tom dashing for cover.

"That's my girl."

She purrs.

My car is where I left it, parked haphazardly against the pavement edge. A bright yellow packet flutters on my windscreen, *Parking Notice* stamped across the front.

"I'm barely touching the stupid line."

At the far end of the road, a uniformed traffic warden scurries around the corner.

I grab the ticket, shove it into a pocket on my overalls, and stomp around to the back.

What now?

Is it safe to open? What if I do and Rayne goes up in smoke?

If the bag isn't light tight, then my only lead is a goner by now anyway. But what if I leave her and something happens? Or if something happens to me and she can't get out? It would be a really bad day for the poor sucker who eventually opened the boot.

Eyes scrunched shut, shoulders drawn towards my ears, I pop the lock and lift.

No bang. No fire. No smoke.

Yay.

And there's the body bag, wrapped in blankets, then covered in four layers of bin liners.

Not graceful, not pretty, but functional.

Norma flutters off my head to lead the way back inside as I heft the lumpy load onto my shoulder.

My knees wobble, my back creaks, but I can move. Slowly.

"Hello, Danika. Not off for a run this morning?"

I stifle a groan.

The lady from the apartment below mine stands in the doorway, with a mop head at her feet attached to a length of leather covered in cubic zirconia. A mop head that promptly barks and growls at Norma.

"Stop that, Shirley. Stop it now." Though stern, her voice is high and shrill, a perfect match for her four foot frame. Couple that with boobs that reach her knees and curly hair dyed a weary shade of purple, and it's no surprise that the mop-dog ignores her utterly.

More barking, until Norma thuds to the ground and roars at the top of her tiny lungs.

Shirley backs off, whimpering.

"Um…" I fight to steady my buckling knees. "No run this morning, day off." Now if only I could remember her name.

"What you got there? Looks heavy."

"Stuff for the flat, bed sheets, rugs—"

"In one bag? You'll get dust all over your sheets."

"Oh. Darn. Wish I'd thought of that."

Mrs. Purple Hair beams and tugs sharply on Shirley's lead. "Don't let me keep you. I'm sure you've lots to do, saving the world, protecting humankind, going on dates."

I smile. Try to. "I like to keep busy."

"Now there's an app my granddaughter uses. On her phone? You look at pictures and swipe the people you like." The way she says *swipe* brings to mind an antique dealer describing pewter cutlery or brass doorknobs. "Must be so much easier these days to find young people like yourself. You know, *those* kinds of people."

Oh, dear.

"You mean SPEAR agents?"

She laughs and waves a knobbly, liver-spotted hand. Each nail is painted devil red and shaped to a clawlike point. "No, no, don't be silly." She lowers her voice and whispers behind her hand, "I mean the gay people."

"Ah. *Those* people." I nod. "Don't worry, every new moon we gather by the river for a big meet-and-greet. Everyone brings a swimming costume and we practise diving off the docks and racing the swans. Then we all get dressed, pair off, and stop for fish and chips at this tiny little Greek place outside Misona."

"How lovely." Oblivious, she pats my shoulder. "I'm glad you have regular meets with friends. I do hate thinking of you alone in this place, all bored and lonely. You're such a kind and polite young woman."

I haven't the heart to correct her. Especially since, despite her dark ages attitude, this virtual stranger is more accepting of the truth than my own mother who is blind or wilfully ignorant. Or both.

"Thanks." This time my smile is real and indulgent. "Have a good day, okay?"

"I always do, dear. Come on, Shirley, stop being so shirty." She yanks at the dog, waves brightly, then totters off.

My knees give another angry wobble, reminding me of the distance still to travel. They hold until, puffing and panting, I reach the service lift…which is out of order.

Of course.

At least I'm only on the third floor.

❖

Whoever gave that advice about using the stairs over a lift clearly didn't have a sack of dead flesh to lug around. I do these steps every day, but now, at my door, my whole body is sheathed in sweat.

My knees give out as I reach the front hall, leaving me to kick the door shut and shunt the body bag through like a rolled-up carpet.

There, finally in the living room…bathed in the sunlight streaming through my window.

Closing the curtains dims the room, but light from the kitchen and bedroom still provides a dangerous glow.

Where the hell do I put her?

I crawl through the last of my floor junk to reach the boiler cupboard in the corner. Too small.

Bathroom?

A shudder tickles down my back.

I'd rather not pee with a dead body watching. Same goes for my bedroom.

Kitchen?

With the blinds shut, the darkness is deeper with no direct sunlight on the lower cupboards.

The first holds all my cookware, pots, pans, and dishes, the one beside it, my crockery and a few dry foods.

I pull the shelf running through the centre of the unit, but it doesn't budge. Norma tries to help by jabbing at the shelf with her beak and complains when I lift her out of harm's way.

"I've got this, girlfriend. Watch and learn."

"Danika Karson?"

One push-kick later, the shelf is in pieces.

The jagged plywood shards would make a handy set of stakes, but I stack them on top of the fridge and well away from Rayne's potential line of sight.

Giggles consume me as I twist, turn, and finally wedge the body bag into the space. Maybe it's shock. Or fatigue. Whatever it is, I can't stop. Tears spring to my eyes and my ribs ache as the giggles become full-on hysterics. Even the ringing of my landline can't snap me out of it.

"I don't see what's so funny," a gruff voice scolds as I answer.

"Pip?"

"Weren't you coming over for breakfast?"

Oops.

"I'm sorry but"—the giggles are back, stupid, girly titters I can't control—"there's a vampire in my kitchen cupboard."

"Come again?"

"Fanger. Cupboard. I wrapped her in a body bag and put her next to the saucepans."

Pippa sighs. "I knew I should have kept you longer after those shots. I'm coming over."

"I'm fine."

"You're cracking jokes about cupboard vampires."

"It's not a joke. It's the one who attacked Jack. I was going to log her and let SPEAR take care of it, but then she told me about this bounty on my head. I'm all, *No, that's bull*, and she says, *Yeah, well check it. And by the way, I'm not registered and neither are any of my hundred nestmates*—Pip?"

Rustling down the line. The jangle of keys.

"No, I told you, you can't come here."

"There's a vampire in your house. A *vampire*, Dani. One that's already attacked a human."

I make soothing, shushing noises. "She's out cold, wrapped in a body bag, and locked in my cupboard. Besides, look outside. She's not going anywhere until sundown."

A long pause. "She?"

"Yeah. Female."

"I see." Pippa clears her throat. "I've never heard you refer to a vampire as anything other than *it*."

I flop on to the sofa. "What? No, I—"

"Yes. Werewolves are skilled hunters, trolls are tanks, fae are a pain in the arse, but vampires? They're dirty-stinking-death-monsters. Never *she*."

The laughter is gone now, the warmth it brought replaced by a prickling discomfort across my shoulders. "She—*it* has information. I can't afford to let the lead go cold."

"Of course. And does *she* have a name?"

Pause. "Rayne."

Pippa hoots as if she's scored a goal. "My big sis, finally getting to know a vampire. Is that where you were all night? With Rayne? Shouldn't she be in a holding cell? How did you get her home?"

"Long story."

"But—"

"I love you, Pip, really I do, but sod off. Sorry I missed breakfast—I'll make it up somehow—but for now, please, please, go away."

"Make it up by telling me about this vampire."

"There's nothing to tell—"

"Is she cute?"

"She's a vampire!"

"So?" Pippa chuckles. "Come on, is she cute? What does she look like? Has she got green eyes, I know that's your thing—"

"Bye, Pip."

"Wait, is she tall? Short? Is she blond?"

I hang up.

❖

A part of me, a strange, rowdy part, wants to check on the body bag stashed in the kitchen cupboards.

No, her eyes aren't green, but that shade of dusky acorn brown is beautiful and one I've never seen before. Not on a vampire or anyone else.

Norma jump-dives onto my shoulder and rubs her beak against my cheek. "Kaaaaaaaarson."

"Yeah, right? Pip is full of crap."

In the bathroom, I spin the taps over my bath and add a generous blob of bubbles. After last night, a long soak sounds like bliss.

While it runs, I grab my phone and dial out to the SPEAR switchboard. "Francine Quinn, please."

She answers on the second ring. "What the hell are you playing at, Karson? These lines aren't toys."

"What are you talking about?"

"Don't play dumb you arrogant little—" She grunts. "I've got work to do. If you've nothing to say, get the hell off my line."

I place my hand over Norma to stop her growling. "What are you talking about? For once I haven't done anything."

"Last night? Ungodly hours of the morning, you decide to dump-dial me? That might be your idea of a fun prank, but I was in the middle of a very important—" Another grunt. "You have no business calling me at that time of night without good cause."

"I do have good cause. That's why I'm calling now. I have a lead on the missing persons and—"

"So? Why are you telling me? I tasked you that case because I thought you could use some initiative. Don't tell me I need to hand-hold you through it?"

Norma snarls. I silently agree.

"You know what, I can handle this. Sorry to…waste your precious time."

"Finally learning some respect? Good. Knew this case would do you some good. Anything else?"

"No."

"Good. Report at the end of the week."

Click.

I toss the phone on the bed. My fingertips itch and tingle, that familiar longing to wrap them around Quinn's skinny throat. Instead, I tug the punchbag from the corner of my bedroom and firmly pummel it while the bath runs.

Norma skirts tight circles around my head, occasionally swooping in to scrabble at the leather with her claws.

"Bitch. Bitch. Bitch. Bitch. Bitch."

With each punch and kick I add an insult until sweat drips into my eyes and my muscles hum with fatigue. Somehow, this is more satisfying than sparring with Noel. Here, I can scream as much as I like and visualize Quinn's face crumpling beneath every impact against the bag.

Another two minutes and I'm done and so is the bath.

Stripping down and sliding into the water is the single most glorious moment of my life. Hot suds wash over me and immediately start to soothe the aches built over the last twelve hours.

I dip low enough to immerse my hair, then pop up again. "Norma?"

She brings me a facecloth, dropping it on my head with a chittering gurgle that sounds almost like laughter.

"Thank you, baby."

"Danika…" She settles on my head and curls her tail tight around her body, a familiar and comforting weight.

Bliss.

Gentle lapping from the water lulls me, relaxes me, and I lean back, allowing my eyes to close.

Just for a second.

CHAPTER SEVEN

C old.
     Dark.
I sit up.
Water laps my chest and stomach.
Huh?
A hand slaps over my mouth.
Terror slices through me. Icy, dagger-sharp panic locks the breath in my throat.
"Quiet."
Can't.
Too confused. Need to stand. See. Think.
"There's someone here."
That voice. I know it. Soft and hushed, but familiar.
Frigid water sloshes around me.
I flail, catch flesh. Yes, punch, kick, fight back.
Attack.
Escape.
Survive.
Loud thudding fills my ears. My skin prickles with goosebumps.
Combat lessons flash across my memory, every training exercise, sparring match, and test.
Move. *Now.*
I plant my feet and push, but the ground is cold and slippery.
Water sprays across my shoulders and face. Into my eyes, up my nose.
"Stop it—"
Again I thrash about, aiming for that voice. My fist catches hard

flesh and draws a grunt of pain. Punch again. Again. My hand strikes air.

They've gone?

No, the hand is still on my mouth.

"Agent, please, stop hitting me."

What?

"Rayne?" I whisper into the fingers mashed against my lips and teeth.

Silence. The hand lifts.

"Yes. Are you okay now?"

The thunderous thudding eases off. It's my heartbeat, slowing as the eruption of adrenaline ebbs to a mere gush.

"Rayne?"

A gentle hand grips my shoulder. "You need to climb out of there."

Climb *out*? Where the hell am I?

I stand. Water sluices off my body.

Wait, I'm naked?

Memory returns, and with it, recognition of the lap of cold water around my shins.

I'm in the bath. I'm naked in the bath. I'm naked in the bath with a vampire standing over me.

"What are you—"

"Shh!" Rayne puts her fingers to my lips. "There's someone here."

I vault out onto the non-slip mat. Freezing. How long have I been here?

I open my mouth again, but Rayne is on the move, pushing a towel into my hands. There's no fumble or hesitation, which reminds me that vampires can see just fine in the dark.

Hands shaking, I wrap the towel about my body. "Rayne—"

"They're sneaking around, trying not to make noise." Her voice hardens.

"Where's Norma?"

"Who?"

"My chittarik. She's usually better than a guard dog and—"

"I've not seen a chittarik."

My gut clenches. "I'll check it out."

"But—"

"I've got this. Stay put." Balanced on the balls of my feet, I slip through the door and close it behind me.

The bedroom is dark; long shadows stripe the bed and the faintest gleam of moonlight shows through a chink in the curtains. Empty, though, which is good.

I reach beneath my mattress and pull out my kaiken, a short, slender blade with a gleaming edge. I'd prefer a gun, but this will do.

Suitably armed, I creep into the living room.

Also empty.

Shreds of shiny black fabric dot the floor. Soft, pale dust. Clothes. DVDs. My usual junk.

Norma lies on the sofa, legs drawn tight to her body, one wing crumpled beneath her.

"No—"

Something hard and heavy cracks off the back of my head.

I fall.

The dagger spins out of my grip.

A growl ripples close to my ear.

I throw a punch over my shoulder, but the angle is off.

Someone grabs my wrist and twists my arm at the elbow.

I sprawl, face flat to the carpet, a scream caged behind my teeth. Can't move.

Hot breath on my back. Drool slides down my neck. "You're weaker than I expected. But I'll still kill you. I'll kill you for her."

More pressure on my arm. Weight across my butt and legs.

Can't move.

My free hand scrabbles across the floor. The dagger is close, barely an inch from my fingers. If I can just stretch—

My captured arm twists. Bolts of agony race up and down my ribs and shoulder.

A dark shape streaks across the sofa. It flies overhead, collides with a thump and…the weight on my back is gone.

I roll clear.

Rayne grapples with a man I don't know, one with the hard eyes and sharp teeth of a vampire.

He bests Rayne with a sly right hook and steps over her fallen form to lunge at me.

I dodge.

Clawlike fingers snag my towel. It sticks on my damp skin then jerks free.

My kaiken lies several feet away, beyond the vampire struggling to free his nails from my towel. Can't go that way. Behind, my kitchen and a joyous assortment of knives and other pointy things.

I run.

He follows.

Three steps from the door he has me again, nails digging into my shoulder. The pain is intense, but fear is stronger and the battle rush has me fired up. Anyway, no bloody vampire is getting away with attacking me in my own house.

I drop to my knees and twist left. Carpet burn—ow—but I'm free and out of reach.

For now.

Up again, run. Dodge. Duck.

He's fast. Nearly lost a hunk of hair to that swipe.

I need a weapon.

Can barely see in the kitchen, just the shine of sharp teeth and the glitter of silver eyes. The vampire kicks out, catching me in the stomach. I fly back, bounce off the sink and sideboard. Cookware rattles above me.

Weapon.

My hand whispers across the surface, seeking something, anything of use.

Frying pan.

Clang.

The vampire stumbles aside, snarling and spitting. Then it comes again. I twist right, end up in the corner against my hob and washing machine.

Nowhere to go.

He grabs the fridge and heaves. The whole unit tumbles sideways and down.

I drop, hook the frying pan over my head, and dive forward on my bare belly.

The fridge slams into the wall unit and lodges there at an angle. Junk I usually keep on top showers the floor around me: papers, spare keys, cereal boxes, and a large pile of plywood shards.

More snarling. Shrieking.

Rayne reappears with a great leap. She lands on the vampire's back and wraps her legs around his ribs, slashing with her fingernails. Blood flies through the air like rain.

I'm up again, frying pan in hand.

Clang.

The vampire falls, Rayne beneath it, crushed and stunned. She moans.

I snatch a piece of plywood and dart in, sharp point aimed for the creature's chest.

My foot flies from beneath me, skidding on a piece of that waxy black fabric. Down again, on my back, head cracking off the floor.

Stars. Buzzing. Blurs.

Pain.

The frying pan is gone, but I still have the plywood. My stake. Must use it.

The vampire crawls over my body to sit on my stomach. He wraps one hand about my throat, the other around a fistful of hair.

No…can't breathe…

I shove up with the jagged spike, but the strike lacks power.

My tongue thickens in the back of my throat.

Again.

It swats my hand aside.

Darkness tunnels my vision.

Again.

The wood slips from my fingers.

Stars are brighter now, the buzzing louder.

This isn't fair. If I could reach a weapon. Even the frying pan…

Rayne slides into view like some crazed, fanged angel and lands a stunning blow with the base of a tall saucepan.

Freedom. Air. Light.

The vampire slumps against the fridge, eyes crossed, head bloody. He roars.

I roll left, catching another piece of cupboard shelf on the way.

The vampire wobbles upright.

I follow, arms out-thrust, all my body weight behind the fresh stake.

The point sinks through flesh like a skewer through lamb and bursts from his back in a stinking gush of black ichor.

Direct hit. Yay.

Flesh bubbles and blisters, inky sores erupting across exposed skin. More of the dark substance spills out, spreading, dripping, oozing until nothing remains but a pool of sticky black gunk and the echoes of a scream.

I flop to the floor, panting, one hand on my chest.

A moment later Rayne slumps beside me, still holding the saucepan. She exhales. "Agent?"

"Yeah?"

"Would you care to explain why I woke in your cupboard?"

CHAPTER EIGHT

Rayne perches on the end of my bed, staring at her cuticles. Though motionless now, she's been busy because my clothes are sorted and folded in neat piles on top of my pillows.

How domestic.

Beside them is a pile of the shredded black material that I finally identify as the body bag.

Weird to see Rayne here, in my room, on my bed. She looks like a normal person, rather than the blood-drinking, throat-munching kind.

Norma is there too, curled up on the bed beside her. Unharmed, just pissed from the crumpling of her wings and a little dozy from the knockout. Well…more dozy than usual. In fact, dozy enough to have no complaints about a stranger on my bed.

Wrapped in a fresh towel, I pause in the doorway and clear my throat.

Rayne's nostrils flare, but she doesn't look up. "You're bleeding."

I take quick stock of myself. Aching shoulders with five deep indentations from the vampire's nails. Back and ribs, sore and bruised. Oh yeah, and the slashes down my shin and calf, bleeding again inside my towel.

"I'll be fine."

"You should dress it."

"I will." When alone. Without a vampire in the room. "Thanks, by the way. I completely misjudged the strength of that thing."

"I didn't want you to get hurt." She trails a finger across something square and yellow on the end of my bed.

She even emptied my pockets? My cheeks warm a little.

"Are you going to pay this?" She waves the parking ticket.

"I have other things to worry about right now."

"You committed a crime."

"I parked with one edge of my wheel hanging over a set of double yellows. Hardly crime of the century."

Silence.

I shuffle back and forth in the doorway, scraping my toe over the line between bedroom carpet and bathroom tile. A thin line of red dribbles down my leg. More blossoms on the white towel. "Rayne…I need to get dressed."

An instant later she's on her feet and at the bedroom door. Didn't even see her move.

"Sorry." Still she avoids meeting my gaze, but her voice has become light and breathy. "Sorry. I didn't mean—I don't want—I'll wait outside." Gone.

My shoulders drop as tension flows out of them.

I clean and bind my calf and mangled shoulder, then work on the rest of my body. Super comfort now makes up for last night's torment: black jeans under a long T-shirt, finished with a cropped shirt and ankle boots. My hair, I hike into a ponytail.

Now I feel like me.

"Norma?"

"Son, son?" she mutters.

I stroke her head. "Don't worry. Stay there. Get some rest."

"Karson."

I find Rayne in the kitchen, scooping lumpy vampire ooze into a bin bag.

"Gross. You don't have to do that."

She shrugs. "Least I can do."

I watch her, stooped low, head bowed. Can she still smell my blood? Her control is incredible, the best I've come across at such a young age. Especially if she hasn't been drinking regularly.

"What now?" Still no eye contract, just tidying.

"We talk. More specifically, you finish telling me about these unregistered vampires."

"But I don't know anything. I'm a youngling—no one tells me anything."

"Bullshit. What were you going to tell me this morning before the sun hit you?"

She hunches up, gnawing her bottom lip like a scolded child.

I wish she'd stop. For some reason, the little dents her teeth make on the edge of her lip send my pulse galloping, fangs or not. She also has a dimple in her left cheek, small, deep, and cute as hell.

"I don't know anything."

"So I should send you to SPEAR? Let them execute you for attacking a human?"

"No, please—"

"I risked my neck getting you here. If anyone finds out, I'm done, understand? Make all this worth it. Tell me what you know."

"I…"

I snatch her hand and shove it into the slick black muck. "This used to be a vampire, Rayne, like you. If you're no good to me, this is what you'll end up when SPEAR get hold of you."

The hand begins to shake. "I can't. They're all I have. My family. They need me." Her eyes shimmer, wavering between that pale amber and the bright silver of vampire anger. "You don't understand. You don't know—"

"Hey, calm down."

"Don't tell me to calm down."

I scoot my foot left, closer to a large shard of my busted shelf. "Rayne—"

A long, low growl spills from her mouth. Her fingers flex.

Shit, shit, shit!

I dive for the plywood and grip it tight, crouched low and ready to fight.

She scrunches her eyes shut. Fists tremble.

"Rayne?"

Both eyes snap open. Silver flares before the usual colour returns. "They attacked you. It's not right. You're only trying to help."

"The bounty?"

She nods.

"What the hell did I do, anyway?"

"You're very good at your job, Agent." She gestures to the plywood gripped tight in my fist. "We all have reason to be scared of you." Her lips part slightly, showing off the gleaming points of fangs.

I tighten my grip on the stake and take a second to remind myself: no matter how cute that dimple, Rayne is a vampire, capable of popping my head from my shoulders and using the neck hole as a champagne flute.

❖

One good thing about Quinn's dick move is that I no longer need to report to HQ. Working with the civvie bashers leaves me free to act as I choose, with check ins by phone at the start and end of my shift. I make the first call, inwardly curse the smug voice on the other end, then return my attention to Rayne.

She's on the sofa, playing with Norma who seems delighted at the attention. More of those growling, gurgling purrs and playful flicks of her tail. She bats with her paws, but her claws are always retracted, clearly intending to tease rather than harm.

What the hell?

"What do we do now, Agent?"

I loop my utility belt around my waist, check my gun, then start to slide knives into various hidden sheaths. Hip, left thigh, right calf, forearms, lower spine…

"I'm expecting more information from a source in The Bowl. We'll go there first."

"We?"

"I'm in enough trouble as it is. No way I'm letting you out of my sight."

"Is this your chittarik? She's very friendly."

I eye them both. "Not usually. This is…odd."

"How so?"

"She hasn't tried to jab your eyes out."

Rayne giggles, a sweet, lively sound. "She'd never do that, would she? No, never, you pretty little thing. She's just like my chittarik, Princess."

"You called a scaly, cat-sized, mini dragon *Princess*?"

She shrugs. "I was fifteen."

I stop secreting weapons and turn to face her properly. In profile, Rayne's face is less doll-like, with a finely defined jaw and straight nose. Her eye corners have the faintest uptick which blends seamlessly into the shadow cast by long, thick eyelashes. Even her mouth from this angle has an adorable pout and a tint as if her lips are smeared with strawberry gloss.

What. The. Hell.

I scrunch my eyes shut. What's wrong with me? She's not a *she*, she's a vampire. A demon. A monster.

Isn't she?

Rayne laughs again and turns Norma onto her back to rub the scaly belly.

Never, in all the time I've had her, has Norma allowed someone else to touch her that way.

I whistle, a sharp burst of sound through my teeth.

Muttering her reluctance, Norma leaves Rayne's attentions and swoops onto my shoulder. She brushes my cheek with her tail and nips at my earlobe. "Karson?"

Nice try, traitor.

Rayne straightens. The smile is gone, her gaze now serious and deep. "We had all sorts of supernatural creatures back home. A few pixies, a water sprite. There was a gnome at one point, though that disappeared when the brownies showed up. For some reason they don't get along."

I know my mouth is hanging open, but I can't help it. "Are you a Rancher?"

"Dad was. Then my brothers took over. Well, three did. Most of my sisters and the other two joined the police."

"How many of you were there?"

"Fourteen."

My hand freezes, part way through stroking Norma's back. "Your poor mother."

Rayne smiles. "We're a foster family. Eight sisters, five brothers, and Mum and Dad living on the ranch. We had mundane pets too, dogs, cats, ferrets, and horses on the wild scrub at the back."

I try to imagine Rayne surrounded by animals and family. It's weird. But nice. "I had no idea."

"I loved them so much. They were as wonderful as any real family—no, they *were* my real family."

Despite myself, I'm intrigued. "Were? What happened?"

She gives me a level look. "I died, Agent."

Shit. When will I learn to keep my foot out of my mouth?

"I need to sort some things and make a phone call. Wait here."

She frowns but stays on the sofa, watching as I stride away.

Norma dives off my shoulder and back to Rayne, calling the whole way.

Traitor.

I retrieve my kit bag from the cupboard as I dial and inspect the contents while waiting on the connection.

Stakes. Chains. Tranq darts. Lead bar. Communion wafers. Silver throwing stars. More knives…

"Hello?"

"Hey, Seb. Sorry...I mean *Mr. Mayor.*"

Silence. Then. "Agent Karson? To what do I owe the pleasure? I've a rally to attend in forty-five minutes with a speech to rehearse, names to learn, and a long car ride ahead of me, all without my PA who picked today of all days not to show up for duty. She'll never work in this city again by the time I'm done."

I wait long enough for the tirade to ebb, then fill him in on the unregistered vampires and the people missing from The Bowl.

Throughout, Mikkleson is silent but for the occasional grunt or muttered affirmation. At the end of my tale, more silence, and a slow exhalation. The man must be made of cigars.

"And what does that have to do with my son?"

"I think it's far more likely he was unlucky. He lives in The Bowl, right? Exactly where all these other people have gone missing."

"So?"

I roll my eyes. "So if he's connected to these disappearances, I need to update the civvie bashers."

"The police? Absolutely not."

"Of course I do. I need to tell them—"

"You're not to breathe a word of this to anyone."

"But—"

"Do you have any idea what's at stake? What this could do to my career?"

"You—"

"Tell no one. Not the police, not SPEAR, no one."

"I have to get backup."

"The hell you do." His voice drops to a furious hiss, loud and deep in my ear. "For what I'm paying you, you'll handle this exactly as I say."

"Now you wait a second—"

"No, Agent, *you* wait. I've worked hard to get where I am. I've given everything. Now this city is finally in a stable position, and you want me to throw it away? I've held up my end of the bargain. Twenty per cent wired to your bank last night. Fifteen each to your mother and sister. Now you do your part and find my son."

"But—"

"I'll have your SPEAR license revoked."

My fingers tighten on the phone. A loud rushing sound fills my ears. "You can't do that."

"Try me."

"But—"

"But nothing. If I discover that anybody else knows about this, you'll never work in this city again. SPEAR will drop you faster than a live grenade, and that's the end of you and any chance at that house in Cipla. I'll personally see to it."

My hand is shaking. I can't make it stop. "Please—"

"Do your job, Agent. That's all you need do to make this go away. Get out on those streets, find my son, and keep your mouth shut."

The line goes dead.

Chapter Nine

Rayne stands beside me with Norma riding her shoulder. She waits several seconds, then whispers, "Are you okay?"

"Fine, I...we need to go."

"I heard the call." She frowns at my frustrated eye roll. "I have exceptionally good hearing."

Shit. How do I keep forgetting she's not human? "It's irrelevant. I still have a job to do."

"And your job is important to you?"

"What the hell do you think?" I unfurl my hands. My nails have left deep red indents on my palms.

Rayne nudges Norma off her shoulder. The chittarik loiters for long moments before flying over to give my face a comforting nuzzle.

"I think I'd be questioning why Mayor Mikkleson is so keen to keep this under wraps. And why he picked you."

"I already know why, he—"

"Do you?" She speaks quietly, but the words hit hard. "I won't tell you your job, Agent, but it's worth considering there may be something more happening here." Rayne holds my gaze for several tense seconds, then walks towards the door. "I'll wait in the car."

I chew the edge of my lip, snagging Norma from the air to deposit her on the sofa. "I'll see you later."

"Ka? Karson, Da?"

"Not a chance. You'll only be all over Rayne, anyway. You like her?"

"Daaaaanika."

"Oh, don't guilt trip me, you scaly slut." I leave the flat, still shaking my head.

❖

In the car, strapped in tight, Rayne runs her fingers over the dashboard. "My dad had a banged up seven-seater saloon. We'd go on field trips all over the country for his Ranching duties, but when it was holiday season, we'd hire something bigger and go camping."

I imagine the huge family, fourteen kids and two adults, riding into the sunset in a giant minibus.

"What was your favourite spot?"

She grins. "There's a beautiful lake on the north edge of Anglesey. Gwragedd Annwn breed there and Dad used to take us to study them. Such pretty things."

"Yeah, and dangerous. You sure none of them ever…"

"With Dad?" She laughs. "No, he was too good for that. But they did try. They seemed to really like him. I think it was the beard."

I grin and pull the car away from the curb, into the flow of traffic. "My dad was nowhere near as cool. We'd go camping, but Mum hated it, so we usually only went to caravan parks. All the amenities, cafés, and Wi-Fi."

"That's hardly camping."

"You've not met my mother."

She fiddles with the broken radio. "What happened to your dad?"

My fingers tighten on the wheel. The car lists as I take a right turn sharper than I should. "He died."

Rayne shrinks back against her seat belt. She clears her throat, then points out the window. "What's that?"

I sneak a glance. Bite back a snort as the building slides through my view. Bright red and purple signage proclaims *Delights of the Night* while the wide windows up front are draped in heavy red curtains.

"*Edane* massage parlour."

Her eyes widen. "Really?"

"Traditional too. All the *happy endings* you could want."

"Just for supernaturals?"

I shake my head. "Humans, mostly. They use places like that to get up close and personal with *edane* men and women in a reasonably safe environment. Vampires too. Though recreational blood loss is something I'll never understand."

Rayne gapes. "But what about the Foundation? I thought we got our blood there."

"Fang junkies donate in person."

She falls quiet.

I keep driving, cursing myself over and over. It's been years now. Surely I shouldn't be so sensitive over Dad. Surely I—no. There's no *surely* where family is concerned.

"There's so many supernatural stores and entertainments here. It's nothing like where I'm from."

I chance another glance at her. "Angbec is pretty forward thinking. We were the first city to recognize *edanes* as citizens, well before the Supernatural Creatures Act forced us to. And we were the ones to spearhead the Interspecies Relations Act."

"I had no idea. Is that why the supernatural population is so big?"

"We're a haven compared to the rest of the country, and with SPEAR based here, generally everyone behaves themselves."

She lowers her head. "I'm sorry. My nest and I have caused a huge mess."

"It's not your fault—" I cough, alarmed at how easily the words of comfort roll off my tongue.

"Maybe not wholly my fault, but I've...done my part. I want to make it right."

"You're making a good start."

Inner Angbec gives way to the weary drudgery of Misona. Lights dim, crowds thin, and Rayne sinks deeper and deeper into her seat.

"Why have you brought me here?"

"I need to see a friend."

❖

Though she seems unsure, Rayne exits the car and stands beside me. Her clothes brush against mine, the soft whisper of her breath cool against my arm through layers of fabric.

"Rayne, are you shaking?"

She steps back.

"You're a vampire."

"But I—"

Soft growls float through the air, coming from the far side of the street. In the shadows, two dark shapes slink close to the ground. Another smudge of darkness, taller and broader than the other two, steps out from an abandoned storefront.

"Agent?" Her voice quivers.

Wendy's familiar shape materializes from the dim beyond the car. He strides towards us with the two smaller figures, now visible as wolves the size of ponies. He takes one look at Rayne, then snarls, his eyes flickering from brown to yellow. "What's this?"

"You told me to come back—"

"No, *this*." He waves a hand at Rayne. "What's this blood sucker doing on pack land?"

The two wolves raise their hackles, baring teeth.

"Calm down, she's with me."

"No, *it* is a vampire and *it* is trespassing."

Rayne wrings her hands. "I—I'm sorry. I didn't know—"

"Lies," roars Wendy. "You've two seconds to get off our land, before I—"

"Enough." I shove myself between Rayne and Wendy, arms outstretched. "You, grow a spine, and you, put your cock away."

"But I—" Rayne lifts a hand.

"It—" Wendy points.

"I said, *enough*. I don't have time to play referee. Wendy, do you have the information or not?"

Rayne puts a hand to her mouth. Her eye corners crinkle with mirth. "His name is Wendy?"

Uh-oh.

I throw myself backward and out of the way.

Wendy hurls himself at Rayne with a bellow, fur sprouting fast from his hands and face. She blocks the frantic charge but goes down, shrieking in terror.

I draw my gun and level it at the two wolves preparing to spring. "Don't."

Snarls. Growls.

"Test me, dog breath. I dare you. No? Then back off."

They share a glance. Step aside.

Wendy and Rayne are still grappling on the pavement. Wendy is part way towards his hybrid form, most of his exposed skin covered in shaggy dark fur. Beneath him, wrestling to keep his jaws from her face, Rayne kicks and screams and growls like an animal. But it's not enough. His teeth close on her forearm with a sick, wet crunch.

"No! Rayne—Wendy, don't—"

Silver sparks in Rayne's eyes. Subtle at first, then a dazzling gleam. She roars, a bestial sound, terrifying from such a dainty mouth.

With her right arm still trapped in Wendy's jaws, she curves her free fist round and punches him in the top of the head. Again. Again. Again. He releases. She rolls free.

The pair face each other, crouched low, fingers flexing.

Blood floods from a cut on Wendy's face. A darker, richer shade streams down Rayne's arm.

"Guys, stop. We can't—"

They collide again, this time with Rayne on the offensive. She grabs Wendy's head with both hands and squeezes, dancing to and fro to steer clear of his swiping claws.

Wendy howls a deep, agonized note.

Again the two wolves creep forward.

"Don't move!"

They pause, but I know they won't stay afraid of me for long. Not while their alpha is in danger.

Rayne's hands are visibly closer together, compressing Wendy's features like putty. I've no idea how much more he can stand before his skull caves.

I aim the gun at Rayne. It shakes.

"Let him go."

She squeezes harder.

Wendy whimpers.

"Rayne, let go."

Her eyes narrow and she looks back at me. The death grip falters.

Wendy shoves off the ground, a powerful leap that carries him free and twelve feet into the air. His slams into Rayne, forcing her back to the ground. Powerful fingers close around her throat. Claws dig into flesh.

I fire.

The shot echoes through the empty street.

A startled flock of pigeons take to the skies.

Rayne stares at me, her eyes round and wide. The silver is gone now, fury chased away by shock. "Agent…" Her voice rasps through damaged vocal cords.

Moaning, Wendy tumbles off Rayne's body. He has one hand pressed to his shoulder, gripping tight against the flow of blood oozing through his fur.

What the hell did I just do?

The two wolves dart past me, fawning over Wendy. They nuzzle him, lick him, paw him, all the while whimpering and whining. Several seconds of this, then they turn to me with low, rippling growls.

Again I level the gun.

"Wait—I—"

Rayne darts off the ground and slides to a stop in front of me, arms outspread.

I freeze.

More growls. Wet teeth gleaming. Muscles tensed to spring.

Rayne tilts her chin. "D-don't. I mean it. Leave her alone."

"Back off, boys." Wendy trudges forward, free hand raised, a soothing, calming gesture. The wolves glare at him. "I said, back off."

They retreat, though continue to watch me, anger and hatred burning in their eyes.

Rayne heaves a huge sigh and drops to her knees.

I stare at the top of her head.

What just happened here? What's going on?

"I—Wendy—"

"It's okay, *Agent*. After all this time I know where I stand." He refuses to look at me, staring instead at the floor near my feet.

Something in my chest is tight and stiff. Again I try to speak, but the words won't come. "Wendy…"

"That's not my name. And you…" He looks pointedly away from me to the figure on the ground. "You are not welcome here. I see you again, I end you. Understand?"

"I'm sorry." Rayne's voice is tiny. "I'm trying to help. Please. I know I did wrong, but I want to make it right."

He gives a rough bark of laughter. "A vampire with a conscience? Oh, holy day, that fixes everything, doesn't it?" Blood continues to drip from his shoulder. "Look, I got what I promised. Do you want the intel or not?"

I lift my hand, then let it drop. "Yes. Please."

Wendy shakes himself, a full body ripple from toes to the top of his head. By the time he's done, most of the fur is gone and his claws have been reduced to mere fingernails. He strains, then my bullet flops out of his shoulder and hits the pavement. "The leader of the vampires is some dame called Vixen."

Still on the floor, Rayne stiffens and clutches her hands to her chest.

"Means something to you, does it?" He snorts. "We hear she's powerful, old, and traditional. Likes to think that we supes should have stayed hidden and secret. But if we can't be that, then we should be in charge." Another snort. "Or the fangers should, to hell with the likes of us."

"But what about the humans going missing?"

"Give an old man a chance, you impatient bitch."

"You wish." The response is automatic, and though there's a flicker of recognition, Wendy refuses to smile. My shoulders slump. "Sorry. Go ahead."

"Word is the humans are a food source to travel with the nest. They're new to Angbec, so they haven't signed with Clear Blood. Don't mean to, neither. They're happy being under the radar because they can plan without bother."

"But what are they planning?" I can't help myself. This information is old—I have it already from Rayne. If I'm going to do something about all this, I need something fresh.

Wendy spits at the pavement. "I don't know, all right? Something big. And political. We heard she has links with Clear Blood and the mayor's office. Don't know what, but I'd guess someone down at City Hall has a bit of a fetish."

"A junkie?"

He shrugs. "Mayhap. Maybe not. Time for some detective work, rather than leaning on us, right, *Agent*?"

"Wendy—"

"That's all I got. Take it or leave it." He rubs his shoulder again, then backs away, still eyeing Rayne. "And remember what I said. This is your one free pass, Vampire. After that, you're ooze."

Rayne takes her feet and stands close at my side again. No longer shaking, she just stares at her fingers with small, timid jerks of her head. "I understand."

"Good. Show yourselves out of pack territory. You get three minutes."

CHAPTER TEN

Never before have I felt unsafe in The Bowl. Wary, sure, but unsafe? Afraid?

I look at Rayne, watching her face work through dozens of complex emotions.

"Are you okay?"

She stares up at me, gnawing her bottom lip. "I didn't mean to cause you trouble. He attacked and I just...It's an instinct."

"I know. I should have warned you about his name."

"Did they hurt you?"

I take the chance to assess myself. "Not a scratch on me. What about your arm?"

She holds it up, inspecting pale skin through the gashes in her ruined sleeve. Her fingers flex. "Mostly healed. It hurts, but no permanent damage. You saved me. Thank you."

Yeah, still confused about that. The gun under my arm feels heavy and awkward, my trigger finger itchy.

Did I really shoot Wendy? To save Rayne?

She smiles, unaware of my thoughts. "Did you get what you needed?"

"Yeah, but I wish there was more. Most of what he said you'd already told me."

"Even the rumour about the mayor's office?"

Shrug. "There's always rumours about that place. Probably doesn't help that Mikkleson is such an arrogant—" I break off, squeezing my eyes shut as my brain races to catch up with my mouth. "Mikkleson. Son of a bitch."

Rayne leans away from me. "What?"

"His son. He's not just a drug addict—he's a fang junkie too. No wonder he didn't want anyone to know."

"It's illegal?"

"Grey area." I start pacing, thinking hard. "I've been trying to figure out why a fifteen-year-old boy would have a vampire in his house. No signs of a struggle, but a vampire clearly kicked it in there, judging from the ooze Mikkleson had in that evidence bag. So the boy was donating blood and…what? It got out of hand? Someone went too far? He changed his mind?"

The thoughts are swirling so fast I can't keep track.

"Maybe he kills this vamp and heads out to get help then gets snatched off the street for his trouble."

Rayne shakes her head. "Is this boy trained? How could he possibly overpower a vampire?"

I study her face. "Have you ever drunk blood from a willing human before?"

"No. No, I promise—I'd never—I told you—"

"Calm down. I'm just thinking, if you had, you wouldn't have to ask." I stop pacing. "When a vampire has a willing donor, something weird happens, they seem to…link. I don't know what the proper word is, but that's why humans get such a high off it. It does something to them. And the vampire gets an echo of the sensations. Both sides end up spaced out for a few minutes, especially if the volume of blood exchanged was high. Then the kid could have easily jabbed the vamp with a wooden spoon or even a pencil. Wouldn't take much."

Rayne's eyes briefly flicker silver. "But you don't know for sure. You're speculating?"

"It's as good an idea as any."

A broad shape, low to the ground, steps out from the shelter of the climbing frame. Two more leap over it, twin points of gold shimmering in the darkness.

I turn.

Three more on the other side of the car, another on top, glaring at us.

"Agent…"

"I see them."

"He said we had three minutes."

"I'd say he's a lying bastard."

The seven wolves form a ring, hemming us in with low snarls and growls.

"We're leaving, guys. Promise."

They advance.

I move closer to Rayne.

"What do we do? What do we do?" Her voice is a panicked whisper.

I fight the urge to roll my eyes. "Don't panic, for starters."

"But—"

"You're a vampire. You just healed a bite on your arm as though it was nothing. Get a grip."

She nods, trembling like a leaf in the wind.

Too late I spot movement from the corner of my eye. "Duck!"

An eighth wolf springs from the darkness, straight over my head. It slams into Rayne and carries her down, jaws snapping at her face.

I roll, coming up with the gun levelled for more dangers.

There are none. The other seven wolves turn and dash at Rayne, snapping at her legs, her arms, her stomach.

"Hey. Get off her. Get off!"

Her screams are shrill and heavy with pain. Arms flail, legs kick, but the sheer number of wolves is too much.

I squeeze off a shot, but my aim is wide and the bullet sings off the pavement towards the play area. My next shot is worse, striking the ground a bare inch from Rayne's face.

She screams.

"Get off her, you idiot wolves. She's no threat to you."

One swings round to me. Growls.

My feet slip on the pavement, then off the edge, into the road. Against a tyre. My tyre. My car.

I leap into the vehicle and slam the door. The wolf collides with the glass, slobbering all over it, scratching the hell out of my paintwork.

I drop my gun on to the passenger seat and start the engine.

The car responds with a roar, startling the wolves into looking up.

In that tiny gap, Rayne finds herself and thrusts upward with hands and feet. Three of the huge wolves spin through the air like toys, thudding to the ground several feet away. She stands, legs planted wide, arms out.

Blood streams from bite and claw marks all over her body. Her clothes are shredded, her hair a nest, but through it all, her eyes shine bright and clear.

Silver. Lively. Angry.

Rayne ploughs through the remaining wolves like a scythe. Nails and fangs drip blood, while clots of fur stick to her fingers as she battles like a creature possessed. Perhaps she is.

The last wolf, the one still baying at my window, yelps as she grabs it by the hind legs. A twirl on her heel and the wolf is airborne, sailing across the play area.

I clamber out of the car. "Rayne? Rayne, it's okay. It's over."

She shrieks again.

"It's over. You won. They're done. Stop."

Her hands close over my shoulders, fingers digging in. Rayne hefts me into the air like a child and slams my back against the side of the car.

Stars dance across my vision.

My boots flail a full foot off the ground.

"Rayne?" My fingers stretch towards the knife strapped to my wrist. Pause. "Rayne, please—"

She stops, open mouth an inch from my throat. "I—I want—"

Panicked breath clogs my throat. Still I can't draw the knife. "Rayne?"

"I-I want to make it…make it right."

Pressure in my shoulders slips away as she lets my body fall. I slide down the car. End in a heap on the Tarmac.

She turns, vaulting the bonnet to flee along the road.

"Rayne? Rayne!"

Shit.

❖

My gears screech as I take the next bend, the rear fishtailing across dashed white lines. I want to slow down, the rational part of me knows I should, but the SPEAR in me knows better.

The trail of blood I'm following is already fading. Much longer and I'll have no way of finding Rayne, until she finds a human to munch on.

The expression on her face, the speed, the silver sheen in her eyes, all classic signs of a vampire on high alert, a vampire mere minutes from blood mania.

I take another turn, clipping the pavement on the exit, much to the anger and fear of the woman standing on the edge with her fake-tanned legs on show in ripped fishnets.

Two drops of blood to my left. Another on the right. A smeared handprint on the shaft of a tall street lamp. A car with a dented bonnet. Nothing.

"Damn it."

I slow, now peering down every side street for more signs.

At a cross road controlled by traffic lights, two cars idle nose to nose in the centre. One has clouds of smoke streaming from the bonnet.

"Hey, what happened?"

Shaken from the conversation and trading of insurance details, the two drivers look my way. "Something fell out of the sky—"

"Not some*thing*, I'm telling you, it was a person—"

"With silver eyes?"

"I know what I saw—"

I gun the accelerator. "Which way?"

They point, still arguing. I miss the rest, guiding my car along a wider main road with two lanes to each side.

Half a mile on, I find her. She's slowed, but only to the speed of an athletic sprinter, rather than a cheetah.

"Rayne!"

She stops in the middle of the road. Traffic is slow, but enough to be dangerous, cars swerving around her in a flurry of horns, screeching tyres, and fist shakes.

Times like this I'd give a lot for a blue light on top of my car.

Still she hasn't moved. Standing. Silent. Waiting.

For what?

I pull closer, flicking on my hazards and hoping that's enough.

"Rayne?"

Silence.

"Rayne, listen to me—"

"Why not drive at me, Agent? Like you did before?"

It takes a moment to pull my thoughts together. "Yesterday? No, this isn't like then."

"Isn't it?" She stares upward. "Everything is so clear like this. I can see every star in the sky, the pits and shadows on that tiny sliver of moon. I see the whites of your eyes and the colours in your hair. I hear your heart. The blood in your veins."

The car rumbles beneath me and I consider revving it up again. Pressing my foot down like I did before, like I intended to do to the wolves.

My leg trembles.

"I can smell you," she mutters. "Your hunger, anger, and fear."

The gun is still on the passenger seat. I grab it and dive out of the car, free hand raised to hold aloft my SPEAR ID. Whether it's the gun or the ID I'll never know, but advancing cars in all directions squeal to a stop and back up fast.

"Your heartbeat is incredibly fast, Agent. It's exciting."

I lick my lips.

My finger tightens on the trigger.

A single ounce of pressure and the shot is clean. She's right there, not moving. A clear, easy target. A chest shot would end this mess in seconds.

So why can't I do it?

Blue lights flicker in the corner of my vision. A siren.

I lower the gun. "Rayne, you have to come with me. Please."

Nothing.

A police car screeches to a stop beside mine. The officer within tumbles out, facing me with one hand extended. The other clutches his chest radio. "Okay, miss, put the gun down."

"You don't understand—"

"Nothing is going to be solved with guns, you hear me? Put it down. Nice and slow. Put it down and we'll talk."

"I'm a SPEAR agent—"

"That doesn't put you above the law. You can't swing a loaded gun around in civilian areas with no supernatural threat in sight."

"Are you crazy, can't you see—" But even as I point to Rayne, I know she's not there. In fact, I can't see her at all. "Damn it. I need to go."

"No, you—"

"And you need to get back in your car. Right now."

The officer frowns. "You don't give me orders—"

"There's a mad vampire loose and I need to find it. Get in your car."

He mutters something into his radio. A coded string of numbers and letters that does nothing but piss me off. "I'll need to see your license, miss."

"It's Agent. And I'm busy."

"You show me your license right now or else I'll—"

Rayne vaults over the squad car, arms spread, legs tucked, an eagle in flight. Her landing drives the officer to the ground and she aims straight for the soft, meaty flesh of his upturned throat.

He screams, flails, kicks, and begs.

I level the gun again. "Rayne."

"Shoot her," he yells. "Shoot her, shoot her."

My finger twitches. Relaxes.

"What are you doing? Shoot her."

Instead, I run straight for them, free hand dipping into a pocket on my belt. Paper packet, marked front and back with a tall cross. Tip the small white disks it contains into my palm and yank at the neck of Rayne's shredded blouse. The communion wafers smoke the instant they touch her skin, sparking and fizzing like fireworks. The stench of burning flesh stings my nose.

Rayne rears off the officer, twelve feet straight up as though off a springboard. She lands on her face by the side of the road, screeching and clawing at her back.

"Move."

The officer obeys, scrambling back on his arse, with tears of terror on his cheeks. Wetness fans across the front of his trousers. "Shoot her. Shoot her."

"Get lost."

He stops, caught by indecision.

"Go away."

At last, he's up and running, back to his car. Within seconds, he's gone.

"Rayne? You need to snap out of it. Rayne?"

More screaming. Growls. Shrieks of mingled pain and fury.

My fingers tingle. The gun beneath my arm takes on the weight of a dozen blocks of lead.

Draw and shoot. Just like the officer said. Like I should have done last night.

Shoot her in the head. Then fire the rest of the bullets into her chest until the holes ooze black.

My hand wavers, then falls. "Damn it."

I run back to the car and heave the boot open, searching for my kit bag. On the right, tucked into a pocket beneath the zip, are three long lengths of chain: iron, silver, and steel.

No time to separate them.

Rayne is up again, the smoke is dissipating, and her gaze is trained on me.

My hip slams the edge of the boot. Stars dance across my vision as my head cracks off the door.

She's fast.

Breath hot and damp on my neck. Nails clawing at my cheeks.
"Rayne!"

I swing with the chains. Can't see which one hits her face, but I make a guess when her cries begin anew.

Back in the bag, fingers closing around a bandolier of rubber balloons.

Again I swing, and the balloons burst against Rayne's face and chest. The holy water splashes everywhere, bringing up welts, pus, and sores.

Her screams shift from fury to pain, and she drops to her knees, clutching her face.

I'm gasping, panting, wheezing...but alive.

"Help me..." Her eyes beg louder than her words.

Shoot her. Stake her. Wrap her up in consecrated steel and pop her head off.

I sigh, and in that moment I know for sure.

"I've got you, Rayne, don't worry. I've got you."

CHAPTER ELEVEN

The Clear Blood Foundation: a five-storey monstrosity in glass, steel, and concrete.

I swing my car against the pavement edge, ignoring the jagged yellow lines beneath me and the parking meter just opposite.

On the back seat, Rayne lies deathly still, skin smoking. Though I tried to avoid it, some of the chains lie against bare flesh, and the blessed steel has already raised red welts on her arms and throat on top of those left by holy water scalds.

My stomach twists in painful knots. "Rayne? Can you stand?"

She lifts her head, wincing as the links brush her oozing cheek. "Agent?"

"You need to get up. You have to get inside."

"Can't...see..."

I touch her ankle. "Then follow my voice. Get up and follow my voice. We're close."

She slumps against the seats.

Standing outside the car, gazing at the bright golden lights of salvation within Clear Blood, I've no idea what to do.

Nothing in my training has prepared me for this.

I can't leave her to get help, but if I unwrap those chains or try to carry her...

A prickle brings my attention to my left cheek. Flakes of dry blood flake under my fingernails.

Rayne twitches.

I wonder...

I'm toying with the crazy idea when a security guard walks around the edge of the building. She takes one look at me, then the car, and leans into an impressive sprint. "You can't park there."

"I have a vampire—"

"This area is for emergency vehicles only."

"What do you think this is?" I grab her shoulder and force her down towards the open rear door. "Vampire. Blood mania. I need to get her inside."

The guard frowns. "Doesn't look much like a vampire to me."

"Get the doors open and warn the cafeteria we're coming. There's only one way I can think of to do this."

I don't wait to see if she obeys. Instead, I unfasten the buckles on my forearm knife sheath and roll back my sleeve. The knife, when I draw it, is sharp and light, balanced for throwing even if that's not my preference. I lay it against my palm. Pray.

At first there's no pain. The blade bites through flesh without effort and there's no blood for several seconds.

Liquid red drops well up at either end of the cut.

One tentative step takes me closer to the car.

"Rayne?"

No response.

I lean in and wave my bleeding hand in front of her nose. Closer. Closer.

Her eyes snap open.

Chains creak.

I run.

I'm at the entrance before the first links break. They spin through the air at speed and pepper the main doors. Glass shatters and sprinkles the ground, startling the security guard loitering inside.

"Move!" I shove past.

More glass shatters.

From the corner of my eye I catch sight of Rayne, struggling to free herself from three sets of chains while following the scent of my blood. Her fangs are longer than I've seen them, her eyes ablaze with silver.

I'm not going to make it.

The guard is yelling, someone else is screaming, but my focus is all ahead.

Down the corridor. Door on the left. Three small steps up.

Footsteps behind me, light and quick. Panting. My heart in my throat.

I'm not going to make it.

Another corridor. Turn right. Right again. Left. There.

The swing doors fronting the cafeteria hold fast as I barrel into them. The impact knocks me flat, and Rayne flies over me, her charge thwarted by my fall. The doors burst open, lock and hinges broken under flailing fists.

Crashes, thuds and shrieks follow.

Back on my feet, I peer through the remains of the frame.

At the far end of the cafeteria, Rayne wrestles to free herself from the twisted remains of a long metal table and several benches. Beyond her, using the larger entrance, an orderly line of vampires queue against the wall with raffle style ticket stubs in hand.

One or two of them look our way. The rest stay focused on the shuttered hatch at the front of the line through which a woman in white dispenses tall reinforced pint glasses of thick red liquid.

A table leg smashes into the wall above my head. The mangled table follows.

More broken links from the chains spin across the floor.

"Here"—I wave my arms—"over here."

Rayne hurls more furniture aside as she wades towards me.

I keep waving, this time staring at the woman frozen in the serving hatch. "Blood bag."

"But I need to warm it—"

"Blood bag."

"Where's her FID—"

"Give me a fucking blood bag." I'm scooting sideways, measuring the distance between myself and Rayne with the few remaining tables. Four. Three. Two.

The woman darts out the side door of the kitchen, a plastic medical bag held aloft. She spots Rayne and skids to a terrified stop.

I cup my hands. "Toss it."

My own blood makes my grip slippery, but I catch the bag as it flies at my face. A second later, Rayne is on me, snapping and snarling, mouth aimed for my palm. I shove the bag against her teeth.

The plastic gives with a muted pop, spraying my face and hands. The rest splatters Rayne who moans and parts her lips. She clutches the bag, shoves it to her face and drinks. And drinks. And drinks.

Slow, wary, I ease away, scooting back across the slippery floor.

Something is drumming, hard and fast, and several seconds pass before I recognize my own heartbeat.

Still holding back, the woman points at the guzzling figure on the floor. "What's going on? Why is she in mania?"

"Long story. Get another bag."

"I can't. There are rules and daily allowances—"

Rayne stops drinking and drops the empty plastic packet on the floor. She stares at me, my hand, my blood.

I stand and back towards the kitchen. "Seriously, get another bag. In fact, make it three."

CHAPTER TWELVE

I'm arguing again. Seems to be something I'm good at.

The security guard stands at reception, fighting to reach the phone. I'm beside her, slapping her hands away, and failing to keep my temper.

"We have a procedure." Again she reaches for the phone. "I have to report the incident to SPEAR."

Again I shove her hand away. "They already know. I'm a Grade Five agent—"

"But my report—"

"Make it to me."

She stops. "You can't bring in a manic vampire without warning us."

"You'd prefer I left her on the street?"

"Where's the rest of your team?"

"Busy."

"You brought her in alone?" Her eyes widen.

"We're leaving now."

"What? No, wait—"

I'm already walking back to the cafeteria where Rayne waits with her hands folded in her lap. Six armed security personnel form a ring around her, positioned to shoot without catching any colleague in the crossfire. I'd be impressed if I wasn't so pissed.

Someone has found her a change of clothes, a frumpy, ill-fitting pair of trousers and a *Clear Blood Clears The Future* T-shirt under a large lab coat.

"Rayne, we're going."

"No." She doesn't look up.

"Of course we are. Or did you forget, we've got things to do."

"I'm not safe. I need to stay here, under guard."

"We don't have time—"

"Agent?" At last she lifts her head. The ripe acorn brown is back, but with it comes pain and fear so strong her eyes shimmer with it. "I could have killed you."

"But you didn't."

"I could smell you. I *still* smell you. Your blood has the finest, sweetest scent—you're a sensory cocktail."

I glance at my bandaged hand. It aches, but the cut is clean and sure to heal quickly. "There's bigger things happening."

Her forehead wrinkles. Shoulders slump. "I…" She sighs. "I don't want to hurt anybody else."

"You won't."

"You can't know that. I have to do right, I need to be responsible—" Her words break beneath a short, sharp gasp. "I know what to do." She stands.

Security tightens their collective grip.

I dash in, hands outspread. "Steady, everyone, steady. I keep telling you, she's not a threat."

One on the far side twitches his gun. "Our procedure says—"

"Screw procedure."

"You don't need to protect me, Agent." Rayne laces her fingers and places them on the back of her head. "Ladies, gentlemen, please be so kind as to escort me to reception."

The guards share startled looks. I know my expression must match theirs.

"Rayne…?"

"I have to do the right thing. I should have done this weeks ago—you said so yourself."

Her voice, usually so calm and soft, is hard now and sure. Her words ring with a confidence and certainty I've not yet heard outside a combat situation, and my heart flutters like a butterfly.

Is this the real Rayne I'm hearing now? The one from *before*?

The guards look to me.

I bite my lip. "We don't have time—"

"We'll make time." She starts walking and the security team part to let her through.

"It's okay, guys, I've got her." I follow.

At reception, behind the large desk, the night receptionist looks up from her computer. She smiles, removes her headset, and slips out to greet us with all the easy, snake-like grace of an *edane*. Not vampire though.

"Good evening, how may I assist you today?" Her voice is a symphony, all highs and lows and harmonies pulled together into one sentence. I could dance to the sound of that voice.

Up close, her hair is long and pale, thick like a spill of eagle tail feathers. Her eyebrows have a similar texture, light and fluffy like a duck's underbelly.

A siren, then.

"I'd like to register my status as a vampire and add my name to the registry, please."

"Of course. Take a seat and I'll bring you the appropriate paperwork."

Rayne sits on the end of a squishy sofa positioned between a pair of tall pot plants.

This part of Clear Blood more resembles a highbrow doctor's office than the public face of a powerful pharmaceutical giant: plush carpets, textured wallpaper, and huge golden plaques in a row above the doors leading deeper into the building. From this distance I can't read them, but the lettering above them proclaims, *Clear Blood Foundation, Board, Benefactors, and Founding Members*.

In front of us, a low coffee table holds a selection of magazines, leaflets, and flyers.

"*Tired of buying new clothes every full moon? Try our brand-new mega stretch fabric, guaranteed to withstand the most violent of lunar shifts*," Rayne reads off the topmost leaflet. "Really?"

"There's a reason Wendy always looks like a hobo."

"There's nothing here for vampires."

I slump beside her and kick my feet up on the table. "Why would there be? Those monsters don't need styling tips and homeopathic pain remedies."

"Monsters?"

Shit.

"Rayne, I—"

"No, you're right. I *am* a monster. But I'm a monster with a conscience, and now I'm going to do the right thing."

I risk looking at her.

She's staring at her fingers, head bowed, shoulders hunched. Her eyes are dim, almost glassy, and her lips turn down at the corners.

And yet...I find myself wanting to touch her cheek, to crack a joke, anything to bring on a smile. To make those dimples reappear.

"You're not a monster."

"I'm a vampire."

The siren returns, holding a pen and clipboard with several sheets of paper already clipped in. The board she hands to Rayne, the pen to me.

I hold her gaze and fold my arms. "She's the one registering."

"I assumed you were the witness." The receptionist smiles. Her teeth are pointed, freaky, especially against such expertly applied lipstick. "You'll require a pen."

Still I hesitate. After everything I've been through tonight, I don't want this creature touching me.

Rayne pins me with a disapproving frown.

I reach for the pen, watching the siren's eyes for any sign of a trick. Nothing happens and I slide it from her grip without incident. "Thanks."

"My pleasure." She returns to her desk.

"What's wrong? Why did you—" Rayne breaks off as a man pushes through the double doors leading deeper into the public side of the building. In scruffy jeans and a band T-shirt, he looks more like a grungy student than a lab technician.

"Are you Rayne?" He stares at me.

"No, her." I point.

"Come with me." He spins on his heel and strides off again.

Rayne darts after him, leaving me scrambling to keep up.

"Just a moment, Agent." The siren waves from behind her desk. "You'll need these."

Two guest passes attached to lanyards, with our names printed in tiny black lettering.

I reach for them, neck craned to see which direction Rayne takes along the corridor.

Cool, smooth fingers grip my hand.

When I look back, the siren is grinning, the lanyards pressed between my hand and hers. Her fingers drape over mine, nails long and blue, filed to cruel points.

"You—"

"Take the third door at the end of the corridor. You may use the stairs or the lift up to Vampire Relations, which is on the second floor."

"I—"

"Remember to wear your lanyard at all times. Wouldn't want you detained by security."

My gut churns like a whisk. Sweat dribbles down the back of my neck.

"Bitch."

The siren chuckles. "Have a good evening."

Not much chance of that now.

I leave reception with the lanyards in hand, the continued giggles of the siren ringing in my ears.

❖

By the time I reach Vampire Relations, Rayne is already seated in a private booth and filling out paperwork. I try to hang back, but Grungy Student directs me to the chair at her side. He doesn't quite shove me into it, but his firm gesture to the high backed seat has a similar effect.

Rayne doesn't look up, even as she loops her guest ID around her neck. Her hand flies across the page, filling in check marks and text boxes with incredible speed. Her expression is one of concentration, tongue tip peeping from the corner of her mouth.

Pale pink. Soft. Moist.

I close my eyes and thread my fingers in my lap.

Just stay calm. Surely there's nothing to worry about? It's not like I have any feelings—

A jolt like an electric charge fizzes up and down my left arm, lighting every nerve ending. My eyes snap open, free hand reaching for the gun, but there's no threat here, just…

Rayne. Her hand rests on my forearm at the source of the continued tingles. The touch is light, but I feel it all the way through my body. The air becomes tight and close.

"Are you okay?" She tightens her grip. "Your breathing, your heart rate, it's—"

"I'm fine."

"You're flushed."

"I said, I'm fine."

The hand trembles, then slips away.

The lack of contact steals my breath. I gasp, bereft and needing.

I know this feeling—intimately, actually. Though the last time I experienced it, I'd been lying in bed, appreciating the morning sunlight on the bare skin of my most recent date. She stood naked by the window, golden beams highlighting her breasts and hips. As I watched, my body tingled, still reeling from the passionate night we'd shared, the sheets and pillows damp with her juices and mine.

No. No, this can't be right.

I slam the chair back, straight into the path of another figure, this one with a white coat, thick rimmed glasses, and all the other boxes ticked beneath the list *What Makes a Stereotypical Geek*. He carries a tray with a huge needle, complete with two-pronged applicator.

"Oh, excuse me—"

"Watch where you're going, nerdlicious." I scramble away from the chair and over to the wall, staring at the laminated posters telling the story of the Life Blood Serum and its creation. A glance shows Jackson in pride of place, his beaming picture included in each of the panels.

I stare, fists clenched, shoulders tight, waiting for my breathing to slow.

Damn, that siren. If she's tricked me with—

"Agent?" Rayne's voice quivers. "Really, are you well?"

"I'm fine."

She's coming closer, I can sense her, actually *feel* her in the air like a soft breeze.

"Stay where you are. Please, stay over there."

Silence, awkward and strained.

Then, a cough from Nerd Boy. "Well, Miss Rayne, I'm your consultant for this evening, and if you've finished the paperwork, we can get on with your sample and FID."

She's still watching me.

I walk left, following the story on the posters.

At last, the prickle of her attention fades away.

I keep pretending to read, now sneaking glances to where Rayne sits. She's removed the lab coat and dropped the shoulder of her T-shirt. There's no bra and her bare skin is clear, smooth, and pale.

A mad urge consumes me, a yearning to rush over and press my lips to her collarbone. Her shoulder. Her neck.

The consultant lifts a small medical pin from his pocket and pricks Rayne's shoulder. A bead of bright red blood wells up which he collects on a slip of white paper with a blue tag on the end. The blood soaks in, and he clips the slip to the top of her paperwork.

"Thank you. Now stage two." He lifts the syringe and removes the cap, exposing a huge needle. "Please hold still, Miss Rayne. I'll only take a second."

"Wait!"

It takes a second to realize that the shrill, frantic voice is mine. Rayne stares, full lips slightly parted. "What's wrong, Agent?"

"I...you..." I scratch the back of my neck. "What is that, anyway? I've seen loads of registrations and there's never been a needle involved."

An indulgent smile from the consultant. "It's new. We're running a pilot on one in every ten new vampire registrations—a microchip in place of the old Foundation ID card."

"A microchip? Like for a dog? You can't do that. She's not an animal."

He flinches. "I know that, but this is the procedure now and—"

"Rayne, you don't have to do this. You're not a monster we have to tag."

She hikes the T-shirt back into place and faces me. "I thought this is what you wanted. I thought I needed to do the right thing."

"You do, but—"

"But what? I don't understand what you want me to do. What do you want, Agent?"

I bite my lip. The question hits me harder and deeper than it should.

The intensity of her gaze sets my skin tingling again. I can barely look her in the eye.

"We've come a long way since the early days of ID cards and fobs." The consultant cautiously steps between us. "During this pilot, we'll track every vampire with a unique chip, which carries all of their registration details, including information on their bloodline. After that, all they need do is present their shoulder for scanning when they come to collect their blood."

No. No, they can't do this. They can't treat Rayne like some pet or criminal.

I want to argue, but the words won't come. Instead I find myself watching as Rayne lowers her T-shirt collar again and offers her shoulder to the consultant. The needle pierces her skin, the plunger sinks, and a second later, it's done.

"Thank you." She scoops her clothing back into place.

The consultant grins. "My pleasure, Miss Rayne. Agent, if you'll countersign the witness statement, we're all done."

The words on the page are a blur. My hand trembles as I angle that wretched pen over the dotted line. I barely recognize my signature. Damn that siren.

The consultant snags the papers and tucks them into a folder under his arm. Another grin. "Sorted. You're free to go whenever you're ready. Thank you, Miss Rayne, for registering with Clear Blood. Please know that your dedication to the preservation of human life is deeply appreciated and that your actions today will ensure you remain a valued member of the community here in Angbec."

And he's gone, leaving Rayne and me to stare at each other across the chasm of the ten-by-eight booth.

Five seconds pass. Ten. Fifteen.

"Agent—"

"Don't."

She freezes, half a pace away. "I know you'll only tell me you're fine, but you should know that I can hear and smell the changes in you. Your heart rate is elevated, your skin sweaty, even your pupils have dilated. What happened at reception?"

Part of me wants to tell her, the rest wants to run off screaming, because how can I? How can I look her in the eye and tell her that bitch of a siren has slapped a *go faster* stripe on my libido?

"Did you touch the siren?"

My head snaps up.

"She seemed very interested in you, and she'd already tried to touch me when I arrived. It was a good attempt, but siren powers don't work on vampires."

"Lucky you." Knowing I'm not alone makes the admission easier. "She caught my hand when passing over the stupid guest passes. Whatever she did, it's strong. It's making me feel all sorts of weird stuff. I'm not myself."

Rayne frowns. "Odd. Sirens only enhance what's present. They don't have the power to add anything new."

"What?" My stomach knots.

"We always had to be careful if we joined Dad on his Ranching duties with young sirens, because they can't control the power. Anyone they touch experiences their emotions tenfold. Older ones pick and choose, and then they tend to focus on sexual desires and feed off them."

"No. No, that can't be right, I…no. It can't. I don't…" My lips are dry, my throat parched.

I find myself staring at Rayne again, the fullness of her lips, the slender arch of her neck as it meets her shoulders. Even the brilliant pale gold colour of her eyes.

"Agent?"

"I need to get out of here." I run.

CHAPTER THIRTEEN

I'm back in reception, glaring at the siren chattering into her headset from behind the safety of her desk.

She pauses the phone call to give me a long triumphant look. Her lips draw back off the sharp points of her teeth. "Are you feeling all right, Agent?"

She knows. She knows what she's done and she thinks it's funny. Bitch.

Words catch in my throat.

My hand twitches towards my gun, then flinches away.

Then I'm running, straight across the lobby and out through the main doors, still being boarded up with thin sheets of plyboard. She's calling, trying to coax me back, but I'd rather run naked through a field of cacti then head back in there.

My mad dash takes me onto the pavement and face first into a tall, long-haired man with vaguely familiar features.

He flicks out a hand to steady me. "Aah, Agent. Tul'a mir han, du sak. Purrek hi han qui nar?"

Cold Blood Tongue?

I catch sight of brilliant purple eyes, the liquid grace of his movements, the arrogant smile.

Oh. *That* guy.

I swallow to ease the parched desert of my throat. "I'm fine, and none of your business. Anyway, shouldn't you be at work?"

He looks over my shoulder to the pile of shattered glass and repair attempts on the main doors. "This *is* my work. Last night I waited tables only to assist a friend. In truth I'm head of security here at Clear Blood. I take it this mess is your doing?"

"Why would you assume that?"

"Am I wrong?"

"No, but—"

"I thought not." A glance over his shoulder, back towards my car still parked haphazardly against the double yellows. "Please move your vehicle as soon as possible. This is a restricted zone, and I'd hate to see it towed."

Yeah, I'm sure you would. Aloud I say, "No problem, I'm leaving."

I know he's watching me climb into the car. I make a point of checking all my weapons, my mirrors, my gears while he waits. Eventually, with an agitated grunt, he slips into the building and out of sight.

Stiffness I hadn't been aware of slides free of my neck and shoulders.

The steering wheel creaks as I rest my head against it, clinging to the leather with my eyes closed.

Why? Why is this happening?

"Agent?"

I scream, bouncing in my seat hard enough to crack my head against the roof. "Damn it, Rayne—"

"I've been calling you. Didn't you hear me?"

"No."

"I'm sorry. I didn't mean—"

"Don't worry about it." With effort, I loosen my clawlike grip on the steering wheel.

She slips into the car and shuts her door. Each movement is neat and precise, quick and fluid. Beautiful.

Silence.

Again.

With her so close, everything is tingling and fizzing inside me. My blood, my skin, even my bones respond to her. I want to pin her down, drag my hands back through that adorable pixie cut, and rough it up with my fingers.

She sighs and the gap between her lips exposes a hint of fang.

The tingling drops lower, between my legs.

"Agent—"

"I'm sorry." The words are run together, jumbled up, but I can't stop. My mouth is dashing off without my brain and I let it, because I know if I stop, if I sit here for one more silent, painful second, I'll end up grabbing her, and kissing her. "About before—what I said back in

Clear Blood. It was thoughtless and I…you just…" I lick my lips. Try again. "You're not like other vampires. I've never met one like you before."

"What do you mean?"

I clench my fists on my thighs. "Good. Kind. Every other fanger I've met has been murderous, insane, or just plain dickish, but you're… nice."

And sexy. And beautiful. And so totally kissable—

"Who's that?"

Oh, good, a distraction.

I follow Rayne's gaze out the side window to the figure stepping out of a black hackney. He looks over his shoulder, pays the driver, then hurries towards Clear Blood.

"Jack?"

Instead of taking the front doors, he slips around the side of the building. But there's nothing down there…except the entrance used by vampires needing their dose of blood.

What the hell is he doing?

My hand is on the door, ready to slip out, eager to follow, when Rayne lunges across the seats.

"Wait!"

Her fingers close over my shoulders and force me up against the door. Her body follows, leaning across the handbrake and gearstick to press her face close to mine.

My body burns. Every inch of skin lights up, and even the tiny hairs on my forearms lift as if to get close.

"What—"

"Shh!"

Her face looms before me, eyes big and round with panic. The faint gap between her lips shows a flash of white teeth and the pale pink tip of her tongue.

I want to kiss her. So much.

"Rayne—"

"Quiet, Danika. Keep very still." She leans closer. The tip of her nose brushes against my cheek.

Wow.

That's the first time she's said my name beyond that first time in the holding cell. It sounds incredible on her lips, the syllables soft and sensual in a way no other voice has managed.

I can't breathe.

My face is aflame, senses filled with the smell of her, the feel of her, the sound of her.

"What's happening?" My voice cracks. Doesn't even sound like me, more a small, breathless version belonging to the child version of me. Or maybe the post-coital one.

Still Rayne presses close, her lips now against my ear. Her breasts rub against mine, hands still firm around my shoulders. I'm trapped... and I never want to leave.

"Vixen's here. I can't let her see you—she'll kill you."

My brain is mush. "Kill?" It sounds serious. It may even be a bad thing, but I'm not sure why.

Fire turns to ice. My cheek stings.

The world snaps back into sharp focus in time to tilt sharply as dizziness swings in and out.

"Sorry, was that too hard?" She's not even looking at me, her gaze on the wing mirror beyond my head.

When she finally returns to her own seat I lean right, watching the doors of Clear Blood.

Silhouetted in the empty frame stands a woman. The light is too dim to give me facial details, but her shape, build, and stride are those I remember well.

My memory flickers back to City Hall, to the wash of papers across the Angbec city crest, many of them reading *Vote Mikkleson*. I remember grey eyes, blond hair, and the seductive sway of slender hips.

"Amelia?"

Rayne peers at me. "Who?"

"Going into Clear Blood, that's Amelia Smythe. Why would she be—Ow. Stop it."

But she doesn't. She grips tighter, her nails digging into the soft skin of my forearm. "You met her? Does she know your name? Does she know who you are?"

"Sure, we talked a bit when I knocked her flying, why?"

"We need to leave." She grabs her seat belt buckle and snaps it into place. "Right now. Drive."

The urgency in her voice is catching. My heart triple steps now with adrenaline. "You're scared."

"That's Vixen. She's my creator, the Angbec queen, and the one who published the bounty on you. Please drive."

I'm laughing now. Can't help it. "I thought you were supposed to be the one with the good eyesight."

"It's the truth. Have I ever lied to you?"

"But I met her yesterday morning." Still I loiter, hand on the ignition key, but not turning. "Morning, Rayne, when all fangers are tucked away and harmless."

She fidgets, constantly looking towards the doors. "Vixen is old enough that she can stay awake for a short period of time when the sun rises. She's strong and incredibly powerful. Please, please, drive."

A chill seeps through my body. "You can't be serious."

"She wants you dead, Agent."

Amelia is still at the doors, glancing at her watch, then up and down the street.

My mind struggles to catch up. "You're telling me there's a vampire that can walk around during the day?"

Rayne buries her face in her hands. "Please."

"No." I know she's right, I know I should get the hell out of here, but I can't compute this. "Rayne, look at me. Can vampires walk around in sunlight?"

"Very old ones. Vampires like Vixen have been around for hundreds of years. They drink blood mostly because they feel like it, but their need is greatly reduced, unlike the rest of us who *have* to drink."

"But—"

She grabs my hand. The powerful jolt of physical contact flares again, untempered by my fear.

"I'll tell you anything you want to know. All of it. Everything. Ask me any question and I'll give you the answer, but please, let's go before she sees us."

I start the car.

Her relief is palpable and she twists to gaze out the window. "I don't know why she's here, but something must be wrong and you can't be part of it."

I watch the woman I know as Amelia give one last glance to her watch, then slip into the building. She moves with purpose, confidence, as though Clear Blood is a place she visits often.

What's going on?

And why is Jack sneaking into his own building?

Rayne nudges my shoulder. "Don't."

"I didn't do anything."

"Your scent just spiked. You're planning something. Or you realized something. Whatever it is, don't. We need to leave."

But we can't.

If Amelia is who Rayne says, then I *need* to know what she's up to. I need some proof to take to SPEAR. More than that, I want to know why Jack is arriving in a cab instead of his own flash car, and sneaking in through the vampire entrance.

I stop the engine.

Rayne sighs and grabs my arm as I try to open the door. "At least move off the double yellows first?"

I stare. Then I'm laughing, that quick, girly type of giggle just shy of outright hysterical.

Only I, Danika Karson, fang hater and SPEAR badass, could fall in with a law-conscious vampire.

CHAPTER FOURTEEN

The siren is gone when we head back in. Some androgynous figure with green hair and piercings mans the desk instead.

"Good evening, welcome to the Clear Blood Foundation. How may I help you today?"

I pull my SPEAR ID. "We're fine, heading up to the research floor." I speak without stopping, trying to recreate the assured confidence I usually feel when I walk into this building for my inoculations.

We stop outside one of the lifts and wait for the booth.

"Rayne, chill. We're having a look around, that's all."

"But if she sees you—"

"We'll deal with it. She already knows my face, so that doesn't make a difference. Do you really think she'll pull something here?"

She shuffles her fingers. "You don't know her. Don't underestimate her."

The lift arrives and I step in, stabbing the button for the fourth floor. "You are the most un-vampire-like vampire I've ever met."

"Meaning?"

"You don't act like a vampire, is all. You're so…timid."

"We aren't all the same, Agent."

"But you have to admit, it's weird. Think about it—what's left in this city for you to be afraid of? Sunlight?"

She watches the numbers change on the floor display. "And wooden stakes, blood mania, bullets to the heart or head, SPEAR. You."

My stomach clenches. "You don't have to be afraid of me."

It's with a jolt that I realize the truth of my words. I won't hurt her. I can't. I *like* her too much.

The lift opens, revealing four closed doors, one on the left, three to the right.

"This isn't the research floor."

"Nope." I cut left. "These are offices and meeting rooms. Do you think you can find places Amelia—I mean, Vixen—has recently been?"

She hurries after me, eyes wide with alarm. "Why? We're supposed to be avoiding her."

"It might give me clues about what she's doing."

"But—"

"Don't worry. You'll hear anyone coming long before we need to panic."

She shakes her head. "I don't like this. You don't have a warrant or justifiable cause to search up here. Speculation and my word aren't enough."

"Why don't you let me worry about the law? I think I know enough about my rights as a SPEAR."

Rayne grabs my arm. "I was a police sergeant before Vixen took me. You have no authority to do this."

"Seriously?" My jaw drops. This explains so much.

I imagine Rayne in civvie basher uniform, complete with hat, baton, and epaulets.

"It doesn't matter. No one is going to catch us. We'll be in and out in a couple of minutes." I take off before she can stop me again, shaking my arm to work out the tingling prickles from her touch.

Bloody siren.

"Here"—I touch the first door—"can you smell or sense anything?"

"I'm not a bloodhound. This building is filled with blood and chemicals, plus dozens of bodies pass through every day. Unless Vixen was here this morning, I won't smell a thing."

"Fine, hard way it is." I try the handle. It gives with a click and opens into an office that clearly doesn't belong to Vixen. Three golf caddies lean against the wall and every available space is filled with golfing paraphernalia: photos, tees, balls, miniature clubs. Even one of those stupid tweed flat caps with a stiff brim.

I didn't think anyone owned this stuff.

The next office resembles my flat—organized bomb site. Papers, books, and pens everywhere. A small wicker bin teeming with tissues. Rayne refuses to enter, adamant it stinks of sickness. A glance at the desk shows me a box of cold and flu medicine, so she's probably right.

I have my hand on the handle of the third office when Rayne gives a hiss of warning. I push, but the door refuses to budge.

"Come on," she mutters.

"It's locked."

"None of the others were."

"Okay, calm down, we'll go back to—"

"No time." She reaches across me and grabs the handle. The locking mechanism gives with a pained groan as she slams it down. An instant later, she's bundling me inside.

She holds the door. Waits with her ear cocked against it.

I leave her to it and study the walls.

Neat. Elegant. Expensive. Big winged chair, leather. Large desk with a flat screen computer. Sideboard dotted with framed newspaper articles, awards, and certificates. Obnoxiously large bouquet of flowers near the window. Two bowls of potpourri on the sideboard, another on the desk beside a round shaving mirror and a small can of air freshener. Photo of Jack, with his arm slung around a movie-star-slim woman with big teeth and fake hair. A second photo, this time with Jack kissing the cheek of a woman in a floor length ballgown. Another, again, Jack posing with a beautiful woman. Another, another—I stop looking.

"Hey, Rayne—"

She slaps a hand over my mouth. How she managed to get from the door to my side in less than a second is yet another reminder of what she is. I struggle to stay calm. Her fingers are so soft.

Long seconds pass as she holds me like that, until I start to wonder if she'll ever let go. At last, her muscles become more liquid and she returns the hand to her side. "They've gone back down."

"Great. Check out Jackson's office."

Rayne wrinkles her nose. "Why so much room fragrance?"

"Probably to hide the lab smell. Look at this junk. I can see why Mum likes him."

"Your mum?"

I pause in my riffling through papers and files in the desk drawers. "She tricked me into going on a date with him last night. Let's just say it didn't go well."

"Last night? So that's the same man I…" She looks away.

"He's fine, don't worry. And you're making up for it. Imagine, if you hadn't attacked him, I wouldn't have known anything about Vixen and her kidnapping ring. We never would have met."

Rayne fusses with the dried petals in a bowl of potpourri. "And that would be bad."

My hand freezes on a black lever arch file. Something about the way she says it, the way her eyes follow my every movement. Could it be that she…? No. I can't let myself think about that. Not now. Hell, not ever.

"You're breathing very harshly, Agent."

"Am I?"

"Do you need to sit?"

"No, I'm good." The heat of her gaze leaves me sweaty and wanting.

She tilts her head, a blend of curiosity and scepticism in her eyes before she walks along the wall, one hand running along the edge of the side unit. I'm hyper aware of her fingers, of the way they glide across the smooth wood. Her glossy fingernails gleam in the dim light, and it isn't until then that I realize the only light source is through the window.

"Agent—"

"What do you think he has on his computer?" I help myself to the desk chair and switch the machine on. My cheeks are so hot they must be roaring, but I keep my sights on the screen.

Rayne perches on the side of the desk. Her breath is low and even, and I find myself wondering what she'd sound like moaning under the glide of my fingers on her skin.

Reports, accounts, lab tests, databases, lots of information but nothing useful.

Two minutes in, my vision starts to fog as the heat of Rayne's body washes over me. So warm. And she smells good too, like lemons.

I lean back. "Nothing here."

"Pity."

"Yeah."

Silence. A car horn honks outside. Loud beeping follows, like a rubbish truck reversing.

She's closer than ever, one hand resting on the desk beside mine, still clutching the wireless mouse. Her fingers twitch. "Should I check the cabinets?"

I open my mouth but no words come. My throat is too dry. Cough, try again. "Yes, please."

"They're locked," she says, after a test.

"Is that a problem?"

Rayne grins, suddenly playful in the silver moonlight. And beautiful. "Not at all."

She pulls and the drawer flies open.

When I join her at the cabinet, her arm presses against mine, constant motion as she shuffles through the files within.

I pull a handful of folders, barely reading the titles before tucking them inside my jacket. She cocks an eyebrow but does the same, lifting the hem of her T-shirt to slip the papers in against her stomach.

Her smooth, flat stomach.

I can't do this.

More silence. The beeping outside has stopped. In its place comes the distant roar of traffic and the closer ticking of a clock.

Several papers flutter free of a plastic wallet and spill across the carpet. Can't see what they say, but most contain long columns of numbers and dates.

We bend at the same moment, reaching for the paper.

Our hands brush.

A charge leaps between us. I imagine I can see it, bright gold sparks like the crackle of live wires.

"I—"

"Agent—"

Again, at the same moment.

I tuck my finger beneath her chin and lift until her head tilts.

Her lips part. Between them, that flash of tongue again, and the shining white of sharp fangs.

Fuck it.

I kiss her, running both hands through that incredible pixie-cut hair and mussing it up, like I wanted to before. The strands are sleek, soft, and silky, but that sensation is nothing to the glorious press of her mouth. Soft but firm, sweet yet savoury with the vague hint of something metallic. Like pennies.

It's blood. Oh, crap, it's blood, it's blood—

Don't care.

The taste of Rayne overwhelms everything and within seconds it's all about her. I open my mouth across hers, delighted to feel her mimic the gesture, stunned to feel her tongue, awed to feel her teeth. The sharpness against my lips is terrifying and exhilarating, a mad mix that makes my heart spin and my head melt.

Yeah, I'm sure it's that way around.

She shuffles close, giving me all of her, breasts pressed tight to mine, thighs rubbing against my own. More of that softness and hardness and I revel in it and the chance to explore that perfect body up close.

My bandaged hand hurts but I can't let go, can't help but hold tighter, gripping as if she might float away.

The kiss breaks, and as it does, so does my heart. We can't do this. "Rayne, I'm sorry, I—"

"It's okay, Agent."

"No it isn't. I…and you—we…"

"I said it's okay. I feel it too."

I freeze, my hand still under her chin. "What?"

"I lied about siren powers on vampires. But I didn't lie about *how* they work."

I can't breathe. I must sound like an idiot, but I can't stop stuttering. The words won't leave my mouth in a coherent way. "Really? But you never…and you're not…"

She cocks an eyebrow. "Aren't I?"

I kiss her again.

This time, she curls her arms around me, crushing my body tight to hers.

Part of me expects her to be hard, all angles and rough edges, but she's not. Rayne has curves and soft bumps, smooth planes and stiff points, just like any other woman. She kisses like any other woman, whimpering her need into my mouth where I can taste it along with the rest of her.

"Rayne?"

"Yes, Agent?"

"Really?" I sigh. "Call me Danika."

"Of course. Danika."

My name on her lips lights a flame in my belly, one that roars with increased ferocity as the kiss intensifies. Her tongue lashes against mine, her hands grip my sides and squeeze, pulling me in, rubbing my hips against hers, a familiar dance I long to repeat without the hindrance of clothing.

This is perfect. So, so perfect and—

Rayne jerks back. The move is a blur, sharp and sudden enough that her fangs catch the corner of my lip.

The stab of pain is nothing to the ache at the loss of her touch, but she doesn't give me time to complain.

"Vixen's coming," she whispers.

The spell is broken. I'm myself again, back in my body, painfully aware of my position, kneeling on the floor of Jack's office in the middle of the Clear Blood Foundation. "We need to hide. Quick, we can—"

She grabs my hand, halting my frantic leap to my feet. "Do you trust me?" She stares into my eyes, lips compressed, eyes intense. "Danika?"

Fuck.

She's a vampire. I watched her mangle half a pack of werewolves. She attacked a policeman—and me—before wrecking an entire room of metal tables and chairs. She necked four litres of cold human blood in a matter of minutes.

And kissed me like the lover I've always dreamed of.

"Danika?"

"I trust you."

She smiles, the smallest flicker of relief before pulling my body back to hers. She wraps one arm around my waist, the other over the top of my head.

Then we're flying.

I have time to remind myself that vampires can't do that, before Rayne's fist punches through a ceiling tile directly above. Her leap takes us into the narrow space between floors. Dust rolls through the dimness, shallow and crammed with pipes, wires, and switches. She pushes me further along with the whispered directive to lie flat, then pulls herself up to join me.

She shifts the bent ceiling tile back into place.

"No, wait"—I wave at her—"leave it ajar so we can see."

A quick adjustment, then the door opens.

Through it storms Jack, straight for his desk. He snags a packet of wet wipes from the bottom drawer and wipes the side of his neck.

Rayne squeezes my wrist. Good thing, because I'd forgotten I'm meant to be hiding.

There's blood on his neck. And his collar.

He dashes away the crimson spots, then drops the damp rag in the wicker bin at his feet. Then he opens another drawer and fishes out a small stick of concealer and a pad of foundation. He applies both while staring into the shaving mirror, muttering the whole time.

As he finishes, two more figures sweep into the room, one already speaking in soft, relaxing tones. "Please calm down, Mr. Cobé." That voice. I'm angled wrong to see the newcomers clearly, but I recognize at least one. I'd remember that voice even after a hundred years. Amelia Smythe.

Jack slams the make-up into his desk. "Cut the foreplay, if you would. I'm not in the mood. How long have you known?"

A soft chuckle. "Long enough. But so long as your supernatural proclivities have no effect on what you do here or how you use my money, I see no reason why I should concern myself. Play with vampires as much as you wish, there's no harm in it. Is there, Marco?"

A second figure steps up to the desk and rubs the sides of his mouth. It's the Cold Blood Tongue speaking creep from downstairs. From the restaurant. "None at all. Indeed, as much as I respect and appreciate the efforts of your companions here at Clear Blood, I sometimes wish humans could offer blood on a more...mutually agreeable basis."

Bile rises in my throat.

Rayne's hand tightens on my wrist, but it doesn't help.

Jackson Cobé, a fang junkie? Mum would be horrified.

"No harm?" Jack snorts. "Clearly you've never been on the wrong side of a hungry vampire."

"And you have?"

"Last night. I barely escaped."

Amelia—no, Vixen—loiters near the door, still out of sight. "Tell me." Her voice is hard and sharp.

As Jack tells his story, Rayne's grip tightens to the point of pain. I nudge her, poke her, prod her until she finally lets go. My wrist creaks as I work the kinks out.

"...and then I drove away." Jack shrugs. "Of course I would have stayed to help, but Danika knows what she's doing. She didn't need my help."

"Danika?" Marco stiffens, his smug smile sliding away. "Danika Karson?"

"That's right."

A lump of dust rolls along the tiles, hurried by my breathing. Small motes tickle my nose. I feel a sneeze approaching.

"I see. Did she arrive when you were leaving? Perhaps running a sweep through the car park?"

Jack, busy double-checking his make-up, fails to notice the faint silver glint in Marco's eyes. "No, I ate with her. You saw her, at the table with her mother. We ordered dessert together."

Vixen hisses softly through her teeth. "So *you've* met her?"

Marco flinches. "I—"

"Tall woman? Dark? Wears her hair in dreadlocks?"

"And smoking hot in red, that's right." Jack grins. "You know her, Amelia?"

"We've met."

At my side, Rayne gives the faintest of growls. Her arm curls protectively around my shoulders.

A cough from Marco. "If I'd known I was speaking to the great Danika Karson, I would have handled things differently. Though I should have known. That level of arrogance could only stem from a reputation like hers."

I wrinkle my nose, a combination of anger and that bloody dust. What does he mean, arrogance? Just because I called him a disgusting parasite and told him to hug a wooden pin cushion? That was the gist of it anyway; Cold Blood Tongue doesn't translate well into English.

"I wouldn't say arrogant, but she is a bit rough around the edges." Jack's voice becomes wistful. "Doesn't stop her doing the job though. That vampire she captured yesterday was tiny, but strong, and she dealt with it quicker than anything I've ever seen. Danika's an incredible agent."

"Yes, she's quite impressive," Marco cuts in with another cough. "Skilled enough to rein in that lone vampire and take her back to SPEAR single-handedly."

Rayne tuts and pushes off the edge of the tile frame. She presses a finger to her lips, then slithers away through the darkness of the crawl space, belly flat like a snake.

I've no idea what she's doing, but I can't follow. They'd hear my clumsy human arse in an instant.

No choice but to wait and watch. And try not to sneeze.

Below, Vixen finally enters my view, glaring at Marco until he turns away, shoulders bowed, head lowered. "I see. I had no idea. Regardless, I'm glad you're safe. Though this does make our scheduled chat all the more important."

"Why? That was a one-off incident. Clearly that vampire was crazed and now she's been dealt with."

"Perhaps, but you and your campaign for mayor are a significant financial investment. I'd sleep better knowing you're safe and protected at all times. Given your encounter last night and the stigma related to your...other hobbies, I suggest you take on Marco as your personal bodyguard."

I gasp. Dust flies into my face and straight up my nostrils.

Jack straightens in the chair. "Absolutely not."

"Excellent idea." Marco, recovered from his subtle scolding, steps up to Jack and lays his hand on the back of the chair. "Obviously in daylight hours, I'll arrange for other, more suitable protection, but for evening meetings and late night lab work, I'd be more than happy to guard you, Mr. Cobé."

"But—"

"Then it's settled." The ice in Vixen's tone leaves no room for argument. "I've other matters to attend tonight, so I'll leave you gentlemen to discuss the finer details. Good evening." She stalks out of the room.

Silence.

The urge to sneeze pounds within me. I cram my fingers into my mouth and use the other hand to squeeze my nostrils shut.

"She seems stressed." Jack scratches the side of his neck. "What's rubbed her the wrong way?"

It's not working. My nose, my mouth, everything itches. I'm going to sneeze. There's nothing I can do.

"I believe Ms. Smythe has received some distressing news." Marco wanders to the window and out of my line of sight. His voice is low and steady, but there's an edge there, and a hint of the Italian accent I heard last night.

My pulse throbs in my ears. My eyes scrunch shut. The back of my throat convulses.

"Mr. Cobé, I think we should discuss how we'll go about—"

I sneeze.

Jack looks up from his desk. "What? What's wrong?"

Marco grunts. "Shh."

I tuck my face into the bend of my elbow. Another sneeze builds at the back of my nose.

A loud siren blares through the air, a two-tone whine directly beneath me.

My yelp of surprise is drowned out completely, though my feet drum hard against the floor tiles.

Marco darts back into view, glaring at the tiny sliver of a gap in the ceiling tiles.

Every muscle in my body locks down, a frantic attempt to make myself invisible.

Can he see me? Am I back far enough?

Jack bolts from his desk. "We need to go."

"But—"

"That's the fire alarm. You may be fireproof, but I'm certainly not.

There's enough explosive chemicals in this building to blow this city off the grid, and I don't want to be in here if it's not a drill."

Still Marco stares at the ceiling.

My second sneeze bursts free, caught against my face by Rayne's hand curving around my jaw. I sag into her, and she rubs small, comforting circles on my back.

"Hey." Jack stands by the door, beckoning. "We need to go."

At last Marco turns and follows Jack out.

Rayne pins me flat for several more seconds before shifting the ceiling tile. She drops back into the office and raises her arms. Both hands close neatly around my waist as she catches me, a bizarre show of strength against her slight frame.

"Where did you go?" I rub snotty drops on the back of my sleeve.

She snags my hand and starts running. "You heard Marco—now Vixen knows *I* was the one attacking Jack last night and that *you* took me in. If she thinks I'm imprisoned or dead, then that's even more reason to kill you."

"But—"

We dart past the lifts and towards the rear stairs, marked with the green and white exit sign.

"I set off the fire alarm. I had to, he would have found you."

Another weak sneeze splatters my chest with spit. "I think he did."

Down the first flight, two at a time, half running, half flying with Rayne in the lead.

"He won't know it was you up there, not with all that room fragrance. So long as we can get out without him or Vixen seeing us."

I stumble on the second flight, tumbling forward with a cry. Rayne snags my other wrist and yanks me back to my feet.

"You okay?" Her eyes shimmer with concern.

My heart skips a gleeful triple step. "Fine."

On the third flight we meet with other occupants of the building. Rayne and I fall in at a more moderate pace, mingling with the flow to ground level.

Outside, men, women, and *edanes* gather in a confused cluster, gazing up at the building. Blue lights from a pair of speeding fire engines illuminate the crowd and street, while the low, two-tone wail of the chemical threats unit fills the air.

Jack stands well back from the rest, almost on the corner of the street, with Marco at his side. He watches the moving vehicles with open curiosity, unresisting as Marco draws him off the road.

Rayne leads us in the opposite direction, back towards short stay parking where she insisted I move the car.

Before I round the corner, I chance a look back. My gut clenches.

Marco is watching us, lips drawn back in a snarl, a bright silver glint shining in his eyes.

CHAPTER FIFTEEN

B ack in the car Rayne is calmer. Still jittery, but no longer clawing my arm.

I pull up beneath a street lamp outside an independent butcher and unlock my phone.

"What are you doing?"

I sigh. "It's time to update SPEAR. Even I have to admit this has gone too far."

"But—"

"Don't worry, nothing's going to happen to you. Promise. But if fangers—I mean, vampires—can walk by day, SPEAR has to know. Can you imagine how much extra work we'll have on our hands? And don't forget the hundred-strong nest of unregistered vamps."

Rayne's lower lip quivers. Both hands clench on her lap, flex, then release. "Okay. Do it."

As I dial, I find myself wondering if I'd still call if she said no. Would have I risked whatever it is growing between us for the sake of following protocol? The answer, just out of reach, is so frightening, that I decide not to chase it.

"SPEAR switchboard. Please state the agent or extension you require."

"Noel González, ID A20280508B05."

"Please wait."

Chirrup. Ringing.

"Hola, Agent González here—"

"Noel, it's me."

Silence. Scuffling. "Dee-Dee?" His voice is hoarse and hushed. "Mierda, what are you doing? Quinn is ready to string you up, sí?"

"Long story, but I need your help."

"Of course, for you, Dee-Dee, anything, but what is all this talk of vampires and breakouts? Rumours here, they say you took a vampire from custody."

Damn that Shakka. When we next meet, he and I are going to have words.

"I had to. She had information on—"

"It's true?" He mutters some more, a sibilant stream of Spanish no doubt cursing me and all my ancestors. Or something like that.

I tighten my grip on the phone. "Please, this is important. There's a nest of vampires here under a single queen. Her name is Vixen, but she—"

Rayne flinches at my side. I don't know what she hears, but she's staring at my phone as if it's about to bite me.

"Karson? Karson, is that you?"

Ah.

"That better be and you'd better explain why you're calling Agent González instead of me." Quinn's voice lashes down the line, a whip crack harsh enough to sting.

I chance a glance at Rayne, then switch off the engine. This is going to be a long one. "I can explain."

"You damn well better. I've just had a call from security at Clear Blood saying they found you snooping around one of the offices. A little before that, we had another call, also from Clear Blood, talking about a vampire in blood mania brought in by a single agent fitting your description."

"There was a vampire in blood mania, but—"

"Right. And I suppose the chase through Misona earlier was something to do with you? The slew of injured werewolves lined up for medical aid?"

"That wasn't my fault."

"And did you smuggle a vampire out of holding yesterday? It's crazy, even for you, but given your behaviour so far, I've got to ask. Did you do something as stupid and dangerous as release a wild vampire?"

"There's dozens of unregistered vampires in Angbec and they're snatching humans off the street, mostly from The Bowl."

Silence.

"Did you hear me?"

"I suppose you have proof of this nonsense?"

"Yes. No, but I have a witness. She's here right now. Her name's

Rayne and she used to be part of the nest. She's been helping me since sundown—"

"Nest? You mean she's a vampire? Oh, Lord, it's true."

"Wait, wait, a second—"

"You get back here right now, and bring that fanger with you. If the reports I have are true, she attacked Jackson Cobé last night. What the hell is wrong with you? Have you lost your mind?"

Deep breath in. And out again. "I know we've got some weird hate-hate relationship going on, but can you put it aside for a second and listen to what I'm saying?"

"Agent Karson—"

"Come on, Francine, you know me. You hate me, but you *know* me. Would I do something this insane without good reason?"

"Thirty minutes. Get back here now or there'll be hell to pay."

Click.

I hurl the phone at the windscreen. Only a quick snatch by Rayne saves it and the glass from damage.

She tucks the phone neatly into the gap beside the handbrake and swivels against her seat belt. "That didn't go well."

"That bitch can't see far enough past her own crooked nose to listen to sense. This is insane. I can't take you in now. She'll make sure they kill you out of spite." The thought ties my stomach in knots.

"Then let's find some proof." She lifts her borrowed T-shirt, and for one wonderful moment, I wonder if she's about to take it off. Then she pulls the stack of files out of her waistband and waves them at me. "There must be something useful in all this."

I remember my own files, squashed against my chest and stomach. "I doubt it."

"What else are you going to do? Take me in?"

I face her, trace my fingers along the curve of her jaw. "Not a chance in hell."

Rayne smiles. "Good. Then let's sit somewhere and go through this."

❖

Fifteen minutes later we're in a café, me nursing a double shot cappuccino, Rayne picking the wrapping off my blueberry muffin.

"You're not about to tell me you guys can eat too?"

She sniffs the baked treat, then pops it back on the plate. "No. But I can enjoy the smell."

I try to imagine being unable to eat. Giving up the taste of all my favourite foods. The idea is horrific. "What do you miss most?"

"Mum's cottage pie." She speaks without hesitation, without guile. "Always filled with vegetables from the allotment and flavoured with different spices. It tasted different every time, but that's what made it good."

I reach across the table, tangle my fingers with hers. "I'm a useless cook. Mum taught me a few dishes, but I'd rather bung some veg in a bowl and throw some chicken on top."

"Very healthy."

"I have to be. I might be tough with a gun or a blade, but even SPEAR agents spend a lot of time running away."

Rayne grins, squeezing on my fingers. "I can't imagine you running from anything."

"I have my moments."

"I won't let anything hurt you, Danika." She looks briefly at my other hand, the one still bandaged tight from the cut across my palm. "Even me. With me here, you won't need to run."

It's sweet. So sweet in fact, I feel guilty for laughing.

She leans back, fingers slipping from mine. "What's so funny?"

"Nothing, I'm sorry." When her glare intensifies, I modify my answer. "You're so gentle and kind—I can't imagine you in full-on protection mode. Oh, don't make that face."

"I could be tough if I wanted to be. I was once a terribly stern police officer."

"I'm sure you were." I hide another chuckle behind a sip of coffee, then look at the files spread before me.

Remembering how I got them, Vixen's sharp voice, Marco's knowing smiles; the thought kills off any amusement.

"How is she getting away with it? Vixen, I mean? Walking around in the day, and you heard what she said—Jack's a financial investment. Do you think she's funding his campaign?"

Rayne leans back in her seat, her lips pursed in the faintest of pouts. It's adorable. "Maybe."

"But then, why was she leaving City Hall yesterday with a bunch of *Vote Mikkleson* posters? Is she playing them both?"

"It would be her style. That way, no matter who wins, she wins. Remember, she already knew about Jack's habit of *donating* blood. Can you imagine what the public would think if that came out? I'd imagine she has dirt on the mayor too, something good for blackmail."

The words are barely free of her mouth before facts click into place. I gaze at Rayne and know she's got it too.

"The kid?"

She nods.

"So she knew Mikkleson's son was an addict and a fang junkie and used it as leverage?"

"Perhaps. But then why take the boy?" Rayne stares at the table, her brow furrowed, eyes distant. Her focus is as admirable as it is beautiful, and instead of thinking about the case, I find myself watching her.

She has freckles, tiny, near invisible ones across the bridge of her nose.

"Who is he? I know he's mayor, but what else does he do?"

I fight the urge to stroke those freckles. "Mikkleson? He used to be a Marine."

"High up?"

"Probably. He doesn't much seem like the type to take orders."

She smiles. "Sounds familiar."

"Hey—"

"So he's strong-willed. Probably doesn't like being pushed around. Used to getting his way?"

"What are you getting at?"

A shrug. "Maybe he didn't enjoy getting blackmailed. What if he started to rebel, and she took his son as a warning? Or perhaps Vixen took his son, and he decided to get rid of her?"

I slump in my seat. Anger burns in my gut. "And I'm the perfect person to do it. It's no secret how much I hate—hated—vampires. I didn't even ask questions. He mentioned Cipla and that was it. I took the money and ran."

"What's Cipla?"

"An estate on the southern edge of Angbec. I grew up there. When Dad died, we left to move closer to Mum's job, but the house is still there. Abandoned."

Rayne stretches across the table. Again our fingers tangle. "So you wanted a way to hold the memory of happier times."

"Easier times."

She smiles. "There's nothing wrong with that."

One of the café staff wanders over to collect our empties. He offers another cup of coffee, and I agree, waiting until he's gone before I speak again.

"There is when I let it get in the way of my job. Mikkleson played me, and now I'm stuck in this big, ugly mess with no idea how to get out."

"Ask for help."

"I've never been good at that." I gaze at her.

"Practise."

I shift my hand until I have all of her fingers gathered in mine. "Rayne, please, help me solve this."

"No, I'm sure you can handle this alone."

I blink at her. Like an idiot. "What?"

Her lips wobble, then stretch into a smile. "Sorry, couldn't resist." Her laughter rings across the table, too bright and cheerful for this dreary, back street café.

"Seriously? Now you joke?"

She drags my hand to her lips and kisses the backs of my fingers. "You're not the only one with a comic streak."

"No shit. Maybe you're not so timid after all."

A wink, then Rayne is spreading the stolen files, snagging one off the top to start reading. She skims the first page, then begins the next. And the next.

"Are you actually reading those?"

She barely looks up. "Vampire."

Of course.

As my coffee arrives, I choose my own folder, open it, and begin to read. Much slower.

❖

Three coffees later, my head is buzzing. Two coffees after that and I'm certain I'll never sleep again. My eyes ache from reading and my fingers have a mind of their own, leaping across pages as I follow the words.

Rayne cuts me off. She seems alarmed at the effect caffeine has on me and pauses often to listen to my heartbeat and breathing. It's cute in a mother-hen sort of way.

Four files lie on the seat beside me, fully read from back to front. Two were useless, some reports of a new drug with a name I can't pronounce. The other seems to be accounts linked to Clear Blood, waiting for Jack's signature.

For the first time I realize that as well as a talented chemist and lab technician, Jack is CEO of the Foundation, only a little way down from the board of directors.

Yep. It's clear now, why Mum decided he was such a perfect match. He's exactly the sort of man she'd wish for me: intelligent, driven, and rich. Shame he's an arrogant, womanizing, conceited, cowardly fang junkie. Oh, and male.

I lick my lips, conscious of the tiny cut on the edge of my mouth where Rayne's fangs nicked me.

And why were her fangs so close to my face? Because I kissed her. We were kissing. Kissing. *K-I-S-S-I-N-G*.

Best kiss of my life. Without doubt.

A wriggle of warmth floods my body and I scrunch up my toes within my boots.

Rayne looks up from her sixth file. "What's wrong?"

"Nothing, I—"

"Your breathing stuttered. I thought you'd found something."

I inhale slowly and let it go through pursed lips. "Sorry, no."

"You're feeling strange about it, aren't you? I can't help it. I'm tuned in to you. I notice everything about you, from the hitch in your breath, to the shifts in your heart rate. Even when your scent changes, though I need to be close for that."

"You're tuned in?" Part of me wants to be freaked out by that, but the rest squeals with inward delight at the thought of anybody paying that much attention to me. It might be the most romantic thing I've ever heard.

She nods. "I can tune out if I want. *If* I want." She clears her throat and returns to the file on her lap.

CHAPTER SIXTEEN

Three herbal teas later—Rayne is adamant about the coffee—I toss the last file across the table and lower my head to my forearms. "There's nothing here. Talk about waste of time."

Rayne touches my elbow. Though the effects of the siren have worn off by now, the contact sends a little thrill through me. Without lifting my head, I shift my hand.

Our fingers dance together, stroking, sliding, whispering over each other, until I can hardly stand it. I look up.

She's staring at me, eyes bright and cheerful, lips slightly parted. I think about kissing her.

"Stop it," she murmurs.

"What?"

"You're thinking something naughty. I can tell, it changes the rhythm of your breathing. Just like before you kissed me." Her fingers shift to trace swirls over the back of my hand.

"You weren't complaining then."

She chuckles. "And I'm not complaining now, but you asked for help." With her free hand, Rayne flips her folder and lifts a page out. "I think I found something."

Campaign stuff. Donations. Rally locations. Allies. Notes on advertising.

"This is nothing to do with Clear Blood."

"No," she agrees, "but look—Jackson received four large donations in the past couple of months. This one is listed as anonymous, but here's the other three, from Fox Light Enterprises, Den Building Ltd, and this last one from Tall Tails Ltd."

I shrug.

"There are also signs of continual funding from one or all of these companies or businesses related to them." She continues to trace shapes on my skin. "You don't see it?"

Right now I can't see anything beyond her skin against mine, the contrast of light and dark. "See what?"

"They're all linked to foxes."

Can't think with my hand on fire like this. I watch her index finger and the path it takes across my knuckles, then down to my wrist. Back again. Again.

"Danika?"

"Hmm?"

"Foxes. Vixen."

"Right." I cross my legs beneath the table.

"Are you listening? Those businesses might be owned by Vixen."

I sit straight, abruptly freed from the spell Rayne weaves across me. "Could be coincidence."

"Check."

"How? I'm more of a fighting, chasing, hunting, killing sort of agent. Fieldwork, y'know?"

She grins. "Yes, and very good at it too. How long have you been with SPEAR?"

"Eight years."

"You don't seem that old."

"I joined really young. It's all I wanted to do."

She cocks her head. "You sound like me."

"Meaning?"

"Don't get upset. I joined the police force back home because it's all I wanted too. Most of my brothers and sisters were older, and Dad always told us that if we could do something worthwhile, we should. They decided worthwhile meant protecting people, and I agreed."

I smile. Though my youth might have been troubled and hectic, helping people had always been front and centre in my mind. Making a difference. Being a SPEAR seemed natural, and despite Mum's fear and veto of the idea, I did it anyway, pushing myself to be the best I could.

I'd made a deal with Mum; if I couldn't get promoted to fieldwork in four years, I'd give it up and find something less dangerous.

I did it in two.

"Give me your phone." Rayne's voice pulls me back to myself. "I want to check those businesses."

After passing her the device I swig from my mug. It's cold now, the peppermint taste giving way to slight bitterness.

A wave towards the counter brings over one of the café staff. Shifts have changed twice since we sat down, and now the figure behind the counter is a whippet slender *edane* with green tinged skin and hair like Christmas tree fronds. A sprig of red berries hangs in a cluster beside their left ear, which is long and pointed.

They approach, smiling and chirpy. "Good evening. What can I do for you?"

"Don't suppose I could get another…" I glance at Rayne. She hasn't stopped searching, but something about the set of her shoulders suggests she's listening to every word. "Tea, please."

"The green tea is excellent. I can make it up with a blend of fruit infusions to give you a truly unique flavour."

"Um, sure. Can I get another muffin too? One of the big yellow ones, please."

Rayne is still searching when my treats arrive. I start on the muffin at once, gobbling half before remembering to share. I break off a piece and leave it near her elbow. She nods thanks, again without looking up, and pauses to inhale.

"Lemon and poppy seed. We used to make those at home."

"They're my favourite."

"Maybe I'll cook for you one day," she says.

It's subtle, but I catch a hint of uncertainty in Rayne's voice. Her gaze flickers off the phone, so fast I might have missed it had I not been watching her.

"I'd like that."

She smiles and keeps tapping the screen.

Watching her is a treat I can't describe. The delicate motions of her hands, the concentration in her eyes, the tiniest tip of her tongue peeping from the corner of her mouth. More than once she stops to rough up her hair, an unconscious gesture as sexy as it is adorable.

I want to run my fingers through it again. Hell, I want to pull it, use it to draw her head back while I lay a trail of kisses down her throat and across her breasts.

"Danika?"

"What, what? Yes, what?" I snatch the fresh mug and hide behind a sip of flavoured tea.

"You're distracting me."

"I didn't do anything."

"I can smell you." She stares, one eyebrow raised. Slow, deliberate, she lowers her gaze towards my legs, then back up again. "I *smell* you."

Shit.

Can't decide if I'm embarrassed or even more turned on at the thought.

I settle for a point between the two and slip out from my chair. "I'm going to the loo."

"Don't be long."

"Funny. I'm horny, not desperate."

❖

In the bathroom, I splash cold water into my face and down the back of my neck. It soaks straight through my bandage, but the faint sting is a welcome distraction to the moist heat between my legs. I'd love to douse that too, but that might be inappropriate.

I stare at the cracked mirror above the sinks, shifting sideways when another woman darts in, all rushed and panicked. She whips off her blouse and drags on a T-shirt with the café's logo embroidered on the left side.

"Sorry, love." She shoves the blouse into her bag. "I'd usually change at home, but our bloody supervisor ain't shown up. I had to do a mad scramble for a babysitter then peg it across town."

I raise my hands. "No need to explain, I just drink here."

"Yeah?" A weary smile. "Don't suppose you want a job? With him off and the new girl vanished, we're mega short-staffed right now."

"I'm a SPEAR."

She looks me up and down. I twitch my jacket to show my gun in its shoulder holster.

"Wow, awesome. You on a sting or something?"

"Or something."

"Well, you guys are awesome. Hope you get paid better than we do in this dump. Right, laters." After fluffing her hair and wiping her mouth, she darts out again.

I'm still staring at the mirror when the realization hits.

Then I'm scrambling, jarring my hip on the sinks in my haste to get out.

The girl is already behind the counter, trying a half apron around her waist while chatting with the sprite. I shove aside a box of gingernut biscuits and lean over the worktop.

"Hey? Hey, you? What happened to that new girl you were talking about?"

She stares at me, wide-eyed. "Meryn? She never showed up. All excited and pleased to have a job, then a no-show on the first day."

"And your supervisor?"

"Who knows? He should be here now, but no one's heard from him. Probably got distracted on the way. Or mugged. I keep telling him to take a cab, especially with all those disappearances cracking off near his house. Even vam—"

I don't hear the rest.

I'm back at the table, waving my hands at Rayne. "Hey, tell me something."

"They're all owned by Vixen." She cuts across me and holds out the phone.

Numbers. Names. Addresses.

"Huh?"

"It took some digging, and the relationships are well hidden, but all three businesses are owned in whole or part by Amelia Smythe. She's involved with much more—property development, research, private security, entertainment, even the Clear Blood Foundation. I think she's on the board."

"But how? She's one person."

Rayne lays the phone on the table. "Vampire. She's had plenty of time to build contacts and make money. Some of these businesses were established in the 1870s."

"What the hell is she planning with all this?"

"I don't know, and it's still not proof. Vixen, or Amelia Smythe, is using her businesses to donate money to Jack's bid for mayor. That doesn't make her a kidnapping criminal."

The word kidnap reminds me of my urgent flurry back to the table. "Tell me, when she took you, changed you, I mean, did she know you were a police officer?"

Rayne stiffens. "Why do you ask?"

"Humour me."

"I…" She toys with a tall metal sugar caddy. "Yes, she knew."

"And? Did she seem interested? Did she ask about what you did or who you worked for?"

"Not really. There wasn't much time for that."

She doesn't look at me. No, she's actively looking away, staring out the window.

"Rayne...?"

"I didn't know. Please believe me. I didn't."

I raise my hands. "No idea what you're talking about."

"We met while I was on duty at a charity event. They wanted extra security because some TV star came to give a speech. I was on the doors. She smiled when she went in and...well, you've met her. You know about Vixen's smile."

I don't want to hear this story. The lowered voice, the hesitant pace, I know what she's about to say. I know, and it brings a lead weight to the pit of my stomach.

"She found me when my shift ended and invited me to her hotel. We didn't talk much, but she was impressed when I told her about my job. She took me to her room and—"

The lid of the sugar caddy pops off. Sugar floods across the table.

"Rayne..."

"It didn't even hurt. I didn't know what she was doing until it was too late. I thought it was just a kiss. Then the sickness came, and the dizziness and the confusion. *Then* pain. By then it was too late."

My eyes prickle at the corners and beneath the lids. I wipe them with the back of my hand and wait for her to finish.

"The next night I had no idea what had happened. She explained, and I didn't want to believe, but then she brought in one of the cleaning staff and I..." The caddy dents. "I was so hungry. I couldn't control it." At last she looks at me. A droplet of red forms at the corner of her eye and slides down her cheek. "After that, I had no choice. There was no one else to turn to, and she became my family. It wasn't until we came here that I started to question her talk about change and equal rights. But I didn't know she was doing this, please believe me."

I stand.

Misery and a weary sense of acceptance fill Rayne's gaze until I skirt around the table and sit beside her.

"I don't care what you did. That's done now, it's over. What matters now is how you act next."

"You don't think I'm weak and pathetic? Letting myself fall for a vampire?"

I tuck my finger beneath her chin. "Seems we have something in common."

She smiles. That dimple in her cheeks reappears. "Guess we both have good taste."

"I certainly do. Yours could use a little work." I kiss her, long, slow, and tender, with all the words I long to say but can't.

She moans. "You taste like lemon. I miss lemon. That's amazing."

"*You're* amazing."

A cleared throat breaks us apart.

It's the sprite, grinning wide as they collect our spent mugs and side plates. "Did you enjoy the tea?"

"Lovely, thanks." I drag myself away from Rayne. "Could you tell me about your supervisor?"

"Oh, dear, must I?" The sprite stops collecting and actually slips into my recently vacated seat on the other side of the table. "Now, I'm grateful for equal opportunities, you understand. All those businesses staying on the right side of the Interspecies Relations Act are wonderful for a weak and relatively powerless sprite like myself, but I truly protest the inclusion of vampires on our staff. No offence to you, my dear." They gesture at Rayne, who shakes her head.

"They're just so unreliable, and he is the worst of them. For the last week or so he's been popping in and out of the shop when he should be working, meeting with dark and shifty characters at the back, and now he's gone. Poof! I called his house, but there's no word. I think he's joined a gang."

"Gang?"

"Come, come, you're a SPEAR aren't you?" They look at my bandaged hand, at Rayne, then back at my face. "The Underworld has been unsettled for weeks—there's a strange power shift happening. Talk of a coup too, as if anybody would be mad enough to try something so foolish. But everyone is riled up in a way I've not seen since the sixties, with vampires in particular acting very strangely. Again, no offence."

This time Rayne growls, showing off a hint of fang in the corner of her mouth. Her eyes darken, and though the silver flickers in and out, it's enough to chase the sprite from their seat.

"Yes, yes, I've done it again. I knew it. I didn't mean to offend you, truly I didn't. But your friend asked and I had to say what I thought and—" They sigh. "My spruce always told me I should learn when to keep my mouth shut. Oh, I'm still doing it, aren't I? I'm sorry. So, so, sorry." They gather up the mugs and plates in record time, then carry the lot away. "I'll be back to clear up that sugar."

Rayne and I stare at each other.

She shakes her head. "His spruce?"

"*Their* spruce. Those sprites are agender. And they're probably talking about the tree they sprouted from. Some sprites simply step out of trees one day, fully grown and speaking the language of who or whatever lives in the area. Sometimes they can't talk at all, though this one clearly doesn't have that issue."

"So another vampire has probably turned to Vixen. Why does that matter?"

"The sprite talked about a coup, but against who? There aren't any other powerful *edane* forces in Angbec. Fae fight amongst themselves too much, and even the werewolf packs can't outnumber the vampires. The only species with bigger strength in numbers is us."

Rayne bites her lip. "Humans? A coup against humans?"

"What else could it be?"

The sprite returns and sweeps away the spilled sugar. Though they apologize again, they take care to stay well away from Rayne and leave immediately.

"A move against humans needs months of planning and plenty of work during the day. There's no way she'd be able to organize anything like that without help." I bury my face in the crook of my elbow. "And of course, she's been getting it." When Rayne gives me a curious glance, I gesture to the counter. "The people going missing, it's not just homeless people from The Bowl. Mikkleson's PA is missing, Pippa has been short-staffed at Clear Blood. Even civvie bashers are missing officers."

"But surely that's just people not turning up for work?"

"No, they're people with information or skills or connections. Even you, Rayne, you were an officer. Vixen probably had plans for you."

She fiddles with her fingers. "Because Dad was a Rancher, I had skills and knowledge lots of others didn't. I was in the middle of forming a specialist street unit focused on supernatural crime. Then Vixen found me."

I start pulling the papers together, gathering the files into one untidy pile.

"What are you doing?"

"This is good, but it's not enough. With Quinn on the warpath, I need more concrete evidence, so we're going to go get it."

"You've got that look in your eye again."

"It'll be fine."

She frowns. "Now I'm worried. Where are we going?"

"City Hall. We have another office to search."

CHAPTER SEVENTEEN

My phone is ringing as we get back to my car. I'd rather not answer, but Rayne snags it before I can stop her.

"Danika Karson's phone."

"Hello? Who's this? You're not my Danika. Where is she? Why do you have her phone?"

Mouthing *Why?*, I take back the phone and press it to my ear. "It's okay, Mum, I'm here."

"Oh, baby, what's going on? You haven't called or checked in or anything."

"I've been working."

"What's all this about Jackson being attacked?"

Rayne ducks her head. I pat her arm.

"It's dealt with. Is that why you're calling? Do you have any idea what time it is?"

She snorts. "Yes, do you? After all that happened last night you couldn't give your poor mother a call? I raised you better than this, I—"

"I've been working. Sorry, but it got the best of me. Are you okay?"

"Yes, I'm fine, mostly I wanted to ask about you."

For a few moments I can't speak. "Really, Mum? Really?"

"Of course. You future is important to me. So come on, tell me about your dessert with Jackson. Did you get on? Is he as nice as he sounds on TV? Did you arrange to meet again?"

I should have known.

"Mum..."

"I knew you'd like him, from everything Pippa said. He's such a gentleman, isn't he? And handsome. I bet he'd take excellent care of you, and with all that money of his, you wouldn't need to work for SPEAR any more."

"I like working for SPEAR."

"Phillipa will be so pleased. Even she's ready to settle down. Has she spoken to you yet? Did she share her news?"

"Actually, no."

Mum tuts. "Hurry up. I'm bursting to talk to you about it, but I know she wants to tell you herself. Anyway, Jackson is so skilled and intelligent. He heads the research team, and did you know he synthesized the first version of the Life Blood Serum when he was twenty-one years old?"

Rayne gives me a sympathetic look. I shake my head and wait for a gap.

"Mum—"

"And he practises judo. Isn't that nice? It would go so nicely with your cap-area."

"It's called capoeira."

"Maybe you could visit the martial arts museum together? Wouldn't that make a lovely second date?"

"Mum—"

"He lives in Harmony Rise. You know, those new apartment blocks Phillipa was looking at. Nice, but not so great for young families. Though I suppose Jackson hasn't had to worry about that until now. But those bear people have done a beautiful job in that area, clearing out the old dross and building up the new estate."

"Mum, please—"

"Shopping too, they're working in Cipla too."

"Who? What are you talking about?"

"The bear people."

I look helplessly at Rayne. "You're not making sense."

"That development company named after bear caves." She clicks her fingers. "Sett Building—no, no, that's badgers. Not warren either…"

"Den?" I tighten my grip on the phone. "Den Building Ltd?"

"Yes, that's them. They're planning to demolish all those horrid old houses and build a new shopping centre. It's going to be great."

I pause. "Backtrack, Mum. Which area?"

"Cipla."

Demolish the houses?

My stomach knots. Even my intent to correct Mum is lost in the face of this new information.

They can't. *She* can't. Those houses are old. Special.

My mind drifts back to a three-floor property with shuttered windows and a scuffed red door. The garden out front is grassy with a winding path from the front gate all the way to the front door which hides behind a raised porch. In back, a swing set, sandpit, and two bikes.

I shake my head. Bite my lip.

Mum's still babbling, something about theatre tickets and ballet.

"I need to go."

"Of course, baby. I just wanted to see how you were. Let me know when you next see Jackson."

"I'm not going to see him again, Mum, I…sure."

"That's my girl. Speak soon."

I hang up.

Rayne stares at me. Her face is a curious mix of surprise and confusion. "She doesn't know."

"Of course not." I shove the phone into my pocket and start the car. "I couldn't tell her about the work I do. She'd never recover."

"No, she doesn't know you're gay."

My foot slips on the clutch. The car gives a reluctant whine as I restart. "Oh."

"Danika?"

"I—"

"Are you embarrassed?"

"No."

"You know there's nothing wrong about it, right? Nothing bad or sinful? People love who they love, and nobody gets a choice in that. Man, woman, *edane*, we all want the same things."

"I know that."

"So why haven't you told her?"

I grip the steering wheel. It hurts, but I welcome the pain. "I have. Time and time again, but—and I say this with love—Mum is a narrow-minded, hardcore Christian who wants her oldest baby girl to give her six squalling grandkids."

"You can still—"

"I don't want children." I don't mean to shout, but it happens anyway, an angry burst in an otherwise calm car.

"Right. Sorry." Rayne's voice is cold. Distant. "I didn't mean to pry."

"Rayne…"

"No, it's fine. I just don't think lying to your family is healthy."

"I'm not lying."

"You went on a date with Jackson."

"You don't understand."

"Don't I? Seems to me, you'd rather put yourself through discomfort and embarrassment to keep your secret. Actually you're right, I don't understand. Why? Why can't you be honest?"

I slam my feet down. The car screeches to a stop, throwing us both against our seat belts.

"She knows, Rayne, of course she knows. Who do you think I am, anyway?"

"Then why is she—"

"Because this"—I sweep a hand up and down my body—"is a *phase*. It's me *testing the waters before fully committing.*"

Rayne arches an eyebrow.

"I know, I know, it's bullshit, but she clings to it like stink to shit." A sigh. "Look, when Dad died, it was the three of us, Mum, Pip, and me. We couldn't even keep our house. Maybe it's different with a foster family, maybe you don't get family love the way I do, but if I told Mum I'm never going to have a family the same way she did, it would break her heart. Again."

"Family love?"

The back of my neck is prickling. Even my fingertips itch. I want to lash out, kick something, punch something. "The kind of love you only get through blood." Bitter chuckle. "And I don't mean that kind of blood."

Rayne folds her hands in her lap. She doesn't move, but her body is tense and rigid, her mouth tight. "You think foster families can't love each other?"

"No, I think vampires can't love anything but themselves and the source of their next haemoglobin hit. Look at Vixen, about to demolish those beautiful houses in Cipla for a shopping centre. How can she? Visit any of them and you'll see growth marks on the doors, names scratched into skirting boards, floors scuffed and stained. Everyone had to move when property developers bought the land, all those families shunted aside like nothing."

A lone car scoots around us. The headlamps flare, briefly lighting the interior before it's gone again.

"Vixen is evil and clearly out for herself, pulling strings everywhere to get what she wants. She's dangerous, selfish, and needs to be stopped. Just like the rest of them."

"Like me?"

"What? No."

"I see. I'm glad I understand you better."

Something's wrong. Her voice, her eyes, her body, it's not like it was a moment ago. She's right beside me, but in that moment the space between us resembles the Grand Canyon.

I reach for her, but she turns her head, glaring at the window with a little huff.

"Fine." Again I start the car. "Let's go. We've got a lot to do before you drop dead at sunup."

Her head whips round. She stares, open-mouthed.

I glare right back, inwardly hoping, wishing, begging her to lash out. That would be easier to deal with. I'd know what to do with that. But this soft, wounded, pitiful look is something else. I can't fight that.

She opens the door.

Before I can speak, or even think it through, she's unclipped her seat belt and leapt out of the vehicle. She slams the door with a thrust of her palm and strides away in the opposite direction.

Long seconds I sit there, mind split by indecision.

I open my own door, but a loud honk from a passing car forces me to close it. By the time I step onto the road, the street is empty again.

Fine. Just fine.

Back in the car. Slam the door. Pump the accelerator.

Speed away.

I try to put her hurt expression out of my mind. Perhaps it's better this way. Besides, it's true, isn't it?

No matter what I feel for her, no matter how *tuned in* Rayne is, she's a vampire and I'm human. The sun will rise, she'll drop dead, and I'll be alone to face what comes next.

Like usual.

CHAPTER EIGHTEEN

I park two streets from City Hall.

My watch beeps, a subtle reminder that night is passing fast, and all I have is more questions and nothing to stop Quinn taking another chunk out of me.

She must be livid by now. Probably sent other agents to look for me. Though that might not be a bad thing. Backup at a time like this would be great.

Instead, I approach the huge Victorian building alone.

It seems larger at night, darker and more ominous. The blue and white pennants are still there, and the stern angles of Mikkleson's face take on a sinister edge in the dim light.

Security trolls still man the doors. One appears to be dozing, the other distracted by a moth fluttering against the glass of the lamp above its head. It rumbles, a sound as close to laughter as it can manage, and extends a huge, knobbly hand. The rumbles cease when the moth is replaced by a dark, lumpy smear on the glass.

At this time of night, the reception desk is unmanned, just a night guard standing in front of the metal detector I used the day before. He raises a hand as I approach.

"Excuse me, we're closed to civilians right now."

"Not to me." A flash of my gun and ID soon changes his tune. "I'm meeting a witness upstairs. This is the only time he could meet."

He nods. "Oh. Uh, okay. I do need to ring it in though."

I pause. "To who?"

"Security." He mumbles into the walkie-talkie clipped to his shoulder, gesturing me through with the other hand. "Everyone's on the second floor today. Stairs around the corner, lift on your left."

"Cheers."

He's watching me, so I make a show of pressing the number two, smiling as he catches my eye. Then I'm in the box and moving, a mechanical ding pinging on each floor.

On the second floor the lights are brighter, the air lively with the presence of live bodies. A glance left and right reveals an empty corridor, and I dart out onto the plush red carpet and to the main stairs. Back down to the first floor, then to the end of the corridor where Mikkleson's office waits.

The door is locked. Of course.

I turn, ready to ask Rayne to break in like she did at Clear Blood. Oh.

Lock picking tools aren't officially part of a SPEAR agent's kit, but I have them because, why not? Another thing to add to the leg-long list of crimes Quinn holds against me.

Two minutes to unlock the door, then I'm inside, pulling it shut after me.

It's dim in the office, only the reflected glow of the street lamp outside. Like before, the air sits heavy with the scent of cigar smoke.

The desk is bare now, except for a lonely fountain pen and a small lamp. The drawers are locked too. My tools make short work of those.

Inside, a wide crystal decanter of something dark, probably whisky. Two tumblers. A cigar box. Matches. Empty note pad. More pens. Paper clips. Elastic bands.

How can there be nothing here? Not even a sheet of paper? Does the man not have letters to sign or paperwork to look at?

The rest of the office is no help—military orders and decorations on the walls, a display case of six fancy medals under glass. Three potted plants. A rifle mounted on a long mahogany plaque. The second door.

I push into the second half of the office.

Smaller and cluttered. Here, it seems, is where Mikkleson keeps all the usual furniture one would expect in a working office. Three filing cabinets, another desk, two computers, and a phone. In and out trays.

Computer first. It boots and immediately requests a password. I try various military sounding words until the machine beeps angrily and displays a message: *Too many incorrect password attempts. Account temporarily locked.* The second computer is older and grubbier so I leave it and work on the cabinets.

Nothing. Just a bunch of city stuff like maintenance, rubbish disposal, and development orders.

That last one catches my attention and snags it when I spot a letterhead bearing the words *Tall Tails Ltd.*

No money, but requests to begin development in Cipla.

The paper crumples in my hands as I read the plans. Vixen has permission to demolish all the houses in a half mile stretch. She'll do away with the school and the little line of shops alongside it, to replace the lot with a multi-storey car park and two-level shopping mall.

No. No, she won't.

"Hey, what are you doing in here?"

I spin around, papers still crushed in my fists.

Another night guard, this one short, fat, and hairy. "Well? Who are you?"

Rayne's words come back to me. Speculation. No concrete proof.

I think again of Quinn and the fury in her voice as she ordered me back to HQ.

"I'm the new night shift secretary." I show him the papers. "Mikk—Mr. Mikkleson was missing some files, so I came to get them for him."

He frowns. "No, you didn't."

"Of course I did, I—"

"No"—he sniffs the air, a huge, nostril rippling inhalation—"you're lying. Not about all of it, but you don't work here."

Great. Just my luck. "I'm a SPEAR agent. I'm on a case and—"

"Half true. And if you're really a SPEAR, you can tell me how I know that."

"Werewolf. Grey Tail pack. You guys can smell lies on humans, I get it. But you have to believe I'm here because I need to be."

He walks deeper into the office. "I also smell vampire and blood on you, not much like any SPEAR I know." That *edane* glide is obvious now, but there's something else in it, something predatory and angry. "Who are you?"

"I already told you—"

"Right, of course, you're an agent. Then where's your case notes? The rest of your team? If I call SPEAR now, will they confirm your case?"

My hand tightens on the Tall Tails papers. The palm of my other hand begins to prickle. "No, they won't, but I can explain that—"

"Explain it to the police, doll. I don't want to hear it. Put your hands on your head and turn around."

I sigh. "I don't want to do this."

"That's the first honest thing you've said to me." He stops on the far side of the desk, both hands resting on his podgy hips. "Didn't you hear me? Hands on your head."

I lift my hands slowly, shifting my weight forward to the balls of my feet. "If you're so good at recognizing the truth, you'll know I mean it when I say I'm sorry."

"For what?"

I toss the papers and throw myself across the desk. The computer and trays slide sideways as I plough through, left leg out, heel cocked. My boot catches him in the chin, momentum and thrust knocking his head back.

He stumbles but doesn't fall, and I skid off the end, landing in a crouch. Then I'm up, sprinting back into the office and out the main door. I'm on the stairs before the werewolf catches up.

Fur sprouts all over his face and neck, and though he's panting, I know he's faster.

"Get back here."

I duck his groping hands and leap on the banister to slide down the thick wooden rail on my belly. Would be fun if I wasn't risking my job.

He follows at a waddle, halfway down by the time I reach the bottom.

Back at ground level, I sprint across the tiled floor, vaulting the side table beside the metal detector. The guard from earlier, startled by my appearance, tumbles back and to the floor.

"Sorry," I call over my shoulder.

The werewolf guard is at the bottom, more fur growing on his hands. He yells something, but I can't hear it over the thudding of my own heart, the hiss of my own breathing.

Keep going. Don't look back. Don't get caught. Keep moving.

My mad dash ends with jarring abruptness as I run straight into the thick, stone-like chest of one of the trolls.

It peers at me as I land on my rear.

"Stop her," the guards yell, still several yards away. "Stop her, now."

I scramble up, meaning to dart around the troll, but the huge creature sweeps down with one heavy hand and hefts me into the air by the scruff of my jacket.

I kick it. Punch it. Wriggle, twist, and pull, but the only thing to give is my jacket which tears along the back seam.

Almost free. Kick some more, push back.

The jacket tears the rest of the way leaving me free to drop out of it and roll clear. My gun clatters on the floor, my knife sheaths doing the same, but I'm mobile and ready to move.

The werewolf guard dives at me, a furious swipe with a hand tipped with long black claws. They miss flesh but hack long holes through my top, shredding the back to ribbons.

I stare, alarmed and suddenly afraid. "What are you doing?"

"You're clearly a threat." He spins around and advances again, slow measured steps on the balls of his feet. "Lying about SPEAR, snooping around Mikkleson's office—"

"But your claws can pass the virus."

He chuckles and kisses each of his fingers in turn. "Scared?"

I grit my teeth. "Pissed. You work for the city—you should know better." He springs again, but I'm ready, rolling clear and pulling two knives on the ascent. My injured hand throbs around the handle of the silver blade, and I know I won't be able to hold it long.

He stops half a pace away. "You're prepared."

"Call SPEAR." My voice cracks as I say it, but what choice do I have left? "I'll wait here without fuss if you call them. Ask for Francine Quinn, leader of the alpha team. She'll confirm who I am and my ID. I'm Danika Karson, A20240119A05."

"I don't care who you are, you're going down."

More security arrives, communicating through those shoulder walkie-talkies. Five of them flood the space and form a loose ring around me.

How did this go so wrong, so fast?

Again the werewolf grins. "So, what's it going to be?"

For one crazy moment I think about fighting my way out. There's one *edane* among the total of seven guards, but that's nothing I can't handle. The other six are human and likely easy to flatten. I could probably do it without hurting them.

The ground shakes. Rumbles.

I spend precious seconds trying to find the reason, then the troll wraps both arms around my arms and ribs from behind and hugs my back to its chest.

It says something, or I think it does, and small crumbs of dry dirt shower my face. It stinks too, a blend of pine bark and wilted poppies.

My legs flail, but I can't move my arms at all. Even if I could, knives are pointless against trolls with their thick, stony skin.

The werewolf guard lopes over, huffing and blowing but grinning, a gesture that only widens as I gasp and drop the blades.

"Now then, *Agent*. Where were we?"

CHAPTER NINETEEN

Grey walls. Grey ceiling. Grey floor. Hell, everything is grey, everything except the bars in place of the fourth wall. No, those are steel and as thick as my wrist, driven deep into the concrete that makes the top and bottom of my cell.

I find myself thinking of Rayne. Is she still upset with me? Is she hurt? Did she find somewhere safe to rest? Has the sun risen? Has it found her outside, unprepared, and burnt her to a crisp? Does she still want to bake lemon and poppyseed muffins for me?

No point worrying about that now.

I tell myself that, but the thoughts keep coming back—Rayne's face pressed to the glass of my car, her lips parted in a silent scream as the sun's light spreads across the road. Her murmurs as I run my hands through her hair and the softness of her lips against mine. Her skin, so smooth and pale, such a contrast to mine.

Distraction. That's what I need.

Even though I've done it several times already, I pace the edges of my cell, mentally logging the contents and their potential uses. Flat, uncomfortable bed, bolted to the wall and too heavy to shift. Toilet, no lid, though the flush is loose and might break free if I pull hard enough. Sink, cracked, stained, and smelly, no good for anything. The taps don't work.

My gun is gone. Utility belt too. And, despite my complaints, yells, and eventual struggles, they took my watch.

Angbec Police Force, nothing if not overly cautious.

The area beyond the bars is spartan, one chair at a table strewn with take away wrappers and crushed cans of cola. An array of playing cards beside the mess looks like a game of solitaire.

A door opens to the right, beyond my line of sight. Quick footsteps follow, then a uniformed officer appears, still fastening his fly. "What are you looking at?"

"Nothing. Just wondering why you guys have me in the supernatural holding unit."

"You're dangerous."

"To who?"

He frowns, then returns to the table. "Give it a rest, eh? I don't have time for you."

"Yeah, because that card game is so important. Come on, what's happening? What time is it? When's breakfast? Do I get a phone call? What's the meaning of life?"

The frown deepens as he shifts a card from one pile to another.

"You know I'm a SPEAR, right? You must have sussed that when you took my stuff. You know I'm one of the good guys."

Still nothing.

"Come on, talk to me. I'm bored."

Another card.

"I can keep this up for hours, by the way. In fact, if you don't talk to me, I'll have to sing. Think you're pissed now, think how you'll feel after twelve rounds of 'Three Blind Mice.' Hello? Hey? Come on, say something. Hello? By the way, you can't put a club on a spade, Meat Stick."

His gaze never leaves the cards, and though he does replace the last one, he neglects to thank me for my correction.

I return to the metal slab masquerading as a bed and sit, chin propped on my fist. "Hey, Meat Stick?"

The officer winces, shifts another card, and keeps his head down.

"Don't like that one? What about Sideburn Sid? Gorilla Arms? Butt Chin? Oh, come on, you miserable sod."

He slams his palm on the table. "My name is Officer Barnabas Watson and—"

"Barney? Like the lizard? Cool." I fight back the giggle brewing and point towards the stairs. "Why don't you run back up to your supervisors and let them know you've made a mistake."

Barney grins and leaves his card game. His swagger over to my cell is both comical and alarming. "There's no mistake, Agent Karson. You were found raiding the office of Mayor Sebastian Mikkleson and then proceeded to attack the night guards."

"Attack? Wait a second—"

"More than that, I hear you've been up to all sorts of no good tonight. What happened to the vampire that attacked Calum?"

"Who?"

He leans against the bars. "The officer you drew your gun on before unleashing your pet fanger."

"What?"

"For a SPEAR you sure seem comfortable with supes. I've heard of you, Karson—werewolf informants, gargoyle plaything. Rumour says you've even got a chittarik living with you."

"Her name is Norma." Thinking of my little baby only reminds me of how long a night it's been. No sleep either, beyond my catnap in the bath yesterday. I can only hope she doesn't wreck the flat looking for something to eat.

Barney's jaw drops. "Norma?"

"Got a problem with that?"

"No." He recovers quickly, turning now to grip the bars and shake them. This close, I can see a scar across his left cheek, long and thin like a scratch from a nail.

"Shouldn't surprise me, really. You SPEAR agents are all the same, puffed up and self-important. Making your own rules while stepping on ours. I don't care what training you have or what languages you speak, you're still human. You should be on *our* side."

I'm up again, crossing the cell and slapping the bars. "What the hell do you think we do all day? SPEAR is all about protecting people."

"If you say so." He turns as if to step away but, at the last moment, swings back, grabs my wrists, and jerks them through the bars, hard enough to clang my chin. "Where were you when my wife died, huh? When the vampires snatched her off the street and tore her throat out?"

My immediate instinct to struggle stops cold. "Wife?"

"She was pregnant, Agent. Do you have any idea what that's like? Not one life lost, but two, but you stand there and tell me it's about *protecting* people? The Interspecies Relations Act is a joke. These monsters need to be wiped out, not coddled and given jobs. And you"—he pulls tighter, mashing my face into the bars—"you need to concentrate on *protecting* your own kind."

By the time he releases me, my face stings, shoulders aching from the strain.

I back towards the bed, massaging my jaw. "They're powerful creatures, Barney. What you're talking about won't work. You think people haven't considered that? There may be more of us, but one of them is worth six humans. We wouldn't stand a chance."

"Then at least we'd die fighting."

"I don't want to die."

He snorts and returns to the table. "Neither did my wife."

❖

I fall asleep at some point. Must have, because when I open my eyes next, Barney is gone, replaced by another officer I vaguely recognize. Just inside the cell bars are a sandwich, a bottle of water, and a packet of crisps.

The water is warm but tastes incredible. Even the BLT is good. I leave the cheese and onion snacks for later and knock lightly on the bars. "Did you bring this? Thanks."

The female officer looks up from her magazine, and in that moment I find the memory of her.

We were running down a dark alley, in joint pursuit of a gnome in the habit of stealing clothes from washing lines. That tricky little bugger led us a merry dance over half a mile before leading us into a den of wild imps less than happy to see us.

I trace the thin claw scars on my arm, twin to the ones I know she has on her hip.

"Tiffany?"

She grins. "Close. It's Tina. Hi."

"Sorry, I—"

"Don't worry about it. I bet you've got a lot on your mind right now."

"No shit."

Tina leaves the table and stands close to the bars, her shoulder towards me. When I give her a curious look she directs her gaze up and to the left.

A winking red light.

She watches my face and, when I nod, smiles and pulls a chocolate bar from her pocket. She hands it over, blocking the exchange from view of the camera with her torso.

"You angel," I whisper.

"You saved my life. Least I can do."

I break the bar into chunks and eat them piece by piece, careful to keep my hands out of view.

"Why are you here? I asked upstairs, but nobody's saying much, only that some SPEAR has gone rogue and attacked Mayor Mikkleson."

"Wow, the rumour mill strikes again. I'm working a case *for* Mikkleson."

Tina chews the inside of her cheek. "Private hire? Didn't think you guys did that."

"We don't. We shouldn't. I never will again, that's for sure. Do you think you can get a message to his office? Maybe if he knows I'm here, he can help when the shit hits."

"What shit?"

I study her face, trying to decide how much to say.

She sighs. "I know SPEAR and APF don't get on, but we're above that, aren't we? We don't have some testosterone-fuelled urge to swing our cocks around."

A piece of chocolate shoots from my mouth, propelled by a giggle. "Such a way with words."

"Well, we don't. I've no idea why you're here, but if you're half the person I remember, then what they're saying upstairs is bullshit. Give me the full story. Let me help."

I open my mouth.

The door opens.

Tina leaps back from the cell, standing to vague attention as two men walk in from the right. They might well be clones of each other, in deep blue suits and white shirts. Only the ties are different, one in red, the other in black. Oh, and one is tall and lanky, the other broad and heavy.

I lean against the bars. "You should have mentioned the dress code. I'd have worn something pretty."

The broad one smirks.

The tall one doesn't. "This isn't the time for jokes, Agent. I need you to come upstairs. I've got some questions to ask."

"Yeah, me too. First up, which one of you jokers took my watch?"

"It's customary to relieve supernatural suspects of all possessions when we—"

"No, it isn't. And I'm not *edane*. Clearly you know that, so cut the crap and start again."

He looks at his companion, who shrugs and shakes his head.

"Fine. You'll have your things back when we're done talking. When we've cleared up this apparent misunderstanding."

"Apparent?" From the corner of my eye I spot Tina gesturing frantically, mouthing *no* and shaking her head.

No. I've had enough.

"If you guys have a problem with how I work, report it to SPEAR. Francine Quinn is the name you want. But if you don't want to talk to her, then—"

"We've already spoken to her." Broad and heavy speaks up for the first time. "In fact we tried to get your people to pick you up, but Agent Quinn thought you might enjoy our hospitality for a while."

Bitch.

I return to the bed and sit, legs crossed, arms folded. "You're not getting more than two stars out of me. This bed is lumpy as hell, and you didn't put a mint on my pillow."

They laugh.

A chill ripples down my back.

For a horrible moment, I'm not sure if they're laughing with me, or at me.

Tall and grumpy opens my cell. "If you come without fuss, we won't restrain you. I'm sure you'd prefer to avoid the embarrassment of shuffling upstairs in chains?"

Again I open my mouth for a smart comeback, but the look in his eye stops me cold.

He'd really do it.

"Who are you anyway?"

"Inspector Bose, and this is Sergeant Hozier."

A brief smile and half raised hand from broad and heavy.

Bose continues, "Agent Quinn will be here soon, but before that we'd like to question you."

I try to smile, but even I can tell it's not my best.

I don't like the sound of this. Not one bit.

CHAPTER TWENTY

I hate these interview suites. They're comfortable and well lit, but I'd be a fool to consider them anything but another selection of cells.

I sit at a table with Hozier and Bose on the other side. Bose sits, Hozier stands near the wall underneath the clock.

Half past three. We've been in this cramped box for two hours, and we're all the worse the wear for it.

Poor Norma must be frantic by now.

Behind Bose's shoulder, a small tripod holds a camera complete with blinking red light.

"Come on, Agent, work with us. Maybe we can help." Bose clasps his hands and leans in. A plastic cup of tepid coffee stands to his left, another on my right, neither of them touched. "What were you doing at City Hall?"

"The merengue."

Hozier snorts.

Bose snarls, an almost animal sound, before leaping to his feet. His fist flies up on its way to my face.

I stay seated, tense and ready to move.

At the last moment he stops and points instead. "And you wonder why relations between SPEAR and this police force are so strained? It's awkward, stuck-up, arrogant little bitches like you." He storms out, slamming the door behind him.

"I'm not arrogant." I sip at the cold coffee. "I just like dancing."

Hozier claims the empty seat and fixes me with a sceptical glance. "Seriously?"

"Sure. Hard floors? Great for all those twists and turns."

Another laugh, and he rubs his jaw. "You're something else. In fact, I'm starting to see why Agent Quinn wanted to leave you here."

"She loves me, really."

"No doubt. You don't have to tell us anything, I know that. Hell, I'm not entirely certain we can charge you, but something must have taken you into that office. Since you're a SPEAR, I can only guess there's some sort of supernatural threat at City Hall." He watches my face. "We can't do much about that, we aren't trained, but civic matters fall on us. Is there something we should know?"

"Probably. But I have promises to keep. Important civic promises."

"Oh. I get it." He smiles, friendly and understanding, but I can't help but ponder if he really does get it.

Probably not.

"Do you need anything, Agent?"

I nudge the coffee. "One of these that doesn't taste like sludge?"

Another laugh. "Sorry, only so many miracles we can pull around here."

A gentle knock at the door interrupts our shared joke. Through it, at last, strides Quinn. Her narrow weasel face is twisted in irritation and distaste.

Hozier stands and blocks the way to the table. "This is a private interview suite. You can't—"

Quinn whips out her ID and tosses it on the table. "I need a moment with my agent."

"That's fine, but let me—"

"Get out."

He blinks, thick lips slightly parted.

I tap on the table. "I got this, Sergeant. Don't worry."

"Sure?" He actually looks worried, eying my supervisor with a wary stare. "We have a camera in here at all times, okay? Always monitored."

This time, when I smile, it's one of gratitude. "I'll be okay."

"Let me get that coffee." Though clearly unsure, Hozier leaves the room.

Quinn shuts the door, drags out the chair, and sits.

She glares.

I stare.

The clock ticks.

"Explain. Now."

For one crazy second I imagine telling her to stick it up her tight, narrow arse. It would almost be worth it, to see the look on her face. Instead, I sit back, spread my hands on the table, and explain.

Everything.

Well, I might have glossed over a few details, like how I got hold of the files from Jack's office and my heated kisses with Rayne. After a little internal fight, I even kept quiet the extent of Jack's relationship with vampires. He might be a sly, womanizing, narcissist creep, but underneath all that, he has some great plans for Angbec's supernatural population, should he be successful in his bid for mayor. From the paperwork I read, he's a forward-thinking, imaginative, and community driven sort of man.

By the time I finish speaking, my throat is dry and my voice hoarse. I down the rest of that disgusting coffee and burp away the bitterness.

Still Quinn stares. "So you're saying you accepted money from a civilian to use SPEAR resources in an unsanctioned investigation?"

"After everything I've said, *that's* what you focus on?"

"Did you or did you not accept money from—"

"Yes, I did, and it's a bloody good thing too." I slap the table. "Vixen is planning something. Mikkleson *and* Jack are compromised by her. Vampires can walk the streets by day and there are dozens of them we know nothing about. Are you hearing me? We need to *do* something."

She smiles. It's slow but wide and flashes all of her slightly yellowed teeth. "You're right. In fact, here's something I should have done months ago." Quinn leans across the table, holding my gaze. "You. Are. Grounded." She enunciates each word with hard, deliberate emphasis.

My heart stops. Or it feels like it does. "What?"

"Grounded, with reduced pay, for a period of fourteen days. In that time you'll be restricted to desk duties and forbidden from any unauthorized *edane* interaction, including Link. You'll report directly to me, confirming each day that you've made no attempts to conduct fieldwork."

"But—"

"I've warned you, Karson. Again, and again. You're lucky I'm not taking it a step further."

My hands curl into fists. "We need to track down that nest and stop Vixen. You need me."

"Yes, you and your miraculous informant. And where is she? This Rayne?"

"I don't know."

"Ah. Had a little lovers' tiff, did you?"

My head snaps up.

She's still grinning, but now her eyes are lively with malice. "You think we haven't been watching you? I gave you the chance to come in and explain yourself. Instead you chose to play kissy faces with that fanger in some café. I should send you to the psychiatric unit."

My cheeks burn. "You saw?"

"You're such a hypocrite, Karson. All this time you've been preaching how dangerous vampires are, and look at you. How long did it take you to stick your tongue in her mouth? I see you've cut your hand too—been donating to feed your little pet? Disgusting. You of all people should know, vampires are for killing, not fucking."

I'm standing on the other side of the table. Not sure how I got there, but Quinn has shoved her chair back and she's glaring at me, head tilted to meet my gaze.

"Do it." She spreads her arms. "I know you've wanted to hit me for years. Do it, then we'll see where you end up."

I lower my fist. Hadn't realized I'd raised it.

The door opens again and through it steps Hozier, steaming mug in hand. He freezes at the sight of us. "Everything okay, Agents?"

Quinn spins on her heel. "Keep her here until I can get someone to pick her up. Gun, ID, and utilities remain confiscated, clear?"

"Uh, sure."

"Quinn, please don't do this. Please. Quinn—"

She lifts a hand. "We're done talking. One of the team will drop you home and tomorrow you report to me." Gone.

I scream, kicking at the table.

The untouched cup of coffee wobbles, then falls, spilling thin brown water across the surface.

Hozier sighs. "It didn't go well."

"There are vampires running in the streets without registration details. Some can walk by day. Yeah"—I nod at his stunned look—"I thought the same, but it's true. We *need* to get out there and find them, and that crazy bitch just chained me to my desk."

"She doesn't seem to like you much."

I snort. "She's just jealous that I bone more girls than she does."

"You—oh. Okay." Hozier sets the coffee on the table and backs away. "You've got another visitor, by the way. Promise you won't hurt him?"

I throw myself back into the chair, cracking my knuckles. "I'll be good."

"Try." He returns to the door and beckons. "I'll leave you two alone."

"Agent Karson." This new voice jerks my head up and draws a gasp from my mouth. "You've really cocked this up, haven't you?"

"Mikkleson?"

The mayor sighs and wags a finger at me from his position behind the camera. "We need to talk."

CHAPTER TWENTY-ONE

Another staring match. I'm getting sick of it, but I've no idea what to say to the man. In the end, Mikkleson saves me by pushing a button on the side of the camera. The red light stops blinking.

I sit straight.

This can't be good.

He helps himself to the chair opposite and leans forward, fingers threaded together on top of the table. "What do you think you know?"

Deep breath. Grit my teeth. "Your son is a fang junkie."

"And an addict." Shrug. "Didn't think it would take you long to figure that out. And?"

I match his pose. It's that or wrap my fingers around his throat. How can he be so blasé and calm?

"I know Amelia Smythe is a vampire. And that you knew."

He sighs. "She's a very rich vampire, Agent."

"She's paying you?"

"Not directly." He strokes his jaw. "Do you own property, Agent Karson?"

The question blindsides me, and several seconds pass before I catch up. "I rent."

"I'd have thought you could afford something more with a nice SPEAR salary."

"I'm saving."

"Of course. So you've no idea what's happening to property prices right now. Angbec is a fast growing city. We'll soon match the capital insofar as national migration."

I sip from the mug Hozier brought me. This coffee is lovely, hot and strong and laced with sugar.

"There's a lot of money to be found in property, Agent."

"You authorized that development request from Tall Tails Ltd."

"And why shouldn't I? New homes are just what this city is begging for, and if they arrive during my term? The voting populace isn't likely to forget how well Mayor Mikkleson looked after them in their time of need."

Something hot and heavy seems to settle in my chest. "But you paid me, knowing I wanted that money to buy a house there. Why would you do that, knowing they would be demolished within the year?"

"Even the most stubborn of mules responds to a dangling carrot."

I lay my hands on the table, fingers flat. Deep breath in, another out. "Why send me after Vixen if she's so great and you're making so much money?"

His lip twists beneath the neat brush of his moustache. "I want my son back. He's a lazy waste of space, but he's still my son. Not leverage."

My fingertips itch. "But I'm a tool you can use?"

"Supernatural Prohibition, Extermination, and Arrest Regiment." He sniffs. "Things were different when I served. We knew who the bad guys were and did what we were trained for—destroy said bad guys. Now? SPEAR is a joke, a bunch of armed, arrogant children fighting fairy-tale monsters. And you're the worst hypocrite of the lot. What happened to turn you so hard against vampires? Why not the werewolves or the fae?"

I look away. "None of your business."

"No? Nothing to do with Charles?"

Everything in me seizes. My fists are on the table again, tight enough to make my palms ache.

"What happened? The reports only said so much—"

"Shut up."

Mikkleson smirks. "Touchy subject, I see."

"I said, shut up."

"Come on. Tell me what happened that got little Danika so riled up. Wrong place, wrong time?"

"Fuck you."

"I hear that's not something you'd enjoy since I don't have tits. Or fangs."

Ice floods my body.

Was *everyone* watching? How many people know about me and Rayne?

Laughing, he stands and walks towards the door.

I'm on my feet. Walking. No, running, three long strides that turn into a flying kick.

My heel strikes him in the back of the neck, propelling him forward into the door. It buckles but holds, so I kick him again, a roundhouse that snaps his head to the side. The door flies open. He falls through, grunting.

I'm after him, then crouched over him, one hand fisted in the front of his shirt.

"No—"

"Stop her—"

"What's happening—"

I hear the voices, in a distant way, but mostly I hear echoes of Mikkleson's laughter and snide tone.

"*Don't.*" One punch. "*Talk.*" Two.

Blood.

"*About.*" Three.

Cracks. Moans.

"*My father.*" Four.

Hands on my shoulders. Grabbing my arms. Pulling my hair. More wrap around my waist. Pin me to the ground.

I'm shouting now, tears blurring my vision. But I can still see Mikkleson. I can see the pulped, red mess of his nose, the wide, terrified eyes.

More yelling. Furious screams, shrill and crazed.

It's me, oh, Christ, it's me.

Then Quinn drops into view, her gun levelled at my head.

Her lips move. I can't hear her over the buzzing in my ears, but I can read the words easily enough.

"You're done, Karson. You're so, so done."

❖

My mind is wandering again. Not that there's much else for me to do in this cell beyond staring at the backs of my eyelids, pondering the new additions to my record.

Assault. Grievous bodily harm.

There's slander too, but Mikkleson will no doubt pursue that separately.

And there's the little matter of my SPEAR license.

I can't remember deciding to attack Mikkleson. Not sure I did. Can't even remember exactly what I did, just the panic in his eyes. There's blood on my top and face. Most has dried now, and the skin on my cheeks and jaw pulls in odd directions. More on my bandaged hand, which throbs in time to the thudding in my head.

My mind drifts back to Quinn, to her furious face as she glared at me over the barrel of her gun.

Her words faded in and out, so did everything else, but one thing stood out above all other sounds.

You're done, Karson. You're so, so done. You're not just grounded, you're dismissed, hear me?

I do remember screaming. Maybe that's why my throat hurts so much. My shoulders too, aching from my frantic lunge across the hallway.

You're dismissed. When the general hears about your conduct, it's over. Given the evidence, I doubt they'll even bother with a hearing. Prison, Karson.

Something wet rolls down my cheek, through the dried tracks of blood.

When I wipe it, my hands come away with crumbly pink smears.

No.

I'm not crying. I'm not.

Pacing again. Up and down, up and down, left right, left right, left right in front of the bed.

The walls blur and I wipe my face again.

Left right, left right, left right.

I reach the far corner of the cell and rest my forehead on the wall with my eyes closed. I focus on my breathing, working to bring that back under control while my hands shudder and shake. More wetness on my cheek. It slides down my jaw and off the end of my chin, splattering the cold grey floor.

I'm not crying. I'm not crying. I'm not—

A whimper bursts out of me, loud and frantic in the silence. It's followed by another, and another, and then I'm sobbing, slapping my palms on the wall while tears rack my body.

No idea how long I've been crying when the weariness of it takes me to my knees.

I'm still like that several minutes later when the door opens, and soft footsteps approach the cell.

I can *feel* someone staring.

"Why are you in supernatural containment?"

My eyes pop open. "Jack?"

He's close, forehead resting on the bars, eyes filled with concern. "When they said you'd been arrested, I figured you'd be upstairs, but they're treating you like a werewolf or vampire. What's going on?"

"How did you get in here?"

"Um…" He scrubs a hand through his hair. "I talked to one of the officers upstairs, Tina or something? She's a cute little thing and very friendly—"

I raise my hand. "Forget I asked."

"Sorry, I know we were—"

"We were what?"

He smiles, all teeth and wrinkled eye corners. "We didn't start well, sure, but I know you felt it too. The spark between us back at the restaurant."

"I'm gay." I scoot my legs round to sit more comfortably on the floor.

He stares. "What?"

"Gay. A bean flicker? Rug muncher? Todger dodger? Lesbo?"

His blank look intensifies.

"I like girls, Jack."

"No, no, I get that, I just—" He rubs the sides of his mouth. "So you're not into guys? At all?"

"Nope."

"Even a little bit?"

"Never have been."

"So when we kissed in the car park—"

"No." I raise a hand. "When *you* assaulted *me*, I used my fists instead of words. Sorry about that, but the training kicks into high gear in the presence of a threat."

"I'm a threat?"

"No."

He looks hurt. "But Teresa said—"

"Never mind what she said. Mum lives in Egypt on this one."

"What?"

"Denial, Jack. She refuses to accept the fact I'm not your traditional little homemaker, to the point that she's still setting me up on dates."

"Oh. Right." Jack tucks his hands into his pockets and rocks back and forth on his heels. "So we won't be—"

"No."

"Ever?"

"No."

"Right. Of course. Shame."

I prop my chin on my fist. "What the hell are you doing here?"

"I heard about what happened at City Hall. Then my bodyguard put me on high alert in the office, saying you'd gone rogue."

"Marco?"

His eyes widen. "So you really were there."

"Yep. Hiding in the ceiling. Heard your little chat with Vixen too, you creep."

"Wait, Vixen? Who?"

"Sorry, did I confuse you? I meant Amelia Smythe."

"From the board?" Jack rubs his mouth again. He's looking back and forth as if searching for help but there's nobody else down here. Not even the pack of cards on the table from before. "Why do you call her Vixen? What are you talking about?"

I sigh. "Give it up, okay? I know."

"Know what?"

So he wants to play the game?

"Know that she's been funnelling money into Clear Blood for the last few years and that she's guiding your research and development. Looks like she learned about your little junkie habit too. Is that why you wear all that make-up? Hiding bites, scars, and bruises?"

Jack hurries up to the bars. "Keep your voice down, please."

"What I don't know is what *she's* getting out of it. Marco clearly reports to her, so she must be getting information from the Foundation, but the rest? Her nest, maybe? Come on, tell me, it's not like I can use the intel any more. What's she buying? Fake FIDs for her soldiers? Or maybe you're sending her blood on the side when she can't get hold of enough humans."

"I have no idea what you're talking about. Clearly you're upset but—"

"I'm a hell of a lot more than upset."

"Okay, you're angry, but let me help."

"Pippa adores you. Wonder if she'd feel the same knowing she works for a two-faced crook." My vision blurs again and I spin away to face the bed.

I won't cry. Not in front of this prick.

"Danika…"

"Get out."

"But I can help you. I have connections—I know the type of person you are. I can vouch for you. Maybe I can—"

"I said, get out."

His steps retreat. Then return. "You won't tell anybody about... y'know? Not that there's anything wrong with it, but I don't want people to get the wrong idea, especially while the election is on and—"

"Get out, Jack. Get out. Get out, get out, get out."

Running footsteps. The door slams.

Alone. Again.

The tears fall faster than ever.

CHAPTER TWENTY-TWO

Early evening. Must be, by now. Someone brought food a while ago, but I've seen more appetizing slicks of puke on the paving slabs outside. It comes with another bottle of water and a plastic knife, fork, and spoon wrapped in a slightly damp napkin.

I drink the water and tuck the plastic utensils into the back of my waistband. Nothing like the comfort of my gun or stiletto, but better than nothing.

Tina's back, sitting against my cell with her back to the bars. Each time I sniff or whimper, she graciously faces forward and keeps talking.

She chatters about everything and nothing, her boyfriend, their attempts for a baby, the trials and tribulations of house buying, even the latest series on TV, some fantasy show about a woman with three pet dragons. Nonsense. Even civilians know dragons were wiped out by the Romans.

When she stops, silence falls again, but for the echo of my own sniffles.

What would Mum say now? After all this time? She'll probably be pleased to see me out of the job. Now I'd be free to join a sewing class, be an attractive young woman, and find myself the perfect gentleman boyfriend.

"What's so funny?"

I look up. Hadn't realized I'd laughed aloud. "Just thinking about my family."

"Have you spoken with them yet?"

"No."

She frowns. "They don't know you're here? Does anyone?" When I shake my head, she stands and tugs a mobile from her pocket. "You're not a supernatural. You can make a call if you want. Is there anyone you want to speak to? Solicitor?"

I trudge up to the bars. Who the hell would I call at a time like this? I have a solicitor, of course, SPEAR gave me one, but the last thing I want right now is to speak to my mother. Although...

Tina hands over the phone and steps away to give me space as I dial.

It rings three times.

"Phillipa Karson, who's calling, please?"

My breath catches in my throat.

For several seconds I can't speak.

"Hello? Are you there? I can hear you breathing." My sister grows increasingly agitated. "Are you being gross? Do I need to call the police?"

"Pip?"

"Danika?"

I don't bother to wipe the tears this time. "It's so good to hear your voice."

"What have you done now?"

The question drags a laugh out of me. "Why do you assume I've done something?"

"Haven't you always?"

"Well, I *have* been arrested and charged with GBH, if that's what you mean." I raise my hands as if to calm her squeal of alarm. "I'm fine, but I might have broken Mikkleson's arm. And nose. And jaw."

"Mikkleson? As in the mayor?"

"Busy day. Anyway, he's a bad guy. I was doing my job. Kinda."

Pippa gasps. "I hate your job." Her voice is rough, almost a shout, so unlike her that I stare at the phone in alarm.

"Pip—"

"I hate it, Dani, so much. All those monsters out there and most of them aren't even *edane*. If something happened to you, I wouldn't cope. I don't want you to miss..." She sniffs. "Why are you always getting in trouble?"

Can't help but smile at that. "I'm good at it. Anyway, trouble usually means I'm doing something right." I open my mouth to tell her more, to explain that I'm suspended and probably up for dismissal, but I can't do it.

Somehow, saying it out loud will make it real.

"Where are you?" Pippa saves me from the pause by breaking in again.

"Supernatural holding unit at the police station. I'll be here a while too, so will you feed Norma for me and give her some fuss?"

"Who?"

I touch my forehead. "Norman's a girl, who knew?"

"I thought you did. I thought you were being weird, like when you named the hamster *Fangs*."

"I was nine."

"Your point?" Her laughter fades to a sigh. "Mum'll go crazy, you realize? Can't believe you called me instead of her."

"Why the hell would I waste my one phone call speaking to her?"

"She's only a pain because she loves you."

My eyes sting again. "I know. Keep her inside, will you? Away from all those *edane* restaurants and bars she likes so much. There's a bounty on me, and I'm not sure how safe it is for you guys right now."

"Dani…" Sniffing. A rough honk as she blows her nose. "What about you? Are you okay?"

"I'm fine."

"Promise?"

I tighten my grip on the phone. "Promise, Pip. On my locs, okay? On my locs and hope to trim."

Another snuffling nose blow. "You haven't said that since we were kids."

"I mean it. Anything happens to me, I'll cut off every one."

"I don't want you to cut your hair."

"Me neither."

"Good. Call me when you're out."

The line dies and I hold the phone to my chest with my eyes closed.

❖

Tina finds me that way, clearing her throat to catch my attention. "Everything okay?"

"It will be." Though as I hand the phone back, part of me acknowledges I'm not sure that thought is true.

"I need to go now. Will you be okay?"

"Sure. Can't get into any more trouble now." I smile.

She doesn't. "I-I'm really sorry. I know what being a SPEAR means to you and—"

"I'm fine. Really. Thanks for being so kind."

"Least I can do for the agent who saved my life. And if there's anything else I can do…"

I nod, hoping this time that my smile is more convincing. Probably not, but she does nod and walk out, leaving me once again with no company but the screaming in my head.

❖

I'd be bored but I'm too wired.

No one has been down since Tina, and though that can't be more than an hour ago, the minutes drag.

I find myself thinking about Rayne.

The sun must have set by now. That means she'll be up and about.

Where? What is she doing? Thinking? Feeling? Does she know how sorry I am?

A rustle by the door draws my attention.

Rayne stands there, staring, pale eyes hot and intense. "Danika?"

I sit up on the bed. "Is that really you?"

She smiles. "Hi."

I'm up in an instant, running to the bars. I hit them hard, but the pain is nothing to the joy at seeing Rayne safe.

She grips my hands, squeezes my fingers. "I came as soon as I heard. I'm sorry. I should never have left. You needed me. I promised to help but I ran and now you're here and—"

I jerk my hands free and grab her chin. When the words stop, I kiss her, hard, long, and desperate. "I'm the one who should be sorry. I was awful to you, I said horrible things."

"It's okay."

My fingers run up through her hair, tousling it. Still soft and silky, though now it smells less like her vaguely lemony scent and more like ash and dirty water. "Where have you been?"

"I…" She looks away. Clears her throat. "I'm not really sure. I wandered around a lot last night, but I could feel the sun coming. It was going to catch me, so I…"

"What? What did you do?"

The points of her fangs are tiny right now, the barest hint of sharpness against the rest of her teeth. "I burrowed into the silt at the bottom of the river. Not great, but better than burning to death."

"So these clothes…?"

"I borrowed them."

The way she says borrowed makes me think of the way folklore speaks of dark fae *borrowing* human children.

I clear my throat.

She winces. "I stole them."

Clearly I'm a bad influence on this woman.

Then again, the neck of her top scoops low and reveals cleavage I never knew she had. Dark jeans nip close at a high waist and hug her slender legs all the way down into tall black boots. She wears a jacket too, long and denim.

In fact, she looks like me.

"Is...do I look bad?"

"No. Hell, no. You look amazing."

She beams and my heart skips.

I pull again and she follows my grip, closer and closer to the bars, until her cheeks press against the metal.

"There's blood on you. Did someone hurt you? Why are your knuckles bruised? There's a graze on your forehead too, how did you—"

"Mikkleson came to see me while I was being interviewed. I may have lost my temper."

Rayne leans closer, brushing her nose up and down the side of my cheek. The gesture is vaguely feline and sends a quiver of something electric up and down my spine to end with a fizzing shock in my groin.

"You smell awful," she continues, "but all I can think is how glad I am you're safe. I dreamed about you."

Her skin on mine is doing weird things to my concentration. Like, obliterating it. "Hmm?"

"While I was out for the day. I dreamed of you in trouble, men all around, shooting, shooting, shooting. You couldn't get away. I tried to help, but I was trapped in place, I couldn't move. You were dying and I was helpless to stop it."

"Uh-huh."

Her nose moves across my cheek and to my mouth. An instant later she tilts her head and whispers against my lips, "You're not listening to a word I'm saying."

I kiss her again. Can't help it. I crush my lips to hers and taste her sweet, sweet taste, elated and confused all at once. How has she done this to me? And so fast? And why am I running with it?

Rayne pulls back, grinning wide.

I pull myself back together with a shake of the head. "Vampires don't dream."

"I did."

"So you weren't dead?"

She shrugs.

I've learned more about vampires from spending two days with Rayne than I managed throughout the entire span of my SPEAR training. If vampires can dream during the day, we've got it so wrong.

I lean it for another kiss, but Rayne is halfway across the room.

"Damn it, don't do that, I can't—"

She puts a finger to her lips. "Someone's out there."

"Probably another copper come to gawk. How did *you* get in, anyway?"

Another one of those meltingly hot grins. "Vampire."

Of course.

"And I came to get you out. We need to stop Vixen."

That name brings back the last few hours like a punch to the tits.

"Can't help you."

She walks back to me. "What are you saying?"

I bite my lip. Again my eyes prickle, but this time anger keeps the tears at bay. "Quinn suspended me. Probably because of what I did to Mikkleson, but mostly because she's a hateful, up her own arse bitch-face."

"But those people...the nest."

I sit on the bed. "Think about it, Rayne. This has only been allowed to happen at all because Mikkleson is in Vixen's pocket. Do you really think he'll allow me out to catch her? She'd be executed without doubt and he'd lose everything."

"But—"

"I gave everything to become a SPEAR. When I was little, I'd watch that fantasy TV show about the vampire hunter and all her friends in high school. Just silly American teenage stuff, but it meant something."

"Danika." Rayne clings to the bars, her expression haunted.

"Girls at school decided I was weird and made those years hell for me. Didn't help that I wouldn't play the chase-and-kiss games with them. Or that when I did, I only wanted to kiss the girls."

I drag my hands through my hair. "Mum wanted me to do ballet and horse riding, can't tell you how much we argued over that. So I got a paper round and bought taekwondo classes. Then kendo. Then capoeira."

"You're amazing."

Though the words are probably supposed to comfort me, they only make it worse. "I've put everything into this job, my body, my mind, my soul. I've been bitten, scratched, crushed, stretched, and stabbed. I learned six dead languages just to communicate with *edane* civilians. I even accepted I was never going to have a family, not the way I was always raised to know it. And now, because of Vixen and Mikkleson and everyone else, I've lost it all."

"So you're giving up?"

Loud shouts from beyond the door save me from having to answer.

There's something familiar about the voice, the high, slightly manic screeching of it.

Rayne gives me a panicked glance.

I shrug.

She bends her knees, then vaults upward out of sight.

Again I try to place the voice.

Ah. Of course.

Two seconds later the door to the holding area opens, and there's my mother, fighting off the desperate grip of a pair of officers.

CHAPTER TWENTY-THREE

Y ou can't stop me seeing my baby—how dare you. Do you know who she is? My Danika is the best SPEAR in the country, and you've locked her up like an animal." When one of the officers opens his mouth, Mum bulls straight over him. "Get me your supervisor. The sergeant or the inspector. I want to speak to someone in charge right now and—"

"Mum?"

She pauses mid-rant, one arm raised high. "Danika! Look at the state of you. What happened?"

"Bad night."

"Why are your eyes red? Have you been smoking?"

I can only imagine how I look: unshowered, bleary-eyed, and blood splattered. The back of my top is shredded too, thanks to that crazed werewolf from City Hall. And there's my bandaged hand.

"Smoking? Seriously?"

"Have you?"

"No. I've been working."

She swells; it's like watching a balloon inflate. "Working. But you're covered in blood. And what about your clothes, did you get mauled? Why is your hand bandaged like that?"

"Mum, calm. You sound like Pippa."

"Because I'm worried about you," she snaps.

"I'm fine."

"No, you're not, you're a state. Have you eaten?"

I have to think about that. "Not for ages, I—"

She yanks a plastic box from her handbag and shoves it sideways through the bars. "Here."

One of officers tries to intercept, but the look she gives him makes even me draw breath. His companion drags him off to the side, and both stay well back.

Inside the box, two foil wrapped packages and a plastic bottle of something red and thick.

For one horrified moment, I wonder if she's brought me blood. Then I pop the lid and the scent of cinnamon drifts out. And cloves. Ginger. Hibiscus flower. And…rum?

I stare.

She winks.

The first square of foil contains chicken, seared crispy and still warm. The taste, as I sink my teeth in, is heavenly, all chilli spice, black pepper, and jerk seasoning. My third present is a serving of fritters— delicious salty cod fried in batter, studded with red peppers, onions, and even more seasoning.

I could cry.

Of all the meals and snacks Mum makes from her time before reaching England, this is my favourite.

"Dani?"

I choke on a lump of chicken and swallow hard to get it down. "Pip?"

She's standing in the doorway, small and wary, watching me eat. I hadn't seen her arrive. Though Mum does have a tendency to steal the show.

"I'm sorry, I tried to keep her away, but—"

"It's okay. I should have known."

A pause. "I fed Norma. She's fine but worried about you. She flew out the door and took off before I could catch her."

"Bloody thing." I roll my eyes. "Hope she's okay."

"Are *you* okay?" A small step closer. "Upstairs they said…" Tears glisten in her eyes. "Assault?"

"Would it help if I said he deserved it?"

"A little." She smiles, though the tears don't stop and her shoulders buck. "What's happening? Jack rang me a while ago, he was so upset and—"

"*He's* upset?" Half chewed fragments of cod fly from my lips. "He's part of the reason I'm in this mess."

"No." Mum cuts across me. "Don't you dare blame him for your mistakes."

I freeze, mouth full. "But—"

"No." She extends her finger, not quite pointing, but using it like a baton. "You think I don't get it? I *know* you, baby, and while I don't understand why, I know relationships frighten you. But throwing around dangerous accusations to avoid him is low, even for you."

"Mum—"

"I thought I'd finally found someone for you. Even you couldn't possibly find fault with a local MP and respected chemist. But now you have this mad conspiracy theory about vampires and blackmail?"

"It's not a theory."

"Do you have any idea what you've done to Phillipa? Jackson's her boss, in case you forgot. She's been up all night and most of the day, worrying about you, feeding your disgusting lizard pet. How can you be so selfish, with her in such a fragile condition?"

"Fragile? From a cold?"

"You are so—"

Pippa darts across the room, hair bobbing as she swerves around the table. "It's okay, Mum."

"It isn't. How's she going to be a responsible aunt if this is how she acts?"

The food slips from my hands. "What?"

Mum glares. "I thought this might help you grow up, but apparently not."

Questions dart through my mind, faster, faster, and the whole time, Pippa stands in front of my cell, clinging to the bars with tears streaming down her cheeks.

Even the two officers are frozen, watching us from the corner like a live episode of some tacky soap.

"What the hell is she talking about? Pip?"

"I've tried to tell you. I nearly did when you came for your shots." She lowers her head. "It's why I suggested dinner, but I was too ill to go. Then I was going to tell you at breakfast, but you never came. I would have told you on the phone, but I wanted to see your face when you heard the news."

My knees feel like whipped cream. "You're pregnant? When?"

"Three weeks. I found out two days ago."

"Pip." My voice cracks. "That's amazing."

Her head snaps up, face brightening. "Really?"

"Yeah, it's what you want, isn't it? This is good news?"

A nod.

"Then, yes. You're going to be a fantastic mother."

She sighs, and only then is it plain how scared she's been. "That means a lot."

I want to hug, her but the bars and my knees have other ideas. I perch on the bed and give my first real smile in hours. "Of course. How the hell could you be anything but incredible? You're such a kind and amazing person. Do you know what it is yet?"

"At three weeks?" She giggles.

"So, no?"

"Adam doesn't want to know and I agree. We want the surprise."

"Smart. That should stop your crazy friends from burying you in blue or pink babygrows." I rub my nose on my sleeve. "You do know I'm going to buy this kid the most badass outfits I can find? None of that fluffy bunnies and squishy elephants shit. This kid is getting skulls, crossbones, and a sword as soon as I can get Link to craft one the right size."

Pippa laughs.

Mum glowers. "So you do care about family." Her voice is glacial.

My heart twists and the tiny hairs on the back of my neck lift in response.

In that moment, I'm nine again, listening to her lecture me about low grades and fights with the girls in my class. And the boys. Fast-forward a few years and that same tone would remind me how weak I was compared to men, and that women don't fight. Mothers shouldn't risk themselves day and night fighting monsters. I could never be a SPEAR.

But I'm not nine any more.

I measure my tone to match hers. "I've always cared about family."

"Could have fooled me. You've done nothing but resist since you were a teenager, ignoring, insulting, or injuring every young man I find for you. Don't you want to be happy?"

My ears prickle with heat. "Of course I do."

"Then let me help. Find a nice man, get out of that cramped flat, and be the best you can be."

I grit my teeth. "I don't need a man to be the best I can."

"It will help." She waves a hand to indicate my whole body. "Phillipa never put me through this. She found Adam without my help and now she's expecting a baby. What have you done?"

"Me? Let's recap." I hold up my hands and tick off points on my fingers. "I've hunted vampires, tamed werewolves, and negotiated peace deals with ancient daemon tribes. I've sweated, cried, and bled for Angbec, which would probably be some dark nightmare apocalypse town if not for me and my agents. I've travelled to lost temples, abandoned cities, and cold ruins for the sake of research and knowledge, the stuff that keeps people like you alive. I've given everything to protecting the people from the dangers all around because I'm one of the few that can. I'm pretty happy with that. What the hell have *you* done?"

Stunned silence.

Soft, sibilant breathing from Pippa. Her eyes are round and wild, as if she knows what's coming. She shakes her head, mouthing, "No, no, no, no," under her breath.

Mum glares, jaw tensed and tight. "But you're capable of so much more. With a husband you could—"

"I don't want a husband." My voice rises. I can't believe she's doing this again. Now of all moments.

Snort. "Of course you do. Every young woman wants a nice man. Why should you be any different?"

"Because I fuck women!"

This time the silence is thick enough to become its own entity. I can feel it beside me, tall, wide, and heavy.

"Mum…" Pippa tries to cut in. She grabs Mum by the arm and tries to steer her away from the cell bars.

I shake my head. This has been too long in coming. "I've told you a dozen times. It's not a phase, Mum. I'm not testing or exploring anything. I know full well who and what I am. I like girls."

"But…"

"But what? I'm human and red-blooded, and one of those men would have caught my interest by now."

She looks like there's something stuck in her throat. Something thick, spiky, and bitter. "That's not possible."

"Mum, calm down. Think this through." Pippa still clings to her arm, still fights to get her away from the cell.

I sigh. "Pip, it's okay."

She frowns. "It's not—"

"You said all along I should put my foot down." A shrug. "You know I like to pick my moments."

"You?" Mum's voice hits new levels of shrill. She whirls on Pippa with her hand raised, and for a terrifying second, I'm worried she might slap her. "You encouraged this?"

Pippa stutters, one hand wrapped about her middle, the other clutching her throat. "I…it…there's nothing to encourage. It's the truth and—"

"The truth is that your sister is a sexual delinquent and you should be helping me fix it."

Boy, these bars are cold beneath my hands. Immovable. Probably for the best, given the itching in my knuckles. "I don't need fixing."

Mum steps sideways, away from Pippa. And me. "Family is all we have. You said you wanted a family."

"I still do."

"And how will you do that with—" She slaps both hands to her mouth. "Have you had sex with a woman?"

"Yes, I have."

I can all but see her mind skimming through Bible passages, picking out the ones telling me how deep into hell I'm about to fall.

"How many?" Her nose wrinkles.

I try to count and fail after thirteen. "A few."

Mum starts to pace. Her hands are shaking, her shoulders stiff, every step rough and jerky. "I can't believe this. How can this be? I did everything right, I gave you everything, all the love I had. How could you end up…"

"Gay? Mum, it's not a crime, it's not a reflection on you. It's what I am."

"What you are is deluded. I should have known. You took it so badly when Charles died. You were never the same after that. Is it because you were lacking a strong father figure? Did you need that masculinity in the house?"

"Mum—"

"I should have tried harder. There were plenty of nice boys at that church back in Cipla, maybe they could have caught you before you became this…this—"

This time when I slap the bars, the loud clang cuts her off.

"I didn't *become* anything. I've been telling you for years, but you won't listen. I may have taken a few years to figure it out, but I was born this way. You don't spontaneously convert after a traumatic life event."

"I think we need to calm down and take a breath." Again Pippa tries to intervene. "Mum, why don't you—"

"You." Mum points a trembling finger at Pippa. "This is as much your fault as it is her insanity."

"Hey." I punch the bars this time. "Don't you dare talk to her like that."

"Why? She's as bad as you. She's—"

"She's the only person who ever listened to me after Dad died." The words are on my lips and gone before I can catch them, but now that they're free, a weight seems to lift off my chest. "All you cared about was family, but you don't know what family is."

"I'm one of six children."

"It's not about how many brothers and sisters you have, or how many children you squeeze out before your ovaries shrivel." I grip my hair. "Family is sharing. Listening. Loving. Family is putting up with crazy phone calls at two in the morning to talk about the latest martial arts movie. It's supporting, even when you don't understand why. Family is standing up for your sister. Family is believing your daughter when she says, *This is me.*"

Pippa hurries back to my cell. She shoves her hands through, and I copy, flinging my arms around her the best I can manage. It's a cold, strained, and awkward hug around those wrist-thick bars. It's also the most loving I've ever experienced.

"I love you, Dani."

I smile. Squeeze her shoulders. "*You* are my family, Pip, and I love you, so, so much."

We pull away, tearful and sniffing, each reaching out to wipe the other's eyes like when we were kids. Like when we stood beside Dad's closed casket, longing to open it, but afraid to try.

"I love you too, baby." Some of the ice has melted from Mum's voice. Her expression remains stony, but there's sadness too. "It's love that makes me want the best for you."

"Best for *me* isn't what was best for *you.*"

"But—"

"No. This is what I am: a foul-mouthed, gun-wielding, high-kick-flinging SPEAR agent who happens to dig chicks. Accept that or don't, but stop saying you love me. *Show* me."

Silence but for shuffling from the two officers at the back of the room.

"Fine." Mum squares her shoulders and tilts her chin. "Fine." A sharp spin on her heel and she's marching away.

I flinch. "Mum?"

She doesn't stop, or even turn. At the door, after a fractional hesitation, she stalks through.

"Shit." My eyes tingle again. "Oh God. No, no, no, what have I done? Pip?"

She touches my fingers through the bars. "What you should have done years ago. I'm so proud of you."

"But Mum—"

"Will get over it. However it feels right now, she loves us."

I nod, like a bloody puppet. "Her eyes...she hates me."

"Never." A last, reassuring smile. "I've got to go after her. See you soon, okay?"

I open my mouth, but the words are stuck, leaving me to watch my sister hurry across the room and out the door.

CHAPTER TWENTY-FOUR

After the officers leave, Rayne drops from the ceiling. Her eyes are wide and round, her lips slightly parted. "Are you okay?"

"I don't know."

The remnants of my chicken and fritters lie beside the bars of the cell. The bottle close by.

I open it and try to avoid the wave of familiar scents. No use. The smell and everything about it speaks of home. I drink anyway, three long swallows that burn my throat.

My head spins. The sorrel is strong and sweet, laced with more rum than I'm used to.

Perfect.

"I'm sorry, Danika."

I lower the bottle. Burp.

Angry responses hang on the end of my tongue but I drag them back. Can't keep using her as a punchbag for my emotions.

"You're hurting," she murmurs.

Shrug. "Nothing new there."

"You don't have to pretend with me. I won't judge you for a moment of vulnerability."

"Thanks."

She approaches the bars. "Your mother will come around. I know you can't see or hear what I do, but her heart was going crazy. And her scent—she's confused and scared."

"Of what?"

"Lots of people fear what they don't know. Or change. With you arrested and your sister pregnant, it's a big piece of news you dropped."

"Not if she had accepted it when I was twelve."

"Danika—"

"I don't want to talk about this." Another swig from the bottle.

"You prefer getting drunk?"

"Yeah, cheers, a great idea."

"What about Vixen? We still need to—" She's off again, back by the door and listening.

Whatever.

I return to the bed and sit with my back propped against the wall, legs up and folded at the ankle. I have enough sorrel to get me pleasantly sloshed, then maybe I can go back to sleep. Not much else to do.

"Something's happening." Rayne's voice quivers. "There's shouting."

"Maybe the doughnuts and coffee have arrived."

She casts me a bemused look. "I'm serious, there's screaming and things breaking. I think there's a fight."

Glug. Burp. "Definitely doughnuts then."

Rayne flinches, one hand slapped to her mouth. "Was that a gunshot?"

"Here? Unlikely." I wave the bottle. "Check, if you're so worried. But don't think they'll thank you for it."

Rayne's expression is one I've never seen on her, a terrible blend of anger, frustration, and…disappointment?

I look away.

"You're better than this. Giving up? I didn't think you knew how. All that stuff you said to your mother, was that a lie?"

"No, but—"

"Then pull yourself together while I check what's happening." She opens the door. "I'll be right back."

I stick out my tongue with a soft *nyah-nyah* sound.

Already my body is warm from the rum, and the spicy taste tingles on my tongue. The bottle is half empty, and I know it won't take long to get through the rest, even for me. I don't drink a lot, but when I do…

My mind drifts back to the first time I got drunk. Must have been thirteen, feeling sophisticated and grown up with alcopops and shandies. My first major crush and I sat on a park bench, swigging from bottles wrapped in plastic bags. She was fifteen and used to drinking, occasionally pausing to laugh at my slurred words and wobbly legs.

Our kiss on that bench was sweet and clumsy, wonderful, until my last shandy made a reappearance in her mouth.

The door opens hard enough to slam into the wall. Through it runs Sergeant Hozier, screaming and gibbering.

❖

"Attack...blood everywhere...they're dead—Vampires came... can't get out." The plain-clothes sergeant crashes into the table and topples over it, landing on his face in an untidy sprawl.

Ha, idiot.

"Agent Karson?" He crawls to my cell. "Help us."

I show him the bottle. "Sorry, no agent here."

"Stop mucking about—you have to help." He fumbles for the keys to the door of my cell. It opens with a creak. "Please. There's dozens of them, all fighting, too many. We can't fight."

A dark blur streaks through the door and skids to a stop near the table.

A woman. Redhead. Pretty.

"Oh. Shit."

Fangs. Eyes gleaming silver and long nails dripping blood.

She snarls and Hozier whimpers like a child. He scrambles to get behind me, but there's no space on the bed.

"Please. Do something. You have to." The pleas turn to screams as the vampire grabs his ankle and drags him from the cell. He kicks and scrabbles at the ground, but there's no way he's escaping.

Calm settles on me.

So this is a vampire attack from the civilian side.

The screams grow louder, punctuated by sobs and frantic pleas. "Help me. Help, please. Why are you standing there? Help."

The vampire smirks. "She can't help. She'll die, you'll die, you'll all die. Angbec is ours."

Through the fog of sorrel, I realize I'm unhappy with the sound of that. We'll *all* die? Like Quinn? Mikkleson? No loss there, but *everyone*? So Wendy? Noel? Mum? Pippa? Rayne?

I sit straight. The world rocks left and right, but a few hard blinks seem to steady things.

"Do something," Hozier shrieks. "You're a SPEAR."

"Not any more."

The vampire drops her prey and turns to me instead. Her smile is wide, her teeth glistening. "Idiot." She steps into the cell. "SPEAR is for life. Until we kill you."

She dives.

I push off the wall and slide down the bed to the floor.

The vampire crashes head first into the wall, growling and snarling. "I'll kill you."

"You'll try."

Another grab, this time at the top of my head. A roll saves me from the worst of it, but my locs catch on her fingers, igniting searing pain in my scalp. When I turn, two long strands of my hair hang from her grip.

"Bitch." Even I can hear the slur in my voice, but it doesn't stop me yelling. "Not my hair. Not my fucking hair."

I make fists and run at her, meaning to crush the smirk off her slobbering lips.

Instead, a single shove sends me flying, through the cell door and into the table, which promptly collapses under my weight. Nails, fragments of wood, and bent screws fly out in all directions, and my head sings with its impact against the floor.

Hozier scrambles towards the door. He trips on a piece of table and lands on his face. Blood streams from his nose.

The vampire steps from the cell, nostrils flaring. "Mm. Dinner."

I'm up again, splintered table leg in hand. As the creature approaches, I pull my arms back and swing it like a baseball bat.

The attempt flies wide, robbing my balance.

"*You're* a SPEAR?" She laughs. "Pathetic."

"Screw you, fanger." I swing again.

Crack. Grunt.

Small chips of something white fly across the room.

She clutches her mouth. "Bitch." Her snarl shows off the three gaps in her teeth.

I choke on a snort of laughter and wag my finger at her. "No more apples for you, young lady."

She blurs at me. Hard hands close over my wrist and throat and squeeze.

The table leg falls. I gag. My legs kick uselessly, two feet off the ground.

"Think you're funny? Think you're so strong and clever? I don't need those teeth to make a meal of you."

My free hand flails, curving round to punch again and again at her grinning face. May well have hit a brick wall.

The fifth punch strikes her cheek and she jerks her head left. Pain spears through my palm and fingers as she bites.

Three of my fingers go numb.

"You taste good, little SPEAR."

The pain makes me dizzy, but it clears the brain fug. I can think.

Her fingers dig into my throat, choking off my air.

Another thirty seconds and I'll pass out.

What can I do? What do I have?

I pat down my ribs. Hips. Waist. My fingers brush the handle of a plastic fork.

Plastic, useless against vampires, unless...

I swing it round, hard and fast, aiming for her face.

"No. No you don't." She sways out of reach then lowers her mouth.

Fresh agony lances through my shoulder.

I scream. Try to.

Bright colours dart before my eyes. The world tips and dips.

But she's not moving now. Distracted.

Again with the fork, angled high, driven hard.

The tines plunge into her right eye socket. Pop. Warm liquid spurts over my fingers.

More screams, not mine.

The hand on my throat flexes and I'm free, stumbling, coughing, wheezing.

Can't stop. Seconds to use. Maybe less.

I drop to the floor and fumble through the table shrapnel for another leg. My shoulder shrieks a complaint but I force myself on. On past the pain. On past the dizziness.

There.

My hand closes around it just as a steel-like grip surrounds my ankles.

It drags me back. My head bounces off the floor like a tennis ball.

The vampire stands above me, furious and bleeding, the fork still protruding from her eye. "I'll kill you slow," she whispers. "I'll take you back to the nest and make it last for weeks. You'll beg me to die."

I throw the chair leg, but she bats it aside with a careless swipe of her hand.

"Please. I'm faster than you, stronger. You can't beat me without all your little toys."

Again she bends over me, straddling my waist. She forces my wrists to the ground above my head.

I'm pinned.

Trapped.

Pissed.

"How does it feel to lose?" She leans close. The end of the fork brushes my cheek. "How does it feel, knowing you're about to die?"

I watch. Steady myself. Wait. "No idea."

She hesitates. "You—"

I turn my head, mouth open, and catch the bobbing fork between my teeth. A jerk rips it free of her eye socket.

The vampire rears forward, elated and confused, and I turn again.

Gooey, bloodied fork tines sink into her left eye, driven deep by her momentum.

Another pop and slicks of clear gunge slide down the plastic.

I let go. So does she, throwing herself back while clutching at her face.

"Bitch," she screams, rolling on the floor. "Bitch, bitch, bitch. I'll kill you. I'll skin you. I'll snap off your fingers for crudités."

I let her roll and pick through the debris for another shard of wood.

A long piece with a jagged end fits neatly in my hand.

By the time I turn back, she's removed the fork and lies flat on her back. Her face is a sticky red ruin, but already her right eye seems to be healing.

"I see you," she hisses. "I see you."

"Good. How's my hair?" I kick her in the face. Her fangs scrape hard against my bare sole, but that minor pain is nothing to the satisfaction of hearing several more bones crack.

She screams.

I lift the makeshift stake. Strike.

Black ooze spurts from the wound, a thick, sticky shower that coats my head and shoulders in stinking gunk.

The vampire thrashes left and right, her single working eye narrowed in fury. Then her hands and face begin to decay, more black ichor oozing from every available hole on her body, including the two fresh ones.

Seconds later, her body is a stinking puddle of ooze, atop a pile of clothes.

I drop to my knees beside the remains and lower my head. That was hard.

❖

A hand grips my shoulder. I turn, fist raised, but it's only Hozier, smiling, pale as snow, but alive.

"You saved me. She would have killed me—I was going to die."

"Chill, you're fine now."

"Because of you. That was incredible. How did you know the fork would hurt her?"

"I didn't, it—"

"You're amazing. I'd be dead if not for you. You're an incredible agent."

"I'm a disgrace."

His fingers tighten on my shoulder. "No, you're the best and I owe you. SPEAR is lucky to have you."

My back straightens. "I...thanks. I guess." I pat his hand and heave a sigh as Rayne re-enters.

She takes one look at the carnage, then streaks across the small space. She slides to her knees in front of me and captures my cheeks between her hands. The kiss she offers me is long and desperate, mingled with the truly awful taste of vampire innards.

I pull back. "Hey, Rayne."

"I'm sorry. I didn't know—I would have been here, but they...and I followed, but they took—"

I touch her cheek. "I'm fine. I dealt with it."

"I should have been with you."

"Why? You think I can't take care of myself?"

Her frantic apologies cut short. "No, I—" A moment later she spots my smile. "You can more than take care of yourself. I just don't want you hurt." Her lips part and a glimmer of silver flickers through her eyes. "You're bleeding."

"I'm okay."

"You smell incredible."

Slowly, I ease my hands away. "What's going on up there?"

The dreamy look vanishes from Rayne's eyes, replaced by her usual timid one. She stares at her hands. "I tried, please believe me. It's why I wasn't here. I tried so hard."

"What are you talking about?"

"Vixen. She sent her vampires. They wanted you but didn't expect so much resistance."

"Civvie bashers held their own, did they?"

"I helped. But there's lots injured. Even Mayor Mikkleson."

Something about her tone tightens a noose around my lungs. "And who else? Who else got hurt?"

"Your sister." Finally, she lifts her gaze to mine. "They took Pippa."

CHAPTER TWENTY-FIVE

I've never been more relieved to have a shower. Never been happier to stand beneath a stream of water, even cold and drizzly like this one. I put my head back and wash away the muck and grime of the last twenty-four hours.

But it's more than that.

Beneath the tepid spray, I'm washing away hate, fear, anger, and pain. The disgusted expression on my mother's face sloshes down the drain at my feet. Quinn's triumphant grin joins Mikkleson's smug taunting, swirling into the plughole with a gulp and a gurgle.

I'm done with it. I'm clean. I'm fresh. I'm me.

A knock on the door draws my attention. Rayne enters without waiting and holds up a heavily stuffed carrier bag. "I borrowed some clothes."

"Borrowed?"

Her smile is forced. "Would you prefer to put those back on?" She points to my old clothes, piled in a stinking heap beside the shower cubicle. The vampire's dying ooze has already dried to a thick grey crust.

"Borrowed is fine." I step out of the shower.

The towel provided is brown and coarse, barely wide enough to go around my hips. Doesn't matter, I've no plans to sit and wait for my hair to dry.

As I pat myself down, Rayne watches me, her gaze hungry, lips slightly parted.

"You're beautiful," she whispers.

Heat flushes my body. My hands shake as I rub the towel across my stomach.

She steps closer. "I can hear your heartbeat." Silver flickers in her eyes. "Your breathing is…shallow."

"Can you blame me?"

Rayne plucks the towel from my hands and stalks around my body. I hold her gaze as far as possible, then close my eyes as she strokes the towel across my neck and shoulders. "We need to dress these bites."

"I'm okay."

"No, you're not. But I'll make sure you are."

The towel shifts to lower back. Lower still.

I clear my throat. "Rayne?"

"Yes?" Her lips brush the back of my neck.

"I—"

The door opens again, admitting a female officer I don't know. She frowns, then peers at me. "Agent Karson?"

"Yeah, that's me." I step away from Rayne and grab the carrier bag. "Kinda."

"We got someone up here asking for you. Hurry up, will you?" She leaves.

By the time I look back, the spell is broken. Rayne has returned to her soft, timid self and is hurrying towards the door.

"I'll wait for you out there. Maybe I can help them clean up." She's gone too.

I breathe deep and let it go slow. I know it's not the time, that I have things to do, but my skin tingles from the touch of that towel, knowing Rayne was the one to hold it. I dress quickly, jeans, boots, and a long shirt over a cropped T-shirt. The underwear doesn't fit right, so I leave it and head out.

In the corridor, that same female officer waits with two sealed evidence bags. She hands them to me before gesturing that I should follow.

"You're giving them back?"

She nods. "Right now we need you armed and ready to fight. We'll sort the red tape and admin later."

My utility belt feels great snugged around my hips again, as do the knives on my arms and legs. Sliding the stiletto back into my hair is like meeting a long-lost friend, but most important is my watch. I wrap the bulky piece of jewellery around my wrist, and only then do I feel dressed.

I make a fist, trying to ignore the tingle in my fingers. They move, but not as well as they should, and though the first aider assured me I'd eventually regain full feeling, he also insisted that I rest.

Oh, well.

The officer takes us back upstairs, along a short corridor and into a suite where the first aiders and paramedics have gathered to help those injured. In the middle of them, subdued and alone, sits my mother.

She leaps up when I enter. "Phillipa—they took her, just carried her away. What's going to happen to my baby? My little girl? How could they—"

"Mum." I grip her shoulders.

Tears stream down her face. "They took her. My girl. Why?"

I could tell her. The vindictive part of me wants to, but I can't. "It doesn't matter. I'm going to get her back."

"You can't—"

"Yes, I can. I'm not a child any more. You don't decide what I can and can't do."

"But—"

"Mum? No."

She sniffs. "Phillipa is everything. I couldn't bear if she got hurt."

With effort, I ignore the pang in my chest. "She won't."

"Promise me." Her hands close around my wrists, trembling and weak. "Promise me you'll get my baby back."

"On my locs and hope to trim. I'm a SPEAR. It's what I do."

Mum return to her seat and covers her face with her hands.

The female officer guides me to a free chair. "Let's get that shoulder and hand bandaged."

Rayne reappears while I'm getting patched up. She crouches on the floor in front of me with her head cocked. "We'll get her back."

It's all well and good making promises like that to my mother, but Rayne should know better.

We know about as much of Vixen's whereabouts as we did last night. How the hell are we going to find them?

Screams. Yells.

I dart away from the first aider still trying to bandage my hand. Those fangers aren't getting anybody else tonight. Not if I've anything to do with it.

❖

I follow the sounds, hand closing around the butt of my gun, Rayne close at my back.

Out in the offices the wreckage is absolute. Chairs overturned, tables mangled, computers, phones, and stationery all over the place. Shreds of paper litter the floor, and along the walls and carpet, there are several slicks of blood. Among the carnage, three piles of shiny black ooze dry to a cracked, gritty finish.

In the middle of it, a snarling, spitting figure drags itself across the ground by his elbows. Instead of legs, two bloodied stumps leave red smears across the carpet.

Rayne bellows, fury filling her eyes with silver.

I point the gun and fire a single shot.

The bullet thuds into the carpet, through the vampire's outstretched hand.

He shrieks, swearing and thrashing as blood pumps from the wound.

Officers scrambling to escape stop dead, swivelling to face me.

"Nobody move."

For a wonder, they obey.

I pick my way through the mess, gun steady and aimed. Right up to the struggling vampire. "Good evening, fanger."

He spits on my shoes.

I kick him in the face.

Bones crack. Blood flies.

"Let's try that again. Good evening, fanger."

"SPEAR bitch—"

Another kick. This time he moans as fangs slice through his tongue.

"I'm not in a very good mood. I'm tired, my hand hurts, and you parasites kidnapped my sister. Test me, fang boy."

He opens his mouth. I can see the indecision in his eyes. Then, "What do you want?"

"Where are your people nesting?"

A snort. "Nesting is illegal, surely *you* know that."

"So is wandering around without *edane* registration, but I bet you're doing that too. Where did your friends take my sister?"

"Dunno what you're talking about."

I fire the gun. The bullet slams into his other hand but doesn't make it all the way through.

More screams, and several of the officers gathered around me begin to whisper and mutter amongst themselves.

"Try again."

He's panting now, struggling to lift himself on mangled hands. His leg stumps wave weakly. "Go to hell."

"Sure. Care to join me?" The gun slides back into my shoulder holster, and instead, I pluck a pencil from the wreckage on the floor. "We can go now." I hold the small shaft of wood between the tips of my index fingers.

Not very long, but long enough.

His eyes widen. "You—you can't. We have rights. Trial, evidence—"

"Not today."

The muttering around me gets louder. The air is thick and heavy with anticipation.

Even Rayne, as she steps up to my side, is stiff shouldered and thin lipped. "Danika…"

"Let me do my job."

"When did torture become part of your job?"

"Right about the time these leeches took my sister."

She steps ahead of me. "Killing him won't help."

"But I'll feel better."

"He gets a trial."

"He doesn't deserve one."

"Agreed." She bites her lip. "But you're not a murderer. Are you? Because that's what this would be. He's helpless. Would you stake him now, in front of these officers? In front of me?"

"He deserves to die."

"And me?"

I inhale sharply. "You're different."

"You can't keep saying that. Why am I different? Because I'm weak? Because I kiss well? I'm a vampire too and we should all be treated the same."

I glare at my boots, watching the shiny bubbles of spit slip down the scuffed leather. "Damn it. Why do you have to be so rational?"

"One of us has to be."

I flip the pencil over my shoulder. "What now?"

"I'll talk to him."

As she bends to do exactly that, I face the officers. "Did he hurt anyone?"

Lots of shaking heads.

Tina pushes her way through the cluster of onlookers, dressed in casual jeans and trainers. She looks me up and down. "You were going to kill him, weren't you?"

I have no idea, and that bothers me more than I'd like. "What are you doing here? Didn't your shift end?"

"They called me back. Everyone's on their way in. We need the extra bodies."

"I'd say you guys did pretty well."

She scans the carnage of the office. "Five officers dead, twelve injured, three critical. That's good?"

"How many vampires?"

"Seven."

"Then yes, that's good."

Her eyes narrow. "What happens now? How do I help?"

"You don't. I call my unit."

❖

"SPEAR. Recite your name and ID." The voice at the other end of the line is coarse and mechanical.

I match it, making my words a dull monotone for the computer to recognize.

"Details not recognized. Recite your name and ID."

I repeat the information, slower this time.

A pause follows.

"Karson, Danika. Agent 20240119A05. Suspended from active duty as of—"

I slam the receiver against the unit. "No. No, you can't do this—"

"You will now be transferred to the civilian helpline."

Tina appears beside me, concerned and curious.

I turn my back and wait, trying to steady my breathing.

This can't be happening. Not now. Please, please, not now.

A click on the line.

"Good evening, this is SPEAR, my name is Cheryl, how may I direct your call?"

"I need field reinforcement, Grade Three and above, Alpha, Beta, and Gamma. Search and rescue. Target, vampires."

Cheryl, whoever the hell she is, clears her throat. "This line is for civilian queries. All agents have access to the private, encrypted line. I'm obliged to inform you that hoax calls are treated with the utmost—"

"This isn't a hoax, you dumb bitch." The phone creaks in my grip. "I'm Danika Karson, my ID is A20240119A05, and I'm telling you I need backup."

Rayne arrives at my other side. She gives a brief thumbs up.

A glance over my shoulder shows the vampire being carried away, his head hung low. No doubt he'll be placed downstairs in another of the supernatural containment units until someone from Clear Blood arrives to check him out.

Another cough from down the phone. "Ms. Karson is currently on leave and knows better than to call this number."

"Ms. Karson is currently losing her shit and needs your help. Angbec police station was just attacked."

"We've had no report of such an incident."

"Because I'm making it now."

Yet another cough. This woman needs a lozenge. "All supernatural crimes should be reported, in the first instance, through the use of the dedicated number nine-oh-nine. Please make your report through the proper channels. Goodbye."

"No, no, wait. Wait."

She's already gone.

I hurl the phone at the wall.

Rayne picks up the broken pieces and stacks them on top of the unit. She stands beside me, one hand closing around mine. She squeezes. "They're below one of the old buildings on Sertral Street, an unused bomb shelter. Call Noel. We can do this."

"Quinn won't let him anywhere near me." I fight back tears. "There's nothing he can do."

"Then let us help." This from Tina, who beckons a couple of her colleagues. Among them is Barney, plain clothes now and as grumpy as ever, though a determined glint lights his eyes.

I back away. "No. No way, you can't—"

"Why not?" Tina shrugs. "We made vows to protect and serve too."

"Vampires. *Edanes* with incredible skill, speed, and strength. You're not trained for this."

Sergeant Hozier pushes through the crowd. "I'm alive because of you." His nose is bandaged, as is his arm, but he appears otherwise unharmed. "If you need help, then please, let me give it to you."

More nods and mutters all around.

"But you can't—"

"We're don't use weapons or speak any crazy languages," Tina breaks in again, "but we can take care of ourselves. What do you think we did for a living before SPEAR came along?"

Rayne's hand tightens on mine. "What was it you said before about asking for help?" She smiles.

I stare at the gathered officers. Some are limping, more are bloodstained, all of them have the glint of steely determination burning in their eyes. Even Barney, who glares daggers, as if daring me to cut him out.

For the first time in hours, I feel a glimmer of hope. "Okay. This is what we're going to do."

CHAPTER TWENTY-SIX

This may be the first time I've ridden in a police car and not felt guilty about it.

Rayne joins me in the back, wedged between me and Tina. Up front, Hozier drives, taking directions from Barney. We're all plain clothes, with weapons, such as they are, tucked into pockets and waistbands.

I'm the only one with a gun.

As if sensing my thoughts, Rayne squeezes my knee, a simple touch but I catch myself staring. I know my expression must be totally goofy, but I can't help it. This woman...

"When we get there"—Hozier pauses for a red light—"how do you want to do this? How do we play it?"

"*We* don't. You guys are here for support and to holler in the cavalry."

"What?"

"You can't do that."

"We want to help!"

"Why do you think we came—"

"...really think you can handle this all on your own?"

"Let us *do* something."

I lift my hand. "I can't risk them turning hostile."

"So you're going alone?" Tina's voice is ice cold.

"No. Rayne's coming."

More cries of anger. Barney particularly swivels in his seat. "Her? A vampire? In case you forgot, that's who we're going after."

"I didn't forget."

"Then why is she here? She's one of them."

Rayne stiffens beside me. Her head lowers.

I grit my teeth. "Shut up. You don't know anything about Rayne."

"I know she's dead twelve hours a day and that she'd happily suck my neck if I let her."

We share a glance.

"She comes with me, end of. Frankly, I'd trust her over you in a heartbeat."

The car rolls on.

Rayne clears her throat. "I'm sorry you feel that way, Officer Watson, but you have my word, I'll do anything and everything in my power to protect Agent Karson and everybody else."

"Even from you?" Barney doesn't look back.

"Especially from me. You're right, I *am* dangerous, but I also know the difference between right and wrong. Vixen is wrong."

"And when the blood starts to run," whispers Tina, "because it will, what will you be doing?"

Rayne's body stiffens against mine.

I hold my breath.

"I'll be kicking seven shades of shit out of anybody who tries to drink it."

A delicious tingle shoots through my body, from head to toes then back again. "Steady, Rayne. For a second there you were almost badass."

She grins. "You've told me time and again I need to be more assertive. How did I do? Was that okay? Did I sound silly?"

"Hell, no. That was good. Really, really good."

The car slows and stops in the sickly yellow light of a dying street lamp.

"Why are we here?" Barney peers out of his window. "We don't have time to hang out with addicts and boozers."

"We're getting backup." I hop out of the car.

"Backup? From this dump?"

Oh, how little he knows.

❖

This part of The Bowl is dingy, with more graffiti, more litter, and more bundles lying in doorways. Most of them contain the people I'm after, but first, I need the leader.

"Wendy? It's Danika."

Silence.

Then a rustle.

Rayne appears at my side, eyes silver, stance loose. Her hands she laces around the back of her head.

"What do you want, girl? And why the hell did you bring that thing back here?" Wendy stands from a nest of bare duvets in a doorway on the right. He has a new jacket, worn over his old ones, through which my bullet hole is clearly visible. Clean, though; Wendy has always been a proud sort.

I rest my knuckles on my hips. "I need your help."

"Is that right?"

Rayne growls.

I put my hand on her shoulder.

Wendy stops in the middle of the road. The mangled remains of a newspaper tumble across the street between us.

Feels like a cityscape Western.

"You've got more nerve than I thought. After what you did—"

"I know where the missing people are. And you were right about City Hall—Mikkleson is in it up to his neck. Jack too."

"Jackson Cobé, eh?" The old werewolf sniffs and spits at the pavement. "Pity. I liked him. He had good ideas."

I gesture to the car. "SPEAR won't help, but I've got the civvie bashers with me. We're going to end this tonight."

He snorts and turns on his heel. "Then good luck to you. Ain't no business of me or mine."

I follow, frantic now, desperate. I don't care. "Please, Wendy? Wensleydale? They have my sister and without my unit I—"

He spins around fast enough to knock me off balance. "They have Pippa?"

My mouth drops open. "How do you know her name?"

"Of course I know Pips." He looks away and his brow furrows. "She always helped when I came to the Foundation." A gentle note creeps into his voice. "Gave me clean clothes, or a toothbrush. Let me have a shower too or cut my hair. She's a good'un, that Pips...perfect she-wolf too."

Didn't think my jaw could drop any further. "How do you know she's pregnant?"

He cocks a bushy eyebrow at me. "I have a nose, girl."

Could Wendy have found out before I did?

If—no, *when* we get out of this mess, I'm going to take Pippa aside and spend a week apologizing. Maybe two.

I shake my head. "She's in trouble. Vixen has her."

Wendy growls under his breath. The bristly growth across his jaw and chin begins to lengthen. "Vixen? No. No, no, no, can't have that." He throws back his head and howls, one long haunting note like a nature documentary. Or a bad horror film.

All around us, fresh voices take up the call, and other werewolves begin to step out of doors, out of alleys, and around cars. They gather quickly, all silent and curious, watchful and deadly.

Click.

I turn. Barney has locked the car doors from the inside. Tina and Hozier seem to be arguing with him, but I can't hear through the glass.

Twenty werewolves stand around us, a mix of male and female, young and old. I look them over, then return my attention to Wendy.

"There's more of you than I realized."

He chuckles. "Worried?"

"Thrilled. The Grey Tail pack is the biggest in the city and they're not as fun as you guys. About time they had some competition."

Wendy's chest puffs out. "That pup calling himself alpha ain't strong enough for those big furry paws he's got. Me and my Dire Wolves will be branching out soon enough. Then we'll see what's what."

"Until then, may I borrow you?"

A couple of the wolves snarl, many of them focused on Rayne.

She still hasn't moved her hands, though there's tightness to her shoulders, like a coiled spring.

"And the fanger?"

I move in front of her and place my right hand around the base of my throat. "I'm Danika Karson and I vouch for Rayne...um...?"

"Just Rayne," she mutters. "Vixen renamed me when I joined the nest."

This new snippet throws me. "What's your real name?"

"That *is* my real name." Her tone suggests I drop the matter. Quickly.

Back to Wendy. "I'm Danika Karson and I vouch for Rayne. I claim her successes and her transgressions as my own and declare my willingness to offer my life as pledge for her actions."

Rayne stiffens.

Wendy frowns. "Where did you learn those words?"

"Not just a pretty face here."

"No kidding."

The wolves around him seem unsure. A couple of them back closer to him, gently touching his arm or his back.

He squares his shoulders and steps closer. Rayne growls, a sound which grows louder as he puts his hand over mine. Around my throat.

I hold my position. "Don't, Rayne."

"But he—"

"It's fine."

He tightens his grip, enough to compress my fingers. "I'm Wensleydale Gordan, alpha of the Dire Wolf pack. I accept your pledge and vow in return that if Rayne should fuck us about, I'll rip her pretty little head off. Then yours."

I laugh, but even to my ears, the sound is strained and nervous. "That's not the official response."

"It's *my* response." He releases my throat and steps back. "Until she proves otherwise, I deem Rayne as trustworthy as our pack-friend Danika Karson. Treat one as you would the other."

Murmurs. Growls.

"And if you don't like it, piss off. We'll discuss it later."

Five of the werewolves break off immediately. Four of them back away from the gathering with their heads down, exposing the backs of their necks. The last, a young male with acne-scarred skin and a nose ring, slowly and deliberately turns his back before walking away.

Wendy clenches his fists. "That boy…"

"I know." I touch his arm. "And if you don't nip it in the bud, he'll be a dick later, but right now we don't have time."

For a horrible moment I worry he's going to ignore me. Then Wendy breathes deep and turns back to me. "Fine, meat sack. Let's go get Pips." He grins.

"After you, dog breath."

CHAPTER TWENTY-SEVEN

Next stop, weapons.
    I hate the thought of giving up the location of a SPEAR safe house, but I've little choice left.

Wendy agrees to take his wolves ahead and wait for us while I take the others to see Shakka.

He's not pleased to see me.

When he attempts to slam the door, Rayne jams her foot in the narrow gap and shoves with all her might. The force catapults him into the far wall where his head cracks the plaster.

Tina and Hozier appear embarrassed and apologetic, but Barney smiles as we walk through, with a condescending glower at Shakka on the way.

I make up my mind to keep a close eye on him. Seems it's more than vampires he has a problem with.

Shakka catches up at the bottom of the stairs to the containment space. He darts ahead and stretches his arms in front of the door. "You can't do this. You can't bring civilians in here."

"They're with me."

"Even the vamp? After the way you treated her? She's from Vixen's nest."

"She *was* from Vixen's nest."

The tiny goblin hawks from the chest and spits at our feet. "You know better than that. She'll always be from Vixen's nest."

"Open the door. All we need is weapons, then we're gone."

"No deal. SPEAR pay me well—I'm too old to risk losing it all for whatever madness you're cooking."

"Saving people isn't madness."

"You're suspended."

Eye-roll. "Don't listen to gossip, Shakka. Anyway, I'm not sitting this one out. Vixen has my sister."

He snorts. "Then may she die quickly. That's the most you can hope for." He steps right.

I follow. "Vixen has dozens of unregistered vampires in her nest. She's been snatching humans off the streets to feed her followers and now she's planning something bigger. We have to stop her."

Shakka stops, one hand raised as if to fend me off. Slowly, he curls long, knobbly fingers down over his palm. "She's powerful. You can't stop her."

"Watch me."

The goblin strokes the side of his nose, rubbing the rough area covered in tough, dark scar tissue. His gaze traces his right hand and the missing middle finger. "She did this, Karson. Said she'd take a fresh piece of me every day I refused to help her."

I'd always wondered what happened to his hand. Every SPEAR has their own theory about how he lost that finger. And the chunk of his nose. And his ear.

I personally thought he'd had a scrap with a dog and was too proud to say, but this?

"What did she want?"

Shakka glares at the closed door to the holding area. His gaze skims away, across the trio of officers and Rayne, before darting back to me. "Covert access to this holding area and knowledge about all the others. She wanted SPEAR."

"When?"

"Six years ago."

A chill grips my chest. How long has Vixen been planning this?

"I escaped, but I'll never forget how she treated me." He breathes deep.

"Then help me stop her."

"You already owe me."

"Don't remind me."

He walks to the steel doors and activates the opening sequence. "If you're really going to stop her, you can clear your debt in one move."

"Which is?"

"Kill her. Tear that bitch up and wash the ooze into the sewer."

The doors swish open.

At the far end, the nursing gargoyle from earlier leaps up with a roar. Both wings spread wide as she dives at the bars.

A sharp crackle fills the air, accompanied by the sickly scent of charred meat.

The gargoyle flies back and hits the far wall, smoking from the palms.

Well, they're always warned about the bars.

Barney keeps back at the top of the stairs, but Tina and Hozier walk straight in, eyes wide with bold and unabashed interest.

On either side of the mother, two smaller gargoyles watch us with open curiosity. These gargoyles are too young to hate and fear humans the way some older ones do and chatter through the bars. One male, one female, both pale in colour with soft wings yet to fully unfurl.

Rayne follows me to the number pad for the weapons store and watches as I enter my code.

The pad flashes a red light. Beeps.

"What?" I type it in again. Slower this time.

Red light. Beep.

Shakka waddles over, expression grim. "What's taking so long?"

"Not a damn clue."

Rayne sighs. "You're suspended, remember?"

Fuck. Fuck, fuck, and fucking bollocks.

I drag my hands through my hair. This can't be happening. Not now. Not when we're so close. And Pippa—

"Rayne, wait!"

She stops dead, fist trembling a hair's breadth from the number pad. "We need weapons."

Slowly, I close my hand around hers and pull it away from the security pad. It's like hauling an elephant by the tail. "If you hurt this unit, the entire building locks down. It'll knock us out." I direct her gaze to the small holes in the ceiling tiles. "Isoflurane. You'd be out in seconds."

"We all would." Shakka backs away. "And I don't feel like bursting facial boils for the next six hours."

I stumble as Rayne relaxes her arm. Though she catches me, I shove away and retreat to the far side of the holding area to press my forehead to the wall.

My mind is spinning, working through different scenarios, coming up with further plans.

There has to be a way we can do this without weapons. We have to make it work.

"Danika?" A gentle hand touches my shoulder.

I close my eyes. "Yes, Rayne?"

Even without vampire smell and hearing, I know her touch. It's familiar and tender, cool yet somehow warm, not with body heat but intent. "We'll get Pippa out."

I grip her fingers. Draw strength from the quiet assuredness in her voice.

Damn right we will.

I turn back to the others. "Change of plan. Without weapons you guys can't come. Rayne and I will go in, covert, and work on getting everybody out. You contact SPEAR and convince them to send backup to Sertral Street."

Objections. Lots of them. All at once.

Doesn't matter. Can't listen.

I have my gun, and the remains of my throwing knives. My utility belt has extra ammunition, and a few other peripherals against *edanes*. I won't need any of it if Rayne and I manage to sneak in, which shouldn't be hard at this time of night. This is the only way.

Tina blocks the door. "You can't do this alone. Wait for SPEAR."

"I can't. Pippa—"

"You won't be any help to her if you're killed trying to be a hero."

I frown. "I'm not trying to be a hero."

"No? Bringing in the werewolf cavalry, bullying your *edane* colleagues? You're half a step from vigilante. You're not supposed to be working right now. This is personal for you on a huge level. You need to be objective and I'm not sure you can."

I think about Rayne. About Mikkleson. Jack. About the house I long to rebuy and the new block of shops that will eventually take its place. I think of Mum and the haunted, desperate look in her eyes as she begged me to save the person we both love more than anyone else in the world.

Personal? Hell, yes it is.

"Hey, Shakka, why is the door open? You can't keep—oh. Well, that was easy, sí?"

Startled, I scoot around Tina to find the source of this new voice.

Oh hell.

Noel stands in the doorway.

❖

Noel edges down the steps, fingers tucked into the waist of his trousers. He smiles, looking hard at everyone before focusing on me. The smile broadens. "When they sent me to find you, I had no idea it would be so easy. I only came for a weapon."

Slowly I step left to put myself between him and Rayne. "Quinn sent you?"

"Naughty, naughty Dee-Dee. What have you been doing?" He cranes his neck. Again I shift to block his view. "Quinn wants you in containment. What is all this? Who are these people?"

Hozier opens his mouth but whatever he planned to say is lost beneath a grunt of pain as Tina stamps on his foot.

"Friends," I tell him.

"You don't have friends."

"Of course I have friends."

Noel wags a finger at me. "No, no, people you choose not to punch can't be counted as friends. I mean people you want to spend time with, sí?"

I feel rather than see Rayne step closer to me. "I have friends."

His eyebrows lift. "Bueno. But you must come with me now."

The officers, tense and unmoving, wait for my response. Shakka backs towards the wall. Only Rayne seems comfortable, reaching up to grasp my shoulder, a silent show of her support.

"I can't. I tried to tell you before—those missing people? The unregistered vampires? They're on Sertral Street. This is my chance to stop them and get Vixen."

"You said this on the phone last night. But it's crazy, you can't mean it."

"It's true." Rayne steps around me. "I know because I'm one of the vampires that helped make it happen. The leader, Vixen, is old and very dangerous. I also know where she is."

In an eye-blink Noel has his gun out and levelled at Rayne's face. An instant later, my own gun is free and pointed at his.

"Dee-Dee? What are you doing?"

"I'm sorry, Noel."

"A vampire? Here?"

"Rayne's the only reason I know so much. I can't do this without her."

His fingers shift on the trigger. In the still, his breathing is a harsh hiss. "What happened to you? First you release this vampire, then you lie and lie and lie. Even to me."

My hand trembles. "I had to."

"You don't trust me?"

"You know I do."

"Then why say nothing? Why wait until you're suspended? I could help. You must know this."

The air in the room is tight and thick. Every muscle along my raised arm trembles with tension. Every part of me is knotted with it, my tongue dry against the back of my teeth. "I'm sorry."

"You did like you do always. You fight alone, you make your own rules." His gun wavers.

"Please, Noel. They've got my sister."

"I have authority to shoot you if I must."

I lower the gun. "If we don't do this now, we don't get another chance. Vixen is in a corner now, and she'll either bust out of it and kill us all, or we keep her there and take her down. You know I'm right."

Voices from beyond the door. The tramp of booted feet.

Tina throws me a panicked glance.

I keep my gaze fixed on Noel. "I wouldn't ask for this if I wasn't certain. Let me go after her. Let me end it."

Louder voices now. Even I can hear the chink and clink of chains, probably from a set of handcuffs.

"Please."

Noel spins the gun on its trigger guard, turns, and puts his head through the door to speak to his team. "I chat with Shakka, amigos. Wait for me, sí?"

"So she's not here?" The voice outside rings with disappointment.

I hold my breath.

Noel says, "No."

The breath whooshes free.

"Shame. Was hoping to introduce her to these cuffs. Bet she'd look great all tied up and helpless."

Another voice laughs. "Would make a change, right?"

"Yeah. Think we'd need to strip-search her?"

"You never know what she's hiding under all those clothes."

More laughter.

Rayne snarls. Silver light fills her eyes.

I grab her by the waistband.

"Go, amigos, go. I'll grab what we need, then follow." Noel pulls his head back in and shuts the door.

I watch him walk down the stairs. Hold my ground as he stops in front of me, the toes of his boots nudging my own.

Silence.

His gaze bores into mine, hard, intense, and searching. I feel like he's flaying my thoughts, one at a time, to reach the tender, bloody centre of my mind.

"Dee-Dee?"

"Noel?"

He lunges, one hand scooping around me, the other flying at my face. I duck it, grab his wrist, and twist until the gun flies from his fingers. Noel grunts. I pull. He stumbles. I take him forward, further upsetting his balance, and flick my leg over his arm. Pull again.

He crashes to his knees behind me, arm pulled awkwardly between my legs. Twist and my gun is pointed at the top of his head. "Too slow," I mutter.

He chuckles. "One day, I get you. One day."

"But not today." I release his arm and kick my leg free. The gun I put away. "What now?"

He lifts his hands to shoulder height, palm out. "We go to Sertral Street, sí?"

I grin.

He slips his gun back into the holster. I lower a hand and Noel uses it to bound to his feet.

"Great. Now, could you open the weapons lock-up? We also need protective vests and access to the toy store."

Noel looks briefly at Rayne before nodding. "Two conditions for my help. First, my unit join us. You will need us and I won't lie to them." Though he doesn't say it, the phrase *like you did to me* hangs in the air.

"Fine. I'd expect nothing less. The second condition?"

His smile returns, all teeth and dimples under twinkling brown eyes. "I get the battleaxe."

Oh hell. That's just not fair.

CHAPTER TWENTY-EIGHT

We're in Noel's modified minivan, since it's the only way we can travel together, loaded down with kit and weapons. And the only way he'll allow a vampire on the team. He seems uneasy, rather than wary, and keeps looking at Rayne with an odd look in his eyes. I can't place it.

She sits beside me, seemingly oblivious, occasionally twitching her leg to allow her knee and thigh to brush mine.

The siren's effects are long gone, but each touch sends my pulse leapfrogging. I can feel it in my throat.

Noel coughs. "You work with Dee-Dee?"

Rayne stiffens. "I…yes."

"How did that happen?"

"I gave her information. After verifying it, she took responsibility for me as a witness."

"Ha, you talk like these." He waves a hand at Tina and the others.

"I used to be an officer."

His eyebrows twitch. "And now?"

"I don't know."

I share my gaze between them, trying to figure out where this conversation is going.

"I do." Noel leans forward against his seat belt. "Before SPEAR I was an engineer for Bytes and Mites Inc."

She studies him. "Nanotechnology? Nice."

"Yes, so I'm smart." He taps the side of his head. "I see things. I see you and Dee-Dee. You'll take care of her tonight, sí?"

"I don't need taking care of."

"Of course." Rayne cuts across me. "I'll protect her with my life."

Noel sighs. "Good." He runs both hands through his hair. "Not what I imagined for my friend, but she smiles in a way I've not seen before. Must be good."

"I hope so."

My cheeks are burning. "Rayne, I don't think—"

She grabs my face. It doesn't hurt at all and I marvel at the self-control she must have to avoid crushing my jaw. Then all big-girl thoughts are gone as she kisses me, long and deep, one hand gripping my hair, her legs rubbing against mine.

Wow. Oh, wow.

Tina giggles.

Barney gasps.

Noel sighs and reaches into one of the pockets on his trousers. From the corner of my eye, I spot him flick a pair of ten pound notes at Hozier, who gathers them up with a smug grin.

When Rayne lets me up for air, I slump in my seat. My body is goo and I can barely lift my head high enough to catch Noel's eye. "Hardly a smart bet."

"No? I know well of your preference for the ladies, but a vampire? That, you must admit, is strange."

I glance at Rayne. "A little. But I'm getting used to it."

Up front, the agent driving takes a sharp turn left. "Nearly there, guys. What's the plan?"

Rayne clears her throat. "They're in a modified bomb shelter beneath the building. We should be able to access it from street level with no trouble."

"Sertral Street, right?" Tina frowns. She pulls her phone from her pocket and stabs at the screen. A moment later, she nods. "Thought so. The only building large enough for what you describe is a nightclub. Are you sure, Rayne?"

"That's what he told me."

Noel throws me a weary look. "I hate working around civilians."

"We could clear them?" I think about how long it might take to do that and know straight away it's a bad idea.

Fiddling with his borrowed gun, Barney snorts and stamps his foot. "Clubs? Are you serious? Why would this fanger make a base in a club?"

"Because it's perfect." Rayne shows off a hint of fang. "Who'd suspect anybody is hiding there if the club is working undisturbed? One of our other locations was the attic of the city library. Public places are perfect and usually accessible." Rayne's voice has a hint of admiration in it. "She's hiding in plain sight. Genius."

"Really?" Barney grunts. "Guys, are we seriously taking this *thing* with us? Listen to her, sounds like she's in love with this Vixen or something. She can't be trusted."

I lean towards the front. "Stop the truck."

"Wait, Dee-Dee—"

"I said, stop the truck."

The vehicle jerks to a halt.

I kick the rear door open and reach back in for Barney. He drops his gun, kicking and yelling, as I drag him out by his jacket and slam him against the side of the van. "Enough. Rayne is trustworthy."

"No vampire is trustworthy. You of all people should know that."

"She's different."

"Because you fancy her? When did SPEAR agents get so twisted?"

"Shut up."

He glares. "She'll show it before long. This act is good, but it can't last. She's a vampire, and none of them care about us except as food."

"She's coming."

"Why? So the pair of you can drop off the next crop of human snacks?"

My fist draws back. It flies.

A hair's breadth before impact, a firm hand grasps my elbow. My attempted punch stops dead.

Rayne. Of course, Rayne.

"Don't."

I suck my teeth. "Why not?"

"Because he's not worth it. Leave him. For me?" Her grip loosens.

I'm free. My arm can move. I can do what I want.

"Why did they come to the station, Karson? What did they want? Picking up their latest human pet?"

I want to punch him. So, so much.

My arm falls.

Rayne smiles.

Together we return to our seats.

Barney stands where I left him, panting.

When the vehicle starts again, he jerks away from the open door, yelling as we drive off.

"I'm trying to help. Why won't you listen? You'll be sorry—all of you. She'll show her true colours and you'll all be dead. She's not safe."

From her seat, Tina leans over and pulls the rear door shut.

❖

Our first pass along Sertral Street reveals a major problem.

The road is crammed with clubbers, both *edane* and human, outside a large building with bright neon lighting.

Club Starshine.

Rayne gives me a startled glance. "He never mentioned this."

"Probably not predisposed to be helpful to us." Hozier frowns through the window. "I'm starting to like your idea of clearing the area."

I shake my head. "And tip off Vixen?"

"But those people—"

"We can handle it." Noel slips off his seat to confer with the rest of his team. Five men, all in tactical gear and weighed down with guns.

Tina clenches her fists. "This isn't going to work."

The minivan turns a corner on to a smaller road. Further along, a narrow alley leads towards the backs of the buildings behind us.

"Stop, stop, stop." I point.

Hidden in the shadows at the back of the alley, Wendy waves us down.

Besides him, twelve werewolves wait in the shadows. They've already shifted, not to their hybrid forms, but full-on wolf, pony sized monstrosities with thick, shaggy fur, sharp ears, and bushy tails. Yellow eyes gleam in the darkness to match the whisper of low growls creeping through the air.

As we exit the van, Wendy lifts his hand. The growls stop, but the tension in the air doesn't budge an inch.

"You took your sweet time." Wendy moves forward.

"Had to pick up some friends."

He looks over my shoulder. "You have friends?"

Noel roars with laughter.

I square my shoulders. "Okay, guys, enough male bonding or whatever this is. Our target is Club Starshine. I want to do this without disrupting the civilians for as long as possible."

"Wait." Hozier lifts a hand. "Surely you don't plan to use them as cover?"

"Do you want to call in the evacuation? Right now there's no reason to do it, and think of the time we'd waste getting permission."

"I'm not sure about this."

Tina clears her throat. "We could go first."

"What's that, guapa?"

Tina rounds on Noel with a glare and spits a stream of passionate Spanish, complete with popped hip and hair flick.

I gape.

He grins. "She has sass, Dee-Dee. I like your friend."

I've no idea what she said, but Noel's appreciative wink convinces me it was something good. Or rude. Or both.

Tina rolls her eyes, though not without a smile. "If Rayne, Danika, and I go first, we can scout the place."

"Perfect." I rub my hands together. "If we find a way through, we'll signal you. It's easy, subtle, and no one needs to evacuate until we know what we're facing. Then, Hozier, we can get the civilians out with some excuse from *inside* the club. Maybe an *edane* fight? Protocols haven't changed?"

"Not that I know." He rubs his chin.

"Good. Wendy, you arrange a distraction with your pack. Something to draw attention outside and away from us."

Tina grins. "Great. Nothing more natural than three girls on a night out."

Noel snorts. "Unless one of those girls is Dee-Dee."

"You don't know her very well, do you?" Wendy chuckles.

"Give me a break guys. What are you saying?"

"I'm saying, chica, that you don't do clubs. You don't know how to act."

"Sure I do."

Wendy throws me a sceptical look.

"What?"

Tina unfastens the strap of her borrowed rifle and hands it to Hozier. "I can handle this. Besides, us girls don't look like agents on a raid."

Noel cocks an eyebrow, then pulls off his protective jacket, revealing the shirt and vest beneath. Utility belt and gun holster he hands to one of his team. He transfers various weapons and tools into pockets, zips, and crevices on and inside his trousers. "Better?"

Tina nods appreciatively. "You've done that before."

"Once or twice."

At a casual glance he's just a guy. A faint bulge or odd wrinkle gives away small details, but only because I know where to look. "Brilliant. Let's go."

Noels snags my arm. "Whoa, Dee-Dee, you next. For me, a man, this look is fine. But you? We need more flesh."

"Screw you, I—"

"He's right, Agent." Tina frees my arm and pulls me aside. "Did you see the other women as we went by? All legs and cleavage. We won't get in at all if we don't look right. Come on, Rayne, we'll all spruce up a bit." She doesn't wait, just herds me further into the alley, scattering the werewolves as we go.

At the end, Tina folds her arms and stares.

I twitch. "Tina…"

She cuts across me. "Take your hair down."

From the corner of my eye, Rayne nods thoughtfully.

Oh. Well, if *she* thinks so.

I tug the elastic from my locs and thread it on my wrist. My hair tumbles from its high ponytail, thick and heavy against my back.

A silver glint flickers in Rayne's eyes. "That will work."

I don't know what she sees, but I want to keep doing whatever it is. Especially if she's going to look at me like *that*.

Grinning, Tina slides back into my line of sight.

"Shut up."

She giggles. "I didn't say anything. Now, do you trust me?"

"Hell, no."

Eye-roll. "Do you trust me to get you into this club with most of your kit?"

I study her face. The giggles have ebbed, leaving her features soft but serious. "Sure, why not."

"Good." She backs off. "Rayne, follow my directions exactly."

The pair of them stand in front of me.

I fight the urge to bolt.

"Shred the jeans," says Tina. "Here, here, and there." She points to my left thigh, opposite shin, and the backs of my legs.

"No, no, wait—"

Rayne's already in front of me. The tips of her fangs flash white between her lips, before she drops to her knees. Her hand swipes across my shin, then thigh.

Eight parallel slash marks show the path of her fingernails.

Breath whooshes out of me. Hadn't realized I was holding it.

"Rayne—"

She's behind me now, steadying my hip with one hand, while drawing her fingernails across the denim beneath the curve of my butt.

Fabric shreds.

Cool air rushes in.

Rayne springs up in front of me, eyes bright, lips slightly parted. "You're not wearing underwear."

I clear my throat. "Yeah. You didn't bring—I mean those ones didn't fit…"

A cough from Tina. "Thanks, Rayne. Now the top. Muss it up a bit."

Still watching me, Rayne reaches for my shirt. She unfastens each button with painful deliberation, circling her finger around each buttonhole. Another chill whips across my skin as she pushes the cotton off my shoulders, but it doesn't last long under the heat of that gaze.

Beneath, the crop T-shirt rides high on my stomach.

Rayne growls low in her throat.

Sweat beads on my upper lip.

She tucks a hand under the hem and feels upward. Her knuckles and the back of her hand graze my ribs.

"Rayne—"

Riiiiiip.

More slashes, this time running left to right across the top. Even I can see hints of my breasts through the gaps.

"When this is over"—Rayne licks her lips—"I want to do this to you again. Properly."

Wolf whistles and applause come from the end of the alley. I tear my gaze from Rayne to find Noel and the others watching.

Rayne scrambles back. She shrinks in on herself and lowers her head, both hands clenched at her sides.

"She looks the part." Noel nods his approval. "Now we hide some weapons on her. Sorry, Dee-Dee, looks like neither of us use the axe today." He stops in front of me, voice lowered. "I take back what I said before. You and Rayne? Fine with me."

"Pervert."

"You love it."

I punch him in the arm.

He swipes for my jaw. Misses.

"Still too slow."

A sigh and playful shrug. "Some things never change."

I glance at Rayne as Noel begins to tuck throwing knives and holy water phials into various places on my body. Some things never change, but others certainly do.

He holds up a Kubotan attached to a slender chain. When I try to separate one from the other, he grabs my hand. "Keep both, chica. Chains? You never know when such things might be useful." He tilts his head towards Rayne. Winks.

Heat flushes my cheeks. "Can we hold off the kinky shit, please?"

"Trust me." He hooks the chain to one of my belt loops, then tucks the Kubotan into the nearest pocket. "Now you're ready."

I turn and twist, bend and stretch. The knives are in odd places; I'll have to be careful how I move and walk, but it's the best I'll get. "My gun?"

"Even I can't find a place for that." After a moment of hesitation, he twirls the weapon and hands it to Rayne. "You take care of this, sí?"

She looks at me.

I nod.

When she slides the weapon into her waistband, I lead the way out of the alley.

We've done all we can. Time to check it out.

CHAPTER TWENTY-NINE

Walking into Club Starshine is like walking into a wall, the music loud enough to feel in my bones.

Rayne spends a few seconds twisting her head from side to side, frowning. "People. Can't smell. Noise. Can't hear."

So plan A is out of the question. Time to search the old-fashioned way.

Noel shoves through us, hand in hand with Tina. They make a big show of giggling and stumbling as they begin their own search.

The music is a living, breathing thing, I can't help but move to it. I'm not much of a dancer, but the room pulses with people matching the rhythm, some human, others not, all engrossed in one thing.

Rayne slips her arms around my neck and pulls me close. She has to stretch to reach that far, but something about her on tip toes is beyond adorable and so, so sexy. I put my hands on my hips and allow her to guide us through the crowds. I could almost forget why I'm here.

Never would have guessed from the soft-spoken, timid specimen I picked up two days ago, but Rayne can dance. In seconds, she's up close, grinding her hips against mine in a way that makes my insides turn to goo.

Her lips move but I have to guess at the words.

"Three doors." She drags my head down and yells in my ear. "Left. Right. Behind." Her dancing swings me round.

First door behind the bar, through which staff move, laden with bottles and pint and shot glasses. Second, at the far end of the club's floor space, marked with a green and white sign reading *Exit*. Third, a narrow, unmarked door, guarded by two men in funereal black. Would have missed it without Rayne's keen eye.

I approach the guarded door, but two steps on there's a mountain in the way. Well, I'm sure he's probably human, but with shoulders and arms like that, I can be forgiven for comparing him to a block of rock.

"Hey, little lady." His gravelly voice is a roar beneath the din. "Dance?"

I shake my head and sidestep, but he follows with a cocky smile. "Sure?" He thrusts both arms above his head and pumps his hips.

Another head shake, a second sidestep, but this time he snags my arm.

Every muscle stiffens. My fist is raised, my legs tight—

The guy falls flat on his back.

The crowd swirls around us, seamless eddies to avoid trampling the little idiot as he grips his nose.

At my side, Rayne draws back her fist with the sweetest of smiles. She slides her arm around my waist and steers me towards the bar.

I'm grinning like an idiot. I know I am, but I can't help it.

Away from the thickest press of dancers, and with distance from the sound system, Rayne's hand hooks around my neck and draws my head down. For a glorious instant, I expect a kiss, but instead, she puts her lips against my ear. "Noel is on your right. Give the signal."

Ah yes. The point of our little field trip.

I fling my right arm into the air and twirl, an apparent dance move with no meaning.

Noel and Tina break off to the doors and the wolves to begin their distraction.

I've no idea what they've come up with, but it better be good.

❖

It takes an age for the Wendy and his pack to show.

Near the bar, making a pretence of chatting and scoping the drinks, Rayne and I watch the main doors.

Where the hell are they?

"Wolf!" The bellow comes from the left, followed by a roar that rattles my ribs.

A man-shaped, furry creature dives *through* the toilet doors, sending shards of wood, plastic, and glass in all directions. It tackles a less furry but obviously *edane* figure.

Revellers scream and shriek, scrambling to get back.

Perfect.

The two hybrid wolves break apart, the second of the pair growing larger and furrier by the second.

Rayne nods. "Wow. Looks so real."

The first wolf slashes with one pseudo-paw. Huge claws cut across flesh, and blood fountains into the air. He roars again and follows with a kick that sends his opponent skittering back across the dance floor.

Fuck.

It *is* real.

"We need to go." I shove at Rayne's back.

"But—"

"That's a dominance battle. We need to get out of the way."

Her eyes widen. "But the humans—"

"Noel can handle it." Again I push. "Go. We have to reach that door before rapid response shows up."

The music grinds to a halt as the wolves plough into the DJ podium, pulverizing turntables, speakers, and mixing desks. In the still, their grunts, growls, and shouts are deafening, but not as loud as the gunshot.

People drop flat, many with hands over their heads.

My instinct demands the same, but Rayne is faster. She shoves me down, then shields my body with hers.

"Everybody out!" Noel's voice is strong and commanding. Through the cage of Rayne's arms, I see him standing on the far side of the dance floor, gun out, SPEAR ID held aloft. "This is no drill, go. We have two lupine *edanes* on the premises, and they are fighting. Go, go, go."

Like a dam breaking, human clubbers surge towards the doors.

The two wolves seem not to notice, struggling to their feet and colliding again.

"Get off, Rayne. We need to go."

On the edges, more figures in uniform black appear to usher the crowds. Six *edanes* of varied types and heights form a ragged half circle around the rear of the rushing crowd, a wall against the battling wolves.

Rayne steers us into the empty space behind the bar and peers out around the edge. "Why aren't they moving?"

I shuffle in for a better look.

The men at our door are still in place on high alert, eyes narrowed, gazes darting, weight forward on their toes.

Screw it. We've got to get through.

"Go." I'm up and out, darting towards the door with a knife in each hand.

The pair share startled glances. Vampires. Young ones, but powerful enough to be fast off the mark.

The one on the left cuts across me, joining his companion to face off against Rayne.

Big mistake.

I follow as they put their backs to me, swinging both knives high and shoving them deep into their napes.

They drop hard, gurgling and clawing. One pulls my knife free before Rayne delivers a pair of powerful kicks.

The crack of breaking bone turns my stomach.

"Wow, Rayne. Take it easy."

She grabs my knives, wipes them clean, and hands them over. "What?"

"I've just never seen you do something like that before."

"We need to get downstairs." She kicks the door open and marches through, leaving me to follow, a prickle of unease teasing down my spine.

❖

Three doors, one on the left, two on the right.

Rayne goes first, head cocked. Her steps are light and silent, even her breathing reduced to nothing. "One person, probably a woman, through the second door on the right." She hands over my gun, slides up to the door, and counts down from five on her fingers.

My stomach gives a little skip.

As Rayne lowers her thumb and shoves the door open, I swing through, gun raised in a two-handed grip.

Security room. Multiple screens. Desk. Chair. Flashing red light. Air scented with greasy chips. A woman.

"Don't move."

She whips her hands into the air. A hot dog tumbles to the ground and spills its innards across her shoes. "Don't hurt me. Please, don't hurt me."

I look again. Not a woman, a girl. A young, frightened girl.

Long blond hair spills over her shoulders, fine and shiny in the artificial light. Ragged sleeves drop down her arms, exposing bruised and puckered skin at the crook of each elbow. And bite marks on her wrists.

"Please, please, please. Don't hurt me, please."

"Calm down." Gun down and pointed at the ground. "I'm not here to hurt you."

The blubbering whimpers pause. "What?"

"I won't hurt you. I'm Danika, I work with SPEAR. What's your name?"

The girl jerks her arms down and yanks her sleeves into place. She looks past me towards Rayne. "SPEAR?"

"That's right. Tell me—"

She dives at me, all shrill cries, fingernails, and gnashing yellow teeth. "You can't be here. No SPEARs allowed."

"Wait." I skip out of reach, but she follows, still yelling.

"Get out. We don't want you. No SPEARs. You have to get out. Get out, get out, get out." Her arms flail, weak slaps aimed vaguely at my face. "Go away."

A shadow of movement flickers in the corner of my eye. "Rayne, no."

She stops dead, one hand raised, a terrible snarl on her face. Silver blanks her eyes, and fangs shine between drawn-back lips.

"She's a kid." I talk while blocking the strikes at my face. "Probably high too."

"I'm not a kid. You sound like my bitch of a stepmum."

I drop my gun and grab her wrists to press on the sensitive pressure points located there. "Stop a second."

"You're hurting me. Let go. Let go."

"Listen to me—"

She stamps on my foot and follows by hawking hard and spitting in my face.

Time freezes.

The damp gobbet on my cheek stinks of mustard and processed meat.

"Did you just—"

Again, with poorer aim. The second sticky missile hits my chin and drips off the end.

"You won't kill my friends. I won't let you."

I spread her arms wide and yank her in for a headbutt. It stings, but she cries out and stomps my foot again. Her knee hikes towards my middle.

A shove sends her careening into the table of monitors.

"She's insane." Rayne starts forward.

"She needs help."

As the girl comes in again, I slide left and grab the back of her head. She struggles, so I pull her hair, meaning to shock her into stillness.

It comes away in my hand, a long line of blond strands on a slim thread, studded with popped stitches.

"No. No, no, no, I only just got those. Bitch."

I toss the extensions aside, snatch her real hair, and tug again.

She thuds into me, clawing at my wrists, bellowing insults.

Laughter fills the air.

"Need help, Dee-Dee?" Noel's voice is a delighted drawl. He stands in the door frame, gun in hand, peering over Rayne's shoulder. "These teenagers can be tricky, sí?"

"I'm a grown woman," yells the girl.

I pull harder, drawing her head back and down, forcing her to bend with it or fall. "Shut up." To Noel, "What took you?"

"The small matter of a dominance battle in a club full of humans. You didn't see?"

"Funny. We need to move."

He shrugs. "My team will join when the wolves are contained."

"And Wendy?"

"He helps."

"But—"

He wags a finger at me. "You know this is how it must be. We are SPEARs, always we protect the people first."

"What about the people here? You don't think all this racket has let Vixen and friends know something's up? What if they're killing people now? Or getting away?"

"Then we follow. We're no use dead, Dee-Dee, so we must wait." His gaze shifts to my handful of hair. "And who is this blond beauty?"

"This?" Another yank of her hair as she tries to speak. "This spitfire knows the way down."

"Spitfire?"

I wipe the cooling spittle clinging to my cheek. "Don't ask."

"I don't know anything, SPEAR fuckers—you won't get in. You can't make me say anything."

Rayne stares at the bank of monitors. "She wouldn't be in here if this wasn't important. There must be something here, is that right?"

"Bite me, bitch," yells the girl.

I cart her to the side and dump her in the chair. "Stay."

"Fuck you."

"No thanks." When I next look, Rayne is studying the area around the monitors.

The screens show offices, bathroom exteriors, entrance, lobby, cloakroom, dance floor all from different angles. The hybrid wolves are still fighting on the dance floor, though rapid response now works with Noel's team and Wendy's pack to keep them contained.

"It's got to be here, there's nowhere else..." Rayne taps the desk with her knuckles, then ducks to crawl beneath it. "I can feel—yes, there's a switch."

Click.

Rayne rolls out from beneath the table, as it and the unit of monitors swing round like a door.

The girl gives a furious wail. "You can't. Not there. You can't go down there."

Noel bends beneath the table and pulls a handful of wiring. Three monitors fall blank when he emerges carrying several lengths of cable. "We can, guapa, and we will. And you? You stay here, nice and quiet." He uses the cabling to tie the girl to the chair, while I hold her down, dodging more spit missiles.

When he's done, I shove the length of blond extensions into her mouth.

"Now," I smile, "be a good little girl and stay there. The grown-ups have work to do."

Noel blocks my path. "Not yet. We must wait for the others."

My palms prickle. "No."

"Of course we wait. Three against how many below? We don't know."

"But we can't stand around waiting."

He grabs my shoulders. "I understand, honest I do. You burn to save your sister, but we must be smart. If we wait, we have my team and the werewolves with us. That is surely better, sí?"

I shove his hands away and retrieve my gun. It slips into my waistband, no longer needing to hide. "I'm not waiting here. I can't. We're so close now. We have to get down there. We can't wait."

"But—"

"Rayne? Are you ready?"

She stares at me, then Noel, indecision brightening her eyes. "Now?"

"My sister's down there."

Noel's shaking his head. His expression is weary, features tight. "Please. We must wait."

"Rayne?"

She presses her hands to her ears. "I don't know."

I walk away from Noel, to the open door. "Then stay, but I'm going. Pippa needs me. I won't leave her down there a second longer."

Warm air drifts from the opening. The metal ladder bolted to the wall looks narrow, dangerous, and long. Don't care. We haven't come this far and done so much to stop now.

I lower myself backward into the hole and secure my feet on the first rungs. "Are you coming?"

Rayne sighs. "I promised to protect you. You can't go alone."

Relief fizzes through me. "And you?"

Noel casts an uneasy look at the door. "I have a bad feeling."

"Yes or no?"

He sighs. "Yes, Dee-Dee, I come. For better or worse, I'll follow you."

CHAPTER THIRTY

It's a long way down. Can't hear or see anything beyond the clatter of my boots on the metal rungs and my fingertips in front of my face. Above, Rayne's steps are light and quick, stuttering regularly as she stops to avoid stomping on me. Beyond, Noel brings up the rear, muttering in Spanish.

The bottom arrives unexpectedly, my left foot slapping on concrete. When I move aside, the wall curves beneath my back, gentle and subtle, arching inwards above my head.

Light comes from a ragged line of hurricane lamps at intervals along the walls.

"What is this place?" Noel's voice echoes.

"Entrance to the air raid shelter. Most of Angbec was built on top of the stuff below—that's how HQ has so much underground space."

He shudders. "Don't like it. Too much earth above."

Rayne points forward. "There's a door ahead. Steel."

"We can still wait. My team, they will come soon and—"

I walk on.

Rayne falls in at my side, a warm, comforting presence. After another stream of swearing, Noel joins us.

The door, when we reach it, appears designed to withstand the heat and force of numerous explosions.

I stand against the wall and draw my gun. "Open it."

"Dee-Dee…"

"Do you hear anything, Rayne?"

She cocks her head. "No, but—"

"Open it. I'll cover."

Noel takes the top handle while Rayne grips the bottom. Together, they pull, and huge gears slide, click, and grind together to open the huge door.

I wait with my gun aimed at eye height, breathing slow, body calm.

I'm going to save Pippa. For me. For Mum.

Light spills out. After the dimness of the passage, I'm blind for precious seconds.

"Who's that?"

"What's going on?"

"Are you expecting more?"

My body prickles. I'm hot, I'm cold. I'm tense, I'm relaxed. I'm everything and nothing all at once.

My vision clears.

Six figures sit around a small table scattered with cards, slips of paper, and poker chips. Three have the deep purple irises of old vampires while two are bulky in a way that suggests giant heritage. The last bends double to avoid the ceiling. It cocks its head and stares through pale yellow eyes with a black, slitted pupil. Beyond them, an arched opening leads into another corridor that curves out of sight.

More swearing in Spanish.

I steady the gun. "Nobody move."

The vampires share a glance.

One, on the far side of the table, tucks the pencil he'd been holding behind his ear. "Is that Rayne?"

A blur darts across me, shoulder height and dark. Familiar.

Noel yells as Rayne's shove to the chest catapults him backward. His body slams into the door, gun spinning away across the floor. Then she's on him, crouched low, head ducked over his throat.

He screams.

I freeze.

Last time I heard cries like that, three members of my team died.

I can't move. Can't think.

Noel's legs pedal. Both hands claw at the air.

Rayne jerks her head.

Silence.

She stands, shoulders low, hands loose. When she turns, my guts threaten to drop out of me.

Her mouth is ringed with blood.

❖

Part of me is screaming, ordering me to lift my gun, draw a knife, something, anything to protect myself.

Rayne steps over Noel and pushes the door. The heavy slab swings shut with a resounding boom.

I find my tongue. "What are you doing?"

"Protecting my family." At last she meets my gaze. Her tongue flicks out, lapping away the blood painting her lips.

I recoil.

That's not Rayne's voice. This voice is soft and cold, confident and…cruel.

She's at my side, a blur of movement I can't follow. One hand closes on the back of my neck, and she thrusts me forward. Like handling a puppy. Her other hand snatches my gun and tosses it over her shoulder.

Can't see where it lands.

Brutal fingers dig into the sides of my throat.

"Please, what are you doing?"

She leans close to my ear. "This is my family now. You know, the one with ties only found through blood? I did a lot of thinking before I dropped dead at sunup."

The paraphrasing sends a jolt of panic through me. At last I can move, I can struggle, but Rayne's grip is firm.

"What have you done?"

"Brought my mother, my *real* mother, a present: the great Danika Karson."

The vampires straighten at the sound of my name.

One shuffles closer, dry washing her hands. "This is her? The bitch with the bounty?"

Another chuckle. "I thought she'd be taller."

"And uglier."

Rayne smiles. "Sorry to disappoint. This is her. This pathetic scrap of nothing."

This can't be happening.

I twist in Rayne's grip, stretching for the holy water phial inside my jeans.

She grabs my wrist. Twists.

Agony arcs along my forearm and elbow, forcing me to the right and down.

I kneel, gasping, wincing, blinking.

I won't cry. Not in front of these animals.

Someone grabs my hair.

The tall creature yanks my head back hard enough to strain my throat. "So you're Danika Karson?" The voice is awful, a cross between marbles in a metal tube and the shrieks of a dying horse. "Interesting. I didn't think you'd be as...*squishy* as the others." It peers into my eyes, blinking over that creepy slitted pupil.

I've no idea what it is. I've never seen anything like this before, but a sense of dread lingers around it, a dark, creeping fear.

I want to scream.

Instead I slam my forehead into the narrow ridge of bony flesh I take for a nose.

No crack, just a wet pop. Thin yellow liquid squirts from the flared nostrils and the corners of each eye.

It releases my hair. "Vicious, aren't you."

With my left hand still in Rayne's grip, I give up using the right for balance. It throws her off, forces her to follow me to the ground, offering precious half seconds.

I reach for my knife.

Fingers close on the hilt. Pull—

A stunning impact slams into my mouth. Teeth click together. Blood bursts across my tongue.

Room spinning. Stars. Bile in my throat.

How did I end up on my back?

I'm wet. Is that blood?

The first vampire stands over me, grin wide and feral, cheeks bristly with coarse stubble. "I've always wanted to taste a SPEAR. You sweet or sour, little agent?"

"Bitter." I kick him in the nads.

He grunts but doesn't fall. "That tickles."

He catches my next kick and twists my foot.

The pressure spins me sideways and I sprawl on my stomach, face down in a patch of dampness that smells of incense. Holy water.

My phials are gone.

In front of the door, still unmoving, sprawls Noel. He really is...

I scream. I shout. I swear.

I twist again and kick out with the other leg, driving my heel into the fingers around my ankle.

Free.

Seconds to spare.

Scramble across the floor. Reach for Noel's gun. Fingers scrape the barrel.

Heavy hands grip my calves.

Concrete grinds against my belly when he reels me in and kneels on my tail bone.

"Leaving? Don't you want to play?"

Hands in my hair again. Head dragged up.

Slammed to the floor.

Up.

Floor.

More stars dance across my eyes. The blood in my mouth thickens.

"Is that all you've got, Agent Karson? Vampire murderer? What a joke."

I grit my teeth. Brace.

My strength is no match for his, but the third impact with the floor is lessened as I slap my hands down.

"So you *do* have some spunk?" He spins me round and wraps his hands about my throat. "I've lost family to your kind. Dozens of them. You and your buddies took my wife."

I'm clawing his wrists, working my fingers between his and my throat.

"She'd been a vampire for three days. Three. Would you murder a newborn for following an instinct?"

The grip tightens.

Air vanishes.

"You and your trigger-happy friends shot her, no warning, no attempted capture. That's murder." His nose butts mine.

Purple eyes blur into glittering silver.

His breath is hot on my face.

My vision dips in and out.

Someone's shouting. Rayne?

Doesn't matter.

Nothing matters now.

Pippa's image floats across my mind's eye. She's smiling, holding a baby. "Look, darling, it's Auntie Dani."

Auntie Dani.

I open my eyes again, struggle to find focus in a fading world.

The vampire licks the blood from around my mouth and cheeks. His fangs lengthen and gleam in the harsh light. "This is for my wife."

I need a weapon.

Knives? Can't reach.

Gun? Gone.

Something small drops off his face. No, not off his face. Off his ear. Behind his ear.

The pencil.

I grope for it. Find it. Grip it.

"Nothing smart to say, Agent?" He presses in on my throat. "No last words? No begging?"

"Closer." It's a waste of my last breath, but I use it anyway. "Closer. Taste."

A pleasured shudder ripples through him. "Don't mind if I do." He leans in.

I bring my hand up, the pencil balled in my fist, pointy end out.

Silver eyes fly open. Mouth hangs slack.

The pencil sinks with effort, but I sit up to help it along, wrap my arms around that fanger's back, and press my chest to his, driving the wood deeper and deeper.

I stop when he coughs and a dribble of black ooze hits my shoulder. His hands drop away.

As blessed air rushes in, he falls back, scrabbling to find the pencil. Too late, fanger.

I leave him melting into ooze and scoot back on my rear.

Still at the table, the other two vampires watch in mingled awe and fury. The part giants talk amongst themselves, slow, ponderous words in a language I can't follow.

The tall thing gives a sibilant hiss and vanishes—actually vanishes—with a puff of smoke that stinks of sulphur.

Rayne walks through the smoke residue, hands on hips, head cocked. "Very good, but you've still lost. It's over."

"Why?" My voice rasps, but I force the words out. "Why are you doing this? After everything we've been through—"

"A few kisses and a quick fondle? Is that all it takes?"

"You promised—"

"I'm a vampire." Her eyes narrow. "Remember? A liar. A monster. An animal."

This can't be true. It must be some trick.

My hand lands in a warm puddle.

Blood.

Noel's blood.

Her smile widens. "Vixen will be thrilled to see you. I seem to remember she had plans if we ever caught you." She pulls me up by my hair and drags me to the other vampires. "Tie her and let's go."

What have I done?

Noel. Pippa. My friends upstairs. I've killed them all.

The memory of Barney's voice rings in my ears, his screams that Rayne can't be trusted.

"What are you growling about?" Rayne leans on the table, watching the other vampires secure my arms behind me at the wrists and elbows. They take my knives too, roughly feeling down my body to locate every one, and dump them in a pile on the table.

I grit my teeth. "Nothing."

"Now I know that's a lie. Remember…I'm tuned in to you."

My breath hitches.

Did all of that mean anything at all?

I straighten and hold her gaze. "I. Will. Kill you."

"Alone?" Rayne's eyes narrow. A silver glint flickers across them.

"When the others arrive."

"The wolves and your SPEAR colleagues? No, they're occupied upstairs. By the time they arrive, you'll be dead and we'll be long gone. But first, there's someone I want you to meet."

CHAPTER THIRTY-ONE

O ur steps echo in the passage beyond the arch.
The single door at the end is guarded by yet another vampire, younger than the others, with a scar across her forehead and down over her left eye.

She arches a misaligned eyebrow at Rayne. "What are you doing here?"

"I need to see Vixen." Rayne barely opens her mouth, but the words are heavy with menace.

"She's finalizing instructions with the ground teams, no interruptions. New snacks can be brought in later."

Snacks? Like a bag of fucking popcorn?

I open my mouth.

Rayne's hand tightens on the back of my neck.

Mouth closed.

"Open the door."

The guard shrugs. "No. I have my orders and—"

A blur across my nose. By the time my brain catches up, Rayne has pulled her fist back and the other vampire leans against the wall, gagging.

"Did you say something? No? Good. We'll let ourselves in." Rayne shoves me ahead of her and leads the other pair through.

Cells. Dozens of them, small and narrow, in a line along the wall on the left. To the right, an open space filled with milling *edanes*. Vampires mostly, but also trolls, goblins, werewolves, and what appear to be a handful of sprites. The long, tall creature from earlier stands in the centre near a low table, talking quietly to a woman in a pale green trouser suit.

I've never seen anything like this. No, I've never seen anything like this outside SPEAR. This is a base of operations, complete with strong holding facilities.

So many vampires. Can't remember the last time I saw so many in one place.

This is exactly why new laws don't allow them to nest.

The woman in green looks up. "Rayne? I knew you couldn't be dead. Not you. Not my little raindrop."

Rayne breathes deep. I know it's a reflex, but she looks so normal in that moment...so human. Except for the lengthening of fangs. Her eyes brighten, jaw softens.

Everyone stops, *edane* and human alike, gazes trained on the action in the centre.

I stumble forward, following Rayne's abrupt dart across the space. She wades through the crowd of onlookers and stops before her mistress. "I'm so sorry. I shouldn't have left. You were right all along, I'm so sorry—"

A kiss cuts her short, long, deep, and passionate.

My chest aches. I look away.

I feel, rather than see, their attention turn to me. A finger curls around the side of my face and pulls my head around.

"Danika Karson."

My jaw aches. "Amelia Smythe. Or is it Vixen?"

A smile. "Now you know. Tell me, how are you feeling?"

"Been better."

The smile widens and there, at last, are the fangs. They add an edge to her otherwise beautiful features, a harshness that ignites a chill in my chest.

"Dani? Danika?" Commotion from one of the cells. Scuffling and shouting.

Everything in my stomach drops to my toes.

Pippa shoves to the front of her cell, one arm stretched through the bars. "Dani, you're alive. I was so scared."

I open my mouth, but Vixen cuts across me.

"You know each other? I thought you worked alone, Agent? At least that's what I've heard. No friends, no teammates. Unless..." She steps away from me and closer to the cells. The crowd of *edanes* parts to let her through.

Pippa holds her ground.

"I know that look in your eye, Human. I've seen it on our mutual friend. Sisters, perhaps?" Nobody speaks, but that seems to be enough for Vixen, who strides back through the crowd to reach my side.

She snags my hair and turns slowly, showing me off. "This is Danika Karson."

A ripple of anticipation zings through the air.

"Yes. You understand. This woman, this one agent is responsible for more deaths among our kind than any other SPEAR in the city."

Murmurs, some impressed, others fearful, most angry.

"Highest kill rate in the country," says a male vampire on the right. "I've seen her file."

I swivel as far as the grip on my locs will allow. How the hell does he know anything about my file?

Wait…I know him. He's a police officer, one of the desk bunnies from Tina's unit.

Oh no.

I look again.

A woman, pencil skirt and torn blouse, dark hair, and a wedding ring. Mikkleson's PA?

Near the back, a man with a mild case of vitiligo on his left cheek. Looks like one of the technicians from Pippa's department at Clear Blood. I don't know him well enough to be sure, but I wouldn't be surprised.

Plenty of others I don't know, but in a cell near the back, knees hugged to his chest, is a familiar figure in black, with smudged goth make-up and bite marks up and down his pale bare arms. Mikkleson's son.

"Good to see you, Ms. Karson. Shinik tir morea nai."

I turn again, facing Marco as he reveals himself from the crowd.

"Think I look bad? You should see the other guy."

He chuckles and moves closer to Rayne, who nods politely at him.

"Don't bait her," snaps Vixen. "Angry blood has a bitter aftertaste." She speaks so matter of factly, several seconds pass before I realize what she means.

Before the thought of escape is fully crystallized, Vixen swings a chair out from beneath her desk and shoves me into it with my arms over the back. It forces me straight and demands I put my head back, off balance and vulnerable. Throat exposed.

Vixen stalks around my chair. "Ladies, gentlemen, others, I had thought to punish SPEAR by killing their prize agent, but that would be an unforgivable waste."

Murmurs. The crowd of *edanes* look to Vixen; even the caged humans look at the tall goddess of a woman with the large grey eyes.

She strokes my hair, like petting a dog.

When I jerk my head away, she cuffs me around the face, a casual backhand that makes stars float before my eyes.

"I'll make her one of us, as I did with many of you. Danika Karson will work with us. For us. For me."

Ice drops into my stomach.

"No. No, you can't." Pippa hammers the cell bars. Shrill notes make her voice dip in and out, but the panic in her eyes is real. "Don't. Please."

Vixen approaches the cell.

Again I try to stand. My weight is up and forward, my butt off the chair, before Rayne forces me down with a hand on my shoulder.

Other captured humans retreat to the far walls. Most are wide-eyed and terrified, but Pippa remains at the bars, face close to the gap. Fire burns in her gaze.

"I should have known you were related, given the trouble you've caused since you arrived." Vixen purses her lips. "You'll have a first row seat. Get her out."

Marco moves in with a key. He opens the cell and grabs Pippa with one slick move. She kicks and thrashes, but he dodges easily. When she makes a second attempt, he slaps her foot down and punches her in the stomach.

"No!" The chair topples as I throw myself out of it. My shoulder slams into the concrete floor but I don't feel it. Can't feel anything but horror for the winded, agonized look on Pippa's face.

She wraps her arms around herself and I know what she's thinking.

Marco dumps her on the floor, not caring, not knowing what he's done.

"Pip?" I worm towards her. "Pip, look at me. It's okay."

"The baby—"

"—is fine. You're going to be okay. Both of you."

Her eyes shimmers with tears. "Dani."

I scream, caught off guard by the hand in my hair. It drags me off the chair and to my knees, then pulls further, not to stand, but to keep me off balance.

"Can I do it, Vixen?" Rayne shakes me hard enough to rattle my brain against my skull. "Please?"

Mumbles from the crowd.

Whimpers from my sister.

Vixen turns aside from her study of Pippa. "You?"

"She tricked me into registering with the Foundation. They put my chip in my shoulder, like some tame, domesticated pet. She even killed one of our cousins outside. Please? I want to do it. Please? For you."

Dizziness rolls over me. A bitter taste fills the back of my throat.

"Please, Vixen. By year's end there'll be no registration, no chips, no insulting blood banks. We'll control the mayor—whoever it is—and we'll make our own laws. We'll hunt in the open, live where we please, be feared, as nature intended. We'll destroy anybody who questions us, all in utter freedom because of you. Let me do this small thing in return. Please?"

I wish she'd stop talking. Her voice, the passion in it, the fire, it turns my stomach. Her grip trembles as she curls her free arm around my shoulders.

Another shake of my hair.

I cry out. Without my arms I can't do anything but hang by my hair, waiting to be eaten.

Marco frowns. He looks at the entry door, then Vixen. "I think maybe we should—"

"Quiet." Vixen raises a hand, then focuses on Rayne. "You'd do this for me?"

"Anything for you."

I cry out again, not from the pain in my head.

Once more Marco tries to speak. He keeps looking at the door, then the cells, but no one is paying attention. Vixen and Rayne only have eyes for each other, and the crowd of *edanes* around us is whispering—no, chanting.

Kill her. Kill her. Kill her. Kill her.

Pippa sits back on her heels, still hugging her stomach. Tears and terror fill her eyes.

"I'm sorry." No way she can hear me with all this racket, but I think she understands.

She presses her lips together. "I love you, Dani."

Marco starts forward. "Vixen, someone is—"

Something small, round, and red flies through the air. It explodes at the top of its arc and shoots pale threads of smoke in all directions.

A familiar scent fills the space, sweet and ancient, laced with something more chemical. Sun cream?

Rayne yells and shoves me down, one hand scooped around my face. The fall is absorbed by her fingers and my teeth mash against her open palm.

Shouting. Screaming.

Thudding feet.

Gunshots.

I struggle but Rayne pins me flat.

Everybody running. Shoving. Falling. Scrambling.

Someone drops in front of me, a vampire, screaming and clawing at her eyes. Blisters sprout on her face and hands, thick, dark, and glistening. They burst an instant later, a foul jet of stinking black ooze.

"Go, go, go! Hostiles front and centre. Straight through. Hostages to the left."

That voice...

"Danika? Dani!" Pippa.

I squirm, but Rayne won't let go.

Damn her. Damn her to the deepest fucking pit.

The smoke spreads further, faster. I recognize the smell now, frankincense and a compound including silver. Not smoke, but a gas designed by SPEAR technicians to incapacitate vampires.

"Dani, where are—no, no, let go. Let go of me! Let go!"

I jerk my body to the right. Rayne follows, but I can see, through the forest of legs, shoes, and boots. Pippa lies beneath Vixen, struggling to keep sharp fangs away from her upturned throat.

She's not going to make it. I know she won't...and there's nothing I can do.

Vixen bites hard, fangs sinking deep. Her throat works as she swallows.

"Pippa!"

I'm coughing, lungs filled with that familiar gas. I don't care, can't care.

Rayne's fingers on my face slacken, then she's moving, a commando crawl across the ground towards Pippa and Vixen.

I thrash against the bindings but there's no give.

The white clouds seem to thicken as they drop, blanketing me, blinding me, muffling my voice. Can't see a thing.

"No, Pippa! Pippa?"

I give up on escape and worm forward instead.

I have to get to Pippa.

A grunt floats through the smoke. A shocked cry. Someone falls, losing their breath. Running footsteps.

What the hell is happening?

"Medic!" Even I can't hear my voice properly, but I call again. "Omega team, on me. Hello?"

The gas begins to break up.

Pippa lies several feet away. Her leg twitches but her arms are loose and floppy. Red stains colour her neck and shoulder.

"Pippa! Pippa, please, look at me. Look at me."

Her gaze lifts. So glazed. Mouth open. No words.

"Pip? Look at my face. Focus on me. Keep looking at me."

I'm nearly there. Six feet away. Five. Four.

Something grabs my bound elbows and hauls me upright.

Rayne. Blisters dot her face and hands. Three have burst, and thick streams of black ooze dribble down her cheeks.

"Get the fuck off me—"

Slash.

Pressure across my chest and shoulders fades. My arms swing free. Pins and needles race across my aching muscles.

"Are you okay?" That voice. Like before. Soft. Gentle. Kind.

Three figures in SPEAR field gear shove Rayne aside. "Agent Karson? Are you okay?"

My legs give out.

I land on my knees, a jolt I feel right to the top of my head.

"Karson, personal status report."

I blink at the first of the three agents. "Quinn?"

"Give me your status report."

Such a simple command. I know the answer. I know what I'm supposed to say, but my lips don't work.

"Karson!" She slaps me. "Hey." Again. "Report."

"Agent Karson"—I lick my lips—"unharmed, untouched. Clear of all known toxicants."

They pull me up. Not gently.

Quinn peers into my eyes and shakes her head. "Shock. Get her out of here. Upstairs with the others."

Upstairs? But Pippa—I can't leave her.

The thought clears my head in an instant.

"Pip!" I barge past the agents and drop beside her. "Pip? Sis? Look at me."

Her eyes roll up to meet mine. Again an attempt to speak, but she can't. Her throat…

I swallow the lump forming in the back of mine and hike a smile to my lips. "Hey, sis. Rough night, huh?"

She smiles. Tries to.

"I know what you're thinking: How do we get all this blood out of our clothes? I'm an expert in that, don't worry. And if I can't, we'll go shopping. You'll want something nice for the christening, anyway."

Tears glitter in her eyes. Again her lips move.

I can't stand it. "Pip, I'm so sorry."

A hand on my shoulder.

I know that grip. In the middle of this madness and pain, I know that grip and who it belongs to.

"I'll break your neck," I tell Rayne. "I'll throw your worthless carcass on a gate spike and dance on your back to drive it in."

"You need to get Vixen."

More blisters have popped on her face. She's weak and slow, but her eyes gleam with familiar fiery silver. "I hurt her a little, but I can't fight any more. You can. Please."

I twist away from her hand. It falls limp to her side.

Another agent hurries up to my side. He lifts the visor on his helmet. "Dee-Dee, sorry for the delay. I had to change, sí? And pick up this little beauty." He pats the head of the battleaxe peeping out over his shoulder, strapped to his back with a harness that criss-crosses his chest.

"Noel?" I grip his shoulders. Touch his face. His hair. His vest. His gun. "How?"

"Your Rayne is more than pretty—she is so, so clever. She gave us time."

"You were dead."

"Then my acting is as good as hers. No, not dead, waiting. Free to call backup." Noel shoves a gun into my hand, *my* gun, and drags a protective vest over my head. "Hurry. Your Wensleydale and his pack will round up the runners, but we must catch the leader."

Too fast. Too much. I don't—

"Dani?"

I spin to face my sister. "Pip? I'm here, yes I'm here."

Each word labours, rough and awkward, past a ravaged throat. "I'm…okay."

"Mierda, what's this?" Noel takes one look at Pippa and slaps a hand to his headset "Omega team, get down here. I have a class two vampire bite, evac needed two minutes ago." Pause. "I don't care, come through now…I said, *now*."

I move closer, but he snags my arm. "Dee-Dee, we have to go."

"Pippa—"

"There's nothing more you can do right now. Rayne will stay with her."

"No. No, I won't let her hurt—"

He shakes my shoulders. "Yes. She protected you, now she protects your sister. Now you have one thing left to do, sí? What are you?"

"I…"

He shakes me again. "What are you?"

"I-I'm a SPEAR."

"Yes!" He squeezes my arms. "And what do you do?"

"I don't…"

"What do you do, Agent Karson? My friend."

"Protect and serve." My voice strengthens. "Learn and understand." Even my back straightens as I shift my grip on the gun. "Hunt and exterminate."

"Oh yes, Dee-Dee." He slaps my shoulder. "Now we go do it."

Pippa lifts her hand, all but her smallest finger curled down. "Don't…let them…win."

"I promise." I curve my little finger around hers. "On my locs and hope to trim. Vixen's going down."

CHAPTER THIRTY-TWO

My head is swimming, but movement helps to clear it. This is what I've trained for, what I've lived for since I joined the regiment. Gun in my hand, trusted colleagues at my back and ahead, a violent threat in need of termination.

Most of the *edanes* have scattered or fallen, caught off guard by the first attack with the incense bomb, or mowed down by advancing SPEARs. A few of the werewolves have tried to shift, but the silver content of the bomb stutters the change and leaves them caught between human and hybrid forms.

Beyond the huge meeting space, another set of tunnels leads further off into the facility. The ones to the left and right are dim and blank, but the centre tunnel echoes with the running footsteps of fleeing vampires. A trail of blood leads the way in.

"You, you, and you, come with us." Noel points as he runs. "You others, relay to Quinn: we pursue the queen. Make sure Omega can get through."

I stop at the tunnel edge, back to the wall. Deep breath in.

Protect and serve.

"Ready?" Noel positions himself on the other side of the tunnel.

Learn and understand.

Slow breath out.

"Let's go."

Hunt and exterminate.

Three of Wendy's wolves bound past me into the tunnel. They spring like mountain goats, using walls and floor in equal measure. My surprise lasts only an instant before I follow, using their huge furry bodies as cover.

The wolves find the stragglers quickly and charge straight through.

Vampires scatter left and right, some falling, others crawling up the walls, all of them yelling and spitting in fury.

Noel nudges my arm and cocks his head left.

I sidestep the snarling, slashing melee on the ground without breaking stride. One of the vampires snatches at my leg, but I leap over it and keep running. Always running.

More vampires ahead.

Noel hurls another incense bomb. Cloudy white strands burst through the air.

Coughing. Cursing. Choking. Dying.

I sprint through, legs pumping, arms swinging, gaze fixed forward.

I know I'm too far ahead. I know the other agents are falling back, unable to keep up with my frantic pace, but I can't stop. There's only one thing left now. One last thing.

"Dee-Dee, down!"

Too slow.

An outstretched arm slams into my throat, and I drop back on my arse, fighting the rush of bile clawing up from my gut.

Can't breathe.

Noel slides ahead of me and fires a single shot.

Nothing.

"Who is it?" I ask. Or I try to. My throat burns and only the weakest wheeze works past my lips.

More smoke swirls around us. Too much. Can't see.

"Stay low." Noel turns in a slow circle.

"Vamp?" Again my voice is nothing. I tighten my grip on the gun, miraculously still in my hand.

"Going somewhere, Agent? Shii re lae?"

I suck in a ragged breath. "Marco."

"Dix sut ma, arri ja'lar pisch?"

"Fuck…you…fanger." I wave away Noel's hand. Anger is enough to get me standing. "You clotheslined me, hardly fair."

A dark shape moves through the cloudy swirls on the right.

"I wish I'd known you back at the restaurant. To think I had you and did nothing worse than serve you a meal intended for an infant."

"To think." Again I wave Noel aside.

He gives up trying to help and guards my back, gun aimed outward.

The wolves behind reassure me we're unlikely to be hemmed in, but their racket also disguises Marco's movements. In that moment, I'd give a lot for the senses of a vampire.

"You're too late, Agents. We've planned this for many years, made precautions. This minor snarl will do nothing to untangle the tapestry of our victory."

Eye-roll. "You done, Shakespeare?"

Marco's face appears on the right.

I scoot sideways on my arse. Not graceful, but quick.

Gun up. Aim. Fire.

Nothing.

"Keep out of my way." I can taste the chemicals in the air. The blend of silver compounds and frankincense are a mild irritant for humans, but Marco must be in real pain. If I could just get a clear shot. "You're not the one I want."

"Perhaps, but I won't let you harm Vixen. She's the oldest, wisest, and strongest of us all. A true queen."

Noel nudges my knee with his toe and twirls his finger at shoulder height before pointing to the far wall.

I shake my head.

He does it again, teeth bared.

No. It won't work. It can't work, it—He's already gone, sliding silently through the clouds of smoke.

I'm alone in the puffy whiteness.

With no distractions, I catch the rustle of fabric, the sibilant whisper of light feet on hard ground.

I twist towards it, eyes closed.

"Vixen isn't a queen." I raise my voice. It drops on the air like a fist, but I need to keep Marco's attention on me. "I've seen more powerful vamps locked up at HQ."

An angry hiss. Behind? When did he get back there?

"You dare—"

"Damn right." I lick my lips. Swivel again. "If she's so powerful, why does she need you to stall me? Why doesn't she face me? Small, insignificant SPEAR with nothing but a gun and an attitude."

A rush of cool air flits across my face.

I hurl myself backward flat to the floor, head cracking off the stone. Marco's fingers graze my nose and forehead before the gunshots fill the air.

Shots?

Mine goes wide, thrown off by my awkward dive. The gun is gone before I get the chance for another, and my wrist sings with agony.

Marco scoots around me like a crab, a terrifying blur of speed.

More shots.

A grunt and soft mutterings in Italian.

"Enough flirting, you bloodsucking European bastard." Noel steps into view. "Didn't you know, Dee-Dee likes the girls?" He keeps firing, above my head now, walking forward with each thunderous shot.

Marco jerks and twists like a puppet as each bullet strikes his chest. Blood dribbles like tears but there's none of the black gunk associated with a heart strike.

"Fucking aim, Noel!"

He laughs, a sound that dies when the gun clicks instead of cracks.

Marco totters in the centre of the corridor. Thin ribbons of crimson stream from his lips and chest, but his eyes shine silver. "When you're quite finished, Human." He darts forward. A blur. A streak. An impossible humanoid bullet dealing pain and death. He slams into Noel with both hands outstretched, leading the way like a spear.

A muted pop, like a microwaved potato, then a grunt.

Laughter.

Not Noel.

"Now, this?" Marco's voice is low and snake-like. "*This* is flirting."

Between him and the brickwork, Noel hangs from Marco's hand against his stomach. No…not *against*.

The vampire swings his hands free in a spray of crimson droplets.

Noel slumps, one hand cupped to the fresh bloody holes in his protective vest.

"So sweet." Marco sucks each bloodied finger with a near indecent moan. "Now, Agent, shall we?"

There's a single knife in my vest, length of a Bowie, shape of a machete.

Not enough.

I draw the blade and settle my weight to the balls of my feet. "Tyr ackt."

"With pleasure." Marco chuckles, then vanishes.

Again, that cool air on my cheek. Then stars and a stunning impact to my jaw. More rushing breeze. A knee in the stomach. Chop to the back of the neck. Jab in the ribs. Strike to the chest.

On the floor again. Crawling. Blood in my mouth.

I spit it away. "Stop playing and fight me properly." I make it to Noel's side before Marco straddles my hips and tangles a hand in my hair. The other he slides around my throat, half pulling me off the ground.

"Right again. I've more important things to do."

My comeback quip gets caught in my throat.

"I'll pop your head like a wine cork. Would Madam prefer red or rosé?"

Pressure builds. My brain is going to explode any second.

Noel's hand drags down my side, snagging on my pocket, which rips along with my belt loop.

He jerks the Kubotan from the torn fabric and swings the chain like a whip.

Marco jerks away from my body, hissing and spitting, swearing in Italian. His face is red beneath a long bloodied gash across his jaw and nose.

That small motion is too much for Noel. He collapses the rest of the way. "Told you...chains...useful."

I snatch the Kubotan in one hand and the end of the chain with the other. Both feel strange, rough and textured as though scratched. Or engraved.

Hope swells within me.

When Marco lunges again, I swing the chain high and twist my hands to loop the links around his neck. As the cool steel makes contact with his skin, the vampire shrieks and drops to his knees. I follow, now pulling my hands apart, closing the loop around his throat.

Smoke pours off his skin, scented of charred bacon.

He shrieks and screams and scratches, but every movement helps my grip.

I sit on his back, pull for leverage, put every ounce of strength into pulling that chain.

Blood trickles through the links.

Still I pull.

The smell worsens.

Heat grows between us as the holy symbols etched into the metal burn skin.

The chain slackens, so I pull again, aware now that I'm searing *through* his flesh.

Screams. So many screams.

I close my eyes but I can't block it out. The agonized chorus goes on, and the sight of that slender chain cutting through Marco's throat scorches my memory.

The chain abruptly gives, a change followed by a thump and a dull rumble.

I know what I'll see when I open my eyes. So I don't.

"Dee-Dee? Come on, get up. You showed that blood sucker."

Instead of Marco, I see Noel above me. His face is pale as chalk, eyes wide and haunted, but his old smile is there, rakish and lively. He waves for me to stand.

"You're hurt." Idiot. But I don't know what else to say.

He shrugs, and though the gesture clearly hurts, the smile never fades. "This? A scratch."

"You need Omega—"

"*You* need to get Vixen. I'll be fine."

I want to believe that. I *have* to believe that.

"Wait, Dee-Dee?" Noel fumbles the huge battleaxe off its harness. "You'll want this."

My own grin grows.

With a nod, I shift the axe to a two-handed grip and walk down the corridor. On the way, I take care to kick Marco's severed head against the wall.

CHAPTER THIRTY-THREE

It's cold down here. Dim too.

Sparse lighting forms strips along the walls, guttering, winking. Small droplets of something dark and glistening form a trail ahead.

A quick touch and a sniff give me the best news I've had all night. Maybe now I'll stand a chance.

The axe droops in my grip. The head is heavier than I remember and my arms ache with the effort to keep it raised.

Or am I just tired?

The tunnel ends at five short steps leading up to a single door.

Deep breath.

"Danika?"

I freeze and wait for my heart to stop trying to burst through my ribs. "Go away."

"Let me help you."

Gritted teeth. The leather grip on the axe creaks. "Rayne—"

"I promised I'd protect you." She stops beside me, close enough to touch.

"I don't need your protection."

"You have it anyway."

I side step. "Pippa?"

"With the medics. I don't know if they—"

"Vixen needs to die. I'm going out there to kill her—no trial, no capture, just dead, understand?"

Her hand closes over mine. "When the time comes, let me say goodbye? She's all the family I have left."

Rayne's skin is so soft, even beneath the sticky coat of half-dried blood and the crust of drying black ooze.

My chest tightens, a new pain I can't shake off. "Don't try to stop me."

"I won't." She releases my hand.

I open the door.

❖

Rain.

The proper stuff, cold and wet.

Looking through to the alley outside, I realize we haven't travelled as far as I thought.

At the end of the narrow passage between two buildings, a steady trickle of traffic roars past. Dim street lamps cast long shadows across the ground. My nose wrinkles at the combined scents of exhaust and litter.

"She's here, I know it." Rayne steps out beside me, careful to keep a good distance between us.

I steady myself and look again. Street to the left. High wall to the right, topped by barbed wire. Rough, pitted concrete showing patches of the old cobbles beneath. Windows high in the walls to the front and back. Large industrial bins against the wall directly ahead. A high-heeled shoe protruding from the darkness behind a stack of bulging black bags.

I heft the axe. "Come out where I can see you."

Rustling. The bags tumble over.

Vixen eases to her feet, one hand pressed tight to her stomach, low down near the hip. Her blouse is stained with heavy, damp splotches. Red, not black.

"I must ask about your companions' ammunition, Agent Karson." She peers beneath her hand. "I've never seen anything like this wound before."

"Probably our explosive rounds." My own voice is a whisper now, rasping across a dry, parched throat. My fingertips tingle. "They won't kill you if we don't hit you right, but they're a bitch to heal."

"I quite agree. But…" Vixen lowers her hand and straightens from her round-shouldered stoop. She smiles. "You've yet to encounter the likes of me. I assure you, bitch or not, I can heal anything you dare throw at me." She puts a finger to her right eye and lifts out a contact lens. Another from the other eye. The light is wrong, but I already know what colour replaces that grey.

"Shall we begin?"

I lift the axe.

A shift on the air drags my attention left, but the blow comes from my right and sends me stumbling forward.

A cool breeze whips sheets of newspaper and food wrappers across the ground.

"Danika!" Rayne darts in and puts her back to mine.

"No."

"Let me help."

Vixen stops on the left again, arms crossed, hip popped. "You dare, Rayne?" Though calm, her tone has an edge of ice. "Betray me for this human?"

Rayne's back stiffens against mine. "I—"

"Shut up." Not sure who I'm talking to, but my outburst silences both vampires. Their attention on me is a prickling blanket across my skin.

"Human, this isn't your concern. Do others of your kind interrupt your mother when chiding you?"

"I wish they would."

Vixen sighs and returns her attention to Rayne. "My sweet, you are my favourite. I have so many plans for you, for your knowledge and skills."

In the distance, a siren wails.

"I can't. You can't do this." Rayne's voice quivers. "It's not right."

Silver brightens in Vixen's eyes, giving her the appearance of a feral cat in headlights. "Is it right that we're hunted and murdered daily? That we're killed for nothing more than the fact that our dietary needs differ from those of the wider population?"

"You kidnapped people."

"I fed my children. As any responsible mother would." Vixen glides closer. "You're a child in a cruel, harsh world." Her eyes glitter to match the pointed smile. "And their world has no space for you. In my world you have purpose. Family."

I dart away from Rayne, axe angled low, and swing for an uppercut into Vixen's face.

She spins to the side, a ballet-like pirouette, and slams her fist into my back, high between the shoulder blades.

Air bursts out of me. Agony races up and down my spine.

I fall.

"See, Rayne?" Vixen continues as though I never moved. "She attacks to silence me. She knows I'm telling the truth."

Great heaving breaths. Nausea bubbles through me. Still I force the words out. "You...bit...Pippa."

"I sought sustenance to heal an injury inflicted by *your* comrades."

My back, open and unguarded, slams into the wall. She holds me there, forearm across my throat, free hand pinning my wrist to the brickwork. She twists. Bones crunch. The axe clatters to the ground.

"Come, my little raindrop." Though her gaze never leaves mine, I know she's speaking to Rayne. "You must be hungry. Join me for a family meal."

Fangs pierce skin below my right ear, white-hot needles digging into my flesh.

My body writhes. Can't stop the hot stream of piss running down my leg.

Is this what it feels like to die?

Vixen moans against me, pulling back to lick at her teeth marks. "So sweet, Agent Karson. I'll make you last for hours yet. Come, Rayne. Join me."

My lips move. No sound.

Fangs in my throat again, the other side this time. Sucking, pleasured moans, and the horrifying sensation of my lifeblood draining away.

Perhaps it won't be so bad. Perhaps it's better to go in the line of duty like this. Mum will get some sort of payout, and without me around to upset her, maybe she'll be happy again. After a while.

Warm now.

Never thought dying would feel like a comforting bath.

Rayne moves closer. Stares deep into my eyes. "Vixen..."

Fire in my lungs.

"Yes, my treasure?"

Pounding in my ears.

Rayne looks away. "Goodbye."

Vixen gasps. Her mouth jerks open against my throat. Fangs slide away.

Pressure fades. Pain sings through me.

I drop, vision spinning, shoulder throbbing.

"So you've made your choice?" Vixen leaves me to face Rayne. No softness in her voice now, no tenderness, just raw, bitter fury.

My axes protrudes from her back. Half the blade has vanished into her flesh, but still she's moving, standing, talking, fighting.

Why won't this bitch die?

Rayne's hands fly to her mouth. "I'm sorry. I had to. I had to." She's gasping. Crying. Begging.

Vixen reaches round and yanks the axe out of her back. Drops it. Near my fingers.

I touch the shaft. Remember the comforting weight in my hands. The power. The strength.

My fingers close over the soft leather.

I'm standing, not sure how, and I can see Vixen. The golden halo of her hair is mussed up and tangled.

"Hey!" I yell. Try to. The word is a strangled groan.

She turns, fury stamped on her features.

I swing the axe.

The blade whistles as it cuts the air, a call of defiance I echo with a shriek of my own.

The edge bites her throat. Shears through.

Black blood jets into the air, propelling her snarling head across the alley. It lands near the bins, lips still moving, eyes still blinking.

The body shudders, then drops like a puppet, jerking and twitching.

My knees fold. Axe slips away from limp fingers.

I chuckle, a weird hiccuping sound through gasps of relief. "Heal that, bitch."

Rayne crouches in front of me. She's crying. And smiling.

"We need to go," she whispers.

I want to lie down. I'm tired. Why am I so tired?

"You need to get to Pippa."

The fatigue clears with a snap. Swirling dizziness vanishes.

Pippa. Oh fuck, Pip.

I scramble up. Leave the axe. Leave Vixen. Leave Rayne.

Back into the tunnel, back to my sister.

❖

The holding area with all those cells is empty. Slick piles of black ooze mark the final resting places of several vampires, while bullet casings and empty incense bomb capsules litter the floor. Blood too. Lots of it, and a smell that takes me back to the crematorium where we last saw Dad.

Rayne clears her throat. "Everyone is upstairs."

"How do you...? Vampire."

She smiles, but it doesn't reach her eyes. "Do you need help?"

It would be so easy in that moment to let her take my arm or even carry me.

"Not from you." I keep walking, though not before I catch sight of the agony in her eyes.

Upstairs, the security office and dance floor are empty. More signs of fighting here, both from the werewolves and SPEAR. More bullet casings, traces of silver nitrate, and the glittering links of broken chain scattered across the tiles.

Through the slicks of blood, twin tracks surrounded by smudged footprints lead to the exit.

Wheels.

A gurney?

I move faster.

Outside, swirling blue lights top three ambulances, two police cars, and four SPEAR vehicles.

Curious onlookers press close to a line of police tape. Many point when I exit the club, others screaming when they see Rayne.

Uniformed officers approach from all sides, so I toss my gun and raise my hands.

"Turn around. Slowly. Lace your fingers behind your head and get on your knees."

I obey, pausing halfway when a sharp voice cuts overhead, saying, "Idiota, she's one of us."

Something in my chest gives a little skip. "Noel? You're alive?"

"Mostly, guapa. I said, leave her alone."

"It's okay, I'm not—"

"Yes, you are. Fuck the rules, fuck these idiots, and fuck Quinn for suspending you. You *are* one of us. Now, you miserable civvie bashers, get the hell away from my fellow agent."

"What about her?" They point to Rayne.

"She's with us too. Now do your jobs and keep those crowds back."

The officers clear out, muttering.

Finally I see Noel. He lies on a gurney, with two paramedics at his head, testing, bandaging, injecting.

He doesn't speak, just points to the ambulance on the left.

Pippa isn't moving when I reach her. The paramedics swarming around her move like ants, busy and tense, quick and efficient.

My heart is in my throat. I can taste my pulse.

They bundle her into the back of the ambulance and slam the doors.

"Wait. I'm coming too."

One figure, pushing a penlight back into his pocket, looks me up and down. "And you are?"

"Her sister. Please, I can't leave her."

"We need to go. Like, five minutes ago." This voice comes from the driver who leans out of her window with a scowl. "Get a move on."

I open the doors.

The paramedic lays a hand on my arm, then jerks it back at a rippling snarl from Rayne.

Climb in. Sit.

Rayne follows, not speaking, just watching, silent and thoughtful.

"Get out. Get out now."

"There's no time." Again the driver. "If we're saving her, we leave now."

Rayne stares.

I sigh. "Let's go."

❖

Something's beeping. It's loud. Shrill.

I look left, right, searching for clues in the expressions of the paramedics who leap into action beside me. One holds a bag of some clear fluid, a tube at its base already linked to a needle inserted in the back of Pippa's hand. The other one checks her pulse against his watch. He swears and starts a series of breaths and compressions.

No. No, no, no, please, not Pippa. Not my little sister.

Fuck, the baby.

Tears are hot on my cheeks as I watch them work, and I find myself praying, something I've not done since Dad died. I pray, not knowing who, if anyone, is listening, and the words pour from my mouth.

"Please, don't die, Pip. Not you, please, not you. You've got to be okay. You're going to live through this, just hang on a little longer. Please, Pip. Please, please, please."

The paramedics count softly, eight chest compressions followed by three deep breaths.

Still she doesn't move.

The beeping continues.

"Please, Pip. You can't leave me. Don't die. Please, don't die."

The compressions become more urgent. Faster.

"We're losing her."

"No, you're not. Keep trying. Don't let her die."

The ambulance takes a corner and throws me into Rayne's arms. She sets me back on my feet and shuts her eyes, head cocked to one side.

"Okay, zap her. Let's go."

They're moving around, pulling out wires, paddles, sticky skin patches. The heart monitor beneath a shelf of bandages flares to life.

They rip her blouse. Squirt contact gel onto her chest. The paddles.

"Clear."

Pippa's body jerks high, then drops.

Blip. Blip. Green line.

"Clear."

Spasm. Stillness.

"More. And three, two, one. Clear."

I can't see. Someone's holding me but I don't know who. I want to talk, beg, but the words are stuck in my throat. They taste bitter and my body locks with panic and pain.

"Please. Please, Pip."

"Clear."

Blip. Green line.

Nothing.

Another corner.

"Again?"

"No, she's gone." A sigh. "Log it, will you? Time of death oh-six thirty-eight."

The sirens stop wailing.

"No!" I hurl myself forward, over Pippa, gazing at her beautiful, beautiful face. "Pippa? Pippa, please, you can't be dead. Please!"

"Miss, you need to stay sitting. Miss?"

Strong, urgent hands shove me back into the little seat near the door.

Pen scratching on paper. Soft whispers. Footsteps. Cloth rustling. I lower my face to my hands and sob like I never have before.

Not Pippa. Not my sweet, loving sister. Not Pip.

"What are you—No! Stop that. You can't. Stop right now."

I peer through my fingers.

Rayne stands over Pippa. Her right arm is stretched above Pippa's mouth which she holds open with her left hand. Shiny red droplets stream from her wrist to splash against Pippa's lips.

Heat darts across my face and neck. I'm up again, pushing, kicking, clawing, punching. "Don't you dare. Don't you dare do this. Not to my sister. Not to Pip."

She doesn't even struggle. My charge slams her into the side of the ambulance and dislodges a shelf of boxes. They spill around us, blister packs and foil packets scattering across the floor. A stethoscope drops across my shoulder. Saline rains from a burst packet.

"Bitch!" I'm crying now. "You monster. You fucking crazy fanger. You won't make her like you. Not Pip, not like you. I'll cut your fucking head off, I swear on my human soul."

Rayne strokes my cheek.

I freeze.

The two paramedics smear themselves against the far wall. Both are pale and shaken.

"It's the only way," says Rayne.

I grasp two fistfuls of her clothes. "To what?"

"For you to not be lonely."

Buzzing in my ears. Blankness.

I slump against the gurney, the fight finally gone.

Vixen may be dead, but the damage she's done will last forever. She won after all.

My vision blurs. "She can't be a vampire. She can't be like—"

"Me?"

I bite my lip. "You're evil."

She looks away. "True. But that doesn't change how I feel about you."

The words are a knife and I gasp as they stab deep. "You don't know me. You don't feel—how can you? You're a dead, soulless monster who drinks blood and pretends to live."

Her shoulders lift towards her ears. "I know. But I still fe—"

"Fuck you!" My voice cracks, but I scream it again. And again. Again. "This is the last pure thing left in my life and you've destroyed it."

"No." Her voice hardens. "No more, Danika. Either you care for me too and you're hurting because you thought I lied, or you accept that I'm a vampire and incapable of feeling like all the others. You can't have it both ways any more."

Something beeps. Not the high, sharp sound of the heart monitor, but something smaller. Closer.

My watch.

Can it really be that close to sunup? Have we really been doing this all night?

Rayne shuffles closer. When she snags my hands, I tug them away, but she tries again, and again, until I'm just too tired to pull away. She squeezes my fingers.

"Am I like all the others?"

"Yes," I snap.

"Really?" She's staring again, that warm, loving look. The one filled with fire, passion, and longing. Her soul is naked in that look. "Do you honestly believe that?"

I stare at our intertwined fingers, my dark ones against her pale ones. "You told them that I was nothing. Worthless."

She sighs. "The moment we went through that door we couldn't win. Giving Noel a chance to call in support was the only thing I could think of."

"You were pretty convincing."

"I had to be, or they would have killed us all. I couldn't let that happen."

My shoulders drop. "But Pippa…"

"I'll take care of her."

"Oh, Christ!" One of the paramedics leaps back.

I turn.

My chest constricts.

Pippa is sitting up. Staring. Breathing. *Living.*

Fangs gleam between her bloodied lips. Bright silver light flashes in her eyes.

Rayne shoves me behind her, arms outstretched. "No." Her voice is clear and strong, the sharp command of a teacher to a student. Parent to a child. A queen to her progeny.

"I smell…" Pippa's voice is soft and dreamy, like her own, but not. "It's sweet…Is it food?"

"Yes. But you need to wait."

"I'm hungry."

A small squeak from the paramedics pulls Pippa's attention towards them. She scrambles off the gurney, a desperate lunge packed with speed.

Shouts and cries of panic fill the back of the ambulance. The vehicle takes another sharp turn, feels like a U-turn, and sirens blare to life once more.

The heart monitor tumbles over. The overhead light dims.

"Pippa, please."

Her head whips round. Lips draw back off sharp teeth.

Rayne shifts to stay ahead of me. "Don't—"

I push past. "Pip? It's Danika. You know me, don't you?"

She scrambles in close to sniff my face. My hair. My throat. Her tongue flicks out to catch the dried flakes choking Vixen's bite marks on the side of my neck.

I clench my fists and force myself to stand still.

This is my sister, she won't hurt me. I have to believe that. I have to believe she can be different. Like Rayne.

"Dani?" Her voice rasps. The silver in her eyes flickers then fades. "What's happening? Why do you smell like that?"

Tears. Can barely see through the blur. "You need to listen very carefully."

Rayne shifts into a ready position on my right, eyes that beautiful shade of ripe acorns. With her fangs at rest, she is calm and as much in control as I've ever seen her.

She's different. Pippa can be too. Please…

"Pip, something really bad happened, and you'll feel different for a few days. But you're going to be fine, I promise. We'll get through this together, like always."

She bites her lip and winces as fangs cut through. "What? How did this…my teeth…? Oh God—Dani, I'm a vampire, aren't I? Oh God…oh no, no, no, no—"

"Pippa." I grab her shoulders and shake them. "Try to stay calm."

"I can smell you," she wails. "I hear waves, but it's the blood in your body. I want it—I'm so hungry."

I shove my wrist beneath her nose. "Then drink."

"No—"

"Shut up, Rayne!" I don't look at her. If I do, my rational mind will kick in and tell me that I'm doing something supremely stupid. "Drink, Pippa. Please."

The fight is in her eyes. Morals versus hunger. Right versus wrong. Human versus vampire.

The victor of the battle springs forward with the return of silver light in her eyes. She grabs my hand and bites on the wrist, rough, hard, and desperate.

The pain fires up my arm and straight through, so much worse than Vixen's bite. The creeping weakness swells fast, and there's no stopping my limp slide to the floor of the ambulance. Pippa never once releases my arm, sucking hard, gulping me down. Killing me.

Dark edges consume the corners of my vision.

Through it, Rayne whispers urgently to Pippa. She tugs her shoulders, pulls her by the waist, but the grip on my wrist never falters.

It's that warm bath again. Deeper this time. Hotter.

Then a sensation like flying. My body is light and airy, while the colours turn bright, fizzing with iridescent sparkles.

So this is the feeling Jack chases each time he offers his throat.

I understand now.

I smile, closing my eyes for the last time while the siren drones on and on.

Chapter Thirty-four

Comfortable. Soft.

Where am I? The stuff around me feels like a cloud, so light and warm.

Cosy. Safe.

Someone's talking, in urgent whispers. Two people talking. No, arguing.

I frown, pissed that someone would bring their argument into this pleasant space.

"Can't stop me seeing her. I want to know she's okay."

Okay, that voice I know. From work? TV?

I flex my fingers, aware for the first time that my eyes are closed.

Damn.

So I've been asleep? And this warm safe place is…where? Not my flat; it smells better and the sheets aren't crisp with a week's worth of sweat.

I realize then, that if I want to know where I am, I'll have to open my eyes.

"You can't stop me, so move before I report you. What's your name?"

Someone really has their tighty-whities in a knot.

The mental image makes me giggle.

The voices fall silent.

"Did she just—"

"Yeah, she did. Danika? You awake?"

There's only one person who says my name like that, a mix of lust and confidence encased in awe.

I open my eyes.

Wow, that's bright.

Close them. Prepare. Try again.

Sloooowly.

Blue and white room, plain walls, one with a tasteful art print framed in dark wood. No windows. Chair beside a low cabinet topped with a jug of water and a single glass with a straw. Small sink. Drip stand. Machines studded with wires all leading to—ah.

I lift my arm to study the drip running into the back of my hand. My chest is tight, skin drawn up beneath the sticky patches linking me to the heart monitor.

A twinge in my neck. Inspection reveals soft dressings, one to each side. More on my forehead, cheek, wrist, and fingers.

"So you *are* awake."

I face the source of the voice. "Hey, Jack."

He waves away the loitering nurse and pulls the chair up to my bed. "How's my little warrior?"

I think about that. My memory is holey, but it's clear I've been hurt badly.

"Water." Ugh, is that my voice? I lick my lips and try again. "Water. Please."

Jack obligingly fills the cup and turns the straw towards my lips.

I stare.

He frowns, sighs, and hands me the cup.

Sipping, I try to remember, struggle to bring the images darting across my memory into some sort of order.

Club Starshine. Werewolves. Hostages. Noel bleeding out. Rayne's sneering stare. Vixen kissing her. Fighting. Smoke. Pain. Pippa—

Water splashes down my front.

"Steady, Danika, you're still weak. Let me—"

"Where's Pippa?"

He tries to take the cup. I resist. More water soaks the sheets.

"You're tired and hurt. We should worry about—"

"*You* should worry about me knocking your bleached, shiny teeth out. Where's my sister?"

Jack stops his attempts to take the cup and sits back, hands raised. "You're still angry, but you've got it wrong. If you'd let me explain—"

"Where. Is. Pippa."

He drags a hand through his hair.

For the first time I notice how tired he looks. How rumpled his shirt is. I've never seen this man look anything less than pristine, even for something as simple as a walk to his car. Even his tie is stained. Waistcoat unfastened. Dark smudges beneath his eyes.

"I know what you think, but I had no idea what Amelia—I mean, Vixen—was doing. I had no idea where that money was coming from or who she really was."

I fold my arms. Tricky with the drip, but I do it anyway. And stare.

"And the blood stuff, I won't be doing that any more. It's too dangerous and I know you don't like it so I..."

Still staring.

"This isn't making any difference, is it?"

"Not a bit." I lift the sheets. Good, seems like I'm dressed. Kinda. I pile the sheets in a damp wedge and toss the lot against the wall.

Jack scratches the side of his mouth. "I'm sorry. I—even if you're gay, I still really like you. I respect you and—"

"Goodbye, Jack." I point to the door.

"Okay. I'll see you around, maybe?"

I smile. "No chance in hell."

He leaves, still wearing that stunned expression.

A moment later, the nurse returns. He holds a small bundle, all flailing legs and flapping wings.

"Karson, Karson, Karson, Karson, Karson!"

"Norma?"

The chittarik wrestles from his grip and dives across the room. She hits my chest hard, then laps frantically at my cheeks, my fingers, my head, my ears. Anywhere she can reach.

I clutch her close, barely feeling the scrabbling scratch of her claws. "Hey, baby, I'm sorry. I'm so sorry."

"Kar. Son son son-kar. Kar..."

"I know, but I'm okay."

She doesn't believe me, that's clear, now sniffing over every bandage and scrap of medical tape.

The nurse stands at my bedside. "That thing has been fighting to get down here for hours. Couldn't catch it, couldn't coax it out. Eventually that Cobé guy said it belonged to you."

"*She* does. Her name's Norma."

"Well, Norma is a pain in my fat black arse. Pretty much like you, Agent Karson."

Ah. So this is a SPEAR hospital.

"I didn't do anything."

"You didn't lose two, possibly three pints of blood? Or dislocate three fingers? You didn't crack your scaphoid"—pointing to my left wrist—"or bruise your ribs and skull? Strain and sprain your shoulder? Damage the ligaments in—"

"I get it, I'm a walking train wreck. So sorry I gave you guys some work to do."

He chuckles. When he next turns, I catch a glimpse of his name tag. Robert.

"While I know sarcasm is your specialty, I'll take that on the nose. Omega team doesn't always have much to do, but when we do, we *really* do. But you're going to be fine."

"Good, then can I have my clothes? I need to find Pippa."

"Agent—"

"Don't. Accept that I'm getting out of this bed and finding my sister. You can help me do that without falling on my face, or you can get out of the way. You can find my watch too."

Norma nuzzles my face again, then crawls up the side of my face to sit on my head. I pet her gently.

Robert sighs. "I'll get you a chair."

Chapter Thirty-five

This chair has no handrims. Not that I have the strength to wheel myself, but I hoped they'd humour me.

Robert pushes me without speaking, twisting back and forth to compensate for the front right wheel that seems determined to run me into a wall.

I keep my hands in my lap, fiddling with the worn and filthy straps of my father's watch. Norma settles happily on my head, her tail occasionally snaking down to stroke my cheek.

I don't have my own clothes, but Robert managed to find a gown that closes at the back, and a pair of nurse's trousers. Getting into them was a painful laugh riot; can't remember the last time I had so many little cuts and bruises. They don't hurt—guess I'm full of the SPEAR morphine cocktail—but my joints are stiff and my muscles over-tense.

"How long was I out?"

Robert stops at the lift and presses the red arrow pointing down. "About eight hours." He notices my little gasp. "I know. Those Clear Blood drugs must really buff you up. That or you're part bull. These injuries would keep most people out for at least a day, but it's barely sundown."

"Then Pippa—"

"No, she's not awake yet. Neither's the other one."

Ah, yes. The other one.

I bite my lip. It's bruised and puffy, but the faint ache helps me think.

Rayne isn't like the others, I know that now. But she *is* a vampire. And so is Pippa.

I run my hands through my hair and find Norma in the way. She nips my fingers.

Pippa Karson, a vampire. What about her job? Her husband? The baby?

My vision blurs as the lift doors slide open.

"Karson?"

I grunt at the sight of the other occupant of the box. "Quinn."

If Robert notices the tension between us, he doesn't mention it. He stabs the button for basement level five and pulls my chair into the corner.

Silence.

Ping. Second floor.

Shuffling.

Ping. First floor.

A cough.

Ping. Ground floor.

Someone tapping their foot.

Ping. Basement level one.

"Mikkleson is out of intensive care." Quinn rubs her nose. "They moved him early this morning."

I keep my sights fixed on the little red numbers showing our progress.

"The officers you stupidly took to Club Starshine are safe too. Shaken, but fine."

Ping. Basement level two.

"I had you brought here because you needed the care, but don't think that changes anything. You're still suspended, soon to be dismissed. And don't think you're keeping that chittarik either—"

"I'm tired, Quinn. Exhausted, actually, and probably high on morphine. I can't deal with you right now. Do me a kindness and shut the hell up."

"Ka! Ka, Karson."

Ping. Basement level three.

Silence.

At level five, the doors swish open to reveal a long, narrow corridor. A security guard nods us through after Robert flashes his ID badge.

My chair wobbles, then starts off again, much faster now, with the accompanying clip-clop of confident, assured feet.

I look back. "What the hell are you doing, Quinn? Pass me back to the other guy."

She smiles, grim and superior. "He's Omega team and has no

clearance past these doors. Were you planning to wheel yourself in?"

"So you thought you'd come down to lend a hand?"

A chuckle. "Not at all. I was called for an execution. Bringing you through to watch is a bonus. I'll even overlook your lack of clearance."

A bitter taste floods my mouth. "Who?"

She pulls a sheet of paper from her inside pocket. "Emily Friedman."

My shoulders drop. I breathe out, slow and steady.

Not Rayne.

My watch beeps. Nearly sunset.

Our holding bay, though larger and more advanced, resembles the one in Shakka's bookshop. Cells fronted with reinforced glass form twin lines to either side of the long space. Most are occupied. Brownies, gargoyles, sprites, and the occasional werewolf watch as Quinn wheels me down the walkway.

Other agents patrol the area, some in tactical gear, others not, all armed with at least a semi-automatic.

Some watch us advance; others ignore us completely.

One woman turns away from her station and trots over to us. She swings her gun round on the strap until it rests against her back. "Karson, you're awake? What are you made of, anyway?"

"Sugar, spice, and all things nice."

She grins. "You're something else. All those unregistered vampires, Amelia Smythe walking around in the day—you've turned everything we know on its head. No one knows what to do."

Can't help but snort at that. "They'll figure it out—their heads are flat enough."

She falls in step beside us. "I hear you've been dishing out blood too. You do know there are proper places to do that, right? With needles, antiseptic, and trained medical professionals."

"I like to cut out the middleman."

"You're crazy, but I'm glad you're okay. And…" For the first time her smile falters. "I'm sorry about your sister."

My fingers tighten in my lap. "Thanks."

Quinn clears her throat. "Prisoner TA865C4, please. I have an execution order."

She cuts a quick glance at me. "Um, sure. This way." She leads us to the cells on the right, her steps slow and unsure. When she points, her eyes are downcast, expression grim.

What the hell is going on?

Quinn pushes my chair up to the glass and locks the wheels in place. "Prisoner TA865C4, otherwise known as Emily Friedman or—"

"Rayne?" I try to stand, but my legs can't handle it. She's strapped to a low table, set at an angle to showcase her whole body. She's exactly as I last saw her, mangled clothes, dried blood.

"What is this?"

Quinn crouches beside my chair. "This vampire attacked numerous individuals over the course of two days. She also broke into Clear Blood facilities, stole private files, and nearly killed Jackson Cobé. She broke into SPEAR facilities too and stole dangerous and valuable weapons. The list goes on." She smiles. "You know what happens when vampires can't be controlled."

"This is bullshit."

"This is law, Karson. Time you started paying attention to it."

She leaves my chair outside the glass, a front row seat to the murder she's about to commit.

Again, I try to stand. I make it halfway before my knees wobble and dump me in the chair. I can't move. Again. Yet again, I can't do anything.

"Quinn? Quinn, don't do this. You don't know the whole story— you don't know. She was working with me. She hasn't hurt anybody, I'm telling you. Don't do this."

Heads are turning my way. Low voices muttering. Curious glances. Even Norma catches my mood, flying off my head to loop my chair, calling in her deep, gravelly voice.

Don't care.

After all we've been through, everything we've done, Rayne can't die now.

The wheelchair squeals as I shove it back, then tips, dumping me on the floor.

Ahead, smirking, Quinn is already inside the cell. She stops beside Rayne's bed and peers at her. "She's pretty, if you forget the fangs and bloodlust. But I told you, vampires are for killing, not fucking. One less leech in the world will make your—sorry, *our*—jobs easier."

I'm halfway across the floor, half in, half out of the cell. The wall helps me stand, but my knees refuse to cooperate. I can't let go unless I want to fall.

Norma flies back, calling me forward, urging me on. "Karson? Karson, Karson, Danika, Dan—"

I grab her tiny body and tuck it under my arm. "Don't be a dick because you hate me, Quinn. You know this is wrong."

"I know my job, something you clearly need a lesson in. Think of the people hurt because of you. How many have died?"

I inch along the wall. "And the people we rescued? All those hostages—"

"No excuse." She draws a slender length of silver chain from her pocket and wraps an end around each hand.

I move faster.

"We're SPEARs. We protect humans, we serve *humans*." She pulls the chain taut above Rayne's throat. "If it's any consolation, she won't feel it. One quick pull and off pops her head, faster than you can say *vamp whore*."

I'm not going to make it. I can tell. I'm too far off, I'm—

My watch beeps.

Rayne's eyes flash open. She strains and sucks in huge breaths. Her back and hips bow off the table.

Other agents arrive. Two catch me under the arms, but I don't want their help. "Quinn, please—"

"Restrain Agent Karson, please." She taps the side of her head. "I mean *Ms.* Karson. She's about to interrupt an execution as directed by the Crown Court of Supernatural Justice. Grab that pest too."

Norma yells as rough hands snatch her from my grip, trapping both wings tight to her back.

"Bitch!" Raging, pulling, slipping, falling. "You know that directive is full of shit."

More murmurs from the gathered SPEARs. The hands on my arms slacken.

"Danika?"

My head snaps up. "Rayne? Yes, I'm here."

She's smiling. "It's okay. There's no space for me here. It's better if I go."

"No." My voice cracks. "You were right, before, in the ambulance."

Deathly silence. Even Quinn appears intrigued.

"And?"

I lick my lips. "You're not like them." I shake away the hands holding my arms and wobble a step closer. "And Vixen lied, there *is* space for you if we fight for it."

Her eyes brighten with the faintest flicker of silver. "We?"

Another wobbly step. "You and me, whatever that means."

She smiles, a real, sunny smile, filled with all the words choked at the backs of our throats.

Quinn growls. "Touching, but the fact remains, I have a job to do." She stretches the chain above Rayne's throat.

"No, please!"

Norma sinks her fangs into the hand on her middle. While the agent thrashes and screams, she pelts forward, beak clicking, wings pumping, straight at Quinn's face.

Quinn stumbles, arms forward to protect her eyes. The chain falls across Rayne's throat.

Smoke. Charred flesh. Screams.

I fall and crawl the rest of the way, reaching up the table to pull the engraved and consecrated chain off Rayne's skin.

Thin wisps of smoke curl up from burnt, crispy flesh.

Still Norma jabs at Quinn, using her claws now and buffeting with her wings. I'd laugh, but Rayne is gasping, straining at the straps, and wincing.

"Rayne? Are you okay? Say something, please." I'm fumbling with the straps, clumsy, awkward fingers shaking too much to handle a simple buckle. "Talk to me."

Her lips are moving. No sound.

"You can heal that? An hour or so and you'll be fine?"

She nods.

I finally unloop the first strap.

Her right arm flies free and pulls my head down for the sweetest kiss I've ever tasted.

She tries to speak again. Fails.

"I know, Rayne. Save your strength."

Quinn scrambles off the floor, holding the back of her head. She points at the ceiling where Norma clings upside down, still yelling and lashing her tail. "Someone catch that thing and remove this crazed civilian from my cell. One of you? Any of you?"

Rayne sits up and tears the straps from their cases. In an instant, she's off the table and gripping Quinn by the throat.

Dozens of guns snap up into position, red dots flickering across Rayne's head and chest.

"No." I leap across them, arms outspread.

Norma dives and flies in front of me, a daring back and forth arc through the gleam of red beams. "Dan-dan. Nika, Karson!"

"They will shoot through you, Karson. And that bloody chittarik." Quinn's voice struggles past the grip on her throat.

I turn to offer the agents my back.

"Rayne?"

She hasn't moved, frozen with Quinn dangling from her grip.

"You have to look at me. Please?"

At last she turns, not to me but the front of the cell. I follow her gaze but there's just the line of agents with rifles and automatic weapons aimed our way.

"What? What's wrong?"

Rayne releases Quinn and laces her fingers behind her head. She's smiling.

Wheezing, gasping, Quinn scrambles away from the floating red dots. "I'm clear, now shoot her. Well? What are you waiting for?"

Uncomfortable looks from the gathered agents.

"Didn't this vampire help—"

"But if she's a civilian—"

"I saw her fighting with us—"

Quinn stamps her foot. "I don't care. Shoot them."

I hold my ground in front of Rayne and close my eyes.

Someone's shouting from far away. There's banging. Scuffling. Yelling.

"Stop!" One voice rises above the others, still distant, but clear. "Stay the execution." More loud voices, then pounding footsteps. "Stop, please. You have to stop."

I open my eyes. "Jack?"

He's running along the walkway, waving a sheet of paper above his head. Two agents chase him down, a flying tackle that slides all three of them across the floor. He struggles, still waving the paper. "Wait, please."

Quinn barges from the cell. "What the hell is he doing here? Get him out."

Jack thrusts the paper forward. "I have..." Gasping breath. "Have reversal order...execution of Emily Friedman."

I glance at Rayne.

She grins.

More murmurs from the gathered agents. Guns lower. Red lights wink out.

"Jack?"

He keeps his gaze on Quinn. "I've read the interview transcripts. Everybody knows Rayne was working with Agent Karson."

"It doesn't matter, she still—"

"Without further investigation you aren't authorized to kill anybody." Again he waves the paper. "I have it here, from the general, and countersigned with all required signatures. Reversal order for Emily Friedman, registered with the Clear Blood Foundation as Rayne. She doesn't have to die."

Quinn, still massaging her throat, snatches at the paper. Her lips twist in an ugly snarl. "Well, you shouldn't be down here. You lot, get this trespassing civilian upstairs right now."

Jack fights free of the grip on his legs and stands. "This *civilian* is now the publicly elected mayor of Angbec and would consider it a huge personal favour if you fine agents would restrain this woman. Attempted murder of a vampire is still a crime."

Silence, then every gun on the floor turns towards Quinn. The red dots make their reappearance.

"Me? No, you can't—I haven't done anything. I'm a SPEAR agent, this is ridiculous."

Jack waves his hand, a lazy dismissal. "Take her upstairs, please."

The floor rushes towards my face, checked halfway by Rayne's arm around my shoulders. She eases me to the ground beside the table. Her eyes ask the question.

"I'm fine." Then I'm laughing and crying all at once. Norma nuzzles against me and I hug her too. "Did you see her face? That stupid guppy look in her eyes? I'm going to savour that one for years. And you, Norma, are a hero."

"Ka-Karson."

Rayne leans in to kiss me, and I let her. One tender hand cups my face and tilts my head to hers, allowing her deep, intimate access to my mouth. Can't help it. I melt into that kiss, slide my hand around the back of her neck and—

A cleared throat.

Sighing, I pull away from the magic of Rayne's lips.

Jack watches us, his expression a mix of wonderment and…lust? "Sorry to interrupt, ladies."

I wipe my mouth. Try to straighten my borrowed clothes. "Jack—"

He shakes his head. "Don't apologize, and don't thank me. It's the least I could do."

"Mayor?"

A nod. "Mikkleson certainly can't perform his duties from a prison cell, and I'm happy to take a win by default. How's Pippa?"

Rayne's hand tightens on mine.

"I'm not sure yet. I haven't seen her."

Jack steps back to free the way out. "Then let's do that now."

CHAPTER THIRTY-SIX

W hy isn't she awake?" Jack's question echoes my thoughts. Pippa sprawls on a low table, one arm dangling off the side. Her head lolls, smears of dried blood still caked about her throat. Her skin is ashy and dry, her features sunken. She looks…

"Pip?" I bang the glass fronting her cell. "Pippa? Wake up."

Nothing.

"Get this cell open. Now. Someone."

The woman from earlier, her gun hanging from its strap once more, gives an apologetic shrug. "You're not authorized with your suspension in place. You shouldn't even be down here."

Jack lifts a hand. "Open the cell."

Tense pause.

She shrugs. "I said it, that's all I'm paid for. Every one of us knows that suspension is bullshit, by the way."

The glass slides up and I'm inside, Rayne with her arm around my waist, Norma clinging to my shoulder.

So cold in the cell. The air is stale with the scent of old blood.

Rayne hisses through clenched teeth and mimes drinking.

"But she did, in the ambulance." I show her my bandaged wrist. "She drank from me."

She waves her hand. Something big and round going up—rising?—something, no, some*one*—someone falling and…

"The sun? You mean the sun came up before she could finish?"

She nods.

My eyes sting.

No. This isn't fair.

I closed my eyes in that ambulance knowing I was going to die and happy to do it if it would save my sister. I had no idea sunrise could interrupt her drinking.

My mind flits back to the first morning Rayne succumbed to the sun, the way she froze mid-sentence and collapsed, utterly and unavoidably dead. Is that what Pippa did? Is that why we ended up at SPEAR rather than the hospital?

The female agent brings my wheelchair into the cell, bumping it over the entrance and lining it up beside Pippa's table.

Rayne lowers me into it, making soft humming noises at the back of her throat.

What would I give to hear her voice right now?

She pats my shoulder, points to Pippa, then leaves the cell.

"Pip." I pick at a corner of the dressing taped around my wrist. "I'm so sorry. You're my baby sister and I promised Dad I'd look after you. One of the reasons I even wanted to be a SPEAR was to protect you. Can't believe what a mess I've made of it."

No movement from the table. No sound.

Norma hops off my shoulder and lands beside Pippa. She peers at me, then back at the table. "Karson? Dan-Danika?" Her voice is sad and gravelly.

"And the worst thing? You never heard me say I was wrong. You died thinking you were like the rest of them. But I don't hate you, I hope you knew that before…"

Drip. Drip. Drip.

"You're my sister, no matter what you turn into, and I love you so much and I'm sorry."

Drip. Drip. Drip. Drip. Drip.

"Fuck, Pip, what now? You're my best friend. Who will I call for a chat at three in the morning? Who's going to head off Mum's matchmaking? Though that's probably not an issue any more."

Drip. Drip.

"I won't tell her what happened. I don't want her hating you too. I'll say…something. One more lie won't hurt."

Drip. Drip. Splat.

I lift my head, finally tuning in to that sound on the edges of my hearing.

Red, thin liquid on the floor. Dripping off the table.

I follow the trail, find my gut clenching when I find the source.

"Pippa? Hello? Help! *Edane* med required. Hello!"

Rayne dashes back into the cell, followed by Jack and the other agent. She lifts a trembling hand to her mouth, while Jack turns aside, holding his mouth. The SPEAR darts forward.

"Where's it coming from?"

"I don't know."

"Let's turn her." She grabs Pippa's shoulders and flips her. Lifts her blouse. "There's nothing there."

My gut clenches. "It's not a wound." My voice is a hollow whisper. "She's pregnant. I mean, she was. Before."

Her face takes on a queer shade of green. "Oh, Jesus."

Rayne tries to pull me back, but I'm not leaving. Not now.

More blood washes from Pippa's body, not the black ooze of vampires, but bright, vibrant red. Like a human.

I try not to look too closely at the mess on the floor.

Drip. Drip. Drip. Drip.

Rayne's arms are around my shoulders, and she's hugging me, shushing me, squeezing me tight, and brushing tears away with the pad of her thumb.

Hadn't realized I was crying.

Three more agents enter the cell, these in the blue and red of the *edane* leg of the Omega team.

"Damn," mutters one.

"She's gone," says the second.

The third frowns, looking first at Pippa, then Rayne, then back again. "Get a blood bag. No, three."

The other two move to obey, though not without raised eyebrows.

I sit straighter. "What are you doing?"

The third medic moves to my chair and nudges Rayne to one side. He pulls me back, well away from the bed. "She was pregnant, right?"

"How did—"

"Did she feed before sunup?"

"A little, but—"

"Good. Vampire bodies treat pregnancies as contaminants, but it's gone now. She may just—"

A shudder ripples through Pippa's body. She gasps, low and hoarse, before abruptly lifting her head.

Her eyes are silver.

Rayne darts behind my chair and drags it back. Norma screeches in alarm and shoots out of the cell. The medic presses himself to the wall. Even the other agent swings her gun round from her back and levels it at Pippa.

"Don't," I yell.

Pippa sits up. She sways once, twice, then looks across to us. Her body becomes statue-still, rigid and silent.

"Pip?"

Her gaze shifts left, then right, scanning the floor and the blood. Her mouth twitches. "I…"

"Pippa, look at me. Please. It's Danika."

The silver of near blood mania flares brighter. "Dani?"

"Yes, it's me. Please, don't move. Sit there and wait. Can you do that?"

She touches her stomach. Not a fast or threatening movement, but I stiffen, and so does everybody else.

Where the hell are those two with the blood bags?

A tear slides down her cheek and she wraps both arms around herself. "All that blood…I lost it, didn't I?"

I nod.

Still she doesn't move.

"Pippa?"

She slides off the bed.

A hiss from Rayne. More back-pedaling. My chair bumps the lip of the cell entrance and sticks.

Bare feet leave slick, glistening footprints as Pippa crosses the cell.

Rayne grips my shoulders, apparently ready to swing me into her arms.

"Don't." I grab the armrests to hold myself in place.

Rayne opens her mouth, but she still can't speak.

"You didn't hurt me. Neither will she. She won't. I have to believe that. Please, Rayne."

A tense pause, then Rayne backs away, close enough to respond, but far enough to offer at least the illusion of privacy.

Pippa creeps forward and crouches beside my chair. The silver in her eyes flickers, then fades, replaced by the shimmer of tears. Her smile is forced and wretched. "You look awful. Green doesn't suit you."

Laughter bursts out of me, shock and relief combined. "But my hair still looks good, right?"

More tears slip down her cheek, slightly pink. "You always had the best hair." Her hand extends as if to touch it, then jerks back at the last moment.

I throw my arms around her, feeling her body tremble to match mine.

How are we going to do this? How are we going to cope? What does this mean? What will Mum say? What are we going to do?

The questions, the uncertainties, the fear swirl through my mind, over and over until even thinking about them is impossible.

"Pippa—"

"This isn't your fault," she murmurs in my ear.

Typical Pippa. Comforting me when she's the one who needs it most.

"I'm going to fix this." Sniff. Rub the snot from my nostrils and upper lip. "I promise. I can't…I won't let you. I'll figure out a way. Oh, Pip. I'm sorry. I'm so, so sorry."

She grips me tighter, sobbing hard against my bandaged shoulder. "I know."

❖

Pippa is gone when I wake next. Rayne too.

Norma snores at the end of my bed, barbed tail tucked in, wings folded down.

Fresh clothes lie on the back of the chair beside my bed. Still not mine and certainly not my style, but better than the gown and baggy trousers. I pull on the jeans and T-shirt, with only a little wincing, and shuffle to the door.

"What the hell, Karson?" Robert again, blocking my path with both hands braced in the frame.

"How did you know I was up?"

He points to the sensors in opposite corners of the room. "Normally we wouldn't use them for agents, but you're known as a live one." He grins.

I match him. "Where's Pippa and Rayne?"

"Both downstairs, in holding." He lifts a hand at my indignant cry. "They're the only places we can guarantee as vamp safe. You know that."

He's right, but the fact irks me. How have I never seen how badly we treat vampires?

"They've been helpful." Robert leads me back to my bed, talking the whole time. "They both gave evidence on Vixen and her plans. She was going to use all that land she bought for food storage facilities and change the new mayor to get them onside."

I have to think that through. "Cages for humans?"

He nods. "We have names, locations, dates, and plenty of other *edane* accomplices…everything we need."

"But she's dead."

"Yes, you made sure of that. But she had lots of contacts and other older vampires in high places. We need to smoke them out and register those who've escaped registration." He tucks the sheets around my hips.

Wait, when did he get me back into bed?

"You'll have to be lucky. There were loads of them."

"Perhaps, but it's our job."

"Our?"

Robert's next smile shows the gap between his two front teeth, and a dark spot on the side of one molar. "They asked me to give you this. It's actually why I came down." He lays a laminated rectangle on my lap.

An ID card. *My* ID card.

The back of my throat prickles. "But I'm not a G6."

"Seems fine to me." He shrugs. "There's the hologram and the issue date—that's today, by the way. Looks like someone got promoted." He leaves me holding the card, mouth open, eyes stinging.

When did I become such a soppy crybaby?

"Knock, knock?"

I dash tears from my eyes and sit straighter. "Noel?"

"The one and only." He wheels through—how come *his* wheelchair has handrims?—and positions himself at the end of my bed. "Guau, you look like shit."

"Screw you, wheels."

He laughs, winces, and wraps an arm around his stomach. Through the open front of his shirt, stiff white bandages cover most of his torso. "Did you hear we have a new Grade Six on the Alpha team?"

Jammy bastard. How did he know?

I hold up my new ID. "Seems they won't take no for an answer this time."

"Or they worry you'll set your pet vampire on them." He rolls back as I raise my first. "I joke, I joke, be calm. When did you get so high-strung?"

"When you became an insufferable arsehole."

"Me? No. Perhaps you're thinking of Quinn?"

I lower the fist. "How are *you?*"

He shrugs. "Internal bleeding, gastrointestinal perforation, cracked ribs. I lost some lower intestine and they accidentally took my appendix."

"Seriously?"

"Ha, no. Drugs make you gullible. But I must hug my desk for a while, no fieldwork for many weeks."

I study Noel's face, the bright eyes, designer stubble, and strong, square jaw. In another place, time, and life, I might have really fallen for him. He's one of the few men able to keep up with my snark and willing to give as good as he gets. Good with a gun too.

"Thanks, Noel."

He cocks his head. "No. Don't do the sentimental woman thing. It's too much for me, sí?" He pats his chest. Hisses through clenched teeth. "Mierda, that hurts."

I arch an eyebrow at him. "Pussy."

"You wish," he shoots back.

Yep. In another place, time, and life.

A tap at the door draws my attention outward.

"Mum?"

She stands in the door frame with one of our ward assistants, handbag clutched to her side. Both eyes are red, puffy. Her cheeks have faint dried streaks on them. Worse than that, her expression is a miserable blend of fear, hope, and pain.

Noel takes one look and wheels his chair out, herding the ward assistant ahead of him. "We speak later, Dee-Dee."

"Good to see you, Mum."

"Mm-hmm." She doesn't move.

"I—sorry I didn't call before. I got swept up in the case and…" Why is she staring? As if drinking me in. "Mum?"

She roots through her handbag and comes out with a small plastic bag. "I came to give you this." She tosses it at the bed. Still standing in the doorway.

I use the sheets to pull the bag closer. Inside, a photo in a tarnished silver frame. Mum, Dad, Pippa, and me, standing in front of our old house back in Cipla. It's spring there; flowers are blooming and the sky is pale blue, streaked with soft puffs of cloud. Sparrows perch in the heavy fronds of jasmine crawling up the side of our home.

I remember that day.

We were about to go on a day trip, some beach down south. Mum hated it, but Dad couldn't wait to dive into the sea and show us how to swim as he did as a child. We came back that night exhausted but happy, covered in sand and crusted streaks of sea salt.

"I have a copy"—Mum points—"and there's another one for Phillipa. One each, so you can remember your family."

I pause my happy consideration of the photo. "What?"

Mum folds her arms. "That is what family looks like, Danika. Look at that and remember what we *used* to be before you broke us."

The words pierce like a blunt spoon. I'm hunched over, gasping as if punched. "I broke? Mum—"

"I know you let that monster bite my girl. How could you? To spite me? To make sure I've no daughters left at all?"

Words stick in my throat. "No. Mum, that's not…You can't mean that."

"You're a sexual deviant and Phillipa is a bloodsucking monster. I'm alone."

I grip the photo hard enough that the frame creaks. "We're here, Mum, nothing has changed. Pippa might be…different now, but she's still our Pip. And I'm still Danika."

Her gaze hardens. "Not *my* Danika. She and my Phillipa are gone. Goodbye."

"Mum? Mum, wait. Mum!"

CHAPTER THIRTY-SEVEN

"W hat the hell is this?"

"My hand, isn't that a flush?"

"No, Rayne, that's a full house. You've won again."

She's never played poker before. No idea how she's come so far in life without ever playing Texas Hold 'Em, but today is as good a day as any to fix that.

"Ah, so cunning, you pretty vampire." Noel drops his cards on top of the matchsticks we're using as currency. "This is a joke, sí? That's the third game you win. In a row."

She shrugs. "Luck?"

"Say what you like, but no more bets." He wheels his chair to the sink, where he splashes his face from the cold tap. "You lovely ladies keep going, but I need sleep. I leave tomorrow. Try not to miss me."

Rayne starts to retrieve the cards. "We'll manage."

"You think? This is the longest I've seen you two stop the touching."

"Jealous?"

He dries his face on a towel. "If I want to watch sexy ladies, I have Wi-Fi in my room."

I toss a pillow at him. It misses by a yard. "Randy bastard."

He wheels away, with a wave and a cackle.

Rayne puts the cards on the table and stops next to Pippa. "You've barely said a word all night." Her voice is soft and gentle, nurturing. "How are you feeling?"

"What?" Pippa's head lifts. Her eyes widen. "Did you say something?"

"Earth to Pip." I wave my hand back and forth. "What's up?"

Stillness follows, broken only by Rayne's soft movements. She finishes clearing up and returns the chairs to their homes against the wall. She even changes the water in the vases left by Wendy and Jack.

Pippa sits, silent and staring, chewing the inside of her cheek. "I haven't been outside since that night."

The bustling stops. No more footsteps.

I look to Rayne and know my expression must match hers.

"Pip, you'll be fine."

"But where will I go?" Her fingers clench on my sheets. "I can't go to Mum, and Adam won't return my calls."

I straighten. "You never told me that."

"I've left a voicemail every night. Texts. Emails. I send them again before sunrise, but he hasn't said a word." A pale pink teardrop slides down her cheek. "He doesn't want me any more, now that I'm…"

"Pippa."

"It's okay." She brushes her cheeks and fluffs the thick curls of her hair. "I know I'd be dead if Rayne hadn't done it. I just wish he'd talk to me."

All my willpower goes into keeping my hands still. "If he hasn't spoken to you in a week—"

"You'll go with me." Rayne's soft voice carries through the room. "Not ideal, I realize that, but I'll take care of you. I won't do to you what Vixen did to me."

"Go?" My hands clench. "You're leaving?"

She avoids my gaze. "I've not been charged. I'm not even under arrest, but people remember me as the traitor from Vixen's nest. I can't stay in Angbec."

"You can't do this to me."

"This isn't about you."

"Right, it's about *us*. You think it's not dangerous for me too? I'm a SPEAR. Do you see me running away?"

"It's not running—"

"Bullshit." I punch the mattress. "Whatever else Vixen did, she brought you to Angbec, and you've got roots now. You've got friends and family. Me."

Rayne's shoulders hunch towards her ears. "I don't want to leave you."

"Then don't."

"And where will I stay? I can't make a permanent home of your kitchen cupboards."

"I don't want to leave." Pippa's voice is low and hollow. "But my life here is gone. I can't work for Clear Blood any more, I've lost my baby, Adam hates me, and Mum is..." She wipes her cheeks. "What's left?"

I throw back the covers and swing out of bed. The movement is easy after a week here, liquid and quick, almost back to my old self. My knees wobble as I put weight on them, but I can walk freely. I fling my arms around Pippa's neck. "I'm here."

She stiffens, still afraid of contact, of what she might do.

"Family isn't a house. Life isn't your job. Both those things are what you make them, and I'm still here. I'll never leave you. Ever."

A hand touches my shoulder. Hesitant at first, then firm, a slow rubbing motion. Two arms slide around me and return the hug with the crushing enthusiasm only a vampire can muster. "I'm scared."

I wipe her tears. She brushes at mine. "Me too. But we'll manage. Like always."

"Promise?"

I pull back to show her my smile. "On my locs and hope to trim."

CHAPTER THIRTY-EIGHT

My flat looks the same as ever: a wreck. I'm glad I insisted on coming alone. Even Norma is with Rayne and Pippa, clearly hacked off at being left behind.

But I have to do this by myself.

The flat seems so small now. There are extras to the mess on the floor, including droppings from Norma and a letter from my landlord advising me of fourteen days' notice. Dated ten days ago. Of course.

The bedroom and bathroom are the only places remotely resembling tidy.

I stand next to the bath, remembering the last time I used it. Rayne slapping her hand over my mouth in the darkness, the explosion of fear in my chest.

Seems like a million years ago.

I fit the plug and turn the tap, watching water bubble and splash up the sides.

Won't be long.

Back in the bedroom, I strip off the borrowed clothes from medibay and sit naked on the end of my bed. The room doesn't even feel like mine. My things are here: the clothes, clean and dirty; the bed linen, also dirty; the handful of books, read and unread; the martial arts and action movie DVDs. But here, like back in the living room, something is missing. A feel. A sensation.

Not sure I like it.

I coil my hair on the back of my head and snag a cleanish towel from the floor.

I climb into the bath with the water still running, sinking into the liquid warmth with a sigh.

Half healed cuts tingle in the heat, the stitches in my neck already prickling in the steam.

Don't care. It's wonderful to lie in my own bath and just soak.

Loud thudding at the door interrupts my interlude.

Pause.

"Nope." I sink lower until the water touches my chin. "Whoever you are, go away."

Knock, knock, knock. Knock.

"Danika? Hello? Are you home?"

What the hell is *he* doing here?

I'm out of the bath in an instant, towel wrapped haphazardly around my body. My feet skid briefly before I find my grip, and then the carpet squelches with each wet step to the front door.

Jack stands on the other side, leafing through a stack of typed papers. At his feet, a thick case bulges with more folders, files, and a slim laptop. He grins. "Bad time?"

I realize what I must look like. "Don't get any ideas."

"Wouldn't dare. I can come back if now is no good."

How satisfying would it be to shut this door in his handsome, toothpaste ad face?

"No, you may as well come in."

He stops dead at the entrance to the living area. "What happened in here?"

"Uninvited guest." His look of bemused horror brings a smile to my lips. "What's up?"

"I need to talk about the future."

I plant my hands on my hips. Water beads on my shoulders and runs down the tops of my arms. "What future? You know I'm not—"

He waves his hand. "No, no, no, I remember." He laughs, and though there's a wistful edge to it—and he gives a quick skim up and down my body—he presses on. "I've got lots to do in the next couple of years, and I was hoping you'd help."

"I don't do private hire. Last experience got me in trouble."

He stares. "Sorry, this is coming out wrong. Do you want to get dressed?"

"Really? You seem to be enjoying the view."

"Oh, I am, but I'd rather not upset your girlfriend. She *is* your girlfriend?"

"Yeah, I suppose she is." I suppose. We have yet to work out what we are.

Ten minutes later, jeans and slouchy T-shirt in place, I'm sitting on the sofa, leafing through the papers Jack dumps in my lap. "All these belonged to Amelia?"

He ruffles his hair. "Every single one. No idea yet what will happen to those businesses, but her assets have already been seized."

"Why tell me? I'm not an accountant."

"Some of the money and property will be converted to funds I can use in my position as mayor." Abruptly lively, he roots through the case for some blue sheets of larger, thinner paper. "It's something I considered years ago, when I first synthesized the Life Blood Serum—a research facility specific to vampires." He spreads the blueprints across the floor and points to different areas in turn. "It would have a shelter, regular blood supply supplemented by the serum, and a lab for us to further our studies in vampire biology and metabolism."

I know nothing about architecture, but even I can tell the building he has in mind is huge. "These locations are properties and land owned by Vixen."

"Yes, she was buying up huge plots of land. I thought, to help me do this. What she actually wanted was a cattle ranch to store her pet humans."

"You heard about that?"

"Should have known it was too good to be true." Jack lifts his hands palm out. "Like I said, if I'd known what she was planning, I never would have accepted the help. These places in the north"—he points to another map—"were areas I planned to use for supernatural social housing."

This man is far more forward thinking than I ever gave him credit for.

"It was all in my manifesto. Homelessness is a huge problem in Angbec, but only in supers. Since these people are recognized members of society, they need the chance to become part of the community, with real jobs and housing options. Most are easy to place, but vampires have particular needs that so far aren't addressed. That's why they often resort to crime."

He's excited now, bright-eyed, clear voiced, and focused. Not once has he made a lewd comment or ogled my body.

"Still don't see what this has to do with me."

"You talk to Rayne." He leans into the sofa. A frown creases his face, and after a quick fumble, he tugs a wired bra from the cushions.

"Shut up."

Wisely, he doesn't comment. "I don't know many vampires. Clear Blood is my creation, but I haven't been involved with the day-to-day for some time. I'm changing that. I want to create things, learn and get involved, but I need people on my side who understand how vampires work. Someone I trust."

"And you trust Rayne?"

Jack snorts. "I trust *you*. You're the strongest SPEAR this city has, and I've seen you in action. If you say Rayne is safe to work with, that's enough for me."

I bite my lip. "She's leaving with Pippa. They go tomorrow and—"

"What? Pippa too? She's the best researcher we've ever had—she can't leave. Why would they do that?"

I give him a level look.

"You've got to convince them to stay."

"I've tried."

"Try again. Please. I'll give them anything they want, whatever they need. But they can't leave this city now. I need them to make this work."

No matter his plans, I'm sure *I* need them more than he ever could. But with nothing to offer them, not even this scabby old flat...

I sit straight. "I'll ask."

"Thank you. Thank you so much."

"You'll need to sweeten the deal, though."

"Of course they'll be paid. I can give them seats on the board, offices, cars, just tell me how to keep them here."

I think of my old home: pencil growth marks on the walls, pictures lining the staircase, dents in the flooring. I remember the smell of frying plantain wafting into the garden at the rear, while Pippa and I played on a rickety swing set made from rough pallets and salvaged plastics.

"My lease is up. Seems my landlord doesn't appreciate unwanted guests."

"How long have you got?"

"Three days."

Jack nudges the blueprints with the toe of his shoe. "I can get you a house. I know the perfect area too, it's—"

"Actually, I know the house I want."

"I'm not an estate agent."

"And I'm not a recruiter. Guess we both need to expand our skill sets."

I let the next pause stretch.

After an eternity, he extends his hand. "Fine, a house. Anything else?"

"Actually, yes." I grasp his hand and shake it firmly. "It's going to need some modifications."

❖

I wake to the soft tickle of cool breath against my ear and the tang of strong black coffee in my nose.

I turn, fumbling across my sheets until my fingers touch a warm, curved ceramic surface. "What time is it?"

"Late," a voice whispers in my ear.

"Not helpful." It's dark, but not so much that I can't see the bedside clock with its dim green digital display: 18:32.

I stretch. "You're early."

"A vampire is never late, Agent Karson."

"Very funny." I sit back against my pillows just as the light flicks on. "Ow."

"Drink up." Rayne stands beside my bed, a steaming mug of coffee extended towards me. Her eyes are bright and lively, her smile warm.

A flush of heat washes through my body. She's beautiful. So, so beautiful.

She cocks her head. "What are you thinking?"

"Um…" I scramble out of bed, flinging the sheets aside to free my path to the floor. "Nothing. Too early for thinking."

"Late."

"It's the night shift."

"It's still morning for me."

I grunt into the coffee mug, hoping that serves as a suitable answer. "Did you sleep well?"

"Really?"

I wince. "I'm still getting used to it. Like I said, un-vamp-like vamp."

As I sip from the mug, Rayne steps around me and begins remaking my bed. "It was fine. Like always. The insulated room is perfectly light tight, so that's no worry. Though the access panel could be closer to the bed so I don't walk into things when I cross the room."

"I thought you could see in the dark."

"Even vampires can take a little while to wake up."

I yank a pair of jeans off the back of the chair in front of my dresser. A quick sniff assures me they're fine to wear a second—or is that third?—time and I toss them onto the bed. A shirt, bra, pair of panties, and T-shirt follow in the same overhand manner.

"If I'm honest…" Rayne's voice quivers. She toys with the corners of my pillow, studiously avoiding my gaze. "I'd much prefer sleeping in here."

The unspoken *with you* hangs over us like a helium balloon.

My chest tightens with desire and need, but I wash both away with another slug of coffee and a shake of the head. "We can chat room arrangements later. I need to get ready."

Even with her back partially turned, I can feel Rayne's disappointment. She rallies quickly and faces me with a smile. "Sure. Pippa is downstairs, so we're ready when you are. I'll wait with her." As she walks by, her hand snakes out to brush my hip.

Such a little, innocent touch, but the contact lights me up in an instant.

I snag her wrist and twirl her in to face me.

Those eyes. That deep, hypnotic ripe acorn colour shimmering with a hard edge of silver.

I kiss her. Can't help it. My mouth opens across hers, owning her, claiming her, and Rayne's hands stretch up to link around the back of my neck. A little growl spills out, no idea if it's mine or hers, but a sudden burst of metallic sweetness jerks us apart.

Rayne looks bashful.

I touch my lip. "Me?"

"No, I had breakfast before coming to wake you. Lifeblood seems to make the taste stronger, even to humans."

No kidding.

"I'll meet you downstairs." As if sensing my conflicting thoughts, Rayne slips away without another word. I watch her go, skin tingling, mouth warm, a breathless sigh on my lips.

❖

Ten minutes later I'm dressed and walking down the stairs with Rayne close behind.

My hand trails along the banister, skipping over dents and dints in the soft, aged wood. On my right, the wall drops back to expose the living area beneath where Pippa sits with a magazine. On my left, a line of photos follow the path of the steps: an older couple, the same couple with a baby, that couple with a younger child, then an older child with a new baby. Halfway down, the pictures have changed again, showing two girls with dark, tightly curled hair and mischievous expressions. One grows tall and willowy, the other broader and tomboyish, curls eventually giving way to spiky dreadlocks.

Can't help but stop at the last picture—three women in a single frame, a mother and two grown daughters.

A pang grips my chest.

Rayne touches my shoulder. "She'll come around."

I'm not sure about that, but I'm comforted to hear her say it.

"I agreed to live with you, not be your live-in alarm clock." Pippa nudges a mug across the coffee table.

I sip. Mmm, more coffee. "I was awake."

"Do you want the lift or not?"

"Someone woke up on the wrong side of the coffin tonight. Relax. It's not like Jack can fire you."

Pippa pulls the spoon from my mug and flicks it across the room. It flies through the kitchen door and lands with a clink, probably dead centre on the sideboard. "We've got new tests to finalize today, but I need the human staff. They leave at eight."

Another glug of coffee, then I'm standing. "Is this the new blood synthesis?"

She nods. "If we crack this, things will change, practically overnight. Can you imagine?"

I want to, but after so long, it's difficult. Vampires drink blood. *Human* blood. Anything else is a dream, something cooked up by those new TV shows springing up in recent months. Nice thought, though.

Rayne walks through, shrugging her coat onto her shoulders. She hands mine over with a smile for Pippa. "You're a great chemist and your team is wonderful. If anyone can do it, you can. Do you need more samples?"

"Not now, but when we do I'll send Wendy to pick them up."

I give a snort of laughter. "Don't let him hear you calling him that."

Pippa deactivates the security on our reinforced front door. "I'm allowed to call him that." The blackout sheeting rolls back and away for another night. "He likes me," she adds, stepping onto the street.

I follow, still struggling into my jacket. "He likes me too y'know."

❖

It's not a long drive to SPEAR.

Rayne sits with me in the back, her fingers entwined with mine. Pippa drives, occasionally sneaking a peep at us through her rear view.

My reflection slides through the image of Angbec, just visible through the shadowed glass of our new car.

It's Angbec like I've always known it, but different. It's brighter and more vibrant, livelier than I remember.

Pippa drops us at the staff entrance like usual. "See you for dinner?"

"You mean breakfast?"

She grins and speeds away.

Rayne opens the doors.

Inside, there's no immediate visible change to the headquarters of the Supernatural Prohibition, Extermination, and Arrest Regiment. Only when we pass security and reach the third floor do the changes start to show—chittarik flying back and forth carrying messages, agents in suits or tactical gear moving on about their business.

And that's the real difference. My field agent colleagues have diversified.

A small red-skinned gargoyle waves hello from his workstation on the ceiling, while a trio of goblins chat beside the junk food vending machine. In the training area, more human newbies go through their basic hand-to-hand, though now they're joined by the larger, furrier forms of werewolves in hybrid form. Link must be thrilled teaching students less prone to broken bones.

I stop at my desk and cage a sigh behind my teeth.

"Norma?"

Fluttering wings. My little chittarik swoops in from her roost on the ceiling and lands on the edge of my desk.

"How many times do I need to say it: use the tray."

She cocks her head. "Karson? Dan-Danika Karson?"

"That's *sorry*, right? I'll take that as a sorry."

Norma pulls a message tube from the flap beneath her chin and drops it before flying away.

Rayne snatches it from the air before it hits the fresh pile of droppings beside my phone. "She only does it to wind you up."

"It works." Grumbling, I take the chair and drop into it, legs up and crossed on the desk.

I open the tube. Read.

"What?" Rayne's eyes are bright and lively, a faint edge of silver creeping in around her irises. "Tell me. Your pulse has shot up and you smell like a kid at Christmas. What is it?"

I wave the curled sheet of paper. "New assignment."

"All of us?"

"Yep." I look again at the paper and the thrilling words at the top: *Special Ops Team: Edane Alpha One.*

Rayne beams and cracks her knuckles. Still smiling, she crosses to her own desk and pulls her utility belt from the top drawer. Into it she slides two knives, a gun, and her own off-white ID card. "Guess we should call the rest of the team."

"Damn right." I loop my own utility belt into place. Check the gun. Ammunition. When satisfied, I leave my desk and stride across the office to the meeting room where my team awaits.

I've got a briefing to give, and we've got work to do.

About the Author

Ileandra Young is one face of Da Shared Brain, who also writes erotica and romance as Raven ShadowHawk. This face writes urban and traditional fantasy, watching the moon at night and dreaming up new supernatural creatures to let loose on her characters. When not writing, Ileandra can be found LARPing (gleefully), snoring (loudly), or playing video games with her twin sons.

Visit her website at www.ileandrayoung.co.uk.

Books Available From Bold Strokes Books

All of Me by Emily Smith. When chief surgical resident Galen Burgess meets her new intern, Rowan Duncan, she may finally discover that doing what you've always done will only give you what you've always had. (978-1-163555-321-5)

As the Crow Flies by Karen F. Williams. Romance seems to be blooming all around, but problems arise when a restless ghost emerges from the ether to roam the dark corners of this haunting tale. (978-1-163555-285-0)

Both Ways by Ileandra Young. SPEAR agent Danika Karson races to protect the city from a supernatural threat and must rely on the woman she's trained to despise: Rayne, an achingly beautiful vampire. (978-1-163555-298-0)

Calendar Girl by Georgia Beers. Forced to work together, Addison Fairchild and Kate Cooper discover that opposites really do attract. (978-1-163555-333-8)

Cash and the Sorority Girl by Ashley Bartlett. Cash Braddock doesn't want to deal with morality, drugs, or people. Unfortunately, she's going to have to. (978-1-163555-310-9)

Lovebirds by Lisa Moreau. Two women from different worlds collide in a small California mountain town, each with a mission that doesn't include falling in love. (978-1-163555-213-3)

Media Darling by Fiona Riley. Can Hollywood bad girl Emerson and reluctant celebrity gossip reporter Hayley work together to make each other's dreams come true? Or will Emerson's secrets ruin not one career, but two? (978-1-163555-278-2)

Stroke of Fate by Renee Roman. Can Scan Moore live up to her reputation and save Jade Rivers from the stalker determined to end Jade's career and, ultimately, her life? (978-1-163555-162-4)

The Rise of the Resistance by Jackie D. The soul of America has been lost for almost a century. A few people may be the difference between a phoenix rising to save the masses or permanent destruction. (978-1-163555-259-1)

The Sex Therapist Next Door by Meghan O'Brien. At the intersection of sex and intimacy, anything is possible. Even love. (978-1-163555-296-6)

Unexpected Lightning by Cass Sellars. Lightning strikes once more when Sydney and Parker fight a dangerous stranger who threatens the peace they both desperately want. (978-1-163555-276-8)

Unforgettable by Elle Spencer. When one night changes a lifetime… Two romance novellas from best-selling author Elle Spencer. (978-1-63555-429-8)

Against All Odds by Kris Bryant, Maggie Cummings, and M. Ullrich. Peyton and Tory escaped death once, but will they survive when Bradley's determined to make his kill rate 100 percent? (978-1-163555-193-8)

Autumn's Light by Aurora Rey. Casual hookups aren't supposed to include romantic dinners and meeting the family. Can Mat Pero see beyond the heartbreak that led her to keep her worlds so separate, and will Graham Connor be waiting if she does? (978-1-163555-272-0)

Breaking the Rules by Larkin Rose. When Virginia and Carmen are thrown together by an embarrassing mistake, they find out their stubborn determination isn't so heroic after all. (978-1-163555-261-4)

Broad Awakening by Mickey Brent. In the sequel to *Underwater Vibes*, Hélène and Sylvie find ruts in their road to eternal bliss. (978-1-163555-270-6)

Broken Vows by MJ Williamz. Sister Mary Margaret must reconcile her divided heart or risk losing a love that just might be heaven sent. (978-1-163555-022-1)

Flesh and Gold by Ann Aptaker. Havana, 1952, where art thief and smuggler Cantor Gold dodges gangland bullets and mobsters' schemes while she searches Havana's steamy red light district for her kidnapped love. (978-1-163555-153-2)

Isle of Broken Years by Jane Fletcher. Spanish noblewoman Catalina de Valasco is in peril, even before the pirates holding her for ransom sail into seas destined to become known as the Bermuda Triangle. (978-1-163555-175-4)

Love Like This by Melissa Brayden. Hadley Cooper and Spencer Adair set out to take the fashion world by storm. If only they knew their hearts were about to be taken. (978-1-163555-018-4)

Secrets On the Clock by Nicole Disney. Jenna and Danielle love their jobs helping endangered children, but that might not be enough to stop them from breaking the rules by falling in love. (978-1-163555-292-8)

Unexpected Partners by Michelle Larkin. Dr. Chloe Maddox tries desperately to deny her attraction for Detective Dana Blake as they flee from a serial killer who's hunting them both. (978-1-163555-203-4)

A Fighting Chance by T. L. Hayes. Will Lou be able to come to terms with her past to give love a fighting chance? (978-1-163555-257-7)

Chosen by Brey Willows. When the choice is adapt or die, can love save us all? (978-1-163555-110-5)

Gnarled Hollow by Charlotte Greene. After they are invited to study a secluded nineteenth-century estate, a former English professor and a group of historians discover that they will have to fight against the unknown if they have any hope of staying alive. (978-1-163555-235-5)

Jacob's Grace by C.P. Rowlands. Captain Tag Becket wants to keep her head down and her past behind her, but her feelings for AJ's second-in-command, Grace Fields, makes keeping secrets next to impossible. (978-1-163555-187-7)

On the Fly by PJ Trebelhorn. Hockey player Courtney Abbott is content with her solitary life until visiting concert violinist Lana Caruso makes her second-guess everything she always thought she wanted. (978-1-163555-255-3)

Passionate Rivals by Radclyffe. Professional rivalry and long-simmering passions create a combustible combination when Emmet McCabe and Sydney Stevens are forced to work together, especially when past attractions won't stay buried. (978-1-63555-231-7)

Proxima Five by Missouri Vaun. When geologist Leah Warren crash-lands on a preindustrial planet and is claimed by its tyrant, Tiago, will clan warrior Keegan's love for Leah give her the strength to defeat him? (978-1-163555-122-8)

Shadowboxer by Jessica L. Webb. Jordan McAddie is prepared to keep her street kids safe from a dangerous underground protest group, but she isn't prepared for her first love to walk back into her life. (978-1-163555-267-6)

Racing Hearts by Dena Blake. When you cross a hot-tempered race car mechanic with a reckless cop, the result can only be spontaneous combustion. (978-1-163555-251-5)

The Tattered Lands by Barbara Ann Wright. As Vandra and Lilani strive to make peace, they slowly fall in love. With mistrust and murder surrounding them, only their faith in each other can keep their plan to save the world from falling apart. (978-1-163555-108-2)

Captive by Donna K. Ford. To escape a human trafficking ring, Greyson Cooper and Olivia Danner become players in a game of deceit and violence. Will their love stand a chance? (978-1-63555-215-7)

Crossing the Line by CF Frizzell. The Mob discovers a nemesis within its ranks, and in the ultimate retaliation, draws Stick McLaughlin from anonymity by threatening everything she holds dear. (978-1-63555-161-7)

Love's Verdict by Carsen Taite. Attorneys Landon Holt and Carly Pachett want the exact same thing: the only open partnership spot at their prestigious criminal defense firm. But will they compromise their careers for love? (978-1-63555-042-9)

Precipice of Doubt by Mardi Alexander & Laurie Eichler. Can Cole Jameson resist her attraction to her boss, veterinarian Jodi Bowman, or will she risk a workplace romance and her heart? (978-1-63555-128-0)

Savage Horizons by CJ Birch. Captain Jordan Kellow's feelings for Lt. Ali Ash have her past and future colliding, setting in motion a series of events that strands her crew in an unknown galaxy thousands of light years from home. (978-1-63555-250-8)

Secrets of the Last Castle by A. Rose Mathieu. When Elizabeth Campbell represents a young man accused of murdering an elderly woman, her investigation leads to an abandoned plantation that reveals many dark Southern secrets. (978-1-63555-240-9)

Take Your Time by VK Powell. A neurotic parrot brings police officer Grace Booker and temporary veterinarian Dr. Dani Wingate together in the tiny town of Pine Cone, but their unexpected attraction keeps the sparks flying. (978-1-63555-130-3)

The Last Seduction by Ronica Black. When you allow true love to elude you once and you desperately regret it, are you brave enough to grab it when it comes around again? (978-1-63555-211-9)

The Shape of You by Georgia Beers. Rebecca McCall doesn't play it safe, but when sexy Spencer Thompson joins her workout class, their nonstop sparring forces her to face her ultimate challenge—a chance at love. (978-1-63555-217-1)

Force of Fire: Toujours a Vous by Ali Vali. Immortals Kendal and Piper welcome their new child and celebrate the defeat of an old enemy, but another ancient evil is about to awaken deep in the jungles of Costa Rica. (978-1-63555-047-4)